THE MAGIC KEEPERS

AN ETHEREAL WORLD NOVEL

E. L. WILLIAMS

Bramble Leaf
BOOKS

First edition

ISBN: 978-1-0686673-0-5

To Katie,
for always being my bestie

* * *

BOOKS BY E. L. WILLIAMS

The First Ethereal

The Blessing of Crows

The Magic Keepers

"All we have to decide is what to do with the time that is given us."

— J.R.R. TOLKIEN, THE FELLOWSHIP OF THE RING

CHAPTER 1

ABERYSTWYTH, JULY 1960

*L*ydia eyed the book on the top shelf and sighed. She wasn't keen on heights, and she wondered whether the book knew it. This was the third time she'd had to reposition the library ladder and her patience was wearing thin. Not wanting to climb down again, she took a deep breath and hooked her left arm through the nearest rung, anchoring herself so that she could stretch far enough to reach the little green book. Just as her fingers brushed against the spine, it shuffled another inch out of her reach.

'Oh, you stubborn little sod,' she growled through gritted teeth.

The book jumped backwards, and Lydia cursed herself. The poor thing was clearly nervous, bless it, but they had enough to do already without new arrivals giving them the runaround.

'Okay,' she said, using her best librarian's voice and softening her tone. She smiled at the book. 'Come on now, lovely, you don't have to be read if you're not ready, but we need to catalogue you, which means I at least need to read your title. Would that be alright?'

1

The book seemed to consider it for a moment, and then slowly shuffled forward.

Lydia smiled encouragingly. She squinted, cursing herself again, this time for leaving her reading glasses somewhere. She could almost make out the title, but the gold lettering on its dark teal-green cover was too faint.

'That's a good book,' she cooed, leaning closer.

'Still giving you the runaround?' a voice from below asked.

Startled, Lydia lost her footing and let out a cry as, for a few vertigo-inducing seconds, the arm she'd looped around the ladder was the only thing holding her up.

The little book shot backwards in alarm, hit the wall and ricocheted into a row of books on the next shelf down. Like a flock of angry geese, they took to the air in panic, rousing other books in their page-flapping wake.

Clinging to the ladder, Lydia found her footing just in time to duck as a hefty old tome, clearly late to the panic, hauled itself into the air mere inches from her face. She screwed up her eyes to avoid the cloud of ancient dust it left in its wake. It was no use. Lydia felt it settle on her face and tried not to breathe in until the worst had passed.

With both feet blessedly back on the ladder and both arms wrapped around it, Lydia opened her eyes and sighed as she watched the flock of books hurtle around the grand old library. She loved this place, with its polished wood, decorative carvings and panelled walls. Granted, it didn't have the ceiling height of her own precious library in Pont Nefoedd. That was often the trouble with basements, but of all the other magical libraries, this was her favourite. Leaving it would be a wrench for everyone concerned, but as the saying went, 'needs must when the devil rides', and in this case, the saying wasn't far from the truth. At least the new library would be more secure than a crumbling old manor house in the middle of nowhere.

With a sigh, Lydia climbed slowly down, her left shoulder throbbing and her upper arm sore. She'd no doubt have a bruise there by the morning. She was also unbearably hot. Her blouse felt pasted to her back and the elasticated waistband of her trousers was digging into her sides. Her stomach rumbled, reminding her to add hungry to the list of complaints too.

They had been re-cataloguing for days, but they were almost out of time. Powerful magical wards protected the library, but at this rate, they would need to be done again before they were ready. While they would have help from a small army of witches and members of the magical community on moving day, they were way behind schedule. If books just refrained from renaming themselves when the fancy took them, there'd be no need for re-cataloguing in the first place, Lydia thought for the umpteenth time in her long career.

'I'm getting too old for this,' she grumbled as her left knee shot her a needle of complaint when she stepped off the last rung of the ladder. The air was still thick with flapping books.

'Ow!' she yelled as a small blue book caught her a glancing blow on the back of her head. It shot off, leaving Lydia to rub the spot, although on reflection, it hadn't actually hurt. She could tell without the aid of a mirror that the heat had undone her efforts to set her hair. She ran her fingers through it as she checked for a lump anyway and thought of her late aunt's honey-coloured standard poodle. Any more grey hairs and she'd look more like a bichon soon, she thought irritably.

It looked like half the books in the library were now on

the wing, but it was far from an ordered affair. This was no murmuration to marvel at. Books, unlike birds, were too independent, some might say pig-headed, to be followers, and so each one was going freestyle. Some were darting above the stacks, pages flattened to fit themselves between shelf and ceiling, while others were swooping in great arcs from shelf top to library floor, looking like gulls diving for fish. The rest, save for a few of the smaller books that were fluttering around ankle height, seemingly confused by the commotion, just bombed around. Lydia sighed. The breeze from their flapping pages was quite refreshing, if you didn't breathe in the dust.

'Nonsense,' Frances said, reappearing, apparently unperturbed by the chaos in her usually ordered library. Lydia jumped.

'You're about half my age and as fit as a flea,' Frances said, peering over her glasses to pin Lydia with a steely look.

Lydia laughed ruefully. 'Unless you're ninety, then no, not quite half,' she said, collapsing into a chair at the reading table just in time to avoid another collision.

'Oh, alright then, you win,' Frances said amiably. 'But I maintain my point about your fitness. You've always been very robust.'

What you really mean is chunky, Lydia thought, but she knew her old friend, who despite her best efforts had the physique of a greyhound, meant it as a compliment.

Frances was a tall, fine-boned woman with poker-straight long silver-grey hair she wore pulled into a tight bun at the back of her head. Her hair had been ash blonde when she was younger, but the style had never changed. Lydia couldn't remember the point when her friend had tipped from blonde to grey, but knowing Frances, she'd barely have noticed either.

The older woman's only nod to fashion were her

bubblegum-pink winged reading glasses. Otherwise, it was a uniform of twinset and a tweed skirt in the winter and twinset and a cotton skirt in the summer months. No matter the weather, the shoes were always the same – a pair of sensible black lace-ups – always polished, but never to the point of being showy.

Without looking up from the book she was examining or raising her voice, Frances said sternly, 'Back to your places, please. Silly time is over.'

Had Frances not been a librarian and keeper of the Aberystwyth Library of Magical Texts, she would have made a brilliant headmistress at some posh girls' school, Lydia thought, smiling as she watched the careering books freeze in mid-air before dutifully gliding back into their places. Who said keepers couldn't do magic?

Lydia remembered coming here as a child when her aunt, the previous keeper at the Pont Nefoedd library, made the trip from their home in the Brecon Beacons to the little seaside town perched on the western coast of Wales. Even as a young woman, Frances didn't hold with the idea of entertaining children, so she'd put Lydia to work, finding or re-shelving books and later, when she was older, doing bits of research for her. No doubt from carefully vetted books known for their good manners. When Lydia's apprenticeship to her aunt Philippa began, Frances had become her third-year mentor, and then later, her colleague and friend.

'Treat them as you would a horse. Kindly, but suffering no nonsense,' Lydia's aunt used to tell her. 'Give them an inch and they will, mark my words, dear girl, take more than a country mile.'

Her aunt would usually follow with the story of the apprentice who had died while trying to manage a difficult book. Lydia had later discovered that the poor girl had tripped and knocked her head on the flagstones, but the story was still being used to instil a sense of wariness and respect for the books into all apprentices.

Lydia looked up just in time to see the new arrival return to its hiding place on top of the shelf. She sighed and massaged her temples to ward off the start of a headache. If only grumpy books were the worst of a keeper's lot.

CHAPTER 2

PONT NEFOEDD, JULY 1960

*M*aggie hopped off the library ladder five rungs from the bottom and sighed as she surveyed the cavernous room. Her mother really should think about smartening up the place. They were forever sweeping up the flakes of paint that seemed to enjoy throwing themselves off the whitewashed walls, the furniture was positively ancient, and the rugs were so drab it was hard to believe they'd even heard of the word 'colour'. Her requests to add a few posters, just for cheeriness, had elicited Lydia's infamous raised eyebrow. Well, infamous in the family, anyway. Maggie knew better than to push it, but it still irked her that her place of work felt like a mausoleum.

According to her mother, their time was better spent looking after the magical books in their care and doing the research required of them. She could hear her mother's voice in her head. 'But Mags, love, it's only us here most of the time. What's the point?'

Maggie huffed as she thought of the well-trodden argument, but stopped herself before she could fall into her familiar list of grumbles. Complaining didn't do anyone any good. That was one piece of her mother's advice that she could agree with – not that she'd admit it to her.

'Doesn't this place get you down?' Maggie said to the Siamese cat lounging on the reading table.

Boudicca blinked slowly in response and then stretched theatrically before rolling over and turning her back on Maggie.

'I'll take that as a no then, shall I, Bodie?' Maggie said, drawing out the cat's nickname and over-emphasising the 'Bo'. She knew Boudicca despised being addressed by anything other than her full moniker. Maggie supposed that if she'd had to suffer the indignity of being called Mr Tiddles for the first year of her life, she might be prickly about names too.

Boudicca flipped around, pinning Maggie with her now worryingly narrowed bright blue eyes. Her whip-like tail slashed back and forth across the table, sending loose sheets of paper sailing to the floor.

Maggie rolled her eyes at the cat and tutted loudly, but she already felt a settling weight in her stomach. She bit her lip, annoyed with herself for being spiteful, because, call it like it is, that's what she'd been. For once, it hadn't been Boudicca who had been in a bad mood – it was her.

'I'm sorry, Boudicca. Really, I am,' Maggie said with a sigh. She already knew it was too late to be sorry. Boudicca hissed, showing off her impressive canines, and turned her back. While she still appeared to be lounging, from her still flicking tail, Maggie knew she'd need to give her a wide berth for the rest of the day unless she wanted to get swiped for her trouble. *Nobody holds a grudge like a Siamese*, Maggie thought. *And I need to learn not to antagonise her*, she chided herself.

Any gratitude Boudicca had felt at being rescued from her father's slightly nutty aunt Deidre all those years ago she reserved for Maggie's mother. With Lydia, Boudicca was still an enraptured kitten – with everyone else, she veered between tetchy alley cat and wannabe velociraptor. *So much for her being my cat*, Maggie thought, the sting of disappointment still real after seven long years.

Glancing at the clock, Maggie felt her spirits lift. Just an hour more and she could go out to lunch with Keith. She smiled, picturing him waiting for her in the pub. Maybe walking her home if there was time. First, she had an essay to finish. She hesitated, considering how missing a deadline would factor in the bigger scheme of things now that she'd made her decision. Or, she corrected herself, had almost certainly decided.

The uncomfortable weight in her stomach returned. Her mother was going to be heartbroken when she told her. The mere thought of it had given her sleepless nights for weeks. But it was her life, wasn't it? She was twenty-one. A proper grown-up, so she didn't need anyone's permission anymore.

Pushing the tangle of thoughts aside, she pulled up a chair as far away from Boudicca as possible. It wasn't unheard of for the cat to exact her revenge with a well-aimed swipe, hours, sometimes days after a perceived offence. Maggie opened her notepad. She'd never submitted a piece of homework late in her life, and so decided that, regardless of the other thing, now was not the time to start.

Alongside her notepad and the books she'd be using for the essay sat a thin manila folder with the words 'Highly Confidential' stamped on the front in fresh red ink. Just looking at the folder made Maggie's stomach churn.

The memory of her mother handing it to her on the morning she left for Aber popped into her head. 'I know it's not the first crime scene report you've seen, but fair warning, love, this one was particularly nasty. The raid on the library was brutal,' her mother had said as she'd held the folder out to her.

Maggie had rolled her eyes and said something snarky that she couldn't remember now. She'd folded her arms and only let them drop back to her sides when she saw her mother's expression change. Not wanting to put a name to the look, Maggie had snatched the folder with an exaggerated sigh before putting it straight back down on the reading table.

'You know that Yolande was—'

Maggie interrupted, her tone sharper and more sarcastic than she'd intended. 'Decapitated by the magic hunters during the attack? Funnily enough, Mother, yes I do remember that little detail from the briefing.'

Lydia hadn't looked angry, even though Maggie knew she was being a brat about it all. Her mother had just looked so incredibly sad, although whether for their fallen colleague in Barcelona or her daughter who was duty bound to read the report, view the crime scene photographs and write up a report on it all, she couldn't tell. Unable to bear it, Maggie had said something flippant and made an excuse about needing the loo.

The truth was that the raids terrified her. The magic hunters raided libraries, looking for a book that could give ordinary people magical power. Some men sought the Holy Grail as they believed it could grant them eternal life and forgive their sins, while others sought power they didn't deserve.

Ironically, none of the scholars in the magical community could agree on whether such a book even existed, but so long as these men believed it did, they would stop at nothing in their quest for it.

Maggie turned her attention back to the notebook. The essay was on the infamous 'Tortured Text'. Discovered in

1945, it had provided a new and terrifying insight into the depravity of the magic hunters. Not content with stealing magical texts and murdering those who got in their way, when the sentient books refused to allow their captors to read them, the hunters tried to force their secrets from their pages.

The Tortured Text had somehow found its way back to the Elders, battered, burned and with a shattered spine that bore the hallmarks of being not just broken but wrung. It had never recovered from its ordeal.

Contained within a velvet-padded rosewood case which protected it and those who cared for it from its uncontrollable rages, a rotation of senior witches tended it around the clock, soothing it with spells and playing it classical music. It liked cello pieces the best, apparently, and somehow that always made Maggie's heart ache. Writing the essay had been a miserable undertaking, and she would be glad to finish it.

Maggie took a deep breath and picked up her pen, but her eye snagged again on the folder she'd not so much as touched in a week. She'd even dusted around it on cleaning day. If her mother came home to find that she'd not written up her report, there'd be hell to pay. Then again, she reasoned, there was going to be hell to pay anyway.

CHAPTER 3

ABERYSTWYTH, JULY 1960

The rattle of china brought Lydia back to the present. Rose, Frances's apprentice, crept into the room carrying a tray in the way one might carry an unexploded bomb. She was a similar build to Frances, although possibly not as tall. It was hard to tell because she was always so hunched, as if she was trying to curl herself into a little ball and disappear. She wore her long brown hair plaited neatly down her back. Lydia winced, and not for the first time, at the thinness of the girl's twiggy, milk-coloured arms. They would not be missing their meal tonight, no matter what, she thought.

Rose was one of the best apprentices they had, although Lydia would never admit as much to Maggie, but her lack of confidence was a serious worry. Some of the old tomes in the collection ran rings around her. They had had to move one of the grumpiest to Pont Nefoedd the previous summer after it cornered poor Rose for hours, snapping at her like an attack dog every time she tried to make a run for it.

Lydia wondered whether the story of the fallen keeper had served not to empower Rose but to frighten her into submission. Like Maggie, she was a full three years into her apprenticeship, but unlike her daughter, Rose still seemed like a fish out of water. Technically and academically brilliant, but still so painfully shy.

Lydia knew it worried Frances. They'd exchanged enough letters on the subject over the previous months, but she just didn't know what to suggest next. Rose didn't fit the mould of a keeper, but maybe that was the fault of the mould and not the young woman, Lydia pondered.

Rose slid the tray gingerly onto the table, the relief clear on her face. Lydia was pleased to see a plate of biscuits amongst the tea things. Her stomach grumbled in anticipation.

'Thanks, Rose,' Lydia said, smiling up at her. Rose flashed a brief smile and then looked at her feet.

Lydia thought of her daughter, Maggie, and felt a familiar squeeze around her heart. She had the confidence to handle even the most obnoxious of books, but Lydia secretly wished she'd chosen not to follow in her footsteps. Theirs was a dangerous world, and she'd rest so much easier if her daughter had been an accountant. Hell, even a trapeze artist would be a less risky profession.

'Stop frowning, Lydia, dear. You will get wrinkles,' Frances instructed as she stood to pour the tea. Almost forty years in this quiet corner of West Wales and her friend still sounded like the Oxford scholar she had once been.

'Oh, now that ship sailed a long time ago,' Lydia said with a laugh. 'Anyway, I prefer the term "laughter lines",' she added pointedly, her gaze straying to the dark corner near the old cargo lift.

Frances snorted and gave a wry laugh as she handed Lydia a cup of tea.

'We still need to change that lightbulb,' Lydia said with a sigh as she took it.

'We do,' Frances said with her own. 'It was a new bulb too. I only put it in a couple of weeks ago. Blasted thing. Typical that it's the one over the lift.'

'This is new,' Lydia said, inspecting the delicate porcelain cup, which was covered in dainty blue forget-me-knots.

'It is actually very old. Wedding present to my parents from the well-heeled side of the family. I decided it was no use to man nor beast sitting in a cupboard,' Frances explained. She took a sip of tea and smiled. 'It's worth quite a bit, apparently. Some collector chap made me a ridiculous offer, but I said no. What do I need money for at my age,' she added with a derisive wave of her hand.

Rose made a noise that was somewhere between a cough and a gulp. Lydia looked up to see her lower her cup to the saucer with trembling hands. Lydia gripped the handle of her own cup more firmly, too.

Frances rolled her eyes but pursed her lips, clearly deciding to keep her thoughts to herself. After a moment, she turned to Lydia and said, 'I think we will all rest a little easier once this move is out of the way.'

'We've just had a bad run of it lately,' Lydia said, regretting the words as soon as they were out of her mouth. They'd lost three libraries and their keepers in the last eight years, and the attack at Winchester a few years ago had left the apprentice and a visiting Elder dead too. And that was just the UK. The Barcelona attack had been only weeks ago. It had come just hours after the relocation. The keeper, Yolande, had returned to search for a book missing from the inventory and walked straight into the enraged hunters. Everyone was on edge, which was why the decision to move the Aberystwyth library was expedited.

The crime scene images flashed unbidden into Lydia's mind, and she took a gulp of her tea. She understood why the Elders felt it necessary to share them with the other keepers.

The Elders were resolute in their commitment to make sure that all keepers and apprentices knew the risks they were facing, but Lydia knew those pictures would haunt her for the rest of her life. That Maggie had to read those reports too made her sick to her stomach. God knows what it had done to Rose's already delicate disposition.

As if reading her mind, Frances said solemnly, 'What has been seen can never be unseen.'

After a moment's silence, Frances spoke again. 'But that we stand as witnesses to our fallen colleagues is no small thing. I find some comfort in that. And who knows, maybe in some other version of what we call reality they are still alive and well.'

Lydia frowned, the question forming in her mind, but before she could ask it, Frances pressed on.

'And we must always count our blessings,' she said. 'Our intelligence people helped to foil the attack on York, and we moved every book in that collection before they tried again. The Barcelona library survives, even if poor Yolande does not.'

Lydia nodded, remembering the week she'd spent in the York library last year, helping with the re-cataloguing. It had been a far more sombre affair, as unlike the Aberystwyth library, which was simply being moved to a more secure location, the removal of the books from York had closed the library for good, ending an institution that had given refuge to magical texts for over two hundred years. Helena, the keeper, had taken early retirement. Nobody could blame her. They'd all thought about it, hadn't they? The risks seemed to be escalating, and without enough experienced keepers to go around or apprentices ready to step up, there had been no other choice.

'Are you going to ask the Elders to top up the wards?' Lydia asked, shifting in her seat.

Frances considered for a moment, 'In theory, they should hold for another couple of days, but yes, I was planning on calling Seren in the morning. I didn't take to the witch they sent last time. There was something about her that didn't sit well at the time, and now—' Frances took a deep breath and turned her head to scan the vast space. She stopped when her gaze fell on Rose and changed tack. 'I'll call her in the morning,' she said, with a lightness in her tone that didn't quite match the tension around her eyes.

Lydia took another gulp of her tea, her mouth suddenly dry. It wasn't like Frances to get spooked by anything.

'While we're on the subject of York,' Frances said, now clearly on a mission to lighten the mood, 'the whole incident led to the discovery of the anomaly, and that is something we can all be thankful for, especially you, Lydia dear. Tell Rose about it.'

All keepers and apprentices knew about the anomaly. Aside from the raids, it had been the biggest news in their tiny, secret community for decades, but Lydia obliged, sensing Frances's need to move the subject away from the wards protecting them.

'Apparently, my library doesn't show up when people use magic to locate the libraries, even though we have records that clearly show that it has been a site of significant magical activity for hundreds, if not thousands of years.'

Rose smiled and nodded politely.

'For once, the boffins and magical folk are all united in their bemusement. Hence the anomaly.' Lydia mimed air quotes around the last word, pressing on just because talking about the phenomenon that kept her family and library safe was a comfort.

'Can you remind me how they search?' Rose asked, clearly playing along with the distraction.

'Excellent question, Rose,' Frances replied, a little too heartily.

Ceding the floor to Frances with a wave, Lydia reached for a biscuit.

'Dowsing, scrying, et cetera, on the magical side of things, and on the science side, we've heard rumours that those government boffins have gadgets that detect energy fluctuations which I suppose might be a bit like radar. Don't ask me for the frequencies, as I don't have time to look it up, but for some reason, Lydia's library is hidden. We're hoping that this anomaly means it's safe from the magic hunters,' Frances said.

'Ah, yes, I remember the story now,' Rose mumbled. 'Wasn't it an—'

Frances blustered on and Rose sank back in her chair. Maybe Rose's lack of gumption was just an inability to compete with the excessive quantities that Frances seemed to possess, Lydia thought. The notion cheered her.

'Moving York was a massive undertaking, and we were a few keepers down. What's-her-name from the Harrow library had flu, and the one from St Ives, I can never remember her name, well she was still on crutches or something similar. We were in a pickle, so the Elders asked Sylvie from the Toulouse library to help. She came over with her witch friend – what was her name, Lydia?'

'Camille?' Lydia offered, feeling almost sure that hadn't been the witch's name.

Frances shrugged. 'Anyway, the important part was that this witch, let's call her Camille for the sake of argument, brought her apprentice. Before they arrived, Valérie, the apprentice witch – we all remember *her* name – was tasked with scrying for and then drawing a map of the magical libraries of the UK. All very basic, first-degree stuff for a witch.'

Rose smiled patiently. Lydia wondered how many times she'd sat through this story. Bless her heart, she was such a pretty young thing when she smiled, and yet something told Lydia that Rose had had little reason to over the years.

'When Valérie presented her list, Camille, who had been to the UK many times, told her she'd missed one. They got other witches to check, and they couldn't find it either. She reported it to the Elders, and, well, the rest is history.

'So, we have an apprentice to thank for finding the anomaly,' Frances said, tapping the table with her finger to emphasise her point.

'But an apprentice witch, not just a keeper,' Rose said with a shrug.

'Did I hear Frances mention earlier that you made the biscuits yourself, Rose?' Lydia asked, not wanting to get drawn into a discussion about the role of keepers. It was natural to look at witches and envy them their magic. She'd been through it herself when she was a girl and she'd seen the signs in Maggie, too, even though her daughter thought she was hiding it well.

Lydia had learned that magic was both a blessing and a curse and had decided at an early age that she was happy with the lot she'd drawn. Rose would learn that in time, as would Maggie.

Rose's head snapped up.

'I did, yes. Not really my forte, cooking, but they don't taste too bad. They're quite dry, maybe, but okay with a cup of tea,' she said, colour creeping into her cheeks.

'Nonsense. They're delicious, Rose,' Frances said, reaching for a second. 'Have some faith in yourself, dear girl.'

While Lydia thought Frances was being generous about the biscuits, Rose was right in that they were fine dunked in tea, and seeing as they'd all missed their lunch again, any food was better than none. Glancing at her watch, she realised it was already gone seven o'clock. They had promised each other they'd call it a day by six at the very latest, so that they had a fighting chance of getting a meal somewhere this evening, so they were way behind schedule. They'd resigned themselves to a bag of chips each last night, arriving at the chippy too late even for a portion of fish. After the conversation about the wards, however, Lydia could do with getting out of here sooner. She'd give it another half an hour and then suggest that they pack up by eight.

'So, tell me, Rose, have you uncovered anything new in the archives?' Frances asked.

'Well, actually, yes,' Rose said, her expression visibly brightening as it always did when the conversation moved on to matters of magical research. 'I found a very interesting spell. The date's hard to decipher, but I'd say we're looking at the sixteen hundreds, based on the paper and overall condition. It's a safe harbour spell and allows a witch to send her magic to another witch for safekeeping. They're used only when witches are in mortal danger.'

'Gosh. You don't see those often,' Frances said, leaning forward in her chair, her interest clearly piqued. 'Rare as hen's teeth. I don't think I've ever seen one. And it was here, in the archive?'

Rose nodded. Frances scowled, clearly annoyed with herself for missing it.

'From what I've read, they're very tricky to get right. Plus, it appears that this one had a whopper of a mistake in it,' Rose said, her eyes wide and the hint of a smile at the corners of her lips.

'Oh?' Lydia said, intrigued. 'What sort of mistake?'

'Well, it looks like a mistake to me. I mean, I'm no expert, but it's probably easiest for me to show you.'

Rose jumped up and, after mumbling something Lydia

didn't catch, disappeared towards the stacks. Lydia bit her lip. If this was going to be a lengthy explanation, their chances of getting out of here anytime soon were dwindling. That said, a new find in an archive was like catnip to a keeper.

When Lydia looked at Frances, the faint smile on her lips was rueful. 'It's nice to see the light in her eyes, and nothing lights her up like research,' Frances said quietly.

Lydia nodded. 'You're doing a good job with her, you know,' she whispered. 'I have a feeling she'll do great things.'

'I hope so,' Frances replied softly, but her expression suggested that she was far from certain.

CHAPTER 4

ABERYSTWYTH, JULY 1960

*T*he old clock ticked, marking the seconds as they slipped past. Lydia's stomach growled, and she gave in and took another biscuit. She'd go back on her slimming plan once she got home. Home. The thought made her heart ache. *Not long now,* she told herself.

Lydia slouched forward, her elbows on the table, fingers drumming. What was taking Rose so long? Frances sat, her back as straight as a die, sipping her tea. She held the dainty teacup in one hand, the saucer on the flat of her other at chest height. She reminded Lydia of the ladies in a Jane Austen novel, and she wondered vaguely if that was the proper way to do it. If anyone had been to a finishing school, she would have put money on it being Frances. She was about to ask, but her friend chose that moment to break the silence.

'I take it you weren't able to read the title of our little friend up there?' Frances asked, inclining her head towards the top shelf of the bookcase. Lydia glanced up and saw the small teal-green book marching back and forth on its edges.

Lydia stifled a laugh. Magical books, just like cats, hated

21

to be laughed at. That was something her aunt had failed to warn her about, and she'd learned the lesson only after getting her fingers pinched in the rusty metal clasp of a fussy old volume during her first week on the job.

Poor little thing, Lydia thought as she watched the book, feeling more benevolent now that she wasn't hanging off a ladder. It looked like a toy soldier playing at guard duty.

'Sadly not,' she said. 'The ink is too faded. Why they're still sending books here when they know you're moving is beyond me,' she added, irritated.

'Maybe to keep up appearances? Throw any watchers off the scent?' Frances suggested with a shrug.

'Do we know where it came from?' Lydia asked.

Frances made a face. 'Ifan's shop. It wouldn't let him read it, naturally, but it must have had a fizz about it, which is why he sold it to the Elders,' she said levelly, although her arched eyebrow spoke volumes.

Lydia snorted. 'Sold for an extortionate amount too, knowing Ifan.'

While the Swansea-based book trader came from a long line of witches, unlike everyone else in his expansive family, Ifan's only power was the ability to sense magic. While technically a part of the magical community, Lydia wouldn't trust him as far as she could throw him. She was far from alone in the assessment, too.

Lydia glanced up at the clock again. She couldn't risk leaving the book overnight. If it took itself off somewhere, there were any number of places it might hide itself. She thought of poor Yolande. Returning to find a missing book … She cut off the thought before those terrible images could bloom in her mind again, like red ink on damp blotting paper. No. They needed to catalogue this book tonight. Only then could they go back to Frances's pretty little townhouse with its cosy, overstuffed armchairs, pot plants and books in every room. She thought too of the lovely magical family who rented the top two floors and warded not just the entire building but half the street.

Lydia tried a different tactic.

Raising her voice, she said, 'I would love to catalogue our new arrival, Frances, and welcome it officially to the Aberystwyth Library of Magical Texts, but it appears not to share our desire to keep this library safe.'

A ruffling of ancient pages from around the library signalled the other books' feelings on the matter. *Bit late, but thanks all the same*, Lydia thought.

'I understand it is unsettling being uprooted and shipped off to a new library, my friend,' Frances said, matching Lydia's tone and volume and turning in her chair to look up at the marching book. 'Please be reassured that as keepers, we all swear a blood oath to protect magic. You are quite safe here with us. I am Frances, and Lydia, here, is the keeper of the Pont Nefoedd library. She is by far our dearest and most esteemed colleague and friend.'

Out of the corner of her eye, Lydia saw the book come to an abrupt halt.

Frances turned back to Lydia, but barely had time to open her mouth before the book launched itself from the shelf and swooped down to the reading table. It landed at such speed that it slid across the wood, the momentum carrying it almost over the edge. Correcting itself, it shot swiftly back to Lydia and flipped itself open, its covers slapping impatiently on the table.

'Thank you,' she stuttered, exchanging a bemused look with Frances.

Lydia began patting down her pockets for her reading glasses, then checked her mop of mousy-blonde curls.

The book fidgeted on the table, its pages ruffling.

'Okay, okay. Hold your horses, my friend,' Lydia said

softly, taking the glasses that Frances had located under a pile of papers. She put them on and started to read.

The book's rough-edged pages fizzed and crackled as tiny blue sparks veined through and around them. Lydia sucked in a breath. She'd seen her fair share of keen books in the past, but this was on another level entirely.

A small red dot appeared under the text, racing along ahead of her at a pace she could barely keep up with. Once she approached the end of a page, it quivered, desperate to turn, which it did the moment her eye had taken in the last letter.

Lydia was dimly aware of Rose trotting back into the room, still wearing her white archive gloves, but the younger woman retook her seat without saying a word. She heard Frances set down her cup for a refill. The sound of a teaspoon on china. The faint crunching of biscuits. The ticking of the old clock on the wall marked out the seconds, but the more she read, the more she felt like time was slipping away from her.

Her mouth felt dry as dust, but she didn't dare reach for her tea. Now that the book was ready to share, it was sparing no detail. It was already clear that it had been the mention of Pont Nefoedd that had galvanised it into action.

Lydia's mind raced as if in competition with her thumping heart. How could this be true? It had to be, of course – the magical texts were incapable of deceit. They were the keepers of the world's truths, not the pedlars of myths and stories. But in her tiny little town of Pont Nefoedd? It just wasn't possible. It couldn't be possible. Could it?

It took her a moment to realise that Frances was speaking to her.

'Are you alright, my dear? You've gone as white as a sheet,'

Frances said, reaching out her hand and placing it on Lydia's arm.

Even though Lydia saw the movement, she jumped at the touch. Taking a deep breath, she tried to steady herself. It felt like waking from a dream. She thought of her daughter, Maggie, and what a beautiful young woman she had become. Of the grandchildren she might have one day. Of the world they might inherit.

She reached for her now lukewarm tea but stopped mid-air, taken aback by the sight of her trembling hand. She snatched it back and laced her fingers together, squeezing until her knuckles turned white in her effort to fight back the tears welling in her eyes. This was not the moment to fall apart.

Rose jumped out of her seat and disappeared, returning a few moments later with a glass of water in one hand, a small tumbler in the other, and a bottle of brandy wedged under her arm. *Not as green as she's cabbage-looking*, Lydia thought, hearing her mother's voice in her head.

She tried to smile up at Rose, but it was all she could do to hold herself together. She bit her lip and focused her attention on the table in front of her. The scratches and dents of decades, maybe centuries of service, to this secret place and to the world. If only people knew of the battle fought every day just to keep them alive – and free. The sacrifices. The lives lost. The dreams cast aside. All to protect something most people no longer believed in – magic. If only they knew that this thing they scoffed at was the very thing that kept the world turning. Oh, the irony.

Lydia nodded when Rose held up the brandy bottle. She downed the generous measure in one and then pulled a face as the liquor reminded her of why she rarely drank more than a sweet sherry at Christmas. She gulped a large mouthful of water, trying to chase away the awful taste. That said, she had to admit that it had the desired effect. She took another few deep breaths and unclasped her hands as she felt the shock dissipate. Holding her hands out above the table, she was relieved to see that there was only the slightest wobble in them now. She reached again for the water and sent the glass flying to the floor.

'I'll sort it,' Rose said, getting up and disappearing towards the kitchenette.

'I'm sorry,' Lydia began, but Frances waved the apology away as she pulled her chair close so that their knees were almost touching. Frances gently lifted Lydia's hands, cupping them in her own. Frances had such lovely hands, Lydia thought. While age had wrinkled the pale skin and peppered it with a few liver spots, her fingers were still long and elegant, her nails short and neatly trimmed.

A flash of memory – Frances playing the piano at last year's Yule party, her long fingers dancing across the keys. Everyone singing. Boudicca sitting next to Frances on the piano stool yowling loudly whenever the song ended. Everyone knew better than to laugh. Her wonderful cat. Her precious, beautiful family. Her lovely friends.

'Tell me,' Frances said, her tone gentle but commanding.

Lydia startled, the memory vanished, and she sucked in a lungful of air as she tried to focus on forming the sentence in her mind.

'It's not a myth,' she stuttered. 'It's real. All real.'

She shook her head, realising that the sentence she'd constructed in her head had come out half formed. She'd missed out the most important part. Her hands might have stopped shaking, but she still felt as unsteady as a newborn lamb.

She took a deep breath. Closed her eyes and tried again. 'The Ethereal. It isn't a myth. It's real.'

CHAPTER 5

ABERYSTWYTH, JULY 1960

*F*rances made a sound that might have been a gasp, but Lydia was still struggling to focus. 'That can't possibly be,' Frances said sharply.

The book shot across the table to rest in front of Frances, the picture of indigence. She couldn't blame it. Doubting a book was as bad as laughing at one. Lydia watched as the words rearranged themselves on the page, the arcane font morphing and expanding. The small red dot raced along underneath the text. It was clearly giving Frances the précis of the revelation it had just shared with her.

'What's going on?' Rose asked tentatively, returning to the table with a dustpan and brush.

Lydia sucked in a deep breath and thought about how to answer. Deciding that there was no way of sugar-coating it, she said, 'There is a prophecy. About a magical being who will decide the fate of humanity. A being who can catapult us into a new age of peace and love – if they feel that there is enough good left in humanity. One of the great texts from the library of Alexandria referred to it directly and named the book that spoke of it.' Lydia pointed at the little teal-green book Frances was still engrossed in.

'As the *Book of Prophecy* was never found, and because the Alexandrian text that mentions it has been firmly behind the iron curtain for as long as anyone can remember, some magical scholars dismissed it as a myth. But here we are,' Lydia said, letting out a long breath.

'What?' Rose gasped, her eyes flying to the little book, which was still lying open on the table in front of Frances. She screwed up her eyes, shook her head. 'Wait. The library at Alexandria was destroyed,' she said, frowning.

When Lydia responded by raising her eyebrows, Rose looked at Frances for confirmation.

Frances was still reading, so didn't look up.

Lydia hesitated. This knowledge wasn't usually shared with apprentices – some things were considered too sacred to divulge before the final oath was taken – but deciding that now was not the time to stand on protocol, she pressed on.

'That was a convenient story our ancestors spread to protect the books that were saved from Alexandria. Many were lost, it's true, but many survived. Where do you think some of these books come from?' she said, gesturing around the room.

Rose's mouth fell open.

Lydia anticipated the next question. 'We don't know why some survived and others didn't. There are lots of theories. As you know, not all books are sentient and not all books about magic contain magic. The origin of the sentient ones is still a mystery to us, but what we do know is that they never lie. Our friend on the table over there is the lost *Book of Prophecy.*'

Lydia's eyes flicked up to the old wall clock, and she bit her lip, aware that her heart was still pounding. This was the find of the millennium.

'Look, there's no time to explain,' Lydia said.

Frances stood up, her chair scraping against the parquet flooring. It sounded so alien, so dedicated was her friend with the preservation of all things historical, even old wood floors in a soon to be abandoned library. *Such a silly thing to notice*, Lydia thought. A lump bloomed in her throat, and she swallowed hard to dispel it.

'Well, thank you, my friend,' Frances said to the book. Then, looking at Lydia and Rose, she said, 'It can't be any clearer, can it. We need to search for it before humanity makes even more of a bloody mess of things.' Her voice betrayed just a hint of a wobble.

'You think it's here then?' Lydia asked nervously.

'That the book has revealed its secret to us here and now rather suggests that it is, yes,' Frances said, and Lydia saw that her old friend was trying to contain the same maelstrom of emotions that she herself was wrestling with.

'Do we dare hope?' Lydia asked, standing up.

'I think, my dear, we must,' Frances replied, her eyes bright as she squeezed Lydia's arm.

Then Frances did something completely out of character. She pulled Lydia into a quick, tight hug. She felt so delicate in Lydia's arms, so at odds with the robust, resilient woman she'd known most of her life. Then Frances stepped away, swiped at her eye with the heel of her hand and said, 'We must get word to the Elders. There's no time to lose. Will you do the honours, Lydia?'

'Of course,' Lydia replied, already heading towards the back office.

'The current password is Hemingway,' Frances called after her. 'You know the location code.'

Lydia hurried through the stacks and into the cave of a room that was lit by one central, bare bulb. It was flanked on three sides by utilitarian-looking bookcases all stuffed full of books with coloured tickets protruding from their tops. Most of the floor space was also taken up with stacks of books in various stages of cataloguing, plus an array of packing crates waiting to be filled. For the last few days, Lydia had felt her heart sink every time she came into the room, but now, moving the library paled almost to insignificance.

She went to Frances's old oak desk in the corner. An island of calm in a sea of organised chaos, it contained just a blotter, a pot of pencils, a desk lamp and a large black telephone. Ignoring the chair, she began to dial the number she'd learned as an apprentice but had never, until now, had cause to use. Her fingers felt too big for the dial and the time between numbers felt like an eternity.

Her heart thumped in her chest as she waited for the line to connect, although whether through fear or excitement, she couldn't tell. She chewed her lip. They were standing on the cusp of history; she could feel it in the air.

'Morgan here,' said a man's voice on the other end of the line, his accent managing to make even two words sound somehow musical.

Lydia made to speak, but her words, when they came, tumbled out in a high-pitched gabble.

'It's Penny, it is. Calling about the Hemingway book you ordered,' she said tightly.

There was silence on the line, then a sharp intake of breath. 'Oh. Penny, you say. Penny. Righto then. I'll be over to collect it quick as I can. Thanking you. Cheerio now.'

She pictured Morgan lowering the receiver. An almost overwhelming urge to shout his name gripped her. She needed to tell him everything they'd just discovered. Her chest tightened as if something was trying to force the words from her, and she clamped her hand across her mouth. To say anything more on an open line would break every rule in the book, and she'd be risking more than just the library. This information couldn't fall into the wrong hands. They had just found the most important book in human history.

'We'll see you then,' she blurted, trying to inject a smile into her voice but finding herself unexpectedly close to tears. It was too late. The line was already dead. She replaced the receiver and stood looking at it as someone might watch a retreating lifeboat. She didn't have time to examine the strange thought because just then someone screamed.

CHAPTER 6

ABERYSTWYTH, JULY 1960

*L*ydia raced back through the stacks as books hurled themselves from their shelves in all directions. A few collided with her, knocking painfully into her shoulder, shin and back. Her heart hammering and her arms raised to protect her face, she swatted away the books as gently as she could as she headed for the reading area. This was no playful display. The air was so thick with fear she could taste it, like ash on her tongue.

When Lydia rounded the last corner, she saw Rose standing stock still, staring into the far corner, her hands pressed to her face. Frances was beside her, chin lifted, hands balled into fists at her side.

Lydia followed their gaze. It took a second for her brain to fully process what she was seeing and hearing. The far corner was nothing but shadows save for a tiny triangle of feeble blinking light. The only sound was that of the old lift, its mechanics creaking and groaning at being pressed into service.

The fear slipped like a stone from Lydia's mouth and

landed in the pit of her stomach. Someone at ground level had summoned the lift.

'Rose!' Frances barked, shaking the young woman by the shoulders. 'Take the tier-ones and use the escape tunnel.'

The *Book of Prophecy*, which was still on the reading table, flew into Lydia's arms. She staggered slightly, unprepared, but clutched it to her chest.

'But who's ...' Rose stuttered. 'We're all here and Lydia only just called the Elders ...'

'Do it now, Rose!' Frances snapped, giving her another shake.

Then, addressing the library, she called, 'Code one! Code one! Emergency evacuation protocol. I repeat. Emergency evacuation protocol!' Her voice, loud but calm, seemed to echo around the vast room.

Lydia stood frozen. Rose didn't move either until Frances grabbed her shoulders and pushed her towards the office. The young woman cried out in shock and took a few stumbling steps before finding her footing.

'Help her,' Frances barked at Lydia as she snatched up a teacup and hurled it into the dimly lit corner away from the lift.

'But it could be ...' The words died on Lydia's lips, because they both knew that nobody with innocent intent would just show up at the library. This was a raid. Every keeper's worst nightmare was here, and statistically, they would not survive it.

The thought felt like a slap to the face, and Lydia gasped.

'Come on,' she said, striding towards Frances and putting her hand on her friend's arm. Frances shrugged off the contact.

The whirring of the lift mechanism stopped, and Lydia let out a breath. Long seconds passed, but then came the clank that could only be the sound of the cage door slamming into place two floors above them. The mechanism clattered into life again and the down arrow blinked as the lift began its slow descent.

'Come on,' Lydia repeated, grabbing Frances as panic rose in her chest.

Frances didn't move.

The down arrow on the ancient lift blinked.

'My car is outside. If I'm not here, they'll search the grounds sooner. This buys us a few minutes, and that might just be enough,' Frances said, not taking her eyes from the lift, her voice flat and emotionless.

'I won't leave you!' Lydia screeched.

'If they find you here, they will trace you to your library – and to your family. And with this' – she pointed to the book clasped to Lydia's chest – 'there is hope for the world for the first time in aeons. Save Rose. Save the books. Get the *Book of Prophecy* to the Elders. Go, please!' Frances said, her voice trembling on the last word as she sent another cup and saucer flying into the dark corner.

'No!' Lydia screamed.

Frances turned, and Lydia knew that she'd see that beautiful, defiant face in her dreams for as long as she lived. 'For Maggie,' Frances mouthed.

Lydia felt the words like a punch to her gut, but her legs responded, even as her heart screamed in protest and a wail of anguish left her lips. She grabbed Rose's arm, and pushing her ahead, ran to follow the stream of tier-one books that had already begun racing to the back office. The rest of the books had, with trembling spines, begun re-filing themselves onto the shelves. Lydia bit her lip, refusing to let her mind think about the fate that awaited the books who would not give up their secrets.

Behind them, the stacks rearranged themselves, turning ninety degrees to lead any would-be intruders to the false office, then the hidden tunnel beyond that would lead them to a locked room on the other side of the property. There was no escape from these men when they set their mind to magic-hunting, but the goal now was to save the books that could do the most damage in the wrong hands. She squeezed the little green book. This one, above all others, had to survive. The thought that she literally held the fate of the world in her hands made her feel sick.

When they reached the office, one of the metal bookcases at the back of the room was already standing ajar to reveal the passageway beyond it. The tier-one books had wasted no time in making good their escape, but Rose hovered at the entrance. Lydia motioned for her to follow the books, and Rose turned and crept tentatively into the darkness.

As Lydia turned the key in the door, she heard a loud and cheery ping. The lift had arrived. She held her breath as she pressed her ear to the door. There were muffled voices and then what sounded like a man laughing. She heard Frances's voice but couldn't make out her words. She let out a long breath and felt the belt of tension around her chest loosen a notch. Maybe it was just someone lost or a visiting witch somehow unaware of the strict protocols. Perhaps Morgan had sent someone in his place.

Lydia's hand was still on the key. She raked her teeth over her bottom lip. Protocol called for them to finish the evacuation procedure once initiated, but if it was a false alarm—The sound of what could only be gunshots pierced her hope. She clamped her hand over her mouth to stop herself crying out. Bile flooded her mouth as her stomach threatened to expel the tea and biscuits. This couldn't be happening.

The sound of shouted commands and running feet

galvanised her into action. She snatched up her handbag from where it lay on top of a packing case, zipped the trembling *Book of Prophecy* inside and plunged into the mouth of the tunnel. The bookcase swung closed behind her, swallowing the last of the light.

CHAPTER 7

ABERYSTWYTH, JULY 1960

*L*ydia had just enough time to see Rose waiting for her at the first bend of the tunnel, the books hovering behind her, before everything went black.

She clenched her hands into fists, ready to fight the panic that always threatened to consume her in confined spaces. The air was damp and cold in a way that only something that had never seen sunlight could be. It smelled of earth and everything that returned to it to rot.

She exhaled slowly and shuffled to the right, feeling along the cold stone wall for the light switch. Every escape tunnel was the same. Memories of the drills she'd done as an apprentice popped into her mind. Her aunt handing her the blindfold, stopwatch in hand, clipboard tucked neatly under her arm. The bruises had been brutal in the beginning as Lydia learned to navigate her own library without her sight, but within a few months she could sprint any route her aunt demanded.

Lydia's fingers brushed the cold metal casing of the switch, and a moment later, a row of amber lights blinked into life above their heads. Rose waited until Lydia caught up, and then they ran together through the narrow tunnel, carved, so legend held it, for those escaping persecution. All the libraries had them. As she fled, the books flying ahead of them, Lydia wondered if Rose had been close enough to hear the gunshots. She hoped not.

Lydia racked her brain, trying to remember where this tunnel ended. All graduate keepers had to memorise the evacuation protocols of all the magical libraries so that they could provide cover for another keeper at a moment's notice. It was one of the first things they did, but the knowledge now seemed buried beneath twenty years of busyness. Of raising her daughter and tending to her library while pretending to all and sundry that theirs was a normal, mundane, run-of-the-mill family and not one tasked with protecting ancient magic from those who might use it for ill.

Lydia felt suddenly desperate to see Maggie and Hywel. To warn them of the danger that had found them, but also to tell them about the *Book of Prophecy*, the promise that it spoke of. A world without wars, without suffering. A world where young men, like her brother, Teddy, got to live out their lives, not lie rotting in a trench in some forgotten part of France.

The tunnel ahead bent sharply to the left and Lydia all but careered into Rose and the gaggle of hovering books as she rounded the corner. Ahead of them stood a flight of old stone steps, their middles indented, worn smooth by the passing of who knew how many feet. At the top of the steps stood a metal door.

Lydia bent forward, bracing her hands on her knees as she tried to catch her breath. Rose leaned against the wall, breathing heavily too.

Rose recovered first. 'This comes out in the old dairy,' she said between breaths. There's a car hidden there. We need to take the old drover's road for just over a mile, but then we can join the A-road just before Moriah.'

'We need to get to Pont Nefoedd,' Lydia said. 'We need to get these books to safety as quickly as possible.'

'How long will it take?' Rose asked.

'Couple of hours, more or less,' Lydia replied, still panting slightly.

Rose was already pulling hessian sacks from hooks on the wall of the tunnel. She held one open, and without hesitation, the books flew in and settled. Lydia grabbed a sack, glad for a distraction from what they had to do next. Once the third sack was full, Rose cleared her throat.

'What do you think they did to Frances?' she whispered. Even in the dim light of the tunnel, Lydia could see the young woman was shaking, her skin as pale as fresh parchment.

They both knew very well what magic hunters had a reputation for doing. Lydia wondered if Frances had made Rose read the reports. It was protocol, but if she'd been worried about Rose's reaction, then maybe she hadn't yet.

The truth was brutal. The hunters were looking for the book they believed would grant them magical abilities. When they didn't find it, they left, sometimes taking non-sentient books with them, presumably if they believed they could be useful in their quest. There had never been a sentient book or keeper that had turned, and the hunters knew it. So they killed keepers and burned books.

Nobody could agree on how the hunters knew what they were searching for. Half of the community believed the book to be a myth, anyway. They suggested the quest was a convenient excuse for bitter, murderous men to kill those who possessed what they coveted. Modern-day witch-hunters driven by spite. Then again, some scholars had dismissed the existence of the book now hidden in her handbag. Humans had a strange and unhealthy ability to believe whatever suited them.

The sound of the two gunshots reverberated in Lydia's memory. She felt a sob rise in her chest but bit down hard on her lip. She had to stay in one piece or they would both be as good as dead.

Rose was still waiting for her reply.

Unable to lie but incapable of forming the words to tell the truth, Lydia said, 'Let's just focus on getting to safety,' her tone sharper than she'd intended. 'It's what Frances wants,' she added, trying to soften her tone but not quite managing it. She had used the present tense deliberately, but the lie felt like a barb in her heart.

CHAPTER 8

ABERYSTWYTH, JULY 1960

*H*efting a sack of books – Rose had insisted on taking the first two – Lydia climbed up the short flight of steps. She had never been more terrified in her life, but there was no way they could hide here. The magic hunters would find the tunnel eventually, and when they did … She refused to finish the thought, and instead turned the well-oiled wheel on the back of the door and pushed it tentatively. It opened soundlessly, the only impediment being the thick carpet of ivy that hung down over it. With a more forceful push, the ivy yielded, and Lydia squinted in the early-evening light.

Pausing, she offered up a prayer to any benevolent entity that may be listening, took a deep breath and then turned back to Rose.

'Listen to me. If anything should separate us, take my handbag – it's got the *Book of Prophecy* in it. Take it and get to my library, okay? Then call the Elders. Nothing matters more than this, Rose. Do you hear me? No arguing, no hesitation. At the slightest hint of danger, you take the bag and you run. Don't look back.'

Rose had begun shaking her head after the first few words. Lydia put down the sack and grabbed her shoulders. She didn't mean to frighten her and felt terrible when the younger woman gasped. She released her at once.

'I'm sorry. I'm sorry, Rose,' Lydia whispered urgently. 'But, please, what this book told us today, it's a chance we're unlikely to ever get again. This is about the fate of the whole world. All of creation, even. We can't let it fall into the wrong hands. Do you understand me?'

Rose looked frozen in fear. Her eyes were wide and unblinking. Her lips were parted as if she'd been interrupted mid-sentence.

After a moment's calculation, Lydia said, 'Rose, Frances is dead.'

Rose recoiled as if Lydia had struck her. Lydia bit her lip against her own tears. It had been a gamble, and there was nothing to be done about it now save to press on.

'Please don't let her sacrifice be for nothing,' Lydia said sternly. 'Get the book to Pont Nefoedd, Rose. Be like the apprentice witch, be the one who makes the difference. Will you do that? For Frances?'

Rose nodded miserably, wiping away her tears with the heel of her hand.

'Good girl,' Lydia said, reaching for Rose's arm and giving her a quick squeeze. 'Come on. Let's move.'

They were just a few steps out of the door when Rose ducked back and grabbed a set of keys from a rusty nail near the exit. She handed them to Lydia and nodded in the direction of the open barn. The hundred-yard dash from door to barn felt like a marathon. With every step Lydia wondered if it might be her last. Would a sniper's bullet find her? What if they shot Rose first? Would she have the courage to do what she'd just instructed the young apprentice to do? Leave her and run?

Confined in their sacks, the books were a dead weight, and even Rose, who had youth on her side, looked glad to set them down when they arrived, breathless, at the covered vehicle.

Lydia yanked off the tarpaulin and pushed the key into the door of a muddied Land Rover. It opened with a satisfying click. Once they'd put the books in the back, Lydia climbed into the driver's seat. She turned the key in the ignition and held her breath until the engine roared into life.

A minute later, with the aid of Rose's directions, they were on the drover's road that led away from the old manor house and the magical library it had hidden in its basement for hundreds of years. Rose wound down the window to adjust the large side mirror when a stray branch knocked it out of position. A blast of cool air rushed in, bringing with it the unmistakable smell of smoke.

The vision of a library in flames, terrified books flying in panic as their precious pages blackened and burned, came unbidden into Lydia's mind. There were many, many reasons to hate magic hunters, but their utter disregard for life in all its forms topped the list. Lydia gripped the steering wheel and prayed that she was wrong. Rose sniffed, and out of the corner of her eye, Lydia saw her wipe her eyes with the sleeve of her cardigan. It was cold comfort that they were probably imagining the same thing.

Rose wound up the window, and they drove in silence until the A-road came into sight. Lydia had never in her life been so grateful to see street lights and other passing cars, but they weren't safe yet. She pressed the accelerator.

They were silent for a long time. Lydia kept her foot down, almost hoping for a speeding ticket if it meant finding a police officer.

'Why did the wards fail?' Rose asked quietly, just as they turned onto the A470.

Lydia had been wondering as much herself. Frances's disquiet over the witch sent to reinforce them gnawed at her. She'd take incompetence over intent. That there was a traitor in the Elders' inner circle was too much to think about.

'I don't honestly know, but we'll need to tell the Elders that Frances wasn't happy with the witch who did it. Did you meet her?' Lydia asked, glancing over at Rose.

The young woman was resting her head against the window. 'No. Frances asked me to collect that last delivery of books from the Post Office. The wards weren't due that day, so we had been planning on picking the delivery up on the way to work. They don't open until nine. But the witch had called the evening before to say she'd be there at eight in the morning. So I dropped Frances at the library and then drove back to town to pick up the delivery. By the time I got back, she had already gone.'

'Do you remember her name?' Lydia asked.

'No, but Fr—' Rose snapped off the name and hurriedly changed the subject. 'Will this road take us all the way there?' she asked.

'Almost,' Lydia replied, glad of the change of tack. 'But I don't think we should go straight there,' she added, giving voice to a new thought.

'But isn't your library the safest place?' Rose said anxiously.

'Yes, but don't you think that escape was a bit too easy?'

She glanced at Rose, who was now sitting bolt upright and staring at her open-mouthed.

'That was the hardest thing I have ever done in my whole life,' Rose said, incredulous. 'How do you mean it was too easy?'

'Think logically, Rose. This was a well-planned attack; they always are. What if they were watching the library? Or that witch who did the wards was working for them. If they know about us, then it follows that they'll be looking for us.'

'But the tunnel is a secret and there was also the false office,' Rose said, although Lydia could hear her certainty fading.

'Granted. If they'd known where we'd come out, they would have taken us right there and then, but what if they were just watching all the roads around the manor? What if they've been watching for days? Or weeks or months? At the very least, they know every keeper has an apprentice.'

Lydia regretted that last comment as Rose visibly shrank into the seat.

'I'm sorry, Rose, but this is where we are, and if we want to get out of this alive, we need to use our heads, okay?'

It took a moment before Rose straightened up again. A quick glance told Lydia that the young woman was still terrified, but terrified and remembering her backbone was an improvement.

'If you're right and they were watching the roads, then we need a different car,' Rose said thoughtfully.

'Agreed. Builth is on the way – we can stop there and find a garage or something,' Lydia said, realising only once the words were out of her mouth that it was probably after eight o'clock, maybe even later. That was a major flaw in the plan, but she said nothing. They'd have to figure something out when they got there.

Lydia checked her mirror and felt the skin on the back of her neck prickle. Hadn't that car overtaken them earlier? She'd noticed it because it was new and just the sort of car that Hywel would have admired. Not that he'd have ever bought one, but he'd have commented on it. Theirs was a life of blending in, something his old, slightly battered Jag did very well. But cars like the one she'd just spotted were designed to stand out. Showy and 'look at me' arrogant. It, or another one much like it, was behind them now. Her pulse quickened, and she raked her bottom lip with her teeth. She had every right to be paranoid, but she decided not to say anything until she was sure.

'Tell me how you'd get to my library,' Lydia said quickly.

Rose blinked at her.

'I need to know that you know how to get there. In case we get separated,' Lydia explained, trying to keep the mounting sense of anxiety from her voice.

For a moment, Rose looked ready to debate the point, but then dutifully tripped off the address. For good measure, Lydia made her recite the emergency-line number to the Elders too, and tested her on the password.

If Lydia had been expecting the test to settle her nerves, it didn't. She checked her mirror again. There was no sign of the flashy car. She sighed. Paranoid then. That was fine. She'd rather be paranoid than dead.

'Do we need fuel?' Rose asked as the lights of a petrol station up ahead shone cheerfully against the darkening sky. Lydia frowned. Maybe it was later than she'd assumed.

In the mirror, Lydia saw that the setting sun had painted the sky with a fiery wash of pinks and oranges. On an ordinary day, she would have commented on the spectacle and delighted in the beauty of nature in all her glory, but today she found no room in her heart for wonder. Today was only about survival.

Lydia squinted at the gauge. 'We have plenty,' she replied, before glancing over to the garage.

Something snagged at her mind as they passed the brightly lit forecourt. It was funny how light often made people feel safe. Marooned on this long, lonely stretch of road, the garage looked like an oasis in a rapidly darkening desert. Maybe that was what had caught her eye.

She was still trying to process the thought as, with the neon lights fading into the distance behind them, she saw the flashy car round the bend. Seconds later, a bullet shattered the back windscreen.

CHAPTER 9

PONT NEFOEDD, JULY 1960

'I heard you were in the Colliers with that lad at dinnertime,' Hywel said as he put a plate of egg and chips on the kitchen table in front of Maggie.

'Dad! I am allowed in pubs now, you know. I'm not a child,' Maggie snapped, realising too late that tone did very little to support her argument.

'I know, love,' Hywel said amicably, adding a plate of bread and butter to the table. 'I was just making conversation. No need to bite my bloody head off.'

Maggie stared at her plate as what felt like a stone shifted under her ribs. *Grow up, Mags*, she told herself. Acting like a spoiled brat would not help convince her parents that she was making the right life decisions. The thought of even forming the words made her stomach turn over. She could just picture the looks on their faces when she told them.

'I'm sorry, Dad,' she said, looking him in the eye. 'I didn't mean to bite your head off.'

Her dad smiled.

'Especially after you've gone and made us another

gourmet meal as well,' she added, trying to smile as she speared an overly brown chip she no longer fancied.

Hywel laughed. 'That's alright, bach. Probably the nutrient deficiency playing with your mind already,' he joked, eyeing his own plate. 'I hope your mam gets back soon or we'll both be looking like egg and chips.'

'You know what Mam would say about your buttering skills too, don't you?' Maggie said, lifting a slice of bread and inspecting it, one eyebrow raised.

'Chapel bread!' they said in unison, then laughed.

'I think she got that from your nan. Nanny Owen, I mean. She was always moaning about how no bugger in chapel ever buttered up to the corners when they did the sandwiches for the service teas. The way she went on you'd think it was a hanging offence.' Hywel picked up a poorly buttered slice, folded it and dipped it into his egg yolk, grinning.

After forcing down a few chips, Maggie said, 'I am perfectly capable of cooking for us, you know. I don't mind, honest.'

'I know, love. I know. But I promised your mam I'd look after you while she was in Aber, and seeing as you're all grown up, this' – he pointed to their plates with his fork – 'plus a bit of shopping is all I can do, really.'

'You've got Bodie to look after too,' Maggie said, but only after glancing around the kitchen to make sure the cat wasn't in the room.

Hywel looked up, his eyes wide. He glanced around theatrically. 'Don't let her hear you calling her that,' he said in a stage whisper.

'Too late,' Maggie confessed, a finger of guilt poking at her ribs. 'I might have tried to be funny earlier.'

Hywel shook his head. 'You're a brave, some might say foolish young woman.'

'I was in a bad mood and being mean and I shouldn't

have. It's not her fault and I shouldn't have upset her. I've been avoiding her all day though, just in case,' Maggie said, pulling a face.

'Very wise indeed. Good job we love her, grumpy as she is,' Hywel said.

Maggie leaned over the table and pecked him on the cheek.

'What's that for?' Hywel said, his bushy eyebrows heading towards his thick head of salt-and-pepper hair.

Mam would be after him to get to the barbers when she got back, Maggie thought.

She shrugged. 'For looking after me. And Boudicca. For being there. Just ...' Emotion caught in her throat, snatching away what she'd been about to say next.

'Everything alright, love?' Hywel asked, his smile falling. 'Is it what's-his-name? Keith, is it?'

Maggie shook her head. Of course, it was him, wasn't it? And her apprenticeship and the rest of her bloody life.

'Your apprenticeship then? Mam says you're a natural keeper.' The pride that shone in her father's eyes tipped the balance.

'Oh, Dad,' Maggie said, her eyes filling with tears and taking her by surprise. 'But I'm not a natural keeper at all. In fact, I don't even know whether I want to carry on with my studies.' Her hand flew to her mouth, shocked that she'd finally admitted what had been playing on her mind for weeks since Keith had unofficially proposed. It had all been so romantic and she'd said yes. Who wouldn't have? He was gorgeous, but now she wasn't so sure.

Since meeting him at Christmas, a life spent in a dusty old library you couldn't tell anyone about, protecting magic you also couldn't tell anyone about, not to mention the possibility of being murdered for your trouble, seemed like a miserable prospect.

Hywel clasped his hands together and leaned towards her. He looked so sad for her that Maggie couldn't bear it. 'I didn't mean that, Dad. Forget I mentioned it, okay?'

As Maggie made to get up, Hywel reached over and gently took her hand. Hers felt tiny in his great bear paw, and she felt like a little girl again, clinging on to him as he walked her to the park.

'Yes, you did, bach, and you can say whatever you like under this roof, you know that. We've all of us got enough secrets to keep from the outside world. In here, together, we tell each other the truth. Always,' he said, his brown eyes serious and locked on hers.

Maggie nodded miserably. Now that she'd said it, she might as well test out what she was going to say to her mother. She felt sick just thinking about it.

'So, it's serious with Keith, is it?' Hywel prompted.

Maggie could read her father like one of her books. He was clearly not a fan of her first boyfriend but was trying incredibly hard not to say as much. She tried to see Keith as her dad might, and she had to admit that he was a bit 'rough around the edges', as her nan used to say. He had a good heart though, didn't he?

Another of her nan's sayings popped unbidden into her mind. 'Deep pockets but short arms on that one.' But so what if she'd paid for lunch again? Keith was right in saying that it was only fair for posh people to pay more than others. He'd grown up in a council house with only his dad's wage coming in, and so she supposed that living in a massive house next to the river and her dad owning a successful business probably made them seem posh by comparison. She had never felt posh, though.

'Sort of. Not really,' she said, tipping her head back to look at the ceiling to stop the tears. Giving up, she looked back at her dad and said, 'He's gorgeous, Dad. All my friends used to fancy him back in school. And he has a normal job. And I'm twenty-one. I just feel like I should be getting on with my life now, you know?' Maggie groaned. She stopped short of telling him about the proposal. 'I'm so confused.'

'Well, that's love for you,' Hywel said with a wistful smile.

Maggie huffed and made a face.

'Oh. Not love then?' Hywel asked, failing dismally to conceal the relief on his face.

'That's the thing, Dad. I don't know,' she said carefully. Surely, if she did love him, she'd know, wouldn't she?

She waited a beat, grateful that her dad wasn't trying to fill the silence. Putting the question of Keith aside for a moment, she said, 'It has made me question whether I want to be a keeper though. I mean, I love the books – really, I do, except maybe a few of the really spiteful ones, but even they settle down after you get to know them. It's just the thought of being stuck here for the rest of my life, you know? Having to get cover even for a weekend in Tenby with Auntie Gill. It's a lot to take on.'

Hywel nodded sagely. 'That it is, my girl, that it is.'

Maggie loved the fact that he wasn't trying to talk her into sticking it out, but she also wished that he would. It would be so much easier if her parents just made her do it, but that had never been their way.

'Mam will be so disappointed in me if I tell her this,' Maggie said, tears finally spilling down her cheeks.

'She will be disappointed, yes, but not in you. She would be utterly heartbroken if she thought for a minute that you were choosing this path for anyone other than yourself. Maggie, love, you're only twenty-one. You have your whole life ahead of you. Me and your mam, all we've ever wanted is for you to be happy,' Hywel said earnestly. 'You've always been so conscientious, but you need to live your life for you – not to please anyone else, including me and your mam.'

Maggie made to reply, but he held up a finger. 'All I'm saying, bach, is that being a keeper is one hell of a thing. You didn't ask to be born into all this. At least I married into it – I got a choice of sorts, but you didn't. Yes, it's a privilege and all that, but it's a dangerous life too. Nobody would think the less of you if you decided that wasn't the life for you. In fact, me and your mam would likely sleep a bit more soundly knowing you were off doing something where the biggest risks to life and limb were a few bloody paper cuts in an office somewhere.'

Maggie laughed despite herself as she wiped away her tears with the fresh hankie her dad had handed to her. He always had a knack for being able to cheer her up. She got out of her chair and threw her arms around his neck. She just wished her mam was here too.

CHAPTER 10

ABERYSTWYTH, JULY 1960

*L*ydia wasn't sure which one of them screamed first. She managed to keep the wheel steady in her hands, but cried out when she saw the car speeding up behind them again. At that moment, two things happened at once. A lorry pushed its way between the car and the Land Rover and one of the old books burst out of its sack on the back seat and landed with a thud on Rose's lap, making the young woman shriek, although whether in pain or surprise, Lydia couldn't tell.

'What's it doing?' Rose cried as the large, ancient-looking tome snapped itself open.

'Trying to help, by the looks of things,' Lydia replied, praying that the lorry wouldn't move until they could find a side road, or a handy police car. Where were the boys in blue when you needed them?

Out of the corner of her eye, Lydia saw the book's pages turn at an incredible speed, then come to an abrupt halt.

'What's it say?' Lydia asked, her voice a breathy squeak.

Rose didn't appear to hear her. Lydia was about to repeat the question when Rose spoke.

'But I'm not a witch! I can't cast spells!' she all but screamed at the book.

The book slammed itself down on Rose's lap and Lydia saw the young woman wince, her face pinched in what was definitely pain this time.

'Just read the bloody spell!' Lydia said, her heart sinking as, in the mirror, she saw the car abruptly swerve around the lorry. When she heard nothing but silence, she shrieked, 'Out loud, Rose! Out loud!'

Lydia wasn't a native Welsh speaker, so struggled to keep up. Rose's voice sounded nothing like her own as she recited the spell. It was deeper, older somehow, and filled with a knowing that Lydia didn't think the young woman possessed. In the mirror, the flashy car closed in.

Any doubts evaporated as the air pressure in the car changed just as the steering wheel stilled under Lydia's hands. The road ahead looked frozen like a photograph. A pigeon heading to its roost for the night was caught in mid-flap. The headlights of a car going in the opposite direction sliced tunnels of light through the gloom. Tentatively, Lydia lifted her hands from the wheel.

She snapped her attention to the mirror. The pursuing car was so close. A man with slicked-back dark hair had reached his arm out of the passenger window. He held a gun that was pointed right at them. Lydia stifled a scream. In some corner of her mind, she wondered where the bullet was. Was it still in the gun? Or already flying through the air towards them?

'What's happened?' Rose breathed.

'Time-freeze spell,' Lydia replied, her lips moving to provide the answer from some deeply buried part of her mind. It couldn't be possible, and yet the evidence of her own eyes told her that, yes, it was. It was then that she realised what she'd seen as they passed the petrol garage.

'Dai Pony!' Lydia exclaimed.

'What?' Rose asked, scrambling around in her seat as if she expected to see him somewhere in the car.

'David Davis, Horse Transport!' Lydia said quickly. She didn't know how long this spell would hold, so they had to be quick. 'Rose! There was a horse lorry back at the petrol station and the man who owns it lives in Pont Nefoedd. He's a good man. We can trust him.'

'We need to get out then!' Rose said, her hand already on the door handle.

Lydia swallowed and willed herself not to get emotional. There really was no time.

'No. The spell won't last long, so they' – she jerked her thumb behind her – 'need to think that nothing's happened. If we both just disappear from the car, they'll start searching other vehicles. We can't risk it.' It was Frances's logic, and it was the only way.

Despite her earlier promise, and just as Lydia herself had done, Rose protested. As if proving Lydia's point about the lack of time, they both felt the Land Rover stutter forward. Up ahead, the pigeon managed a single flap of its wings.

'Hurry, Rose, please,' Lydia implored, handing over her handbag with the *Book of Prophecy* zipped inside. 'Take the books from the back, hide them. Ask Dai to pick them up as you pass.' The wheel stuttered again beneath her hands and, much to Lydia's relief, Rose leapt out of the car, flung the back door wide and opened the sacks to let the books fly out.

Oh, clever girl, Lydia thought. What she said out loud was, 'Run!'

Lydia's heart thundered in her chest, and she bit her lip to stop it from trembling. She thought of her daughter. Her wonderful husband. Her library and her beloved cat. She had never been more terrified in her life. With an effort of will she didn't know she had, she swallowed the fear that felt like a hand around her throat. She had to survive this – for them.

She watched Rose and the books dive into the scrub at the side of the road, and then, all at once, the spell collapsed and the car lurched forward, taking her breath as the seatbelt bit into her chest. She slammed her foot on the accelerator and watched as the speedometer climbed. The Land Rover rattled in protest but obeyed.

There was a sudden change in pressure. A spark of blue light flared for just a heartbeat in her peripheral vision, and then something landed gently in Lydia's lap. She glanced down to see the *Book of Prophecy* she'd zipped into her handbag just hours ago. The same handbag she'd just given to Rose!

'What? No! You're meant to be with Rose! It's not safe with me!' she wailed, a wave of fear and panic breaking over her. She looked back to the road just in time to see red tail-lights looming. She swung the wheel, barely swerving around the car in front. The sound of the indignant horn faded into the night as she gunned the accelerator. 'Sorry, sorry, sorry,' Lydia muttered. What was she meant to do now? 'You need to go back to Rose!' she screamed at the book in her lap, not daring to take her eyes from the road.

The back window on the driver's side shattered, showering her in glass. Lydia shrieked.

In the rear-view mirror, she saw the man in black lean out of the window again. She cried out and gripped the steering wheel, ready to swerve, but to where? There were no side roads that she could see, and how was she meant to dodge a bullet?

As if in answer, the car lurched violently to the right, almost yanking the steering wheel from her hands. *Oh god, not the tyres*, Lydia thought, but it was too late. She fought with the wheel, but the Land Rover felt like a wounded beast in its death throes. Her plan, such as it was, involved getting off the main road and hiding. She couldn't do that on foot.

I'm not going to survive this. The thought felt like a punch to the chest. She cast around, frantically looking for somewhere to hide the book. There was nowhere they wouldn't find.

'You need to go back!' she screamed as she wrestled with the wheel. 'Go back to Rose! They can't find you! What you told me, it's too important. You are too important! Save yourself!'

The book didn't move from her lap, but Lydia felt a heat radiating from it. She risked a glance down – the book was haloed in a golden light. She caught her breath.

Just then, the pressure changed again, and everything stopped. The steering wheel stilled in her hands. Lydia looked in the mirror to see the pursuing car once again, frozen behind her. Maybe the time-stop spell had reasserted itself? She grabbed the book and reached for the door handle, ready to run, but with a sickening lurch, the car shot forward again.

'No!' Lydia cried. But there was something different this time. It took her a second to realise that the engine had died. Panicked, she checked the mirror; the pursuing car was shrinking into the distance. Was it slowing down? If so, it was doing so at an incredible rate.

A flash of bright golden light from beyond the windscreen made her wince. She screwed up her eyes until it dimmed enough for her to risk a glance.

'Oh, bloody hell,' she murmured, reaching for the book on her lap.

Just beyond the bonnet of the Land Rover, a ring of golden light, large enough to drive through, hung in the air. Delicate threads danced around its edges, but it was what Lydia saw at its centre that transfixed her.

Clutching the book, Lydia opened the door and stepped out of the vehicle. The light was warm, welcoming. Like an old friend. Familiar and safe.

I'm already dead and hallucinating as my brain shuts down, she thought, as people and places she'd never seen flashed before her eyes as clearly as if she was sitting in the front row of the Roxy cinema.

People laughing and dancing in a strange-looking coffee shop. A young woman in a cloak galloping across fields on a raven-black horse. A murder of crows surrounding an old woman with a walking stick. A coven in a forest glade, a barn owl ghosting high above them. A kaleidoscope of butterflies against a leaden sky. The last thing she saw was a woman with wings of light erupting from her back. As she turned her face towards Lydia, darkness fell.

CHAPTER 11

PONT NEFOEDD, JULY 1960

*W*hen Keith phoned after work, suggesting a drive to his mate's pub near Brecon, Maggie told him she had a stomach-ache and needed to stay home. Keith had pretended not to hear her and droned on about how he needed some fun after his long and stressful day.

Hywel pulled a funny face as he walked past her in the wide, wood-panelled hallway where she sat perched on the telephone table. She rolled her eyes in reply and gestured to the phone.

She heard the pips sound and hoped Keith had run out of money for the phone box he was calling from, but the sound of more change sliding into the slot told her he likely had a row of coins lined up.

Once he'd finally paused in his complaining, she tried again to tell him she had a stomach-ache. His reply was dismissive and the comment about taking a tablet for the pain put the tin lid on things.

'Keith, I'm not well, so no. You'll have to entertain your-self tonight,' she said. Then she hung up with a little more force than was strictly necessary. She felt bad about lying to him, but when he refused to listen, she felt she had no choice.

'You busy studying this evening or can I interest you in an evening on the settee with your old man watching the telly?' Hywel asked when she went into the living room. He was already on his feet and halfway to the kitchen door.

Maggie brightened. Her dad always found a way of making her smile. 'You're on,' she said as she followed him into the kitchen. She began opening cupboards and drawers, determined to root out some biscuits. Lydia was always on at them about eating healthy food, but her dad usually had a packet of biscuits squirrelled away somewhere.

'They're in my toolbox under the sink,' Hywel confessed.

'Oh, that's super sneaky!' Maggie said, turning to see Boudicca draped across the draining board.

'Should have followed the cat. She's always trying to get me into trouble, that one,' Hywel said, reaching out to stroke the reclining feline. She bumped her head up to meet his hand and then, in one fluid movement, sprang deftly to perch on his shoulder.

Maggie sighed. What she'd give to get a shoulder perch. Maybe one day, once she'd reined in her spiteful human tendencies. 'Sorry, Boudicca,' she muttered.

They were watching *The Sky at Night*, one of her dad's favourites, when the cat let out a strangled yowl from her perch on the back of the settee. A few moments later, the doorbell rang.

Maggie glanced at the clock on the mantelpiece. It was after eleven.

'Stay there,' Hywel said as he jumped to his feet, instantly on alert.

Maggie knew that he'd go into the dining room on the other side of the hallway to check who was at the door before opening it. They might be a so-called anomaly in magical circles, but nobody took any chances these days. Besides, as nobody knew how this so-called anomaly worked, they didn't know how long it had protected them or, indeed, how long it might last.

Getting up, Maggie lurked by the living room door, straining her ears. As she knew from the countless drills her mother made her do each month, it would take her twelve seconds to make it to the kitchen larder and the hidden staircase down to the library.

The doorbell rang for a second time. Then her father's voice, 'Coming,' and the sound of his slippers scuffing along the wooden floor. She heard the locks being released, the clatter of the chain as he let it fall. Images of the local police officers at the door shot into her mind just as her heart leapt into her mouth. Her mother. *Please no*, she thought as she strained her ears.

'Hiya, Dai,' her dad said, loud enough to make sure Maggie heard him. She let out a breath, her shoulders relaxing and her heart rate returning to normal.

'Maggie!' her father called, and she jumped. Her legs were already weak with relief by the time she joined him at the front door.

Instead of the police officers of her imagining, she saw Dai Pony, a diminutive man in his late fifties who was renowned for being able to load any horse into his trailer with nothing more than a gentle word and a handful of pony nuts, hence the nickname. He touched his cap in welcome.

'Hiya, Maggie, love. Didn't wake you, did I?'

'Hiya, Dai, alright?' she said. Then added, 'No, we were up watching the telly.'

It was only then that Maggie noticed a mousy-looking young woman standing behind him.

'Friend of your ma's,' he said, nodding to her. 'Her swine of a boyfriend – excuse my French, ladies – he left her on the hard shoulder of the A470 with all her heavy bags and all. What do you think of that, eh? What a rotter! Took us ages to find her bags, too.'

Maggie and Hywel both replied at once, commenting on the awfulness of it all. They were making all the right noises, but the thumping in Maggie's chest told her that something was very wrong here. She had never seen this young woman in her life, and whoever she was, she looked terrified.

Dai was still in full flow. 'But as luck would have it, I was in the garage, see. I always stop at that one for diesel as it's cheaper than the one in town. Angela runs it, I forget her married name now, but she's belonging to the Sullivans. You know, them that used to have the cobblers in town. Married that chap that used to own the fish shop in Aber. Anyway, Rose here...' He faltered then and turned to the young woman. 'How is it you came to know I was from here, again?' he asked, lifting his cap to scratch his head.

'Oh, every bugger knows you, Dai,' Hywel laughed, stepping outside and clapping the other man on the shoulder. 'And the dirty great big sign on the lorry might have been a clue, eh?'

Dai cast a glance at the horse lorry standing in the shadows, then, frowning in confusion, looked back at Hywel. 'But—'

'Tell me about this new grandson of yours, Dai,' Hywel said, walking him towards the lorry. 'Called him Dafydd after you, haven't they?'

Nice one, Dad, Maggie thought as she turned her attention to the newcomer standing on the doorstep. She was about Maggie's age, tall, rake thin and with long brown hair hanging in a plait across her shoulder. She wore a thin cotton checked blouse underneath a plum-coloured cardigan, an unfashionably long corduroy skirt that looked at least two sizes too big for her and sensible lace-up shoes.

She also had a handbag pressed to her chest like a life preserver.

'You'd better come in,' Maggie said, stepping aside. 'Rose, is it?' she tried again when the young woman didn't move. Her eyes flicked from Maggie to the sacks sitting in the driveway. Just by looking at them, Maggie could tell they were full of books. She swallowed hard.

'You go in, I'll bring these,' Maggie said, stepping past Rose and hurrying to pick up the first sack. The crunch of the gravel under her slippers felt impossibly loud in the darkness.

With the third sack safely deposited in the hallway, Maggie turned her attention back to Rose.

'Is it my mam?' Maggie asked, barely able to form the words.

Rose let out a choked sob. Behind them in the hallway, the telephone rang.

CHAPTER 12

PONT NEFOEDD, JULY 1960

'*P*hone's ringing, love,' Hywel said, putting his hand on Maggie's shoulder as he manoeuvred around her on his way into the house.

Maggie turned in time to see Dai Pony climb into his lorry. Rose remained rooted to the spot, her chin bent to her chest so that Maggie could only see the crown of her head. She had a very neat parting. Precise.

'Pont Nefoedd two six five eight.' Her father's voice seemed to come from somewhere a long way away.

There were two moths circling the outside light. Pale paper wings beating against the glass walls of the lantern. Maggie hoped they wouldn't find a way inside and get burned by the bulb. The wind picked up, sending stray strands of Rose's hair flying around her face. She didn't seem to notice. Maggie's skin prickled in the night air, the chill creeping down her spine and into her bones. She shuddered.

'Maggie!'

Hywel was suddenly in front of her, his hands on her shoulders, shaking her gently. She caught her breath, reality rushing back to meet her. Her father's face looked pained, and even in this light, she could see that he had none of his usual colour.

'Come on, both of you. Let's get you safe inside,' Hywel said, giving Maggie a gentle nudge towards the door.

When Rose still didn't move, he shot Maggie a helpless look.

'In we go now, Rose,' Maggie said, adopting the tone she'd been cultivating for the harder-to-handle books.

Rose looked up, her gaze shifting uncertainly between Maggie and Hywel.

'You're safe now, cariad,' Hywel said, standing aside and gesturing into the house.

Like a cautious mouse, Rose crept forward.

'Who was that on the phone, Dad?' Maggie asked quietly.

'It was Morgan, love,' he said with a sigh. 'Let's get her settled and I'll tell you.'

In the living room, Boudicca took one look at the stranger, hissed and stalked out of the room, her tail like a lightning rod.

'Don't take it personally,' Hywel said to Rose. 'She's a bit temperamental with people she doesn't know.'

Rose didn't seem to even notice the cat.

'You sit yourself down by here. Do you want a cuppa or something stronger?' Hywel asked as he gestured to the battered old settee in the large living room.

When Rose didn't reply, Hywel touched her shoulder, and she jumped as if his hand was a cattle prod.

'I'm sorry, love,' he stuttered, holding up his hands. 'You sit down and I'll put the kettle on.'

Rose lowered herself onto the settee. She glanced up, and the look Maggie saw in her eyes made her catch her breath. She'd seen no one look so lost in her life. She swallowed hard. 'Are you from the Aber library, Rose?' she asked tentatively.

Rose curled in on herself again, hugging her handbag to her chest, her head bowed. Maggie gritted her teeth. Tea. Sweet tea. If the girl was in shock, it would help.

Her dad was filling the kettle when she rushed into the kitchen.

'Morgan's on his way here,' Hywel said, his eyes fixed firmly on the kettle as he placed it on the cooker. His next sentence came out in a rush. 'He said your mother called from the Aber library using the code earlier today.'

Maggie's hand flew to her mouth.

Hywel crossed to stand in front of her. 'He said there was no indication that anything was wrong. She used the standard alert code, not the emergency one. You'll know better than I will what that means.'

Maggie forced her brain into gear. She screwed up her eyes, trying to remember.

'The standard alert is a call from a bookshop about an order. It means they've discovered something of interest that needs immediate attention. Otherwise, it's just included in the monthly report,' Maggie said. 'But what about Mam? What aren't you telling me, Dad?'

Hywel turned back to light the gas under the kettle, but Maggie could see his jaw clenching. She felt her stomach drop. She didn't want to hear any more. If he didn't say the words, then maybe it wouldn't be real. But before she could instruct her legs to move, he continued.

'By the time Morgan got there, the old manor house was on fire.'

Maggie gasped. 'No. No. No,' she said, backing away, her feet readying themselves to bolt.

Hywel grabbed her hands and held them gently but firmly.

'Your mother wasn't in there,' he said, enunciating every word clearly while holding her gaze. 'Have you heard me, love? She wasn't in the house when the fire brigade searched it.'

'But what about the—'

'The Elders sent our own people in to search all the tunnels and secret places plus the surrounding areas, and there was no sign of your mother anywhere. Rose in there is the apprentice from Aber.' Hywel let out a long breath and let go of her hands.

Maggie cast around, looking for the nearest chair, as her legs threatened to rebel in the task of holding her up. Before she could move towards one, her dad swept her into a bear hug.

'Raid,' was all Maggie could manage between her sobs.

After a few moments, Hywel steered her to a chair and pulled out another to sit beside her.

'Definitely a raid. They …' Hywel raked his hands over his face and Maggie braced herself when she saw his expression.

'Love, I don't know how to tell you this, so I'm just going to have to come out with it. Frances is dead,' he said, his voice catching.

Maggie let out a cry that was something between a sob and a scream. Then the rage came. She jumped to her feet, her anger propelling her forward. She paced, like a caged lioness who wanted nothing more than to rip the head off her captors and feast on their remains. This felt better than fear. Anger she could work with.

Hywel watched her for a few moments before he spoke again. 'As I said, though, there's no sign of your mam, and as Rose is here with a few sacks full of books, then we can only assume that they both escaped before the raid and your mam is making her way back here now.'

'She'll not come direct,' Maggie said, busying herself with the tea-making for want of something to do with her hands. Despite her fears, the logic of what her father had just told her was clear. There was no evidence that anything had happened to her mother, and besides, she would have felt it, wouldn't she? They were mother and daughter. There would be a connection.

'Mam won't risk leading anyone here,' Maggie said, aware that her voice didn't sound quite like her own.

'You're right there,' Hywel said. 'Your mother wouldn't do anything to risk your safety or the library's.'

'Or yours or Boudicca's,' Maggie corrected.

His tight smile and faraway look brought a threat of fresh tears to Maggie's eyes. She turned back to focus on the tea-making. The sound of the cat flap announced Boudicca's return. The cat leapt silently onto the worktop and stalked along it. In a show of affection usually reserved only for Maggie's parents, she butted her head into her arm, which sent the second teaspoon of sugar she had been about to drop into Rose's mug spilling. Ignoring the mess, she put down the spoon and stroked the slow-blinking feline. Her fur smelled of darkness and the chill of unseasonably cold nights.

'Thanks,' she said to the cat, looking into her deep blue eyes. She meant it too. Boudicca made a noise that might have been something between a chirrup and a yowl, then turned on her dainty feet and launched herself onto the table. It was clearly Hywel's turn for her feline pep talk.

Maggie went back to her task. Her anger had slowed to a rolling simmer, giving the first bubbles of grief a chance to move in. Memories of Frances slipped into her mind. Games in the library when she was a child, Yule parties, her birth-day, and earlier in the year, a rare research visit to Aber. Rose had been off sick that day and Maggie had been secretly pleased to have Frances all to herself.

She couldn't remember a Christmas or birthday when Frances hadn't sent her a book. Always accompanied by a

handwritten letter explaining precisely why she thought
Maggie might enjoy it – and she had never been wrong. She
was – had been, Maggie corrected herself – a kind, generous,
if occasionally formidable aunt. And now she was gone.
Killed by the worst people imaginable.

The anger rose again, and Maggie welcomed it. Anything
was better than grief. As soon as her mother made her way
home, they'd know the entire story. Maybe then she could
find time to grieve for Frances, but now wasn't the moment.
She had tea to make and a terrified-looking apprentice to
quiz.

CHAPTER 13

PONT NEFOEDD, JULY 1960

Rose had only been in the sea once in her life. She was ten when they went to Rhyl on their first and last ever holiday. Her mother's boyfriend, a stout Mancunian with a hairy back but a bald head, had thrown her into the sea.

Her mother had, for once, tried to help, explaining that Rose couldn't swim, but he'd shoved her so hard she'd fallen backwards onto the sand. Rose remembered the smell of him – stale sweat, cigarettes and cheap beer. He'd flung her into the water like she was a rag doll he needed to drown.

She hadn't even had time to scream. One minute she was in the air, the next she was being pummelled by waves that felt determined to take her last breath. She didn't know how long she'd fought for breath, but she remembered the moment she knew she was going to die.

It was a teenage boy who saved her, pulling her from the depths and then dragging her back to the shore while her mother's beer-bellied boyfriend stood watching, a fresh can of lager already in his hand. Her mother behind him, wringing her hands.

Rose was back in those waves now, not knowing which way was up. Even sitting on this settee in this big house that smelled of fresh laundry and furniture polish. She didn't feel like herself. It was as if she'd been shaken apart and put back together all wrong. Was this what shock felt like?

The sound of rattling china made her jump. Unbidden, a picture of Frances hurling her precious teacups into the dark corners of the library burst into her mind. She flinched, closing her eyes against the image as her breath hitched in her chest.

'Brought you tea, love,' the man said. Rose tried but failed to remember his name.

'I'm Maggie, and this is my dad, Hywel,' the young woman said, as if reading her mind.

She held a mug out to Rose, which she took with shaking hands.

'Are you feeling up to telling us what happened?' Hywel asked gently as he sat on the armchair opposite. He had a kind face, Rose thought. Olive skin, bushy eyebrows, and thick dark hair peppered with silver.

Rose opened her mouth to speak, but nothing came. She frowned. Cleared her throat.

Maggie took the armchair closest to her. She looked so much like Lydia. The same roundness to her features, the pale, clear skin and intense blue eyes. Maggie's hair was lighter than her mother's, almost blonde, and straight, whereas Lydia's was curly. They had the same air about them, though. Kind but quietly confident. In control.

Rose took a sip of her tea, which was almost unbearably sweet and so hot she winced. She looked from Hywel to Maggie. The hope in their expressions was almost too much to bear. Of course, they would be worrying about Lydia. Why was she being so slow? She tried again to form the words, to tell them what had happened, but she had nothing. Her eyes filled with frustrated tears.

'It's okay, bach. You're in shock.' Hywel paused and took a breath before continuing. 'Forgive me though, love, because I've got to ask you,' he said as he clasped and unclasped his hands nervously.

Rose was already nodding vigorously. They wanted to know about Lydia. Even if her words were failing her, she could give them that much.

Maggie put her hand on her dad's knee. 'Was my mam alive when you left her?' she asked, the words tight and rushed.

Rose frowned. Had she left Lydia? No. It was Lydia who had made Rose leave, wasn't it? Her thoughts jumbled again, tossed around in the darkening sea of her memory. Sitting in the car. Lydia driving. Smoke in the air. The flash of lights. Someone screaming. There was a pigeon. What did the pigeon have to do with everything?

'Was she, love?' Hywel prompted, sounding desperate. 'I know it's hard, but you don't need to be afraid to tell us the truth. You're safe now,' he added.

Rose stared at him for a second and then her mind cleared, the confusion carried away by a fresh tide. She nodded vigorously.

'She was alive?' Maggie asked, leaning forward and peering at Rose with an intensity that made her shrink back into the settee. Rose nodded again, quicker now, first at Maggie and then Hywel, desperate to reassure them. She tried again to say yes, but all that came out was the sound of strangled air.

'Oh, thank God,' Hywel cried, burying his head in his hands.

Beside her, Maggie let out a stuttering breath. She patted

Rose's knee as she stood. 'I'll fetch you some biscuits,' she mumbled.

Rose tried again to speak. To explain that they had been in the car together. That the big spell book that was now in their hallway had cast a time-freeze spell all by itself. But inexplicably, the words just weren't there.

CHAPTER 14

PONT NEFOEDD, JULY 1960

*M*aggie loosed a breath as she made her way down the stairs, relieved that their new house guest hadn't protested when her dad had suggested she turn in for the night. Maggie's knowledge of dealing with shock stopped at sweet tea, and she only knew that because she'd seen it on the telly. It would have to be enough until the Elders arrived.

Hywel was standing at the bottom of the stairs next to the sacks of books. He raised his eyebrows in question.

Maggie waited until she was on the last step before speaking. 'She's as okay as she can be,' she said, keeping her voice low. 'I told her where the bathroom was and left her one of my nighties. Maybe her voice will come back after a sleep and she can tell us the full story.'

'Let's hope so, poor dab,' Hywel said.

Glancing down at the sacks, Maggie said, 'We'd better get these down to the library. Mam won't risk coming to the front door, nor will the Elders. We'd best wait down there.'

She grabbed a sack of books and headed for the kitchen.

Once in the larder, Maggie swung open the back shelves to reveal the door down to the basement library.

She turned in time to see her father, a sack of books thrown over each shoulder, set his jaw as he pulled in a deep, deliberate breath.

'I've never understood this lot's obsession with tunnels and small spaces,' Hywel huffed. 'It's not bloody natural. I thought librarians were more like owls, not ruddy moles.'

Ironically, for such a bear of a man, her dad was not great with anything vaguely cave-like. She wasn't about to point out that the library beneath their feet had the footprint of a football pitch and fifteen-foot-high ceilings to ensure proper ventilation for the precious books.

Admittedly, the stairs that connected house and basement were narrow. There had been talk a while back about putting in a cargo lift like they had in Aber, but as theirs was a house in the heart of a busy town, such work would never go unnoticed, and attention was the last thing they needed. Plus, one of their tunnels was big enough to drive a car through, which was something Aber didn't have.

'Mind the—' Maggie didn't get to finish the sentence. Her dad cursed under his breath as his head collided with the single pendent bulb that hung above the first step.

Every time, Maggie thought as she steadied herself against the now undulating amber light on the stairs.

'What I've never understood is why they can't just put them above ground and hide them with spells and stuff,' Hywel grumbled.

Maggie wasn't about to point out that she'd overheard her parents having this exact conversation a hundred times, always when Hywel had to brave the library stairs. A memory of her mother rolling her eyes theatrically leapt into her mind and she bit her lip. She loved her parents' easy banter. The way they teased each other, then danced in the kitchen when the radio was playing something from their courting days.

Maggie swallowed and cleared her throat. She didn't want to think about that now. Couldn't, in fact, think about what it might mean if …

'There is some magical protection,' she said, forcing herself into apprentice mode. She had to give this exact speech to novice witches when they visited for research trips.

'The books themselves do some of the work, but trying to conceal an area this vast' – she strained on the last word as she heaved open the heavy metal door at the foot of the stairs – 'would take way too much energy, even for the strongest witch.'

Just inside the door was a bank of eighteen metal light switches. She usually only turned on the top row, which illuminated the reading area and the route to the kitchenette, but not tonight. Tonight, she flipped every switch.

She stood aside to let her dad enter first, and Hywel huffed out a long breath the moment he was through the door. He strode to the long reading table in the middle of the room, set down the books and sank into a chair like a man who had just scaled a mountain.

'Thought you'd be here, your ladyship,' he said as Boudicca landed silently on the table beside him. 'Should have known you'd want to be in on the welcoming committee when your mam gets home.'

'She could be hours yet,' Maggie said, glancing at the old clock above the notice board where she and her mam left messages for each other. She saw a note in her own handwriting. *Mam, please call Joan in Edinburgh.* Then another below it, in Lydia's looping script. *Mags, remember the report on the Barcelona raid is due on Friday. Sorry, darling. Love, Mam xx*

Maggie felt her lip tremble as she read it and had to bite down hard to stay in control. She checked her watch against the clock. Nearly one in the morning. Rose had arrived just over an hour ago. If her mother was following along separately, she might be here any minute. Her mam's voice echoed in her mind. 'Hope is a powerful magic, Maggie, my love.'

Maggie snapped back to the present when she realised her dad was speaking. Joining him at the table, she lifted the sack of books up onto it.

'And when are you going to tell us how you get in and out of here, madam? This place is like Fort Knox, but you find a way, don't you?' Hywel asked the cat as he tickled her under the chin. Boudicca blinked slowly at him, purring, then abruptly turned and began grooming her outstretched back leg.

Hywel smiled and then yawned, rubbing his palms over his face.

'I'll make us a cuppa to keep us awake,' he said, bracing his hands on his knees as he pushed himself to standing. 'Tea or coffee, love?' he asked as he turned towards the small kitchenette that had been caffeinating keepers for decades.

Maggie was about to reply when the peal of a bell stopped them both in their tracks. She bolted for the storeroom, her heart hammering as she swerved around the old wooden stacks she could literally navigate blindfolded. As she burst into the large square room, the old butler's bell rang again from its perch above the Welsh dresser on the far wall.

Weaving through the forest of metal shelving units, Maggie felt a lump catch in her throat. This wasn't the time to fall apart, she told herself. That would be the last thing her mother needed, given what she'd likely been through. Hell, she might even be injured. No, she had to stay strong. But, oh, how she wanted to fling her arms around her.

Still panting slightly from the run, Hywel helped her push the dresser aside to reveal the door behind it. She hadn't needed any help. It glided easily on the hidden rails she grumbled about oiling each week. Never again, she promised herself.

Hywel stepped forward and turned the door's heavy iron wheel. Maggie could have opened it with one hand, but she let her dad do it. She heard the mechanism clank and then the door was opening.

Time seemed to slow down from that point. She was dimly aware of stepping backwards as the door opened towards her. Of finding herself caught between it and one of the metal racks, her view of the passage beyond obscured. She saw her father take a step to the side. Saw his shoulders fall, and in an instant, Maggie knew it was the Elders at the door, not her mother.

CHAPTER 15

*T*he weight of her disappointment seemed to pin Maggie to the spot. She heard the muffled greetings from the Elders. Morgan and Seren were both using the sort of tone reserved for hospital bedsides and funerals. Someone said something about this being 'an awful business', but the rest was lost to her.

Maggie knew the protocols following an evacuation. She also knew that her mother was a stickler for the rules, so there was no way she'd risk leading the magic hunters back to Pont Nefoedd. It may be hours still, even a day, maybe two, before she got home.

Maggie startled as someone patted her arm. She looked up to see Morgan looking at her intently. If his face was a map, it would be a river basin, laced with lines and tributaries that all seemed to lead you to the pale pools of his watery-blue eyes.

She tried to smile in welcome. Despite her disappointment, it was good to see him. Was it her imagination or was he more stooped than before? The joke, in happier times, was that his back had started to curve after giving up the battle with books, maps and all the bending to examine the rocks and wildflowers he found so fascinating. Her mother used to tease him that walking anywhere with him was like walking with a puppy who stopped to inspect every blade of grass.

'I said, I know it's nigh on impossible, but please try not to worry about your mother, Maggie dear,' Morgan said. 'She'll be making her way back through a convoluted route as per the protocol. And rest assured, we have everyone in the community out looking for her.' He had such kind eyes, and even in the dim light of the storeroom, Maggie could see that they were red around the rims. As he was at pains to tell all the new apprentices, everyone was entitled to their tears, even him, the chair of the Council of Elders.

Maggie bit her lip. She wouldn't cry. She tried to think of a suitable response, but her dad saved her.

'Chris not with you?' Hywel asked.

Morgan turned to answer. 'Just me and Seren for now. Chris is on call at the hospital, so she'll follow on when her shift is done.'

'Hello, Maggie,' Seren said, stepping around Morgan.

Tall, long-limbed and with the grace of a dancer, Seren managed to make black capri pants, flat pumps and a thin black jumper look catwalk elegant. Her long dark curls were pulled into a ponytail that just served to emphasise chiselled cheekbones that Maggie would give her high teeth for.

'Hi,' Maggie said.

It was reassuring to have a witch in the house, but whether it was her magic, her looks or her otherworldliness that intimidated Maggie, she could never tell.

'Rose is sleeping upstairs,' Hywel said. 'Well, I hope she's managing to get some sleep at least, poor lamb. Do you want to talk down here or go up to the house?'

'The house, please,' Seren said.

Morgan glanced at Seren. He looked as if he was about to say something but changed his mind.

'The house then,' Morgan said with a nod.

Boudicca was sitting on the edge of the reading table when they entered the main library, her front feet buttoned together and her tail curled neatly around them. Maggie should have guessed who was at the door. Had it been her mother, the cat would have beaten them both to it.

'Greetings, Boudicca,' Seren said with a slow nod that was almost a bow. The cat rose to her feet, stretched theatrically and made her strange Siamese chirrup. Seren smiled warmly and stepped closer to the table.

Boudicca, a witch groupie of long standing, leapt deftly onto Seren's shoulder and then settled around her neck, purring at a volume that Maggie thought bordered on the indecent, given the circumstances.

Hywel led the way to the stairs, the Elders behind him. *How come Seren doesn't look like the hunchback of Notre-Dame?* Maggie thought, remembering her mother's complaint every time Boudicca demanded a shoulder carry.

After closing the library door, Maggie followed them up the stairs. Seren was walking slowly but quickened her step as they neared the top. Once in the kitchen, she cast around as if she was looking for something.

'May I?' she asked, gesturing in the air with both hands.

'Go where you like, love,' Hywel replied.

Maggie shot her father a questioning look. He raised his eyebrows and shrugged.

They followed Seren from the kitchen into the living room. She stopped in front of the settee and bent to put her hand on the spot where Rose had sat. With one graceful move, she stood and left the room. She was halfway up the stairs by the time Maggie caught up with her. Seren went straight to the guest room Rose was in and stood outside the door, her eyes closed. Boudicca hissed and leapt from Seren's shoulder.

Before Maggie could speak, Seren held a finger to her lips.

Maggie bit back the question and felt her cheeks heat.

Pointing at the closed door, Seren inclined her head and mouthed, 'Rose?'

Maggie nodded. *Oh, to be a witch*, she thought.

Apparently satisfied, Seren turned and headed back down the stairs to where Hywel, Morgan and Boudicca were waiting.

Maggie joined them just in time to see Seren nod solemnly at Morgan. His expression darkened.

'Oh dear,' he said with a heavy sigh.

CHAPTER 16

PONT NEFOEDD, JULY 1960

'Oh dear what? What do you mean?' Maggie asked, looking from Morgan to Seren and back again.

Morgan glanced up the stairs, but before he could say anything, Hywel said, 'Why don't we have a cuppa and talk in the kitchen.'

Maggie started making the tea while Hywel searched for any hidden biscuits he might have forgotten about. The toolbox stash was already long gone. The opening and closing of cupboard doors and her father's mumbling mingled with the only other noises in the kitchen. The ponderous tick of the old wall clock. The quiet hiss of the painfully slow-boiling kettle. The jingle of milk bottles when Maggie yanked open the fridge door.

With nothing more to do with her hands until the kettle boiled, Maggie grabbed a dishcloth and wiped the already clean workshop. Irritated, she flung the cloth into the sink. As glaring at the kettle didn't seem to help any, Maggie tried twisting the knob on the gas stove. It was already as high as it would go. She snorted in frustration.

'I can help,' Seren said in a tone that was part statement,

part question. Boudicca sat curled in her lap, her eyes squeezed shut as her dainty cream paws flexed back and forth, kneading an invisible loaf of bread, as her father was fond of saying.

'Yes, please,' Maggie said, standing back and staring at the witch, unsure of what might come next. Would the tea make itself? You never quite knew with witches.

Seren tilted her head and a piercing shriek let rip from the kettle. Maggie jumped. If ever a household item was mis-named, it had to be whistling kettles. 'Hysterical screaming kettles' would be far more accurate.

Maggie spun around just in time to see the whistle at the end of the spout lift, silencing the hideous noise. She reached for the knob on the stove but found that it was already off.

'Thanks,' Maggie said, feeling that she should probably say more but not knowing what. She hated how tongue-tied she was around witches.

She noticed Seren had her hands hovering around the cat's ears. Boudicca hadn't moved a whisker. *Bloody witches think of everything*, Maggie thought, but was glad of the kind-ness. She hoped it hadn't woken Rose. She made the tea and placed the mugs, teapot, milk and sugar bowl on the table.

Hywel joined them empty-handed. 'Sorry, there's no biscuits. With Lyds away I've been a bit lax on the shopping front,' he said, sinking wearily into a chair.

He looked down at his hands, and Maggie felt a lump in her throat. She leaned in and kissed her father on top of his head before taking her seat.

'What did you mean out there?' Maggie asked, unable to wait another moment. 'Morgan, you said, "Oh dear," as if something was wrong.'

Morgan nodded slowly, his gaze fixed on the table in front of him. After taking a breath, he looked Maggie in the eye and said, 'We think there is something. Not necessarily to do with your mother, mind, but something that needs, well ...' He paused, sighed, and then said, 'I think Seren better tell us. I don't want to make a dog's dinner of it.'

Seren got straight to the point. 'There are spell particles in the living room, across the hall, up the stairs and outside the room where Rose is sleeping. I'm assuming your bathroom is the door directly opposite hers, as there was a trail leading there, too.'

Her accent was a curious mix of her Welsh and Irish parentage, but together it afforded her a soft, lyrical voice that was nonetheless commanding. Maggie couldn't imagine anyone ever interrupting Seren when she spoke.

When Hywel and Maggie exchanged confused looks, she continued.

'We found similar particles on the road from Aberystwyth. As neither Lydia nor Rose are witches then the only conclusion we can draw is that one of the books helped them with a spell.' Seren took a sip of her tea.

'What!' Maggie shrieked out the word.

Boudicca let out a low, rumbling yowl of irritation from her spot on Seren's lap.

'Sorry,' Maggie said, lowering her voice. 'Can the books even do that?' She then worried that, as an apprentice, maybe she should already know that. She felt her cheeks flush.

'Some of them can but only when they're in dire straits. As the protocol dictates that the most powerful books are evacuated first, then we can only assume that one of these books helped them escape with magic,' Seren said.

'And that isn't common knowledge, by the way, not for apprentices anyway,' Morgan added kindly.

'Wow,' was all that Maggie could think to say as something shifted uncomfortably in her gut.

'But surely that's a good thing, isn't it?' Hywel asked.

'It's a good thing that the book helped them to escape,

yes,' Seren said. She looked to be choosing her words carefully. 'But it can be dangerous for a person without magic to cast a spell. That there are particles here and out on the road means that the spell fractured towards the end.'

'What? Like the spell wasn't finished properly?' Maggie asked.

'It might have been that. Or it might have been confused during the incantation. When that happens, the books try to self-edit to keep the spell viable, but that can lead to problems too. I must stress that this is so rare that all we have are theories. Another possibility is that the spell caster might have been so afraid that they accidentally absorbed some of the magic. That's rare, but it can happen,' Seren said.

'You mean like swallowing water when you get out of your depth swimming?' Hywel said.

'That's a good analogy, Hywel, yes,' Morgan said.

'I'll need the address of the person who brought Rose here. The spell particles will dissipate relatively quickly, but we can't take the risk of a civilian being adversely affected by them, especially if they were near Rose for an extended period,' Seren said.

'I'll take you over to Dai's in the morning,' Hywel said.

'What does this mean for my mother?' Maggie asked, trying to keep her voice from wavering. She only partially succeeded.

Seren put down her mug and looked Maggie in the eye. 'Hopefully nothing. I'll need to speak to the book in question, but I think it's most likely that it was Rose who cast the spell. Your mother was probably driving, given that we found the largest concentration of the particles on the road. All indicators point to the fact that the spell somehow allowed Rose to exit the car with the books and Lydia to drive away. I picked up her energy for another hundred yards past the point of highest concentration.'

'So, you're sure my wife is still alive?' Hywel asked, his voice little more than a strained whisper, his head resting on his steepled hands, his eyes on the table.

Maggie's breath caught in her chest. She bit her lip hard.

Seren took a breath before she answered. 'My powers don't extend that far, I'm afraid,' she said, reaching out to place an elegant hand on Hywel's shoulder. 'But what I can tell you both is that there is no evidence that she has come to harm. Violence of any form leaves an energetic stain, and I detected nothing at her last known location.'

'Hywel, everyone in the community is on high alert,' Morgan interjected. 'There's a search party going out at first light to scour the area too. They're preparing as we speak.'

'Please, God,' Hywel said with a sigh so heavy that Maggie feared it might cleave her in two.

'We won't rest until Lydia is home where she belongs,' Morgan said. 'You have my word on that.'

Maggie was relieved when Seren changed the subject back to Rose.

'Can you please describe Rose's demeanour when she got here, Hywel?'

After a quick glance at her father, who looked like he'd aged a decade in just a few hours, Maggie jumped in to reply.

'Quiet. Scared. Obviously, scared. She's not said a word since she arrived, but she's been trying to speak. I thought it might be the shock, you know. Bill the Bread, one of dad's drivers, couldn't speak for a while after his wife died suddenly.'

Hywel's head shot up, and Maggie instantly regretted her choice of example.

'It's interesting that you used the analogy of swallowing water earlier, Hywel,' Seren said as she stroked her chin with her long, elegant fingers. 'Sometimes, when people are saved from the sea, they can die from what's called secondary drowning. Their lungs fill with fluid to flush out the salt water and they drown on dry land. Magic can be similar for the untrained. Rose is quite a sensitive soul. She was almost rejected as an apprentice because of that.'

Morgan cleared his throat pointedly.

'My apologies,' Seren said. 'That is to stay confidential, please, but the point is relevant. A spell of that magnitude would have likely overwhelmed even an adept witch, so the impact on a young, sensitive, non-magical person could be catastrophic.'

Maggie gasped. 'Can you help her?'

Seren held up her hand. 'I said could be – there are no certainties here. For now, sleep is the best remedy. Her body needs to rest, and with any luck, that will be enough. Chris will be here in the morning. Once we know she's okay from a medical perspective, I'll see what else I need to do to help. Hopefully, it will be nothing at all.'

'So that's the protocol for this sort of thing?' Maggie asked.

'Well, that's the devil of it, really,' Morgan replied. 'We don't have a precedent for this.'

'The only reference to fracturing spells was in a text that was either taken or destroyed in the raid on the Truro library back in 1932,' Seren added. 'By chance, it was one of the texts I used for a thesis I wrote a few years earlier, but from memory, it didn't contain any detail on the effects of a fractured spell on people, magical or otherwise.'

Maggie stared at the witch, who had turned her attention back to stroking the cat. At a push, Seren looked to be in her mid-twenties, so either she was writing magical theses from her cradle or was much older than she appeared.

'We need to keep a very close eye on our Rose,' Morgan said. 'A very close eye indeed.'

Silence fell. The clock ticked. The cat purred. Maggie

thought of her mother. Wondered which route she might take to get home. If indeed she was heading here – maybe she'd go to one of the other libraries or safe houses. The thought of her out there, alone somewhere, made her feel sick to her stomach.

Maggie startled when Seren broke the uncomfortable silence.

'Shall we have a word with these books, Maggie?'

CHAPTER 17

PONT NEFOEDD, JULY 1960

*M*aggie led the way down the narrow stairs to the library, Seren gliding soundlessly in her wake, immune to the creaks and squeaks of the old wooden stairs that always complained under Maggie's feet. Boudicca was once again draped around the witch's shoulder like a scarf, her purring amplified in the enclosed space. That cat really was a tart around witches.

Maggie had been glad of the distraction when Seren had asked to see the books recovered from the Aberystwyth library. Morgan had opted to stay in the kitchen with Hywel, suggesting that too much of a crowd might unsettle the books. She wondered if that was the real reason or if Morgan needed to speak to her father alone. The sick feeling returned to her stomach. Hope, she told herself. That was the one thing never to give up on.

'I don't suppose you've looked at them yet,' Seren said as Maggie pulled open the heavy metal door to the library.

Maggie shook her head. 'No, we brought them down still in their sacks. I thought it better to wait ...' She trailed off, stepping into the library and switching on all the lights, which blinked hesitantly into life.

'Let's hope they've all stayed where they were put,' Seren said, arching her eyebrow.

The sacks were hard to miss, sitting on the end of the long reading table in front of them, their necks tied fast with the ribbon her mother salvaged from gifts and birthday cakes to be stashed in the kitchen drawer. Her dad must have grabbed it tonight as the first thing handy to secure the sacks. She remembered her mum winding the ribbon around her fingers as everyone sang happy birthday. Had her twenty-first only been four weeks ago?

'You okay?' Seren asked.

Maggie nodded, although she felt anything but. She tried to swallow down the lump that rose in her throat. Were they really the only survivors of the Aberystwyth library? The keepers could trace their origins back to ancient Egypt, but despite close to two millennia of study and their enduring efforts to protect the books, the consensus was that they were still barely scratching the surface. They couldn't explain why some books were sentient, although scholars had filled their own libraries with theories.

She thought about her essay on the Tortured Text and the concluding line that she'd been rather pleased with. *What does the tragic story of the Tortured Text tell us? When offered the opportunity for euthanasia, the book, despite its obvious physical, mental and emotional suffering, chose life. I believe the story stands as testament to the power of enduring hope.*

Boudicca yowled, snapping Maggie back to the moment. The cat slipped soundlessly onto the end of the table, well away from the books. While her reputation for feistiness preceded her, even she knew better than to take one on. She buttoned her feet and sat, waiting, the chocolate-tipped end of her tail swaying back and forth.

As if sensing their approach, one sack stirred. Seren stepped aside and gestured to Maggie. In her mother's absence, she was the keeper, and as such, anything to do with the books was her responsibility. Maggie stepped forward and undid the knot, sliding the lilac ribbon into her cardigan pocket. The sack lurched forward, the books suddenly desperate to escape their confines.

'Steady,' Maggie cooed, putting her hand on the top of the sack to prevent them from flying into the room. Once the movement had stilled, she eased back the hessian and addressed them.

'You're safe. You're in Pont Nefoedd library,' she said as she carefully lifted the books and placed them gently onto the table. Some were visibly shaking. Her mother had told her it happened, but she'd never seen it for herself. Poor things.

'We'd be grateful if you could tell us what happened,' she said, making her voice as soft and as calm as she could manage.

Maggie saw Seren tense as she pulled the largest book from the sack. It was disproportionately heavy for its size, and she had to resort to sliding it onto the table. It was tan leather, stained dark in patches by time, water or substances Maggie didn't want to think about. Two heavy-looking fili-gree bindings wrapped horizontally around it. The ornate clasps were missing the padlocks that some books insisted on, but even without them, it looked to be closed as tight as a clamshell.

This one wasn't shaking. Thread-like blue veins sparked across the cover, appearing and disappearing randomly. She reached out to touch it but drew back as the energy nipped at her fingertips. There was something else too that Maggie couldn't name. She thought again of the Tortured Text. Its rage and grief. Was that what she was sensing here?

Maggie glanced at Seren, who nodded in reply to the unspoken question. This was the book that had helped her mother and Rose escape.

'May I?' the witch asked, gesturing to it.

It took Maggie a moment to realise that in her mother's absence, she was acting keeper and needed to grant permission to anyone wanting to address the books.

'Oh. Er, yes,' she stuttered.

Seren placed one palm on the top of her chest, the other at her sternum, and closed her eyes. Maggie bit her tongue to bite back the question. She'd love to know more about witches and their practices, but now was definitely not the time. Feeling like a spare part, she turned her attention to the other sack. After once again pocketing the ribbon, she busied herself with unpacking the books, whispering reassurances to them and placing them as gently as possible on the reading table.

Seren opened her eyes and made to sit down. Maggie opened her mouth, about to cry out the warning about the space the witch was already falling into, but a chair from the far end of the table glided into place just in time to seat her. Maggie closed her gaping mouth, feeling like an idiot.

Her hand hovering at least a foot above the old book, the witch cocked her head as if listening, her beautiful features knitted into a frown. Boudicca, clearly deciding that this might take a while, lay down, Sphinx-like, at the end of the table, her blue eyes trained on the witch.

With the rest of the books unpacked and unsure of what else she could do for them, Maggie pulled up a chair and settled in to watch. The old clock marked the seconds and then the minutes as the witch sat, unmoving, her right hand hovering above the book. After twenty uneventful minutes, Maggie got up and wandered to the kitchenette. Before she could spoon the coffee into the mug, a loud and unmistakably pained 'Ow!' came from the library.

She rushed back to see Seren standing, her chair knocked backwards onto the floor. The witch was sucking the outer edge of her little finger as a trail of bright red blood snaked its way down her hand and forearm.

'I'm sorry you feel that way,' Seren said to the book. There was no anger in her tone, such was the control of a witch, Maggie thought.

Boudicca, still on the far end of the table, was bent double, her back arched, eyes wide and tail like a bottle brush. The book looked tensed to strike again. The fine blue threads of energy had been replaced with white flashes more akin to tiny bolts of lightning. The hiss Maggie had assumed to be emanating from the cat, she now realised, was actually coming from the book. She swallowed. She'd never seen a book so incandescent.

'You okay?' she asked Seren.

The witch nodded and took a step back, still trying to stem the flow of blood.

Book bites were rare, but apparently extremely painful. The only saving grace, Maggie supposed, was that they healed quickly, even on non-magical people. She guessed witches would heal even quicker.

There'd be very little chance that the book would speak to anyone while it was in this mood, but she would have to try. Taking a deep breath, she stepped forward. The hissing continued, slow and menacing. Maggie adjusted her chances from slim to almost non-existent.

'I'm Maggie, the apprentice keeper here at Pont Nefoedd,' she said. Unlike Seren, all her communication had to be done the human way. 'My mother is Lydia, the keeper, who I believe you met at Aber.' She hesitated, unsure of what to say next. She took a deep breath and hoped that the right words would come to her.

'I understand that you've been through a great ordeal today, and I want to offer my condolences for the loss of your keeper. Frances was very dear to us too,' she said, her voice almost failing her on the last sentence. She cleared her throat. The book was still hissing, but, she fancied, it was slightly quieter than before.

'We're going to leave you now, but I just want to say thank you for whatever you did to help my mother and Rose escape. We have twenty-six magical texts here today, twenty-seven including your good self, who survived because of your actions. Frances would be so very proud of you, as are we.' Maggie's voice faltered, and it took a monumental effort not to cry. The hissing stopped abruptly. Maggie waited, but the book remained quiet.

When Maggie could trust herself to speak again, she said, 'It would help us enormously if you'd tell us what happened, and which spell you used. My mother is still ...' She didn't finish her sentence because the book chose that moment to glide silently into the air and disappear into the stacks.

Maggie sighed. Not getting bitten was something, she supposed, but it wasn't enough. Not nearly enough, in fact.

Boudicca trotted along the table and surprised Maggie by bumping her head into her hand. Another rare show of affection, but although welcome, it did nothing to lift Maggie's spirits. If the cat was feeling sorry for her, then things really were as bad as she feared.

Seren laid her hand lightly on Maggie's shoulder. 'Well done, Maggie. You're a natural, just like your mother,' she said. 'Good job of calming it. I'm sure it will share when it's ready – and that will be all the sooner, thanks to you.'

Maggie nodded and managed a tight smile, although she

didn't trust her voice to reply. With Boudicca once again draped around the witch's shoulders, they headed for the library stairs.

CHAPTER 18

PONT NEFOEDD, JULY 1960

*R*ose woke gasping for air. Her heart was hammering, her back slick with a cold sweat. She shivered. Where was she? On a bed, that much she could feel, but where? The room was ink-well black and a far cry from the sodium-filled nights of her childhood. This darkness was so thick it could choke you.

In her mind, inky fingers peeled away from the darkness and probed at her nose and lips, looking for a way in. She screwed up her eyes against the image and focused on breathing as quietly as she could. After a few minutes, she felt her heart rate slow. Cracking open first one eye and then the next, she relaxed at the sight of a thin ribbon of moonlight peeking through a gap in the curtains. When the weight on her lids became too much, she surrendered to sleep.

A floorboard creaked next to the bed. Rose's eyes shot open, the rest of her body frozen in fear. There was nothing but blackness. No trace of the sliver of light that had calmed her just moments ago. The smell of stale tobacco hung in the air.

Rose held her breath, but the sound of breathing

continued. Then the unmistakable weight of someone sitting next to her on the bed, so close that she felt the cover grow taut beneath her as it stretched. Heart hammering and a scream ready in her chest, Rose screwed her eyes shut and started to pray to a god she'd never believed in.

Tap. Tap. Tap.

'Rose. Rose. Are you awake?' Maggie's voice sounded from the other side of the bedroom door. Rose jumped, pedalling her feet against the bedspread until she was sitting pressed against the headboard. The room was flooded in bright sunshine, making her squint. Had she left the curtains open? She held up her hand to shield her eyes. It was just a nightmare. She heaved in a deep breath. The room smelled of beeswax and washing powder.

'Rose?' Maggie called again. Rose could hear the tension in her tone, even through the closed door.

'Just a minute,' Rose croaked, her voice sounding nothing like her own. It took her a moment to realise that she could speak. Relief washed through her, and she whispered a thank you to whichever higher power might have had a hand in her healing.

Maggie couldn't have heard her reply because a moment later, the door creaked hesitantly open. She looked bleary-eyed and pale to the point of greyness, her brow creased with concern.

Rose raised her hand and tried to smile as she shuffled off the bed, feeling self-conscious.

'Oh, thank goodness,' Maggie said, some of the tension in her face sliding away. She eyed the still made bed. 'Did you manage to sleep at all?'

How could Rose explain that she'd not wanted to mess up the covers by getting into the bed? 'It was quite warm last night,' she said croakily.

Maggie's face broke into a smile. 'Your voice has returned,' she said with obvious relief.

'Is your mum here yet?' Rose asked haltingly. It was an effort to form the words. She could see them there in her mind, but she had to focus on each in turn in order to form the sentence. She exhaled, feeling as if she'd just sprinted up a flight of stairs.

Maggie's face fell. 'No. Not yet,' she said. 'Soon, I'm sure. She'll be coming the long way to keep us all safe. There are people out searching now too. They're all over the place. All looking for her.'

Rose wanted to say something, reassure Maggie somehow, but her thoughts felt sticky in her mind, like someone had emptied a tin of treacle in there, clogging it all up. She saw Lydia in the car telling her to go. Frances in the library throwing those pretty little teacups into the dark corners. The sound of them smashing. Frances.

'I brought you some fresh clothes to borrow. You're a bit taller than me so I thought a dress would be best,' Maggie said, putting a neatly folded pile of clothes on the foot of the bed next to the unused nightdress and towels. 'The knickers are brand new from Christmas,' she added, looking awkward.

Rose nodded her thanks.

'Look, the Elders are here now,' Maggie said. 'Morgan and Seren came last night, and Chris arrived about an hour ago. Are you up for talking to them?'

Rose nodded again. There was something she needed to tell them, wasn't there? She tried to think, but Maggie was talking again.

'Right. I'll put the kettle on. Dad's been out for bread already, so we've at least got food in the house again. He's had the immersion on all morning, so there's loads of hot water for you too. Come down to the kitchen whenever you're ready, but there's no rush,' Maggie said.

When she was nearly at the door, she turned and pulled something out of her back pocket. 'Nearly forgot. Dad got you a toothbrush from the chemist too.' She rattled it in its box before scooting back to place it on the pile of clothes.

Rose tried to muster a smile, but when she looked up, Maggie was already closing the door behind her. Picking up the toothbrush, clothes and towel, Rose crossed the large landing to the bathroom.

While she would have given anything to have a bath, it didn't seem right somehow, not in someone else's house, so Rose settled for what her gran would call a good wash. She dressed quickly, pulling on the tan cardigan over the plum-coloured corduroy dress. It was a bit short for her and nothing that she'd normally dare to wear, but it was a relief to be in fresh clothes.

As she was brushing her teeth in front of the mirror, something small and beetle black darted across the skin under her right eye. The sensation was akin to brushing past nettles. Rose flinched and peered at her reflection. Had it been a bug? It was long enough to be a millipede. She stepped closer, studying her face in the mirror. There was no sign of it now. She brushed her fingertips against the spot, but the skin was unmarked and seemingly unaffected by whatever it had been, if indeed there had been anything at all. Rose was no longer too sure. Maybe seeing things was something that happened after a shock. She finished her teeth, dried the brush and popped it back in the box.

Back in her room, she left her old clothes folded neatly on the chair, straightened the bedspread and restacked the pillows. She turned slowly, looking around. When her eyes fell on the dresser, she caught her breath. She'd hidden Lydia's bag in the top drawer last night. Rose crossed to the dresser and pulled open the drawer. There, poking out from under some fluffy pink towels, was the strap of the handbag. Reassured, she closed the drawer but kept her hands on the knobs. Something sharp and persistent picked at her mind. Wait. Why had she hidden it in the first place? In fact, why did she even have Lydia's bag? She screwed her eyes closed, trying to remember.

The blackness fell like a dropped stone. One minute she was standing in the brightly lit bedroom and the next she was in the ink-well, her lungs full of blackness with no room for air. Then it was gone. She gasped. Falling forward, she clutched the chest of drawers for support as her legs weakened beneath her.

'I'm fine. I'm fine.' She stuttered out the words, her breath hitching. They did little to reassure her. She stayed still until the weakness in her legs subsided. The book! The memory hit her like a slap. Of course! That's why she had the handbag. She needed to give it to the Elders. Now!

Yanking the handbag from the drawer, she hurried out of the room and down the stairs towards the murmur of hushed voices and the smell of toast.

CHAPTER 19

PONT NEFOEDD, JULY 1960

*F*ive pairs of eyes turned to Rose as she appeared in the doorway. Maggie and Hywel were at the kitchen counter, busy with breakfast-making. The two strangers at the table must be the Elders.

The elderly-looking man with a beaky nose smiled and nodded a greeting from where he sat at the end of the table. He looked familiar, at least. He had interviewed her for her apprenticeship. The other was a strikingly beautiful woman with long dark curly hair and skin that could have been porcelain.

The fifth set of eyes, narrowed to slits, belonged to the Siamese draped around the woman's neck. The cat's tail moved like a swaying cobra. Rose felt something tighten in her chest.

Already feeling the colour rise in her cheeks, Rose opted for a smile and a nod of good morning. There had been something she needed to say, hadn't there? Before she could think of it, Hywel was at her side. She hadn't noticed him move from the counter. There was something comforting about him, Rose thought. Like high ground in a flood. Maggie was very lucky.

'Everyone, this is Rose from Aber,' Hywel said, addressing the room. Turning back to her, he added, 'Rose, meet Morgan and Seren and...' He cast about the large kitchen.

Just then, a petite woman in her thirties with short-cropped blonde hair pushed open the back door, a cloud of cigarette smoke following in her wake.

'And this is Chris. Or Doctor Roberts, if you want to be formal about it,' Hywel said. 'Although she's not setting a good example on the smoking front,' he added pointedly.

Chris ignored the jibe and held out her hand to Rose. 'Chris will do just fine. Nice to meet you, Rose. And he's right about the smoking. Filthy habit. Don't do it,' she said, smiling. Her tone was light, but her eyes were appraising.

Rose swallowed, her mouth dry as sand. The doctor's hand was small, but her handshake was strong. Rose tried to return the smile, but it felt awkward on her face. Like the time she'd tried a mud pack to help clear up her spots. *Smile, you miserable cow. It won't crack your face, you know.* The voice in her head was another of her mother's boyfriends. He'd been called Chris too. Although she sensed this woman was a world removed from the likes of him.

'Sit yourself down, love,' Hywel said, pulling out a chair for her opposite the woman with the cat. 'We've got teacakes and crumpets, and there's toast already on.'

Rose tried again to smile, but settled for nodding. The woman with the long curly hair – she had already forgotten everyone's names – had eyes much like the cat's. Bright blue and almond-shaped. Her gaze had a weight to it, and Rose felt as exposed as she might had she been stark naked. The cat continued to glare at her with narrowed eyes.

Rose lowered herself onto the edge of the seat, rolling the

fabric of Lydia's handbag between her fingers. She looked down at it, confused. This wasn't hers. Why did she have it?

'Did you manage to get some sleep, Rose?' the man with the beaky nose asked.

The question startled her, and her reply took a lot longer to form than she'd expected, but she had to answer with more than just a nod. These were the Elders, after all. The people who set the course of her studies and decided whether she passed or failed in her chosen profession.

'Yes. Thank you,' she said haltingly, her eyes flicking between him and the scrubbed wooden tabletop.

Chris had taken the chair next to her. Even without looking up, Rose could feel the doctor's eyes on her. It felt like everyone in the room was waiting for some sort of diagnosis or pronouncement.

'You'll feel better after breakfast,' Chris said, just as Maggie placed a large plate of toast and crumpets on the table and Hywel added a big red teapot with a chipped lid.

Rose hadn't thought she was hungry, but after picking her way through her first crumpet, she surprised herself by accepting a second. The conversation around the table seemed to avoid the elephant in the room that was Lydia's disappearance and Frances's murder. She wondered vaguely if that was for her benefit, but then the thought was gone.

Maggie and Hywel barely ate a thing, Rose noticed. Their eyes strayed frequently to the old butler's bell above the larder, which, she guessed, must be connected to the emergency tunnel in the library. She thought about her own mother and how she'd so often dreaded her return home. Hearing her key in the door or, as was so often the case, her fumbling attempts to locate the lock. On those occasions, Rose had to get to the front door before her mother's good humour turned as sour as the cheap cider on her breath. She didn't like to remember the days she wasn't quick enough.

Rose studied Maggie and wondered if she had any idea how lucky she was. Nice parents, still together. Big house. She probably had lots of friends, too. Proper friends who cared about you – not just pretended. Maybe she had a boyfriend. She even had a cat.

Lydia had talked endlessly about Maggie as they'd worked through the cataloguing. Rose wondered what it was like, having that sort of closeness with your mother. She felt mean for being envious. Maggie, like Lydia, had been nothing but kind to her. She was happy for them, really; she was. Other people's good fortune just sometimes reminded her of the unfillable hole in her own heart.

'If you're feeling up to it, Rose,' Chris said, 'after breakfast, I'd like to take your blood pressure and ask you a few questions.'

'Okay,' Rose said, still feeling as if her words had to fight their way through the treacle in her brain.

She took her time finishing the second crumpet, but when she could delay the moment no longer, she pushed back her chair and stood up. It was only as the handbag fell to the floor that she remembered the book. *Idiot!* she scolded herself, feeling her cheeks burn at her stupidity. The one thing Lydia had told her to do, and she was here stuffing her face with crumpets while Lydia was God knows where. She dropped to pick it up.

It's not the book. The thought was so loud and clear in her mind that she stood up abruptly to scan the faces around the table. It hadn't sounded like anyone here. She licked her lips and focused on her breath. Everyone was watching her. Her cheeks burned. She squeezed the bag to her chest and closed her eyes. It was as if her thoughts were on a merry-go-round, passing in and out of her grasp. She knew there was something there, some thought or thing she had to grab on to, but it was all moving too quickly. Everything blurring together.

She concentrated hard, willing the thoughts to slow down. And it worked.

'Your mum's bag,' she breathed, holding it out to Maggie.

Breathe, Rose told herself. *Just focus and breathe and the thoughts will become clear again.*

Maggie took the bag but frowned, clearly not recognising it.

'New one,' Rose said with an effort. Her tongue felt too big for her mouth. 'Strap on hers snapped,' she added, feeling slightly lightheaded. Something tracked across her forearm. Looking down, she gasped as she pulled the sleeve of the cardigan over it. She just needed more sleep. Her mind was playing tricks on her.

'That's no surprise. She's got everything but the kitchen sink in her handbag,' Hywel said affectionately. 'I told her too much weight would snap the handle.'

A memory flashed into Rose's mind. Lydia telling her to get the book to the Elders.

Rose gasped. 'Important magic book inside,' she said, her words slurring as tiny black dots swam in her field of vision.

She sank back down heavily in the chair and rested her head on the table. Someone pressed two fingers to her wrist.

'Code was Hemingway,' Rose said with an effort, as she fought the waves of fire and ice racing up and down her sweat-slicked spine.

She felt the tracking sensation at the side of her neck. It was more pronounced now. Like the legs of an insect marching, not across her flesh but in it. She slapped her hand over it, and it subsided.

'The book in the bag is the one Lydia called us about?' someone said, their voice urgent and accompanied by the scrape of chair legs on tiles.

Rose lifted her head and tried to turn towards the voice, but her vision swam, making everything a blur.

'Yes. Important book. Save the …' she slurred.

Rose fought to finish the sentence, but the words just wouldn't come.

'Okay, we need to get you back to bed, Rose,' Chris said briskly. 'Hywel, give me a hand, please.'

Rose felt pinned between sleep and wakefulness in a netherworld of shadows and half-truths. Her body was simultaneously as heavy as lead and so insubstantial as to be carried away by a light breeze. The voices in the kitchen faded in and out, but she heard one thing clearly.

Maggie's voice. 'There's no magical book in here.'

Rose tried to cry out, but she was already sinking into the darkness.

CHAPTER 20

PONT NEFOEDD, JULY 1960

*M*aggie stood staring at the contents of her mother's handbag spread across the kitchen table. Boudicca, who had opted to remain while the others went to help Rose, prowled, stepping dainty paws between the items.

'Mam's always prepared for anything,' Maggie said to the cat, stroking her slinky back as she passed.

Along with her purse, keys and make-up bag, there were four handkerchiefs, twelve pens, three pencils, two spoons, a tin of mints, a ball of string and two small screwdrivers. There were two paperback novels, both Agatha Christies, a crossword book and a plain black A5 notebook, but there was no sign of a magical book.

Seren had inspected each before joining the others just in case the magical text Rose had mentioned had been so fearful as to disguise itself as a contemporary book. Maggie had never heard of such a thing, and even Seren had confessed to never having seen it, although rumours of its possibility had apparently persisted through the ages.

Maggie picked up the purse and held it to her cheek, the

large metal clasp cold and smooth on her skin, the chunky weave of the pink-and-green wool warm and rough. It had seen better days, this bringer of pocket money and cornets from the ice cream van on the way home from school. 'Fetch me my purse and we'll see.' The memory of her mother's voice was clear in Maggie's memory. Inside would be photographs of them all. Her as a baby. Freddie the Labrador, who had died before Maggie was born. Her parents' wedding photo, both looking ridiculously young, and one of the four of them sitting in the garden last year. It had taken most of a roll of film to get one where Boudicca, perched on her mother's shoulder as if she was the star of the show, was looking at the camera.

The cat leaned in to sniff the notebook before sinking down onto it and rubbing her chin against the cover. Maggie waited until the chin rub turned into the roll she knew would follow. She'd earned herself enough swipes over the years to know that Boudicca did not like being moved or interrupted, so she had no option but to wait until she was done.

Once the notebook was in Maggie's hand, the cat jumped up and continued rubbing her chin against it. She then sank her teeth into the corner.

'Boudicca!' Maggie scolded. 'You can't chew Mam's book.'

The cat took a step back, her eyes narrowed. Maggie prepared to step out of swiping distance, but after a moment's thought, Boudicca turned her attention back to the other items. As Maggie stared at the notebook, she heard the familiar sound of a pencil falling onto the tiled floor. She looked up to see the cat idly flicking another off the table with her paw.

She bit her lip. It felt wrong to read her mother's notes, but what if she'd written something in there for them to find? Told them where to come and look for her? 'Sorry, Mam,' she muttered, before reluctantly opening the book.

She reached the last filled page and snapped it shut. Shopping lists, catalogue references, things to do, but no scrawled message or clue about her whereabouts. She checked it three times before putting it back in the bag along with the rest of the contents. She left the remaining pens and pencils on the table so that the cat could entertain herself.

As Maggie walked into the hall to hang up her mother's handbag on the coat stand, Boudicca stalked ahead of her. *There really is no pleasing her some days*, Maggie thought, but decided to keep it to herself.

When she reached the landing, her father and Morgan were speaking in hushed tones outside Rose's room. Her father looked like he'd not slept in a week. He reached out his arm to her as she neared and drew her into his side while keeping his eyes on Morgan.

'Maggie, love, we were just saying that if Chris and Seren can't stabilise her, we might need to move Rose to a hospital,' Morgan said.

'What?' Maggie said. 'What's happened?'

It was her father who replied. 'Morgan, if I understand it correctly, they're saying that the spell was so powerful that bits of it have sort of broken off and embedded themselves into poor Rose.'

'That's right,' Morgan said, nodding gravely. 'The magic is interfering with all her body's systems, sending them haywire. Like a short circuit, I suppose.'

'Will that have happened to my mother too?' Maggie asked, fear twisting her gut.

Hywel pulled her in closer as Morgan replied, 'We can't rule it out, but we're working on the theory that it was Rose who cast the spell while your mother was driving, so we think it's unlikely.'

Maggie sighed. 'Have the search party people checked in yet?' she asked. Unlikely was good news, but her mother was still missing.

'I called the co-ordinator at first light and every hour since. No news yet, but I'm due to call again' – Morgan checked his watch – 'in about ten minutes. I'll go down to the library, if that's okay with you, Maggie?'

'Of course,' Maggie said, not knowing what else to say. That everyone was deferring to her as if she were the keeper of Pont Nefoedd unsettled her in ways she couldn't quite articulate.

CHAPTER 21

PONT NEFOEDD, JULY 1960

*T*he rest of the day dragged by. Every clock in the house seemed to Maggie to have stopped working. She turned on the radio for the lunchtime news just to check the time and clicked it off again as soon as it was confirmed. Whatever was happening in the wider world paled into insignificance compared to what was happening in her own.

Seren and Hywel went off to check on Dai Pony after lunch and returned an hour later, Seren satisfied that Dai hadn't been affected by any remnants of the spell. She'd removed his memory of the whole Rose incident though. Maggie was sad to hear that. Dai was a kind man who, like all kind people, found comfort in the memory of his good deeds. He'd no doubt have another story to replace it with soon, she told herself. Albeit not such a strange one.

Chris spent the day monitoring Rose. Maggie took her a fresh mug of coffee every hour and tried not to notice the hope leaching from the doctor's face. Morgan stationed himself in the library's office, and Maggie and Seren tried twice more to coax the old spell book from wherever it had hidden itself in the library, but without success.

Maggie switched on the radio in the kitchen to wait for the six o'clock news. She was scrubbing and organising the cupboards for something to do when Chris trudged into the room and headed for the kettle.

'Any change?' Maggie asked, throwing the cloth into the sink. She knew she must sound like a stuck record, but it was all she could think of to ask.

'She's deteriorating,' Chris said wearily as she picked up the kettle. 'Her heart is showing signs of struggling, which is the one thing I hoped wouldn't happen.'

'You sit down,' Maggie said softly, moving to take the kettle from Chris. She looked utterly exhausted, and Maggie belatedly realised that she'd come straight here after a night shift at the hospital.

The doctor did as she was told, slumping heavily into a chair.

'Is there really no way of helping her?' Maggie ventured.

'According to Seren, not unless we know what kind of spell was cast, no,' Chris replied. 'Seren's with her now. She's trying to grab some of the threads of the spell to see if she can slow it down.' Chris waved her hands. 'Or something like that, anyway. Not my specialism, I'm afraid. I can only speak to the effect the magic is having on her physical body. If this wasn't magical in origin I'd admit her, but there's nothing we can do for her unless we find that spell.'

Maggie frowned as she filled the kettle, an idea hovering at the corners of her mind.

'Why that bloody book won't just tell us what it did is beyond me!' Chris fumed, thumping the table. 'I know they're beyond the reach of us mere mortals, but we have a young woman's life at stake here!'

'Book!' Maggie said, more loudly than she intended. She all but dropped the kettle into the sink and ran to the library stairs.

She was dimly aware of Chris calling after her, but there was no time to waste.

CHAPTER 22

PONT NEFOEDD, JULY 1960

*M*organ was on the phone when she burst into the library. His voice echoed off the stone walls, but she ignored him. Her heart leapt in her chest when she saw that the books they'd unpacked from Aber were still sitting on the reading table.

'Clever things,' she said as she began gathering them up and placing them carefully into the sacks they'd arrived in. Without the huge book that had cast the spell, the one now hiding somewhere in the library, those that remained fit into just two sacks. Maggie placed the last book and heaved one sack into her arms then grabbed the other by the neck. Panting with the effort, she hurried up the library stairs.

'Whoa there, where you going?' Hywel asked as she all but collided with him in the kitchen.

'No time to explain. Come with me,' Maggie panted, a mixture of adrenaline and exertion stealing her breath.

Hywel caught her shoulder and stopped her just long enough to take the largest of the sacks from her arms. She stepped out of reach before he could make a grab for the other one.

'Rose's room, quick,' Maggie said over her shoulder.

'What's going on?' Chris asked, jogging up the wide stairs beside them.

'Got an idea,' Maggie spluttered between breaths as she gestured to the bedroom door.

Chris knocked once and then opened the door a crack to peer around it before letting it swing open.

Maggie caught her breath when she saw Rose. The young woman was barely recognisable. Her skin was deathly pale, her eyes ringed with huge dark circles, and she looked as thin as a wraith. Was it even possible to lose weight in so short a space of time? Maggie stared as Rose appeared to fight for every breath she took.

A movement across Rose's left cheek caught Maggie's eye. She blinked and stepped closer. Something long, black and no thicker than a pencil snaked across the young woman's chin. A second, shorter one joined it, darting down her cheek and disappearing under the sheet that partially covered Rose's neck. Another pushed its way from the outer corner of her eye.

Maggie watched, frozen in horror, as more appeared, slipping across Rose's face as she opened her mouth to cry out in pain. She made no sound, however. There was just a stuttering of air being sucked into her lungs, as if her body couldn't decide between the chores of breathing or sobbing.

Maggie bit her lip. It would be too easy to turn away, to leave it to the Elders, but she forced herself to step closer to the bed. The smell almost stopped her in her tracks – like meat left out to rot in the sun. Her stomach churned, but she gritted her teeth and stepped closer. As she caught sight of another long black thing sliding slowly over Rose's lip, she realised what she was seeing. She felt her stomach drop.

'But they look like—' Maggie started, but clamped her lips

shut, unwilling to articulate what she thought she was seeing – they'd think she'd lost her mind.

'Words,' Seren said wearily as she pressed a flannel to Rose's brow. 'Some are symbols, but the rest are letters and words. They've embedded themselves in Rose like shrapnel. I've tried to remove what I can, but their intent is too strong. Whatever spell was cast is of a magnitude I've never seen.' She sounded just as defeated as Chris.

Maggie watched as the small black letters streaked across Rose's face and neck. Were they all over her body? It didn't bear thinking about. Maggie felt her anger rise again for the men who had caused all this. Frances was dead and it looked likely that poor Rose would soon be next. And what of her mother, would she—Maggie snapped off the thought before it could take root and turned her attention back to her idea. If there was even the slightest possibility that this could help Rose, then she had to try.

'I need to try something,' Maggie said as she pulled the first book from the sack and laid it carefully next to Rose. Hywel, following her lead, did the same. There were twenty-six in all, some so small they'd fit in her palm, one the size of a church bible, and everything in between.

She was dimly aware of three sets of eyes on her. Chris, Hywel and Seren watched without comment. Maggie waited, but whatever she had expected to happen next didn't. The books remained completely still. Rose's laboured breathing continued, and Maggie could all but feel the life slipping away from the young apprentice. She had been so sure. Yes, it was a long shot, but if even the Elders were out of ideas, then she had to at least try something. This was her best shot – her only shot – and yet it wasn't working. Panic hovered around her. Was Rose about die in front of them all? Maggie searched for the anger she'd felt burning in her gut just moments ago but found only a bottomless bit of fear.

Before she could reach for the nearest book, Boudicca landed silently on the bed. Maggie jumped and almost fell over her own feet, righting herself just in time.

'Not the time or place, pusscat,' Hywel said, stepping forward, but Maggie saw Seren raise her hand. True to form, Boudicca ignored him, elegantly sidestepping his hands. She sniffed the air above Rose's left hand, opening her mouth and tilting her head upwards, clearly not wanting to get too close but needing to get a strong sense of whatever she was smelling. Then she turned her attention to the books, and Maggie held her breath. The cat sniffed the air above each, stepping around them as if they were landmines. Maggie's heart thumped loudly in her chest. *Please. Whatever's happening now, please let this work*, she begged silently. The cat had played no part in the half-formed plan she'd had just minutes ago, but they were running out of options and hope was the only thing left now.

Boudicca stopped her inspection and peered at a thin blue book with a delicate silver clasp. Maggie hoped she wasn't about to try chewing the end or rolling on it as she'd done with her mam's notebook. Instead, she let out her slightly strangled-sounding Siamese meow and sat next to the book, her front paws buttoned. She purred, clearly pleased with herself.

'Oh, you clever girl,' Maggie said, swooping in to lift the book she'd identified. It opened itself, the clasp sliding apart as she cradled it in her hands.

'Well, I'll go to the bottom of our stairs!' Hywel said from somewhere behind her.

'I'm Maggie, keeper of the library at Pont Nefoedd,' Maggie said, speaking at twice her regular speed and addressing the book in a whisper. There really was no time. 'We need to know what spell was cast by one of your, er, friends, please. It seems like you were the closest to the book that cast the spell, and so we were hoping you saw what happened and could—'

Maggie didn't need to finish; the book was ahead of her. As she watched, the pages filled with words written in a slanting, elegant violet script.

'Oh my good god!' Maggie exclaimed. She'd read about such things, but that a book had cast such a spell alone was nothing short of miraculous.

'What?' Chris said impatiently.

'May I?' Seren asked, obviously itching to see what the book was sharing but ever mindful of her manners. The book popped and fizzed in Maggie's hands, and the words 'You may' appeared briefly in the text.

'Book says yes,' Maggie mumbled, her head now crowded with impossible thoughts.

'What does it say?' Chris demanded.

It was Seren who spoke. 'It was a time spell,' she said, sounding almost winded. 'Our magnificent, biting friend downstairs stopped time.' The awe in the witch's voice was clear. 'Goddess above. No wonder it's feeling out of sorts,' she added.

'What does that mean for Lydia?' Hywel asked. 'And Rose?'

'It means we need to get to the scene of the spell,' Seren said, her eyes resting on Rose's prone figure in the bed. 'And quickly!'

Everyone began speaking at once, but they were interrupted by the appearance of Morgan, pink-cheeked, gasping for breath and gripping the door-frame for support. 'Search team found the car,' he panted.

CHAPTER 23

PONT NEFOEDD, JULY 1960

*M*aggie stood in the hallway watching her dad inch down the stairs, Rose in his arms, wrapped in a white sheet. Seren and Chris stood by the bottom step, waiting. Morgan was at the front door, holding it open as if at any moment it might slam shut and trap them all inside.

A warm breeze blew into the house, carrying with it the scent of summer flowers and the ease that usually came with the season. It seemed all wrong, somehow. The day was too chipper for what was happening here.

Her dad's old Jaguar stood just outside, its back door open, waiting. A lump bloomed in Maggie's throat as she watched them manoeuvre Rose into the car. The thought that her mother might be suffering the same ordeal somewhere, but alone, was just too much. They said it was unlikely, but unlikely wasn't the same as impossible.

Boudicca yowled, and when Maggie turned, the cat sprang into her arms. Maggie took a steadying step backwards, partly because the cat had caught her off balance and partly from the shock.

'Wow. This is new,' Maggie said as the cat rubbed the top of her head against her chin, purring. Maggie had to bite back the tears that sprang to her eyes. Swallowing hard, she said, 'You did brilliantly, you know, Boudicca. With the book. Rose has a chance now because of you, and we're a step closer to finding Mam.'

Boudicca leaned back in Maggie's arms and, still purring loudly, slowly blinked her reply.

'Come on, Maggie love,' Hywel called from the driveway. Maggie craned her neck to peer out of the front door. Her dad had one hand on the driver's door of the car, the other tapping the roof impatiently.

'Will you stay here and wait for Mam?' Maggie asked the cat. 'I've left you extra food and water out, and if we're delayed, you know to go to Mrs Thomas down the lane, don't you.'

Boudicca bopped her head against Maggie's chin before leaping soundlessly to the ground. She walked into the kitchen without a backward glance.

Seren and Morgan were already pulling out of the driveway when Maggie ran to the Jaguar.

'Cat flap definitely unlocked?' Hywel asked as Maggie closed the front passenger door as quietly as she could, not that Rose looked to be in any danger of waking up.

'Checked it three times,' Maggie replied as the Jaguar's tyres crunched on the gravel.

Maggie turned again to look at Rose. A flash of something long and black skittered across her ashen face and the young woman grimaced, her mouth opening in a silent cry. Chris pressed the flannel to her forehead and soothed her. 'It's alright, sweetheart, we know how to help you now.'

Maggie and Chris exchanged a look. The quicker they got to the source of the spell, the better.

CHAPTER 24

NEAR ABERYSTWYTH, JULY 1960

*T*he drive to Aberystwyth was excruciatingly slow. Hywel had given up trying to find something on the radio to listen to. The news seemed irrelevant, and music just felt inappropriate. They had fallen into a silence shortly after leaving Pont Nefoedd that was so heavy it was like another passenger in the car.

Question after question about the spell tumbled around in Maggie's mind, but as Seren was in the other car with Morgan, they would have to wait.

Instead, she tried to construct a reverie in which they'd get to the site of the spell to find her mother, somewhat exhausted but otherwise alive and well, waiting for them by the Land Rover the search team had located. They'd all be crying, and her dad would say something about getting his girls home.

An anguished cry from the back seat snapped Maggie back to reality. Rose's face was twisted in pain, her complexion grey. Poor Rose. She dreaded to think what she was enduring. Her thoughts drifted to the story of the Tortured Text.

'There, there,' Chris said softly, stroking the girl's forehead with one hand while pressing the fingers of her other to her neck, her eyes on her wristwatch.

Maggie held her breath, not wanting to interrupt. When Chris met her eyes, she didn't need to say anything.

'How much longer, Dad?' Maggie asked.

'Five minutes, tops,' he replied, his eyes flicking to the rear-view mirror. Maggie felt the car speed up.

The seconds ticked by in silence. Chris pressed a stethoscope to Rose's chest. Maggie looked away.

Up ahead, a petrol station came into view. Hywel accelerated again. Maggie could just make out Seren's willowy form climbing out of the car they'd followed all the way here. Seconds later, they were pulling up alongside. Hywel rolled down his window and Seren leaned in, her eyes on Rose and her expression grave. 'Park around the back. The search team is there with a stretcher to carry Rose to the spell site,' she said. 'The Land Rover Lydia was driving is about half a mile away. They're scouring the area but there's no sign of her yet. We'll head there next.'

Minutes later they were all following the stretchered Rose, Chris at her side whenever the terrain allowed. Seren led the party through the fields and tracks next to the road, her pace and focus akin to a bloodhound with a fresh scent.

Morgan hurried along after the stretcher, speaking to a woman wearing khaki shorts and heavy-looking walking boots who was coordinating the search. She had been first to jump out of the muddy minibus waiting for them at the back of the petrol station, an unruly mop of frizzy blonde hair poking from beneath the type of hat Maggie saw local ramblers wearing. The vehicle had 'Mountain Rescue' painted on the side, and Maggie wondered if they were indeed part of a genuine search team or members of the magical community trying to blend in. She asked her dad.

'No idea, love,' he puffed, struggling to keep pace with the rest of the group.

Maggie was out of breath too. The sun was at full strength now, and she felt the cotton of her blouse stick to her back. Up ahead, Seren had come to a stop. Maggie hurried to join her.

'Is it here?' she asked, casting around, scanning the scrub that divided the narrow path from the busy A-road beyond.

'It happened on the road,' Seren said, 'but this is close enough. You can lay her down here,' she instructed the men carrying the stretcher.

Chris ran her hand over the scraggly patch of yellowed grass before nodding her consent. Rose looked so close to death's door she doubted a stray stone would have even registered, but the gesture brought a lump to her throat.

Hywel, still breathing hard, put a hand on Maggie's shoulder and gave it a brief squeeze when he caught up. The plan was to stop here and help Rose, then for Hywel, Maggie and Seren to go with the search team to where they'd found the Land Rover Lydia had been driving.

'Please make sure we're not disturbed,' Morgan said to the woman in the khaki shorts.

She nodded, and gestured for two of the stretcher bearers to head on along the path, while she and the remaining two went back towards the petrol station.

'So, how is this going to work then, Seren?' Morgan asked as he dabbed at his nose with a large handkerchief. His eyes were resting on Rose, his face pinched into deep furrows.

Seren's gaze was skyward, tracking something in the air above them, although Maggie could see nothing, not even a wandering fly.

'The spell was cast near here. There are threads every-where. The air is choked with them,' Seren sighed, frowning as she turned in a slow circle, her eyes narrowed on the patch of sky above their heads.

'What does that mean for Rose?' Chris asked.

'Honestly, I don't know. I've seen nothing like this before. It's—' Seren's gasp cut off whatever she had been about to say next.

'What?' Chris asked.

'I thought the spell had just stopped time, but that doesn't explain all these threads –that does, though,' Seren said, pointing at the air above their heads.

Maggie was relieved that nobody else seemed to be able to see what she was pointing at either.

'What does?' Morgan asked irritably.

Seren stared at them. 'The portal,' she said, shaking her head either in awe or disbelief – Maggie couldn't tell. 'The spell punched a hole through time and space, creating a portal. I've encountered nothing as powerful as this before.'

'Great, but does it help with getting the spell fragments out of Rose?' Chris snapped.

Seren dropped to her knees in one fluid movement and knelt beside Rose. Maggie watched as the witch's hands hovered over her, lips pursed and a frown creasing her forehead. On a couple of occasions, she winced and snapped back her hand as if she'd touched something hot. Long minutes passed, and then Seren huffed out an exasperated breath.

She shook her head miserably. 'No. If anything, they're burrowing deeper. Their intent is so strong.'

'But, Seren, they're going to overwhelm her,' Chris said, her tone close to pleading.

'I know that, Christine.' Seren ground out the words slowly. 'But she doesn't just have the energy of the spell over-loading her body, she has the portal pulling at her now too.'

'You're saying that rather than helping her, being here

near the portal is just making things worse?' Morgan asked, his voice a cry.

Maggie groaned. So much for her wonderful idea.

Seren shook her head. 'Until we got here, my working hypothesis was that the book likely panicked and poor Rose was just caught in the crossfire.' She paused, her eyes resting on Rose, who had gone remarkably still. 'Now I'm not so sure it was accidental.'

'What, you think the spell intended for this to happen?' Maggie asked. 'But why?'

Seren shrugged. 'I wish I knew, child,' she said, and Maggie tried not to bristle at the insult.

'What's to be done then, Seren?' Morgan asked.

'I can't lie, Morgan, I'm not sure how much I can do,' the witch said, her voice barely audible as a lorry rumbled past.

'What do you mean?' Maggie asked, appalled. 'You can't just let her die!' she added, her voice louder and shriller than she'd intended.

'Come on, love,' her dad said quietly. 'There's no talk of that.'

Seren looked Maggie in the eye as she replied, 'Nobody wants that, Maggie, believe me. We could get a hundred witches here and they'd all tell you the same thing. Magic always has a purpose, and this spell is buried so deep it's not letting her go no matter—'

Maggie saw the moment the thought struck the witch. Her eyes went wide as her lips rounded into an 'O'.

On the ground, Rose groaned.

'What? Seren?' Chris asked, hope lighting her eyes.

'No time,' Seren replied, her voice a rasp.

CHAPTER 25

NEAR ABERYSTWYTH, JULY 1960

*R*ose opened her eyes. For a second, she was back on the beach in Rhyl, coughing up water onto the sand as an awkward young boy with worried brown eyes patted her back and said, 'You'll be alright, kid,' repeatedly. She'd never thanked him for saving her life. He'd run back to his friends when her mother had scuttled down the shoreline, full of false concern. That had always bothered Rose. A complete stranger risked his life to save her, and she'd been too busy coughing to say thank you.

She'd just experienced the same surge of hope that had roared back into her body that day on the beach. Life was not done with her yet. She frowned, trying to organise her thoughts. She remembered the kitchen in Lydia's big house. She remembered the cat. She'd hissed at her, hadn't she? Then eating crumpets with Maggie, Hywel and the Elders, but after that, it was all blackness.

Had she been alone in the dark, she might have been better able to bear it, but she knew she hadn't been. The remnants of horrors she couldn't name faded now like mist below a midday sun.

Rose's senses returned in a rush and she wondered if some monster had chosen that precise moment to finally loosen its grip on her. She was freezing cold, despite the touch of warm air on her skin. Crows on the wing, sounding an alarm. People arguing. Someone mentioned her name.

She recognised the voice of the witch. She remembered it from the darkness. How the sound of that calm, gentle voice had helped drive away the other things that she didn't want to name. Kindness and hope during the most desperate night of her life.

The witch was blaming herself for not being able to save her. Her questions tumbled around in Rose's mind like a spin dryer. 'Why can't I save her? What am I not seeing?'

Rose wanted to reassure her, to tell her it was okay – to thank her for trying, for being there to comfort her in the darkness – but she didn't know how. Her body no longer felt like her own. The pain had subsided. She was glad of that. All she felt now was a curious ache around her breastbone. A golden light crept under her lashes and she pried open her eyes.

The witch and the others were arguing, but her attention was solely on the ring of jagged golden light that hovered above her, its edges rough and tattered as if someone had just plunged their fingers through the old cotton of reality and ripped a hole in the air. Hundreds of threads fluttered from it like streamers in a parade. They danced in the breeze, catching and refracting the light so that she could see not just gold but a kaleidoscope of iridescent colours haloed in the air.

The ache in her chest became an insistent tugging sensation, and she leaned towards the light. A thin gold thread, shot with peacock blue, caught her eye. Without hesitating, Rose grabbed it. She gasped as the thread wound its way up and around her arm, then carried on, coiling itself around her body. She sighed at the warmth of it against her frigid skin. It hummed with power. The others were still arguing. They'd glanced at her, but nobody, not even the witch, seemed to notice the light.

The light appeared to be closer now. She was pretty certain that she couldn't move her physical body, had no idea how any of this was possible – and yet it was. Peering past the fluttering edges of the ring of light, she saw a thick forest bathed in dappled sunlight. It smelled new, somehow, as if it had recently rained, rinsing out the troubles of the day. There was a hint of wood smoke drifting through the air too, mixed with what she thought might have been honeysuckle. Rose closed her eyes, drinking it in. It smelled like home, she thought, although it was as far away from the concrete council estate of her childhood as it was possible to be.

She leaned closer and felt the warm breeze from the forest caress her face, the trace of a lover's hand across her cheek. The trees seemed to whisper a welcome as they swayed, their leaves shifting in the canopy so that the sunlight danced on the forest floor.

A sudden white-hot pain detonated in her chest and a sound that she had taken for granted all her life fell horrifyingly silent. She knew at once that her heart had stopped. The golden thread tightened protectively around her body, holding her.

Behind her, she felt the warm pull of what she knew instinctively would be a bright light of a different kind. She smiled as relief and knowing washed through her.

The golden thread squeezed her gently. It felt like a question. She closed her eyes against the memory of Frances throwing teacups, of Lydia's trembling lip as she told her to run. The sight of her mother lying dead on the sofa in their old flat.

The witch was speaking to her again. This time her voice

seemed to come from a long way away. It didn't matter. Rose knew she was no longer part of this world. She felt it in the stillness of her veins and her slowly cooling bones. Life was giving her a choice.

* * *

SEREN CROUCHED CLOSER TO ROSE, ignoring Chris's repeated question.

'Rose, if you can hear me, I think maybe the spell fragments also include bits of time. If you let them lead you, maybe—'

Seren didn't finish the word because in that moment, Rose vanished before their eyes.

Maggie gasped. Chris swore. Seren fell back on her behind in the dirt, her eyes still trained on the spot where Rose had just been.

'Dear mother in heaven,' Hywel said. 'What the hell just happened?'

'My question exactly,' said a man's voice from behind.

Maggie turned to see three men in black military uniforms striding towards them.

CHAPTER 26

HAY-ON-WYE, JULY 1841

'*L*ydia. Lydia.' Someone was shaking her shoulder.

Lydia stirred; the movement of her head made her wince. She moved her hand and found not tarmac, as she'd expected, but dried leaves. Frowning, she tried to open her eyes but shrank back to avoid a bright shaft of sunlight coming from somewhere above her. How long had she been unconscious? Hadn't it been nearly dark when … Lydia gasped and levered herself upright as the memory of the car chase returned to her fully formed in all its horror. She clutched her head as what felt like a bowling ball collided with the inside of her skull.

'You're okay,' said a familiar voice as delicate fingers squeezed her shoulder.

Leaning away from the sunlight, Lydia prised open her eyes, still squinting. The light felt like a lance through her skull.

'Rose!' she gasped when the figure swam into focus. 'Where are the books?'

Rose hesitated. 'Safe,' she said as she leaned over and offered her hand. Lydia took it gratefully, hoping that being upright might bring back her equilibrium. Once she was on her feet, Rose handed her the little green book.

Lydia sighed and hugged the *Book of Prophecy* to her chest.

'Where's the Land Rover?' she asked, casting around. She could see nothing but old broadleaf trees. 'How long was I unconscious? Where's my handbag? Why didn't you go to Dai Pony like I said?' She knew she was babbling but couldn't help it. Maybe she'd hit her head when she crashed. She ran her hands over her skull but couldn't feel any lumps or bumps, not even any sore bits. A memory formed of her stepping out of the Land Rover. She wanted to look at something. She'd not crashed then.

Lydia bent forward and braced her hands on her knees as a wave of nausea swept over her. She took a deep breath, held it, and then let it out slowly through her mouth. She was just confused, she told herself. Her head would clear soon and she'd be able to think clearly. There was something different about Rose too, although she couldn't quite put her finger on it. Breathe. She just needed to breathe.

Once the nausea subsided, Lydia, still bent over for fear of moving her head too quickly, asked, 'Any ideas where we are, Rose? Are we far from the road? If we can get back to the garage, maybe they'll have a phone and we can try the Elders again.'

Before Rose could reply, Lydia felt the thunder of hooves approaching at speed. She straightened up to see a reedy-looking man with a bulbous nose pulling on the reins of a large grey horse.

'Stand where you are!' he barked.

Lydia saw Rose press her lips into a flat line before she turned towards the voice.

'I said stand still, woman,' the man snapped.

Lydia levelled her gaze at him, which took some effort given the height difference and the pounding in her head.

'Who are you and what's your business here?' he demanded.

'We're a bit lost. We're looking for—' Lydia began.

'Wood anemones,' said Rose, moving to stand in front of her. 'For the church flowers.'

Lydia felt something shift uncomfortably in her gut. Something was very wrong here. She studied Rose's back. She wore a pale blue high-collared dress fastened with a line of tiny buttons. She looked like she was about to pose for one of those olde worlde pictures they did at Barry Island fun fair. The rude man on the horse was also wearing clothes you only saw on the telly.

The blare of a hunting bugle sounded in the distance. The thin man swore under his breath and cast a glance over his shoulder.

'We're ever so sorry if we've inadvertently trespassed,' Rose offered, her voice clear but her tone deferential.

The man glared at them both, his lips pulled into a hard, flat line as he ran his tongue over yellow teeth. Lydia repressed a shudder and lowered her eyes.

'You're the niece,' he said, staring at Rose. It wasn't a question.

Rose nodded but said nothing else.

Lydia had so many questions, but the air all but crackled with tension, so she bit them back and tried to focus on steadying her roiling stomach.

'A hundred yards that way,' the man said, pointing with his riding crop to his left, 'is the path that leads back to the village. You'll know where you are from there.'

'Thank you,' Rose said. 'You're very kind.'

The man snorted as he yanked on the reins to turn his horse. 'Kindness is for women and the feeble-minded. I don't want you ruining the hunt by distracting the hounds – his lordship is in a foul enough temper as it is. Go. And don't let me see either of you here again.' He turned and cantered away.

'The bloody cheek of it,' Lydia said.

'Come on, we need to get back,' Rose said, steering her towards a path. Lydia took a few steps, but then stopped and turned to Rose. 'Wait. Get back where? To the car?'

Rose looked at the ground, clearly in two minds about what to say next. Lydia waited for a few seconds, but then her patience snapped. 'For pity's sake, Rose. Just tell me. Am I losing my mind? Where are we?'

Rose took a breath and looked Lydia directly in the eye. 'The question you need to ask, Lydia, is not *where* we are, but *when.*'

CHAPTER 27

HAY-ON-WYE, JULY 1841

*L*ydia stared open-mouthed at Rose. Even though the younger woman's explanation had just settled in her gut as truth, her brain flatly refused to accept the idea. She swallowed as the nausea returned.

Lydia studied Rose. Her dainty black leather boots poking out beneath the floor-skimming skirt of her dress. Her neatly pinned-up hair, in place of the long plait she always wore. The clothes the rider was wearing. His manner. The rest of the picture seemed to slide into place like some sort of enchanted jigsaw. She knew then that she was as far away from the people she loved as it was possible to get.

She swallowed hard as acid flooded her mouth, but it was too late. She lurched forward and vomited as Rose patted her back.

Rose waited until Lydia had finished retching and spitting before guiding her gently to sit on a fallen tree trunk. Lydia sank gratefully down onto it, unsure how much longer her legs would hold her up. Rose held out a neatly folded lace handkerchief.

Lydia wiped her lips. Her mind was racing, but she simply

couldn't form the words. Her head was pounding. She pressed the little book to her chest and felt an answering thrum of vibration.

'I've been coming back to this spot for weeks, hoping I might find you. It's where I landed too,' Rose said quietly.

She waited a beat, but pressed on when Lydia remained silent. 'The big spell book that landed on my lap saved us by casting a spell that threw us back in time.'

Lydia nodded. She felt ridiculous, but knew in her marrow that what Rose was saying was true.

The blast of a hunting bugle, this time accompanied by the baying of hounds, made them both jump.

'Come on,' Rose said, jumping to her feet. 'I'll fill you in on the way.'

CHAPTER 28

HAY-ON-WYE, JULY 1841

*L*ydia stumbled after Rose, her feet numb and clumsy. Tree roots snaked across the narrow woodland path, some so proud of the soil they looked determined to trip the inattentive traveller. Around them, the trees crowded in like gossips in search of secrets. After tripping twice and almost losing her balance the second time, Lydia kept her eyes trained on the ground in front of her. She stared at the hem of Rose's dress as it brushed over the hard-baked soil, tiny plumes of dust dancing in her wake. No puddles, not even here in the shade.

Lydia thought of Morgan and his love of nature. He could probably name every tree and plant in the forest. The thought of her old friend brought a lump to her throat. The sound of his voice on the phone when she'd called with the alert.

The crack of gunshots made her gasp. She spun around, panic catching in her throat like a barb.

'Lydia?'

She looked back to the path to see Rose frowning in confusion. Lydia sighed. The memory had felt so real. She waved Rose on and followed, working hard to steady her breath and calm her racing pulse.

They emerged from the shadows of the wood into a wide country lane. The sun was warm and there wasn't a breath of wind. The sound of horses' hooves made Lydia spin left and right. She caught a glimpse of a horse-drawn cart disappearing around the bend, a cloud of dust drifting into the air obscuring the driver.

'It's this way,' Rose said, pointing in the opposite direction. She was already a dozen steps ahead.

Lydia looked around, trying to get her bearings. The wood was in full leaf, and the hedgerow across the lane looked fat and full of blackberry flowers intertwined with something she couldn't identify. Beyond the hedge and the fields behind, a tree-covered mountain she didn't recognise. Lydia felt her mouth go dry. Some part of her had hoped that she'd find some sense of familiarity once they were out of the wood.

'Where are we, Rose?' Lydia asked.

'Hay-on-Wye,' Rose replied. 'Come on. You'll feel better with some tea inside you, I promise,' she added, smiling. Lydia started, having no memory of seeing the other woman walk back to her. 'I was very disoriented when I first got here too, but it passes. Dilys will help, just like she helped me.'

'Who?' Lydia managed to ask. Her head was pounding.

Rose looped her arm through Lydia's and guided her up the hill. 'Dilys is the one who found me,' she said, her voice barely more than a whisper. 'She's a witch, although she doesn't use the word. I've been staying with her. She foresaw my arrival and then, about a month ago, yours. That's why we've been coming back to this spot every day since. If you'd arrived yesterday or tomorrow, it would have been Dilys who found you.'

'Wait,' Lydia said, stopping in her tracks. 'How long have

you been here?' She waved her hands in the air, noticing that, like her aching legs, they too felt leaden. 'The raid – it only happened a few hours ago.'

Rose nodded, her face carefully neutral as she retook Lydia's arm and continued the slow walk up the hill. 'I think we both used the same portal, but what was hours ago for you was much, much longer for me. I'm not sure why and neither is Dilys.'

'How long, Rose?' Lydia asked, her tone more forceful than she'd intended.

Rose took a breath before she replied, 'I got here three months ago.'

Lydia's mind reeled. It was all too much. Maybe she had hit her head. With any luck, she'd done it falling off the library ladder this morning and every terrible thing since was some sort of hallucination.

Rose stopped at the brow of the hill and pointed to a small white house in the distance, partially swallowed by the thick dark wood that arced around it.

'That's Dilys's house,' she said brightly. 'Come on. Not far now.'

Lydia opened her mouth, but the questions seemed to get stuck in her throat. She took a deep breath and tried to focus on her surroundings as she walked. The cottage disappeared from view behind a tall hedge as the road turned and dipped before climbing again a few minutes later, affording an even better view of the landscape.

From this vantage point, Lydia could see that the wood behind the house was further away than it first appeared, separated by a large garden and, beyond it, a field filled with some golden crop.

Lydia was unbearably hot. Sweat prickled her scalp and her blouse lay pasted to her back. She cursed the nylon in her elasticated trousers and her sensible slip-on library shoes. If she could just sit down in the shade and rest, maybe her head would stop thumping. A gust of wind, as welcome and timely as a lifeboat to a drowning man, made her shudder with relief. It brought the smell of wood smoke and honeysuckle. The memory fell like a punch.

Maggie as a baby playing in the garden with Hywel. Her daughter's squeals of delight as she plucked the honeysuckle flowers and dipped them one by one in her watering can, her shorts baggy at the bum where they stretched over her nappy. Maggie was a woman now, but the memory felt like it might have been yesterday. Hot tears welled in Lydia's eyes. No. She wouldn't cry. She squeezed the little book tighter to her chest. Took comfort in the feel of it against her heart. Whatever this was, be it hallucination or magic, she would get home to her family. No matter what.

CHAPTER 29

HAY-ON-WYE, JULY 1841

The cottage sat just off the lane at the bottom of the hill. Small, neat and so white it glowed in the sun. As they drew nearer, Lydia realised that the greenery she'd spotted from the hill was actually a climbing rose. The baby-pink blooms were a wash of colour around the windows and a frame around the porch that stood at a right angle to the body of the house.

There was something both wild and yet controlled about how the roses grew, as if an artist's brush had taken great care not to let a single petal cover the glass of the downstairs window, or the two on the upper floor.

The breeze picked up, delivering the musky scent of sun-warmed roses. Lydia sighed out a long breath, feeling some of her tension leave on the breeze.

'Almost there,' Rose said from beside her.

Lydia nodded, aware that she must have stopped walking as she gazed at the cottage. She set off again, taking in the other details.

A low grey stone wall wrapped itself around the cottage, a whitewashed wooden gate at its centre. The wall was almost a garden in its own right. Great tumbles of bell-like purple phlox, a carpet of pretty pink saxifrage and tufts of ferns and flowers spilled from every available crevice. At the foot of the wall, a veritable sea of yellow Welsh poppies bobbed in the breeze.

Rose released Lydia's arm to push open the gate. Standing on the tiled path, which was flanked with creeping thyme, she held the gate and waited. Lydia hesitated.

The box hedge below the window was likely pruned with the aid of a ruler. There wasn't a stray leaf or fallen petal anywhere. Lydia stroked her hand over the nearest tuft of saxifrage, deciding that she much preferred the untamed chaos of the wall.

Lydia took a deep breath and stepped onto the path. Rose beamed at her, then strode to the door and waited, hand on the handle, for Lydia to stand beside her.

The brass fittings on the dark green door were polished to a shine. She couldn't remember the last time she'd even wiped her own front door, let alone polished it. Maybe such things were the norm in—She stopped the thought, not wanting to surrender to the idea that she was in another time, despite the evidence. Had she asked which year? She couldn't remember; her thoughts still felt slow and treacly.

Before she could finish the thought, Rose disappeared inside.

'Aunt Dil, we have a visitor!' she called excitedly. She said something else, but her words were swallowed up by the house. Rose was different here, Lydia thought. Older in her ways, somehow. So much more confident and self-assured.

Lydia felt her skin prickle with gooseflesh as she stepped over the threshold. Whether it was from the drop in temperature because the cottage was cool after the warmth of the day or something else, she didn't know. She wrapped her arms around herself, pulling her cardigan close.

Lydia followed Rose down the passage, past a closed door to her right, which she assumed must be the sitting room, and into a neat-looking kitchen, dominated by a large scrubbed-wood table, then on again into what must be the scullery at the back.

A tall, solid-framed woman stood in front of the open window, a silhouette against the bright sunshine that flooded the room. Lydia blinked, her eyes taking their time to adjust to the change in light.

Bunches of flowers and herbs hung from the ceiling and swayed in the breeze. Lydia felt the fine hairs on her arms stand up as if they were iron filings reacting to the sweep of a passing magnet.

'You must be Lydia,' the figure, who must be Dilys, said. Her voice was low-pitched for a woman's, each word enunciated as clearly as a church bell on a quiet morning.

Lydia's mouth was dry. She nodded, her eyes still trained on Dilys's shadowy form. A warm breeze swept in through the window, bringing with it the scent of the honeysuckle Lydia had smelled on the hill. Above their heads, the bunches of drying flowers rustled as they swayed.

Lydia lowered her gaze, just in time to see a small bird, it too only a silhouette, land on Dilys's shoulder. Too late, Lydia realised that the movement had been too quick, releasing the bowling ball to career around inside her skull once again. She winced.

'It seems our first meeting is blessed,' Dilys said levelly as she clasped her hands together at her chest and held them there, as if in prayer.

'I'll make us some tea, Dil,' Rose said, already turning for the kitchen.

'Welcome, Lydia,' Dilys said, stepping forward. Lydia had the sensation of watching a ghost take on human form as the woman's features took shape before her eyes. She knew it was a trick of the light, but it was unnerving all the same.

Dilys was tall for a woman but held herself with the poise of someone entirely at home within herself. She wore her dove-grey hair pulled back into a tight bun, leaving not even a stray wisp to wander onto her sallow, softly lined face. She had no eyebrows that Lydia could make out, and if she had eyelashes, they lay hidden under the folds of her hooded lids. Her eyes were so dark they might have been black, but Lydia saw kindness in them. Sadness too. As she studied the woman's face, the robin perched on her shoulder peered back at her, head cocked and appraising.

Lydia smiled at the bird, delighted at the sight of it, and she felt another wave of tension leave her body. She sighed before she could stop herself. She was so exhausted, she accepted the steadying hand Dilys placed under her elbow as she steered her gently to the kitchen table.

While the tea wasn't the builder's brew that Lydia was hoping for, she was grateful for the sweet-smelling herbal concoction that Rose handed to her. She felt some of her weariness slip away as she sipped, wrapping her hands around the cup and watching, transfixed, as the robin hopped around the table, presumably looking for crumbs. The silence wasn't uncomfortable, but she had so many questions she needed to ask – if only her mind wasn't so muddled.

'You'll probably be wondering why you feel a bit foggy in the head,' Rose said as she topped up Dilys's cup and then her own from a large brown teapot.

Lydia looked up and felt a lump rise in her throat. Three women, sitting around an old oak table drinking tea. Two of them had done the exact same thing this morning in the library at Aber. The third, her dearest friend, Frances, was now dead. The echo of the gunshots cracked in Lydia's mind, and she flinched as her breath hitched in her chest.

The robin fluttered onto the edge of her cup and chirped at her, sending the echo of the gunshots sliding back into the shadows. She exhaled slowly.

'He'll sit on your finger if you hold it out,' Rose said.

Lydia slowly removed her left hand from the cup and extended her finger just in time to receive the robin. He hopped back and forth on it a few times then burst into song.

'And a song too,' Dilys said when at last the bird fell silent. 'You are honoured indeed, Lydia. He won't sing for everyone.'

'Thank you,' Lydia said to the robin. She wanted to say more, but her brain was still finding it hard to process her thoughts, so she just smiled instead.

'And my thanks too, my friend,' Dilys said to the bird. 'Your work here is ably done for now. If you've other business to attend to, then we'll not keep you from it.'

Lydia gasped as the robin took off in a flurry of wings and flew straight out of the back door. She tried to remember what they had been talking about before the robin sang. She frowned.

'I was confused at first too, but after a few hours, my head cleared and I was myself again. Please try not to worry. I only have my experience to draw from, but it does seem to be temporary.'

'That's a relief,' Lydia sighed. 'And how do we ...'

'Get home?' Dilys offered.

Lydia nodded.

'That question, among others, has occupied our every waking moment since Rose arrived,' Dilys said, inclining her head in Rose's direction. 'And now that you're here too, we can start putting our plan into action.'

Lydia looked from one to the other, her brain still

refusing to supply her with the clarity she needed to take it all in.

'When I arrived, I felt miles better after a sleep,' Rose suggested. 'There's a bed already made up for you upstairs. Clothes in the wardrobe too.'

Lydia felt herself nodding. She wanted nothing more than to sleep. With any luck she'd wake in her own bed next to Hywel, with Boudicca purring on her chest and the sound of Maggie playing her records too loudly from her bedroom. Rose helped Lydia to her feet, and she shuffled, glad of the steadying arm, towards the door. As she reached it, a question formed in her mind. 'What year is it then?' she asked.

It was Dilys who answered. 'It is the year of our Lord 1841.'

CHAPTER 30

NEAR ABERYSTWYTH, JULY 1960

*M*aggie was glad of her dad's arm around her shoulders as the men in black combat fatigues approached. Everyone in the magical community knew the government had a unit that worked on paranormal things, but she realised that until now she'd not quite believed they were real. Not flesh-and-blood human beings.

Do not trust them. Tell them we're here to look for Lydia. Rose left in the night. We assume to go home. Do not tell them about your library. Seren's voice was as clear in Maggie's head as if she had heard her speak out loud. When Maggie looked over at the witch, she gave an almost imperceptible nod. Maggie returned the gesture, although she doubted she was as subtle. Everyone else was looking at Seren too, so Maggie assumed her warning had been broadcast to them all.

'Commander Hawkins,' Morgan said tightly, addressing the man who had spoken moments before. There was no trace of warmth in his voice.

'Morgan,' the commander said, his smile broad but cold. He wasn't much younger than Morgan, Maggie thought, but looked like he still spent his spare time lifting weights and shouting at young recruits on a parade ground. There was a steeliness to him that made her shiver.

'I hear we have some trouble. Thought you could use a hand,' the commander said, smiling as he gestured to the men beside him.

Morgan snorted, and with an obvious effort straightened to look the commander in the eye. 'Thoughtful as ever, John, but we can do without the sort of help the government provides.'

Maggie stared. She had known Morgan all her life and had never seen him so openly hostile before. If these men were from the government, then maybe they could help find her mother. Surely they needed their help. She pulled in a breath, but her dad squeezed her shoulder. She glanced up at him, and he shook his head in warning.

The commander huffed out a dry laugh. 'When will you people learn that co-operation is the way forward here?' he said, his hands on his hips, head shaking. 'You have a missing civilian, maybe two,' he added, his eyes falling to the empty stretcher. 'We've had reports of an arson attack on an old manor house outside Aber and a car chase with guns fired on the A470 just hours later. Admit it was a library raid and we'll help you.'

Maggie could barely contain herself. *No!* Seren's voice was loud and clear in her mind. *For your mother's sake, Maggie, be quiet.*

Maggie bit her lip and leaned into her father, cheeks flaming.

'Alice Walker. Denzel Parry. Abigail Darlow. Jacob and Josephine Griffith.' Morgan recited the names solemnly. 'Should I continue, John? As you know, there are more than a dozen others who never saw the light of day after volunteering to work with Her Majesty's finest.' Morgan looked to be having a hard time containing his temper as he glared at the commander.

Maggie glanced up at her dad, but he stood with his head bowed, eyes closed. Chris and Seren too had their eyes on the ground. What was she missing here?

The commander barked out a dry, exasperated laugh. 'Good god, man, let it go. There was a war on! Would you have preferred Hitler raising a swastika over the Houses of Parliament? We did what was needed. They knew the risks.'

'The hell they did!' Morgan spat through gritted teeth, stepping forward so that the commander had to lean back. 'They were lambs to the slaughter and you knew it!' Chris jumped forward and took Morgan's arm, pulling him away.

'I think, Commander, you and your men need to be on your way,' she said, levelling her gaze at the man. 'We were just out for a walk, but if we hear of anything unusual, we'll be sure to call you.'

The commander stared at her, stony-faced. Chris didn't blink.

Maggie's heart thumped in her chest. She had always known that there was no love lost between the magical community and the government unit, but she'd never thought to ask why. What had happened to those people? Who were they? And why didn't she know about it?

'Have it your way,' the commander said at last, his tone artificially light. 'But remember, magic isn't always enough to stop bullets,' he added, before turning and striding off down the path, his men at his back.

CHAPTER 31

PONT NEFOEDD, JULY 1960

*I*t was close to midnight when Seren appeared in the kitchen, her beautiful face drawn and tired. Maggie had been washing the dishes for something to do while Morgan and Hywel cradled cups of slowly cooling tea. Chris had been persuaded to the guest room to catch up on two consecutive nights without sleep.

The remnants of another barely touched fish and chip supper meant Boudicca would be dining on cod for at least a week, although even the cat seemed to have no appetite tonight.

Hywel's eyebrows shot up in question when he saw Seren.

The witch shook her head as she walked to the table.

'Nothing of use, then,' he said, almost to himself.

Maggie turned back to the sink. She'd told them as much when she'd returned from the library an hour ago.

'I still don't think it's time travel,' Morgan said. 'In all my years, I've never heard of anything like it. And why? What was the book trying to achieve?' He shook his head as he let out a long sigh. 'There's got to be a simpler explanation. There has to be.'

Maggie turned in time to see Seren grip the back of the kitchen chair. Her expression was unreadable as she fixed her eyes on Morgan. He shrugged and said, 'The books say it's possible, yes, but there's been not one recorded case of someone, magical or not, who's experienced it.' He held up his palm to signal that he had more to say, not that Seren looked inclined to reply. 'All I'm saying, Seren, is that if you're right and Rose has disappeared into time, then this might be the first time in recorded history that it's happened. That in itself leads me to believe that another explanation is more likely.'

'Such as?' Seren said flatly.

Morgan shifted in his chair and looked down at the table before meeting her eyes again. 'Such as ...' He faltered, his eyes flicking to Maggie, then Hywel.

'You can say what's on your mind, Morgan, don't mind us,' Hywel cut in.

After sucking in a breath, Morgan said, 'Rose was very poorly, so perhaps the simplest answer is that she simply passed away.'

Seren muttered a curse under her breath. 'What? And took her physical body with her?'

Morgan opened his mouth to reply, but closed it again with a frown.

'We can, of course, wake Chris and ask her for the medical view, but to my knowledge, Morgan, that's far from usual,' Seren snapped.

Maggie stood frozen at the sink. She had never seen an Elder lose their composure, but first Morgan and now Seren. Did Morgan think her mother was dead too? If so, how seriously were they searching for her? She felt the anger begin to bubble in her gut and tried to focus on listening to what the others were saying in the hope of containing herself.

'That was unusual, yes,' Morgan conceded, 'but isn't it a bit of a leap to assume that Rose and Lydia are now in another time?'

'It's a logical conclusion in the face of the evidence, Morgan. The book that witnessed the spell told us as much, and granted, you couldn't see it, but trust me when I tell you there was a portal alongside the A470! Why is that all so hard to believe?'

'I'm not doubting you, I'm just saying that we don't have scientific evidence—' Morgan began, but Seren's muffled scream cut him off.

'You can't ask for empirical evidence of something that operates outside of the laws of empiricism, Morgan! We're talking about magic here!' Seren snapped, pushing away from the chair she'd been leaning on and leaving scorch marks on the wood.

'All I'm saying is—' Morgan began.

Maggie couldn't bear to listen to another word. She slammed the plate she'd been drying to the floor, where it shattered, the noise stealing all other sound from the room.

Shaking with temper, her voice little more than a growl, she said, 'What we need to be talking about is how we find my mother and Rose. Let your mediums ask the spirits if they've crossed, but until we hear that they have, I for one will be working on the assumption that they are in a different time.'

She headed for the door, sidestepping her father's open arms. In the living room she switched on the TV, realised that everything was off air and snapped it off again. The touch of silky fur against her ankle made her start, but she felt some of her fury melt away when Boudicca blinked up at her.

'Hey, Boudicca,' she whispered.

Maggie sank onto the settee and was touched almost to the point of tears when the cat hopped on her lap. She certainly knew how to pick her moments, Maggie thought as she gingerly stroked the cat's back and heard an answering purr. 'Thank you,' she mouthed, grateful for the solidarity.

Seren pushed open the door a few minutes later and came to join her on the couch. Maggie tensed, readying herself for the disappointment, but the cat stayed curled on Maggie's lap.

'I'm sorry I got emotional,' Maggie said, annoyed with herself for apologising even as the words left her mouth.

Seren waved the words away with an elegant hand. 'Never apologise for love. It should be me apologising for losing my temper. I can't remember the last time Morgan and I disagreed so strongly,' the witch said as she curled her long legs beneath her. 'I think we're all just tired and upset,' she added sadly.

'If they have gone into another time, how do we get them back?' Maggie asked.

Seren's eyes fell to Boudicca, and she didn't answer for what felt like an age.

'I'm not sure we can, Maggie. Morgan is right to say that we've never had anyone return to this time with evidence of having been to another. He takes that as proof that time travel isn't possible, whereas I think it's more likely that once someone slips into another time, the door closes behind them.'

'So, what? You're saying they're stuck there? Forever?' Maggie asked, heat rising in her chest.

'I'm saying that portals like the one Rose went through today look to be incredibly fragile. We don't know how they work or if it's even possible to use the same one for a return journey, especially for someone without magic.'

'What if someone with powerful magic used it to go after them?' Maggie asked, looking Seren directly in the eye as her heart hammered in her chest.

Seren's shoulders fell, and Maggie saw the answer on her face even before the witch replied, 'That wouldn't be possible. At best you'd have three people trapped in the wrong time. At worst, using the portal again might collapse it completely, removing any hope of them finding it from the other time.'

'But there has to be something we can do!' Maggie's voice rose into a shout and Boudicca hissed, her back claws digging into Maggie's thighs as she launched herself from her lap. Maggie winced.

Seren shook her head, her eyes on the blue velour of the old settee. 'I will keep researching this, I promise you,' the witch said, looking up and reaching over to put a cool hand over Maggie's hot, clammy one. 'I'm going to speak to our community in Bombay. There's an Elder there who wrote his doctoral thesis on portal theory.'

Maggie stood up. 'That's your answer? More research?' She was shouting now but didn't care. 'You have magic, Seren. Powerful magic. You could go right now and bring them back, but your answer is a trip to India to speak to some academic?'

'Maggie.' Seren said her name as if it weighed a ton.

Maggie walked to the door, unable to stomach any more of the witch's excuses.

'Enjoy your bloody field trip,' she said over her shoulder.

CHAPTER 32

HAY-ON-WYE, JULY 1841

*L*ydia woke to the sound of birdsong and the smell of baking bread. For a few glorious moments she wondered why Hywel, who despite owning a bakery business was useless at bread-making, had decided to try again. She knew it wouldn't be Maggie; she had no interest in cooking. Reality landed like a lead weight. Opening her eyes with a start, her nightmare was confirmed. She was lying on an iron-framed bed in a small room with a low ceiling that sloped towards a deep-set leaded window. The window was held open on an iron fastening, the breeze moving the thin cotton curtain backwards and forwards, bathing the room in bright sunlight and then restoring it to shadow.

Lydia lay back down, fighting hard to steady her breath and wrestle down the wave of nausea creeping up her throat. Shoving her hand under the pillow, she felt the edge of the little green book and exhaled slowly. She pulled it out and clasped it to her chest, focusing on her breath. Once she was certain that she wasn't about to be sick, she forced herself to open her eyes again. 'A good keeper observes the book before trying to read it, Lydia,' or so her aunt never tired of saying.

Levering herself up to sitting, the springs of the bed squeaking as she moved, Lydia looked around the room. It was sparse, but clean and tidy. A small table with an oil lamp next to the bed. A small fireplace on the opposite wall, its hearth laid ready for cooler nights, and to its side, a narrow, walnut-coloured wardrobe in the alcove. The only other furniture was a chair and a washstand, complete with a pretty blue-and-white china bowl. It was real.

Lydia collapsed back onto the feather pillows and decided to give in to the tears. Best to get it out of the way now, she reasoned. But despite giving herself permission to sob her heart out, her mind clearly had other ideas. She had to do something – anything – to get home to her family. She flung back the sheet and blanket and grabbed her clothes from the chair.

Lydia was halfway down the stairs when she heard singing. She couldn't place the tune, but whoever it was had a voice that would win talent shows the world over. The skin on the back of Lydia's neck goose-fleshed at the sound, as if the music were caressing her skin and settling into the soft parts of her soul. A memory of her parents, aunts and uncles singing together in the parlour of her grandparents' house at Christmas flashed into her mind. She had been too young and shy to join in, but she remembered the feeling. The lump in her throat. The tingling of her skin.

The singing stopped abruptly when she entered the kitchen as Rose, her hands in thick oven gloves, hefted a large black kettle from the range and poured water into a blue-and-white jug.

'I heard you get up. This is for you to wash,' she said brightly, inclining her head towards the jug. 'Phew!' She huffed out a long breath as she set the kettle back on the range. 'They weigh a ton even when they're empty,' she said, smiling as brightly as a sunbeam.

'Was that you singing?' Lydia asked.

'Hmm?' Rose asked absentmindedly as she pulled a towel from the dresser. 'Oh, singing. Yes.'

'Rose, you have an incredible voice,' Lydia said as she sank into a chair.

Rose wrinkled her nose and giggled, and Lydia noticed her cheeks turning pink. Rose was so different here. So far removed from the timid young woman she'd spent the last week working alongside at the library.

'Thank you,' she replied. 'Can you believe I never even knew I could sing until I got here. Now I love it. How are you feeling?'

'You were right about the sleep,' Lydia said. 'My head is a bit clearer this morning, although this still feels like a bad dream.'

'I know,' Rose replied, the bright smile falling from her face. 'But we'll get you home, Lydia.' After a long beat, she said, 'But first, breakfast.'

Rose set a fresh golden loaf of bread on the table, and Lydia's stomach gurgled its reply. She pulled a face, embarrassed, but Rose just giggled as she bustled around the small kitchen fetching butter, jam and honey.

'You're different here, Rose. More ...' Lydia left the rest of the question hanging, unsure how to finish it.

'Self-assured? Happy? Content?' Rose offered with a beam that was a mile away from the twitching of the lips that had passed for a smile in Aber.

'Yes,' Lydia said, 'but it's more than that too. You're almost glowing. It's wonderful to see.'

Rose beamed. 'It feels wonderful too. I thought at first that I was just glad to be alive after what happened—' Rose paused in her bread-slicing as Lydia stilled.

Rose cocked her head as if listening to something, then added, 'I'll tell you the whole story after breakfast, but I died in our time. I actually felt my heart stop, which is the strangest feeling.'

Lydia clamped a hand to her mouth, horrified. Had the magic hunters caught her? Shot Rose as they had poor Frances? Why did she tell her to run? They should have stayed together.

Rose reached out and squeezed Lydia's hand. 'They didn't shoot me. It was the spell. And you told me to run because it was the best thing to do at the time.'

Lydia opened her mouth, but Rose answered her unspoken question before she could even form the words.

'There's that too. For some reason, I seem to be able to hear people's questions before they ask them.' Rose threw up her hands in a shrug. 'Dilys thinks it's a spell fragment, but we can talk about that when she gets back. Now. Eat something, please. We have so much to do.'

CHAPTER 33

HAY-ON-WYE, JULY 1841

*L*ydia was on her third cup of tea by the time Rose had finished her story. Rose had decided that the edited version, minus the worst of the horrors that had stalked her in her perpetual darkness, would get the job done well enough.

Lydia had looked close to tears when Rose explained how Maggie, Hywel and the Elders had tried to look after her, and so she made an effort to lighten the tone by recounting how the Siamese cat had hated her on sight. Lydia had rolled her eyes and made an apologetic face then, and Rose had been glad that the distraction had worked.

'Why did we land in Hay-on-Wye, though? It's miles away from where the spell happened,' Lydia said. Rose had heard that question too, but didn't interject.

'We're not sure about that, to be honest. Our best guess is that these ...' Rose shrugged. 'Portals, tunnels, tears in time, whatever we call them, well, they're not straight lines. Maybe they connect to sources of magical power, or maybe they're random. We've ruled out any family ties as I don't have anyone here, not that I know of anyway, but honestly, we have no idea.'

'Dilys, Rose said you foresaw our arrival?' Lydia asked.

'I did. First Rose and then, just after midsummer, I saw you joining us,' Dilys said evenly, although Rose knew her well enough now to detect the hesitation at the end of the sentence.

Rose caught her eye and nodded for her to continue.

'Lydia, you must know, given your line of work, that visions are not always accurate. I was never a gifted seer – in fact, for many years I considered myself lacking any talent for that part of the craft – but as you and young Rose here are the very embodiment of what I was shown, I have come to revise my opinion.'

Long seconds passed, and Rose waited for Dilys to continue, to share the content of the third and most important of her visions. She was about to mention it when Dilys spoke.

'Tell Lydia about your visions, Rose,' Dilys said pointedly.

Rose took a sip of her tea then leaned forward in her chair, choosing her words carefully.

'My nightmares started that first night at your house,' she began, deciding not to mention that by the next morning she felt like something was eating its way through her flesh. Bite by agonising bite, the pain had been unbearable, and yet it was a memory now, as far removed from her actual experience of being as it felt possible to be. It might have happened to someone else, or a character in a book, for all the connection she felt when recalling it.

'I remember waking and thinking, "I'm dying," but then this picture flashed into my mind of a caterpillar in a cocoon, and I thought, "Oh, so I'm not dying. I'm changing."' Rose paused, smiling at the memory. Lydia looked horror-struck, so she pressed on.

'After that, I started to smell things. Tea roses, honey-suckle, thyme, tomato stems after you nip off the side shoots. Then I started to see more pictures in my mind, the woods, the flash of a robin's wing and other creatures.' Rose paused, feeling silly, and changed tack. 'I'd catch a glimpse of a garden full of flowers through an iron gate. An old black kettle on a range. I knew it was all real, Lydia. Don't ask me how, but I knew I was seeing somewhere else, and that gave me hope.'

'And you think you were seeing glimpses of here? Of this time?' Lydia asked.

Rose was already nodding. 'Me and Dil have talked about this a lot over the last few months, and I think the book knew exactly what it was doing.'

Lydia looked confused. 'But you said Seren thought the spell fractured?'

'I heard her say that, yes. She was angry and upset at herself that she couldn't get all the fragments out of me, couldn't save me. She assumed that the spell book got it wrong and that's why the spell fractured.'

'But you don't think the book did get it wrong?' Lydia asked carefully.

'Magic doesn't make mistakes,' Dilys said. 'Witches, yes, but this spell didn't come from a witch. It came from the source itself. Your arrival just proved it. That book wanted you both here, in this time, in this place, for a reason. We need to know what that reason is if we stand a chance of getting you home.'

'Do you think it was something to do with the prophecy in this?' Lydia asked, holding up the small green book.

'Stop!' Dilys commanded, raising her hands. 'Tell us nothing of what that book shared with you in your time. Do you hear me? Rose cannot remember the details, and I do not believe that is an accident either. We have no idea what your presence here in 1841 might do, Lydia, or how your knowledge of the future might somehow change it. So, I beg of you, keep your counsel – for everyone's sake.'

Lydia looked taken aback by Dilys's tone, and Rose couldn't blame her. She remembered well how disoriented she'd felt those first few days after arriving. But there was one more vital piece of information that Lydia needed to know. Had a right to know.

Rose took a deep breath and let it out slowly. She looked Lydia in the eye and said, 'Dilys is right. We need to find out why the spell book sent us both here. And we need to do it before the hunter picks up our trail.'

CHAPTER 34

HAY-ON-WYE, JULY 1841

*H*unter. The word ricocheted around Lydia's mind like a stray bullet. Crack. Crack. The memory of gunshots sounded so real, she flinched. Her breath caught in her chest as if someone had slipped in extra valves while she wasn't looking. She fought for air, her breaths increasingly shallow and hard won, the imaginary valves closing shut, as if turned by a sly hand. Her chest tightened, her heart now hammering beneath her ribs, as panicked as a snared rabbit. Her vision blurred and a chill slipped, snake quick, up her spine. She began to tremble, her limbs no longer under her command.

Rose knelt by her side. 'Breathe out, Lydia. Long breaths,' she said, elongating the words and then exaggerating her own out breath. 'They're not here. You're safe. Just breathe.'

It took what felt like an age to reclaim her body from the panic that had engulfed her. She propped her elbows on the table, her head in one hand, the *Book of Prophecy* gripped tightly in the other. She could feel the power in it, and it soothed her. So long as she had it, she had at least part of the puzzle.

When at last she sat back in her chair, Dilys reached over and patted her hand. She said nothing, and Lydia was glad. She was suddenly too exhausted to think.

'I'm sorry, Lydia, but we had to tell you. It's not fair to keep it from you,' Rose said, getting up and retaking her seat.

Lydia nodded. 'Did they follow us?'

Rose shook her head. 'Dil. You're best explaining.'

'I had three visions. One for each of you and a third about a man who will pursue us. Frustratingly, that vision wasn't as clear as the first two, so I can't make out his face. I do know two things about him, though. He's from this time, so no, you weren't followed here.'

'What about the second thing?' Lydia said, unable to wait.

'I also know that he hunts magic in all its forms,' Dilys replied, her eyes falling to the book in Lydia's hand.

* * *

THE NEXT TWO days slipped by as if they had been oiled. Much to her relief, Lydia's panic hadn't returned during her waking hours, but her nights had been fractured. When she did sleep, she dreamed of her family – scenes so fleeting they might have been snipped from a photo album. Hywel in a dinner suit. Maggie pushing a doll in a red pram, even though the one she'd owned as a child was blue. It wasn't what she saw that threatened to break her, it was how she felt when she woke. Scraped raw and freshly hollowed. Lydia had watched the sun rise twice now to avoid sleeping again, unable to bear it. She'd sleep for a week once she got home to them.

She'd tried over and over again to ask the *Book of Prophecy* for help, but the answers were all in the negative.

'Please tell me again about the Ethereal.'

No.

'How do we get home?'

No reply.

'Why are we here?'

No reply.

'Can I tell Dilys about the prophecy you shared?'

NO!

Lydia had given up then. She spent her days reading the only other book in the house, Dilys's family grimoire, retrieved from its hiding place in the attic. It was fascinating but offered no insight into their present predicament. She wondered whether Dilys had suggested she read it as a way of occupying her while she made arrangements for them to travel to Cardiff. The man in Dilys's vision had arrived just after a new moon, she said. They had two full weeks yet, not that they'd need them.

Lydia sat back in her chair by the window, the grimoire open on a small table in front of her. The light was too poor to read now, and so she watched the birds in the garden. On the ground, a male blackbird, feathers the colour of night and a beak as yellow as a sunflower's petal, hopped between the vegetable beds, eyes trained on the earth, looking for a last worm for its supper. Sparrows bathed in the dust on the path, and in the corner, a squirrel drank deeply from the old stone bird bath Dilys filled every morning.

She'd miss this when she went home, Lydia thought, stroking the *Book of Prophecy* through the fabric of her dress. She hated the constriction of Victorian clothes, but the hidden pockets were a touch of genius in an era when women didn't carry handbags. The book wasn't exactly purring, but the resonance felt similar, and that brought her some comfort.

Stifling a yawn, Lydia closed the huge, dusty grimoire and sighed. At close to six inches thick and double that in height, it wasn't exactly easy to hide. Just possessing such a book had been enough to see people murdered for witchcraft back in the burning times. How the family had kept it hidden so long was remarkable.

Lydia got stiffly to her feet and rolled her neck. She needed to move, to do something, but there was nothing to be done until tomorrow. Dilys had made the arrangements, although she remained tight-lipped about the details. Rose had baked extra bread for the journey and written notes for neighbours asking them to look after the garden while she and Dilys travelled to London to care for Rose's ailing mother. Lydia had to hand it to them, they had thought of everything.

Rose bustled into the kitchen, singing a song Lydia didn't recognise, an empty basket resting on her hip.

'Find anything interesting second time around?' she asked, pausing in front of Lydia and eyeing the closed book.

'Lots of interesting bits and pieces, but nothing of use to us,' Lydia confirmed, pulling on the high collar of her blouse.

'Help me get the veg in if you like,' Rose suggested. Lydia grabbed a spare basket from the scullery as she followed Rose out of the back door. The sun had moved into the west, throwing a welcome shadow over half of the kitchen garden.

Rose stayed in the sunny part. She sang sweetly to herself as she moved around the vegetable beds, pulling carrots, picking herbs and plucking peas from their poles as the birds continued to flutter around her. Lydia tried and failed to reconcile the image with the timid mouse of a girl she knew in Aber.

Lydia headed for the shade, pulling at her collar as she hoped for a cooling breeze. By contrast, Rose looked entirely at home in the high-necked blouse and long skirt. Maybe it was just because she'd been here longer and had had more time to adjust, Lydia mused, but it felt more than that. There was a rightness about her somehow. She looked like she belonged.

Lydia was about to ask what else they needed when the robin let out a warning call. Rose stopped singing abruptly and spun around. The sound of the front door knocker, hard and heavy like a falling hammer, made them both jump. The birds scattered. Rose locked eyes with Lydia, and she knew at once that they were thinking the same thing – the grimoire was still on the table. Lydia moved first but Rose was quicker, disappearing into the house in a flash of skirts.

By the time Lydia reached the kitchen, the table under the window was empty.

'It's hidden,' Rose whispered.

'I thought Dilys said you don't get callers,' Lydia hissed.

'We don't,' Rose replied, sounding more confident than she looked. 'I'll get rid of whoever it is.'

'Wait!' Lydia caught Rose's arm. 'What if it's—'

Rose put her hand over Lydia's. 'I doubt the man from Dil's vision is going to knock politely on the front door,' she said, her conviction visibly waning even before she'd finished the sentence.

The knock came again. Heavy, insistent and anything but polite.

Lydia and Rose locked eyes.

The voice from the scullery behind them made them both jump.

'He knows you're here, Lydia. Remain calm,' Dilys hissed, not breaking step. Her breathing sounded laboured, as if she'd been running. She crossed the kitchen swiftly, paused for a single heartbeat at the threshold and straightened her back. Then she marched down the passage to the front door.

Rose and Lydia huddled behind the kitchen door, listening.

'Reverend Evans,' Dilys said evenly, her voice carrying up

the passage from the front hallway. 'Our second meeting of the day. I am blessed indeed. Please, do come in. It slipped my mind earlier, but you have picked an auspicious day to visit as my cousin arrived late yesterday.' Dilys sounded calm, but Lydia hadn't missed the flash of fear on her face in the kitchen.

The reverend mumbled something in reply that Lydia couldn't hear. She felt her breath stick in her chest. Her back slicked with sweat. Her hand found the little book in her skirt pocket, and it pulsed at her touch. Mouth dry, she glanced at the scullery door and the back door standing open beyond it. A dozen paces and she'd be in the garden. She had to get away before—Rose grabbed Lydia's arm and held her in place. Her eyes held Lydia's, a sweet, sad smile on her lips. She shook her head slowly.

The parlour door creaked on its hinges and Lydia let out a breath. Of course Dilys wouldn't bring a visitor into the kitchen. They'd take tea in the front room, the one with the velvet armchairs with lace covers over the arms. The panic slunk back into the shadows, chased away by the light.

'You okay?' Rose mouthed, her hand on the kitchen doorknob.

Lydia nodded, relieved that this time she'd been able to control the panic before it took hold. She smiled and nodded. 'Go,' she mouthed.

Moments later, she heard the parlour door creak again as Rose went to welcome their guest. Lydia heard the murmur of voices and then Rose was striding back into the kitchen, her expression grave.

'Is this normal? Him calling like this?' Lydia asked quietly.

Rose shook her head. 'Definitely not. And there's something …' Rose hefted the kettle onto the range, hesitating as she appeared to choose her next words carefully. 'We always try to get away swiftly after chapel each Sunday so that we don't need to talk to him much, because he gives me the creeps. But there's something else about him today. Something...' She trailed off, busying herself with tea things.

'Do you think he's the man Dilys saw in her vision?' Lydia asked.

Rose frowned, then shook her head thoughtfully. 'Dil didn't know the man from the vision. She knows him,' she said, jabbing her thumb in the direction of the parlour, 'so it can't be him.'

Lydia felt her the knot in her stomach loosen.

'What do you think he wants then?' she asked.

Rose took a deep breath and let it out slowly. 'Whatever it is, I don't have a good feeling about it.'

CHAPTER 35

HAY-ON-WYE, JULY 1841

*R*ose picked up the tea tray and waited by the kitchen door for Lydia to go ahead of her. Lydia looked milk pale as she hesitated, chewing her bottom lip. Rose remembered the cold dread she'd felt the first time she'd had to pass herself off as a native of 1841 and not the time-travelling refugee of magic she really was.

Rose was anxious too, but not for the same reason. She'd not wanted to frighten Lydia so had shared just enough to make sure she was on her guard, but this unannounced visit was not the happy coincidence the reverend had claimed it to be.

His arrival felt like a low, slow-rolling fog that stole the ground beneath your feet and silenced the world, so that all you could hear was the thump of your own heart pounding in your ears.

At the parlour door, Lydia turned. She looked terrified, poor lamb. At least the story they'd created for her wouldn't require too much pretence. To anyone who asked, Lydia was a cousin of Dilys's late husband, taking the country air as a tonic for her nerves.

Rose mustered up the most confident smile she could manage. 'Ready?' she mouthed.

She saw Lydia swallow before she nodded hesitantly.

'You'll be fine,' Rose whispered.

Lydia didn't look convinced, but stepped forward to open the door.

Rose set down the tea tray on the table in the middle of the room. She turned to see Lydia creep into the parlour, looking like a mouse hopeful of evading a cat. The reverend wasted no time in pouncing, stepping forward and squeezing Lydia's hand, his greeting too quiet for Rose to hear.

He wasn't an unattractive man, Rose thought, even though he must be in his sixties. He was shorter than her by a good few inches, so she guessed he must be around five feet five, but he had the build of a workman, not a preacher. His hair was slate grey shot with silver. Had he lived in 1960, he might have been a news reader. Yet there was something sly about him that always made Rose look for the nearest door. She schooled her face into the benign half-smile Dil had made her practise when she'd first arrived and poured the tea.

'And how long will you be staying with us in Hay, Mrs Malone?' the reverend asked Lydia. His speaking voice was so at odds with his chapel voice, Rose mused. When he preached, he left no one in any doubt as to what he was saying, such was his gift for both volume and projection. But one to one, he all but whispered. It was a clever tactic, Rose supposed. It meant you had to lean closer to hear him.

'Just until I feel stronger, Reverend,' Lydia replied meekly.

'We will all be in chapel on Sunday, of course,' Dilys put in. 'Do you have news of how poor Mrs Price is, Reverend?'

Rose saw a flash of irritation cross the man's face, but he smiled before he tore his eyes away from Lydia and replied.

'Better, I hear,' the reverend said tightly. 'Tell me, Mrs

Malone, you are a cousin on Joseph's side, am I right?' he asked, smiling at Lydia.

'Yes,' Lydia replied. Then added, her eyes downcast, 'God rest him.'

Nice touch, Rose thought, suppressing a smile.

'It was a tragedy indeed. For him to be cut down in his prime like that, and before the good Lord could bless the marriage with the gift of children too. Tragic,' the reverend said, shaking his head with all the sincerity of a brick.

Rose wrestled her expression into something she hoped looked like sadness. Joseph Lloyd had been a wife-beating drunk who had finally picked a Friday-night fight with a man capable of defending himself. He was no loss to the world. Dil had told her the story months before, her eyes only glistening with tears when she mentioned the pregnancies his beatings had ended.

Rose glanced at Dilys, sitting straight-backed and looking almost regal in her chair. Sitting properly had been one of Dilys's first lessons, and it had taken Rose weeks for her back to stop aching with the effort of it. If the reverend's words stung, her expression betrayed nothing.

The conversation moved on to preparations for some local fair in the village, but the reverend looked distracted. His eyes flicked repeatedly to Lydia.

He quizzed her relentlessly, slipping in questions whenever Dilys paused for breath. Which of Joseph's brothers had she married, again? Oh yes, foolish of him to misremember, she'd just told him. Had she said they lived in Cricklewood or Bricket Wood? He was testing her story as surely and as blatantly as if he'd taken a pin to her flesh. Lydia played her part perfectly, though, and didn't miss a beat when she answered.

Rose watched him from under her lowered lashes, feeling increasingly desperate for some crumb of information that would help them understand why he was here. Dilys launched into her pet topic – how the chapel could better help those families struggling to feed themselves – and it happened. The reverend's focus slipped.

How long will it take him to get here?

Rose stilled. Hearing people's unspoken questions had been getting easier by the day, but she was still not adept. Had it been Lydia or Dil she'd heard? She doubted it, but she had to be sure. She waited.

What will he pay me?

Will he take the three of them?

What will I tell the village when the old mare disappears?

Rose let out the breath that had caught in her chest slowly and silently through her nose. She waited a beat and, apologising to Dilys for the interruption, offered to make more tea.

The reverend was on his feet in a flash, keen to send word to whoever his paymaster might be, Rose thought.

'Very kind of you, Rose, but I must get back and start on my sermon or Lord knows what I'll be saying on Sunday,' he said genially.

'It was a pleasure to meet you, Reverend Evans,' Lydia said politely, the smile tight on her lips.

'Delighted to meet you too, Mrs Malone. Delighted,' he said smoothly.

Rose gritted her teeth against the shudder that ran down her back when she saw the look in his eyes as his gaze slid across them. Like a man sizing up a cow and calculating how much he could make from each chunk of its flesh.

Dilys walked him to the front door, and the moment it closed behind him, Lydia collapsed back into the chair and sighed out a long breath. Rose went to the window and peered through the lace curtain at the reverend's retreating form. He was all but running down the lane.

'He knows something, and he's planning to sell the information,' Rose announced the moment Dilys appeared in the parlour doorway. 'He was wondering how much a man would pay him and whether he'd take all three of us.'

Dilys snorted. 'He has always been a snake, that one.'

'But how would he even know anything?' Lydia asked.

'Maybe Dil isn't the only one who has visions,' Rose suggested, shrugging. 'If whoever this hunter is has put the word out to his cronies to be on the lookout for strangers, well, maybe that's all he needed.'

Dilys was nodding, her jaw tight and her lips pursed.

Rose looked around the familiar room. The cottage had felt like home from the moment she'd arrived, but it felt tainted now. As if something cold and oily had slipped into the sunny little house with the reverend's arrival, leaving a mark that could never be scrubbed away.

'So, what do we do now?' Lydia asked, looking anxiously between Rose and Dilys.

'We leave,' Dilys said flatly. 'Tonight.'

CHAPTER 36

HAY-ON-WYE, JULY 1841

*S*uitcases in hand, the three women slipped out of the back door as soon as the first shafts of moonlight lit the world. Waiting for the cover of darkness had felt like torture, but Dilys had been adamant. The garden was just as beautiful under the grace of the moon as it was under the blessing of the sun. The air was warm and heavy with the scent of jasmine, the only sounds the rustling of the leaves in the trees and the occasional hoot of an owl.

At the end of the garden, they slipped through a gap in the hedge that was completely invisible from any angle bar the one they approached it from and into a field of waist-high wheat that swayed and rustled in the breeze. Surely Dilys didn't mean for them to cross it? They'd trample the crop and give any pursuers a clear trail to follow.

Lydia caught her breath as a cloud scudded across the nearly full moon and the light of the world snuffed out. She stopped, unsure of her next step. When the light returned seconds later, she startled at the sight of a barn owl circling high around Dilys's head. The older woman nodded at it, and as Lydia looked back to the field, the wheat parted, leaving a straight, narrow path into the woods beyond. The cloud returned, turning the world dark again.

Rose squeezed Lydia's arm. 'It's okay. Just magic,' she whispered. 'Come on,' she added, pulling Lydia along behind her as they followed the ghost of the bird along the path, towards the woods. When they reached the trees, the moonlight returned. Lydia glanced back just in time to see the path disappear beneath the wheat. She smiled, and something loosened in her chest. It occurred to her that in the four days she'd been here, this was the first magic she'd encountered. She had no idea of Dilys's powers, but asking wasn't the done thing even in her own time.

The owl left them at the tree line, and Lydia half hoped, half expected another creature to arrive to guide them, but from the pace Dilys set, she clearly knew these woods blindfolded. The moonlight cast just enough light for her to make out the shadows of the two women walking ahead.

'Stop here,' Dilys said after they'd been walking in silence for what felt like an hour but was likely only half that. 'We need to climb up onto a ridge now to get to the hollow, and then we need to climb down into it. It isn't very high, but it is steep, so follow me exactly. Take your time and remember to stop when I do at the top of the ridge. It would not be pleasant for any of us to take a tumble here.'

Dilys hadn't exaggerated. In places the incline was so steep they had to pull themselves forward using the roots and branches of the trees. The wood was thicker on the top of the ridge, the flashes of moonlight through the gently shifting canopy the only light. Lydia was panting by the time they reached the top, her hands slick with sweat.

Heaving herself up onto the ridge to stand behind Rose, Lydia huffed out a long breath as she marvelled at the natural hollow that lay before them, bathed in moonlight. It was almost cauldron round, with three-quarters of its perimeter formed by earth and the roots of the huge trees that stood sentinel around it. The remaining quarter looked to be sheer rock, but as Lydia's eyes adjusted, she could see that there was also a cave in the cliff wall.

'Keep moving,' Dilys whispered as she turned and began clambering down the steep sides of the hollow. Rose motioned for Lydia to go next.

The feel of soft, solid earth and old leaves beneath her feet at the base of the hollow almost made Lydia cry out with relief. Her hand felt raw from where she had clung to roots, and she'd considered flinging the suitcase into the void on more than one occasion just to have the benefit of both hands.

Rose landed beside her, having jumped the last few feet. She gave Lydia a quick squeeze on the arm, but then she was off, striding after Dilys, who was already at the cliff end of the hollow. Lydia hurried to join them and was only a few feet away when she saw Dilys begin to climb again. *Dear god*, Lydia thought, *when will this end?*

There was a faint squeak of iron, the rasp of a match striking sandpaper and then the soft glow of a lamp above her. Rose was already clambering up the rocks to join Dilys, who was standing on a flat shelf about six feet above Lydia's eye line.

Lydia followed, glad of Rose's hand when she offered it. Heart hammering, she just had time to see that the shelf they were on was wide and flat before Dilys and the light were swallowed by a darkness so complete it made Lydia want to bolt in the other direction.

Rose retraced her steps and laid her hand gently on Lydia's back. 'Nearly there now,' she whispered in a tone that suggested they were on a ladies' day out and not hiding in the woods from some horror nobody wanted to name.

Taking a deep breath, Lydia forced herself forward,

following the light until she saw, of all things, a rough wooden door set into the cliff. Dilys pushed it open and disappeared inside. She must have turned up the lamp because a small window glowed into life next to the door and the picture arranged itself in Lydia's mind.

A small wooden shack, weathered and grey as the cliff it was built into, its side all but obscured by the trunk of a large oak, its roots in the base of the hollow twenty feet below.

Inside, it was more cave than cabin, but whoever had built it had done a good job of maximising the space. There were just two wooden walls, both the shape of cheese wedges, set at right angles to one another. The one at the front contained the door and window. The one to the side, behind the trunk of the oak, kept the wind out and the lamp-light in.

To the right of the window, the cave tapered sharply, pinching off the space at almost ground level and leaving just enough room for a small iron stove, a table and a few chairs. Directly in front of the door, the cave offered plenty of head room and looked to sink back into the belly of the cliff.

Lydia turned around slowly, taking in the place as Dilys lit another two lamps and Rose fixed a wooden board to the inside of the window. As the light grew, Lydia saw three narrow beds at the back of the cave.

Question upon question jostled for position in Lydia's mind, but before she could decide which to ask first, Dilys launched into an explanation. Rose, who looked like she'd already heard the tale, focused on lighting the stove.

'My great-grandparents built it, or I should say re-built it, as there's been a home here for as long as any of us can remember. It is not something anyone in the village would know about though,' she added quickly.

'History has not been kind to people with magic. Having somewhere safe to hide from those who wish you harm has always been important to my family. My grandmother maintained this place even when my mother decided to renounce her magic for fear of divine retribution.' Dilys snorted and pulled out a chair from the table.

Lydia smiled. 'My mother used to say that a God that had to be feared was not one to be trusted.'

Dilys chuckled. 'She sounds like a wise woman. The task of keeping this place for those who might need it is now mine. The cave stretches back another twenty feet or so beyond the beds. We have another two beds and chairs stored there. My gran hid a family of six here for a month once.'

'Are there any more ...' Lydia paused, searching for the most tactful way to phrase the question. She started again. 'Are there other people with magic in the village?'

Dilys snorted. 'There were, once,' she said quietly. 'Most families either left to find greater strength in numbers elsewhere or, like my mother, they abandoned their magic. Caved in to the pressure of the Church, who told them their God-given gifts were really the work of the devil. Imagine that. A God who, in his grace, in his perfection, makes people the way they are but then tells them they're wicked for it. I have lived a long life, Lydia, but I have never been able to understand how any loving father would do that. No. If it was God who gave me my magic, then he meant for me to have it.'

'You're a believer, then,' Lydia said, feeling the need to say something in response to Dilys's openness.

The older woman didn't answer at once, her unfocused gaze on something over Lydia's shoulder.

'Not in their corruption of God, no. I am a daughter of the old ways,' she said, turning her hooded gaze to Lydia. The lamp light reflected in her eyes, turning them into amber pools. 'I sit in chapel every week, and I sing and pray and smile and bow my head, but I leave every time feeling tainted by the wickedness I hear spewed from that pulpit in the name of the God of love. Their so-called lessons teach us only how to fear our creator, the Church and, most wickedly of all, each other. They school us all to feel ashamed of who and what we are, and then they tell us how to live, who to love and who to hate.'

Lydia asked, 'Why do you put yourself through it?'

'Because I am selfish. Because I want to live in peace, and for women like me, widowed and alone, the only way to survive is to pretend,' Dilys said with a sad pull on her lips. 'I say my own prayers when I'm there. I pray for love. And kindness and an end to wickedness and fear in the world. And, of course, I pray for the souls of those men and women who were murdered for their magic.'

'It's not selfish to want to live, Dilys,' Lydia said softly. 'I think living our lives is by far the best way we can honour those no longer with us.'

Dilys drew her lips into a sad smile, then rose from the chair.

'Water's hot enough for cocoa,' Rose said from her spot near the stove.

'Cocoa and then we will need to sleep. We have a long day tomorrow and an early start,' Dilys announced.

Lydia sucked in a deep breath as she scanned the sanctuary. A night sleeping in a cave would certainly be a first. She tried not to think of what might be happening at Dilys's cottage. Her skin iced at the thought of who might be searching for them in the dead of night. She had to stay strong. This was the next step on her journey home to her family. She was still thinking of them ten minutes later when, curled on the narrow bed, she fell into a dreamless sleep.

CHAPTER 37

PONT NEFOEDD, SEPTEMBER 1960

'*B*ut haven't you got work to do here, Mags?' Hywel asked, trying to keep his tone level. Since her mother's disappearance, he couldn't look at her sideways without setting her off. He was worried about her. Not so much about the late nights spent down in the library – he'd learned long ago that the women in this household had form for that – but the long days she spent away from home. The trips to Cardiff and now borrowing her friend's car to go God knows where. He'd stopped pressing the point for fear of another argument. It wasn't like her. He longed for the days when all he had to worry about was her awful boyfriend, Keith, but he was long gone. Maggie had ended things with him within days of Lydia's disappearance.

'Of course I have,' Maggie snapped. 'I'm not about to let Mam's library go to hell, am I? I'm the acting keeper until she gets back, and it'll be perfect for her.'

Hywel bit back the retort. Was it his imagination, or did she look older all of a sudden? Eight weeks of waiting and longing and searching and hoping had added years to his beautiful daughter. There were shadows under her eyes that had never been there before. But there seemed to be an even greater shadow enveloping her. He felt it too, the presence of the unknown that stalked their every waking moment and haunted their dreams. How the phone all but stopped their hearts every time it rang. Walking to it, mouth dry, palms damp. Hope. Dread. Disappointment – again.

'I've no doubt of that, Maggie love,' Hywel said, offering her what he could muster by way of a smile.

When she didn't return the smile, he tried changing the subject. 'Will you be home for tea?'

'I'll get something while I'm out, so don't wait for me,' she replied as she rummaged in her handbag.

'Okey-doke, love. Well, drive carefully.' He stepped towards her, arms ready for their usual farewell hug, but she ducked around him.

'Will do,' she called over her shoulder. A moment later, the front door slammed behind her, the letterbox rattling.

She had every right to be angry. The police had given up. Not that they'd be any help anyway if Seren's theory was correct and Lydia had been thrown through some sort of tunnel in time, but their callousness had upset them both.

Hywel had arranged their last meeting for a day he thought Maggie would be out, but she'd come home just as the officers arrived. It hadn't gone well. Maggie had been furious with Hywel for excluding her, and he had to concede that he'd miscalculated on that front. For their part, the police officers had been offhand and dismissive, suggesting that in the absence of physical evidence of harm or a ransom, it was likely that Lydia had just chosen to get away for a fresh start. Maggie's temper had slipped its leash at that point and Hywel had to order her out of the room. In the furious argument that followed the officers' departure, they had both said things they'd live to regret.

Boudicca landed beside him on the kitchen counter with a chirrup.

'Hiya, pusscat,' Hywel said, stroking his hand from her forehead to her tail. She arched her back in pleasure and then climbed into his arms. He rocked her slowly as he sighed, glad of her soothing purr.

'Fancy coming to work with me today, sweetheart?' Hywel was only half joking. While there was no way it would happen, not least because it wouldn't be fair on the cat, he felt reluctant to leave her here. She had become the one constant in their lives. The last pillar standing as everything else crumbled around them. He thought about telling the office he couldn't go in, but quickly dismissed it. He had a meeting with one of their biggest customers this afternoon and he couldn't delegate that. Ruining the family business wouldn't help bring Lydia home any quicker.

Reluctantly, he gave Boudicca a last tickle under the chin before setting her gently on the counter. After refreshing her water and filling her saucer with food, he went to get ready for work.

CHAPTER 38

PONT NEFOEDD, SEPTEMBER 1960

*T*he man watched the old Jaguar pull out of the driveway. He checked his watch. The daughter would likely be out all day if she'd borrowed a car again. The father too, if their past patterns held. He'd been watching for weeks now. Making notes. Waiting. Biding his time. The witch Elder was still abroad, but his source said she would be back by the weekend. It would have to be today. Once the witch had returned, he'd have no chance of getting in. It would have to be now.

The house was easy enough to get into. The trees that surrounded it provided all the cover he needed to get to the back of the house, not that the neighbours were close enough to snoop. He spotted the open window within seconds. Why people thought that leaving first-floor windows open was safe was beyond him. It was like they were asking for trouble. The thought made him feel better about what he was about to do. As if he was suddenly only following some inevitable path that these people had laid out for him. An invitation, almost.

It took all of two minutes to find the ladder in the shed.

Another minute later and he was standing in a bathroom bigger than his whole flat. He curled his lip. That was the thing about money, it never went to the right people. He wondered how much this sort of house was worth. Enough to pay his debts ten times over and still have a small fortune left for the occasional flutter on the horses, he imagined.

He crept out onto a wide, panelled landing that reminded him of the hotel they'd taken his mother to in Brighton that time. The doctor said the air would be good for her chest and his brothers had insisted they do the holiday in England, as if Welsh air wasn't good enough. Two nights in a fancy hotel, all five boys and their miserable wives, not that he had one. They'd blown a packet and his mother still died. Miserable cow. Like she did it to spite them. Or him anyway, the only one who wasn't worthy of the family's magical inheritance. His brothers called him the Dud, but they'd be laughing on the other side of their miserable faces once he found this book.

He should have realised what it was when it came into the shop in that consignment, but he'd been full of cold and dosed up on whatever the chemist had given him for the coughing. He knew the book was hiding something; they all were, smug little bastards. The likes of him would never be worthy enough to read their precious secrets, but he had a nose for power, and even in his weakened state, he'd noticed something different about the small teal-green book with the faded gilt lettering. If he'd been well, he might have spent more time examining it, but then Cliff had sent his boys around to remind him of the next payment, and he'd added bruises to his list of ails. He'd needed to sell what he had, and the Elders paid handsomely for magical texts, so he'd done the only thing he could do. By the time his head was clear enough to think about it all, the book had already been collected.

Then the bloke in the expensive suit had shown up. He could spot a lackey for the magic hunters a mile away. They'd chance their arm every now and then. Come into the shop, all charm and innocence. He would take the business card, promise to keep his eyes peeled and then call it in to the Elders, but nobody ever did anything.

That day had been different though. Four hours after they'd lowered his mother's coffin into the ground and two hours after he'd been thrown out of the wake for fighting with his brothers, an opportunity had walked in the door. An opportunity to start again. To forget all about his so-called family. To pay his debts and finally get as far away from Wales as it was possible to get. Fate was giving him another chance. A man asking for a book that he knew in his gut was the one he'd just sent to the Elders. All he had to do now was get it back.

The carpet on the landing was faded in places. A row of family photos stood on a small table, but he quickly looked away. He couldn't think of this as a family home. This was just a library with a house on top. He needed to get in, find the book and get out again. Once he handed it over, he could start afresh somewhere nobody could ever look down on him again.

That he had even made it this far was impressive. He knew that. It was just a shame he had nobody to brag to. His granddad used to go on about there being a magical library nobody knew about, but he was a drunk no one listened to. It wasn't until he met another drunk in a pub, prattling on about searching for a missing woman from Pont Nefoedd on the A470, that he started to put the pieces together.

When the man in the fancy suit came into the shop again, he asked him if he knew a witch willing to bend some rules. He did. It had taken months of watching, listening and asking just enough questions to fly under anyone's radar, but here he was. He'd been right.

He found the stairs to the library hidden in the larder. He put on the head torch he'd brought and switched it on, just in case the lights were connected to some sort of alarm. Then again, the police turning up would be the least of his problems if the charm he'd bought from the witch didn't work like she'd promised. One book bite was agony enough; he dreaded to think what an entire library could do to a man.

He felt the surge of magical power grow as he crept down the stairs. His whole body thrummed with it. It was like nothing he'd ever felt before. He stared at the door. Once he opened it, there would be no going back. He imagined himself sitting on a plane going somewhere, anywhere. Spain, maybe. He could run a bar or something. Maybe he'd even meet someone.

He pulled the black velvet pouch from his pocket. It pulsed in his hand. Tipping the medallion into his palm, he cried out as it touched his skin, the magic running hot from the silver disc. He slipped the cord over his neck and took a deep breath. He'd have ten minutes maximum, maybe less if the witch's magic was anything like her willpower when it came to gin. He sighed and wondered how many more people the magical community was failing. How many of their own were breaking ranks and metaphorically selling their souls to survive because their leaders were too blind to see what was happening.

He took a deep breath and pulled open the library door. He stood for a long moment just inside the threshold, waiting for a reaction. If the spell worked, his energy would be invisible to the books. Heart hammering, he ventured another step. Nothing. Another. Still nothing. He hissed out a long, quiet breath and tuned in to the memory of the book that had come into the shop. The wall of noise exploded in his mind like someone turning on a few thousand radios all tuned to static. He slammed the mental gate shut, biting his lip to stop himself from making a sound. He'd need to get closer then. His heart hammering, he turned slowly, letting his head torch illuminate the vast space. He'd never be able to search the entire place in the ten minutes the medallion would give him. Sweat began to bead on his forehead. But what other option did he have? To leave now would guarantee only failure. He thought back to the bloke in the pub, the chance visit from the hunter, the witch. The gods were urging him on. He was overdue some good luck.

He sprinted for the stacks at the furthest wall so that he could work his way back to the door should he need a quick exit. This was going to work. He could feel it. He walked quickly down the lengths of sleeping books, arms outstretched but careful not to make contact with the shelves for fear of waking them.

By the third row, he picked up his pace. This was taking too long. Behind him, something shifted in the shadows. He checked his watch. He'd been here barely five minutes. He waited but felt nothing more. It might be his mind playing tricks on him. No time to lose. He searched the next few rows at a jog, focusing all his attention into his hands, waiting for that tell-tale tingle that signalled he'd found the book that would set him free.

He was almost at the halfway point when he felt the presence again. He checked his watch – just a few minutes more. He touched the medallion, and while the sensation was uncomfortable, it had none of the bite of earlier. Losing power for sure. A sliver of panic slid into his mind like a splinter, and he began to run. The door was ahead, but he wouldn't give up now. Not when he was so close. He took the next row at a near sprint, then the next. Blood pounded in his ears, his heart racing, although whether through exertion, concentration or just plain old fear, he wasn't sure.

The shadows shifted again, and he stopped, bending double to suck in a breath as quietly as he dared. Eleven minutes. He touched the medallion and was relieved to find it unchanged. The spell was holding. Just a few more rows to go. He was so close he could feel it. He straightened up and listened. Silence. He was about to launch into a fresh sprint when he heard a hiss at his shoulder. He felt his bowels loosen at the sound. There had always been stories of things that even those with magic feared. Unnatural things. Creatures that couldn't be explained but that could flay a man with a thought. He swallowed hard as sweat trickled down his forehead.

At the next hiss, his body reacted before he could instruct it. He whirled around, the beam of his torch catching the—He stopped dead. Sitting on a shelf in front of him was a cat. A skinny, exotic, pedigree-type cat, granted, but just a cat. Not a monster. He couldn't contain the laugh that burst from his lips, rocketed as it was by a sense of relief so palpable he could all but taste it. That's when it happened. The first swipe sent needles of red-hot pain searing through his right eye. He screamed and backed away, but not before the cat struck again, briefly attaching itself to his head, biting his ears and kicking with an unnatural fury with its back legs, claws shredding the skin on his neck. Then it was gone.

In his blind panic, he was dimly aware of the medallion falling, but then the sound of the waking library filled his senses. His head torch had fallen in the attack, but by some miracle was not only still shining but was lighting his path to the door. He bolted for it, holding his ruined eye as he ran and praying with every step that the books wouldn't reach him before he got there. They were all waking now. The air was thick with dust and fury.

He hauled open the door and slammed it shut behind him just as something heavy thudded against it. He took the stairs two at a time. He fell twice but barely registered the fresh pain. He headed for the front door, pulling at the bolts while praying that there wouldn't be a deadlock to thwart him. He sent up a prayer of thanks as the door yielded with just a turn of the Chubb lock and another as he ran into the bright sunshine. All he could think about was getting to his car and finding a hospital. He couldn't lose his eye. He sprinted for the end of the drive and the quiet lane beyond – emerging just in time to step into the path of the van.

CHAPTER 39

PONT NEFOEDD, SEPTEMBER 1960

'He was pronounced dead at the scene, I'm afraid,' Hywel said to Morgan as he handed him a glass of whiskey. 'I got the call at work. Came home to find the ambulance and the police in the lane. He was lying in the road still, poor dab.' Hywel shook his head, his eyes on the living room carpet but seeing the man's ruined eye. The lacerations to his neck. Ears that looked like a Rottweiler's chew toy.

Boudicca chirruped from her perch on the back of the sofa. 'Looks like you saw him off good and proper,' Hywel said to her. He should be thanking her, but the man was dead. She jumped down and put a paw on his lap, readying herself for a cuddle. Hywel hovered his hand over her back, then stroked her. 'In a minute, pusscat,' he said, getting to his feet. He looked down in time to see her narrow her eyes at him, then leap off the settee and stalk out of the room.

'And you're sure it was Boudicca?' Morgan asked.

'No doubt about it. She stayed hidden from the police, but when I found her in the library she was still covered in blood. It was all over her face, her belly. All up her paws,' Hywel said grimly.

'Well, gruesome as it was to see, Hywel, you can't blame her for protecting her home. Ifan had no business being here, and had he found whatever he was looking for, well, we know he wasn't here to help,' Morgan said gently.

'They've identified him then?' Hywel asked.

'Not officially, no, but they found papers in his car. He's one of the community. Bit of a black sheep of a very old, very well thought of magical family, actually.'

'Why was he the black sheep?' Hywel asked.

'It was sad, really. He was the youngest brother of five, and the only one born without the gift. He could sense magic, but that was all. He became a book dealer. Owned his own shop. Used to sell us any magical texts that crossed his path. For obscene amounts, of course, but …' Morgan trailed off, the sadness in his voice evident. He swirled his whiskey.

'I suppose that could turn a man,' Hywel conceded, although he couldn't imagine how. Lydia had lived her whole life surrounded by magical people, but he never heard her complaining about not having magic herself.

'You're sure the police didn't go into the house before you got here?' Morgan asked.

'Certain. By luck, Dennis Powell was the first officer on the scene.'

'One of ours then,' Morgan said, his expression lightening just a fraction. 'Practically magical royalty. Well, that's something to be glad of. He's a good man.'

'Will the medallion give you any clues about the witch who helped him?' Hywel asked.

'Possibly, but they rarely do. We'll be better off questioning all those with the power and motive to do such a thing. We can make our deductions from there,' Morgan said.

'My money's on the witch who signed the wards record book at Aber.'

When Hywel frowned, Morgan sighed. 'We found it in Frances's house. That she'd taken it home suggests that maybe she had her suspicions – but it clearly shows that the wards were redone ahead of schedule. Problem is, only the Elders have the authority to send a witch to re-ward a library, and we have no record of it. She must have been sent by the hunters to disable, not reinforce them,' he said bitterly.

'And you think the same witch might have given Ifan the medallion?'

Morgan gave a noncommittal shrug.

'Bloody hell, Morgan. Don't you have checks and balances for that sort of thing? Can any bugger just walk into a library, claim they're a witch and have the bloody run of the place?' Hywel worked hard to keep his temper in check, but he could barely believe what he was hearing. Frances was dead, for pity's sake!

'Now hang on a minute,' Morgan said, visibly bristling. 'I don't like what you're insinuating here, Hywel.'

'Morgan, Frances is dead, and Lydia and Rose are missing, so, old friend or not, I don't give a monkey's whether you like it or not. This Ifan fella shouldn't have even known about this library or been able to search for it if what you've been saying about this anomaly is true. But he was here, in my house! In the library where my little girl works on her own every bloody day!' Hywel thumped his whiskey glass down onto the coffee table, taking a chunk out of the polish. He got to his feet.

'You're right,' Morgan said wearily. 'The evidence speaks for itself. The Elders have failed to keep people safe, and we will need to answer for that. And we will. You have my word.'

'I need more than words, Morgan!' Hywel snapped. 'I need you to find Lydia and I need you to make sure my daughter is safe in her own bloody home!' He growled out the words, trying to keep a lid on his anger. Morgan bowed his head and nodded as Hywel ranted.

Has it really come to this? Hywel thought. He was shouting at an old man, blaming him for the acts of others. Guilt snaked in his gut. He ran his hands through his hair and groaned. 'Morgan, I'm—'

'You have every right to be angry, Hywel. I would be too in your place. I think it prudent for you and Maggie to have a few days away while we investigate. I'll get our people to tighten the physical security. I think we might have relied a little too much on the idea of the anomaly – taken our eye off the ball, so to speak,' Morgan said, setting down his whiskey glass on the coaster.

Hywel thought of the open bathroom window and mentally kicked himself. He opened his mouth to say as much, but Morgan ploughed on. 'Seren is coming back early, and we'll be holding an all-coven meeting as soon as we can get everyone together.'

Hywel huffed out a breath in surprise. He knew enough about the community to know that such meetings, where the most powerful witches from around the world were brought together, were as rare as hens' teeth. They must be really rattled to have called one so quickly.

'This' – Morgan gestured towards the floor and the library hidden beneath it – 'might be our last line of defence. We will protect it at all costs. You have my word. And we have not stopped looking for Lydia or Rose.'

Hywel felt some of the tension slip from his shoulders. The relief was short-lived as the crunch of gravel on the drive heralded the approach of a car.

'Maggie?' Morgan asked, glancing towards the bay window.

Hywel jumped up and pulled back the net curtain. 'Yes,' he said, relief and dread washing over him.

'Do you need me to stay?' Morgan asked, already on his feet.

Hywel considered his old friend. He looked exhausted. But tempting as it was to tell him to get home for some rest, Maggie would have questions.

'Can you stay an hour? I'll explain, but she'll have questions for you,' Hywel said.

Morgan nodded. 'I'll be in the library when you're ready for me.'

'Dad?' Maggie called from the hallway.

Hywel took a deep breath. How was he even going to begin?

CHAPTER 40

HAY-ON-WYE, JULY 1841

*L*ydia hadn't expected to sleep on the narrow cot bed, tucked into the belly of the cave, but she awoke feeling more rested than she had in years. It was still dark but for the warm glow of the oil lamp. Rose and Dilys were already up and moving around, their shadows dancing on the walls in the lamplight. Lydia threw back the blanket and coaxed her feet into the boots by her bed.

After stowing her blanket and thin mattress in the trunk, she joined the others at the front of the cave. The small window was uncovered but was nothing but an obsidian disc in the wall.

'What can I help with?' she asked as she took in the scene. The small table was set with three plates and the same tin cups they'd drunk their cocoa from the night before.

'All done,' Rose said, placing a small loaf of bread on the table, still partially wrapped in cloth.

Dilys added three apples and a small pot of jam. 'How did you sleep?' she asked, with what Lydia could swear was a hint of mischief in her eye.

'I can honestly say that I had the best sleep of my life,' she said, knowing for sure now that she was missing something.

Dilys offered her a rare smile. 'You are not the first to say that. My grandmother believed that one of our ancestors spelled the cave to ensure that all those who sought refuge here would sleep soundly. My grandfather believed that the cave itself was chosen because of some innate power to heal and soothe.'

'What do you believe?' Lydia asked.

'I believe it doesn't matter,' Dilys said, gesturing for her to sit down. 'I am just glad that we have such a place.'

They ate their breakfast quickly, each of them keeping an eye on the window and the promise of dawn beyond it. Once they'd tidied everything away, they gathered up their things.

'Wait for me,' Dilys said, nodding towards the door. 'I have to hide the grimoire before we leave.'

Lydia frowned. She'd not realised Dilys had brought the book with her. It made sense – the cottage was likely no longer safe – but how she'd carried the heavy tome along with her case was a mystery.

Rose and Lydia picked up their bags and stepped out into the cool pre-dawn inkiness. They picked their way across the flat plane of the cave mouth and stood at the top of the descent, waiting. Lydia racked her brain, wondering where Dilys would be able to hide the book. The trunks were the only option for concealment, but wouldn't they be the most obvious place a thief might look? Lydia was about to ask Rose, but a sudden gust of wind stole her breath and the light from the lamp Rose was holding. Lydia spun around on hearing the thump of wood on stone as the door to the shack swung open. She blinked, her eyes clearly deceiving her. It was a trick of the light, naturally, but it looked for all the world as if Dilys had just walked into the stone wall of the cave itself. Confused, Lydia scanned what she could see of the space, but then Dilys reappeared, walking as calmly through stone as she might an open doorway.

Rose put a hand on Lydia's shoulder and gave it a gentle squeeze. 'Looks like the gods want you in on the secrets,' she said, her voice soft and playful.

Lydia could think of nothing in reply, so just nodded to herself in the darkness. Why, she thought, was the sight of a witch walking through stone so shocking when her daily life was filled with flying, sentient books? She was surrounded by the most impossible magic every single day and yet she could still be awed by the sight of it. She decided that was a good thing.

They walked the first hour in total silence. Lydia focused on the path, following the apple-sized smudge of light from Dilys's lamp up ahead. The silence felt protective, conspiring with the darkness to keep them hidden. Safe. The dawn broke like a betrayal, revealing the thickness of the wood that crowded around them. She hurried to walk beside the others.

Lydia felt her discomfort grow with the light. The thought that someone might be following them slipped into her mind like a thief. What if he was out there? Watching. Waiting. Her breath hitched in her chest.

'My abilities are modest,' Dilys said, not breaking her stride, 'but there is nobody following us. I am sure of that.'

Lydia sighed. A wave of fatigue accompanied the relief. Her feet were hot in her boots and her legs ached from the unrelenting pace. Her case was heavy, despite its meagre contents, and her right palm was scratched and sore from the roots and branches she'd clung to the previous night. She bit her lip and reminded herself that every step was moving her closer to her family. Closer to home.

CHAPTER 41

HAY-ON-WYE, JULY 1841

*T*he wood ended abruptly, depositing them onto a dusty dirt road. Lydia had been so lost in her thoughts of home that she wondered if she had somehow conjured the sight before her. Pen y Fan, the highest peak in the Brecon Beacons, rose in the distance, Corn Du, its faithful understudy, at its side. Lydia would recognise them anywhere. Her pulse quickened. She really was home. She could walk to Pont Nefoedd from here, as she and Hywel had to do once when his first car conked out on the way back from Brecon.

She let out a laugh, feeling almost giddy with relief. Home. She was going home.

'Lydia!' Dilys's voice was like a whip cracked.

Lydia turned to see that she was already twenty feet away from her companions. She hadn't even remembered moving.

Rose hurried to her side. 'They're not there,' she whispered, her hand on Lydia's back. 'Not yet.'

The truth of it landed like a fist. Of course they weren't. Lydia bit down hard on her lip, but her body was already juddering as it wrestled down the sob that was fighting to be released. When Rose pulled her into a hug, she didn't resist.

Once her tears were spent, they walked back to join Dilys, who stood in the shade of a hill so steep even sheep would struggle to graze it. A few strands of her hair had worked themselves free of her bun and floated around her, alive to the eddies of the breeze. She gave Lydia a sympathetic smile but said nothing.

'Are we waiting for someone?' Lydia asked, needing to break the silence and focus on something other than her misery.

'Indeed we are. And if I'm not mistaken, here he comes,' Dilys said, inclining her head towards the road.

Lydia turned in a slow circle but could hear nothing but the occasional bleat of a sheep in the distance. She looked to Rose, who pulled a face and shook her head. Then she heard it. A distant clop of hooves and, she thought, the sound of someone singing.

A few moments later, a carriage appeared around the bend, drawn by four night-black horses with braided manes. Lydia gawked and was pleased that for once Rose looked to be just as taken aback. The driver, in waistcoat and shirt-sleeves rolled to the elbows, was at odds with the finery of the carriage. Its lacquered black paint shone in the sun, and delicate gold flourishes around the handles and trim looked like they might still be wet to the touch. The driver smiled warmly when he spotted them, and while Lydia might have missed it, he didn't utter a word of command or so much as twitch the reins before the horses came to a halt in front of them.

'Good morning, Mr Chapel,' Dilys said, a smile in her voice beneath the formality.

'Good morning, Mrs Lloyd. Ladies,' he added with a nod

at Lydia and Rose. His eyes lingered a second on Rose before he said, 'Go on and say your hellos. They love a fuss.'

Rose beamed and stepped towards the horses, who snorted in greeting.

'What a coincidence it is to bump into you and your companions, Mrs Lloyd. Can I offer you a lift?' Mr Chapel said, a wide grin tugging at the corners of his mouth.

'Why, that would be most kind of you, sir,' Dilys said with an exaggerated nod that was almost a bow.

Mr Chapel let out a wheezing guffaw and jumped down from the carriage. Dilys hugged him, which was so at odds with her usual demeanour that Lydia couldn't help but gawk.

She bit her lip as it occurred to her that he reminded her of Hywel. An older version by maybe twenty years, but the resemblance was clear. It was something in the eyes, she decided, just as tears pricked in her own.

Lydia snapped back to the moment when she realised that Dilys was speaking to her. 'William is an old and very dear friend,' she explained as Rose rejoined them.

'Bill, please,' he said. 'Yes, we all enjoyed many happy years together. Me, my lady wife, Peggy, Dil and—' He seemed to swallow whatever he was about to say next, and Lydia saw the briefest of looks exchanged between him and Dilys. The playfulness vanished and sadness scudded across their faces, a cloud chased across the sun.

'We best get on if we want to get home tonight,' Bill said, the smile returned, although some vestige of the sorrow still lingered in his eyes, Lydia thought as she watched him load the cases.

'All set?' Bill asked.

'Almost. Climb aboard, ladies,' Dilys said, 'while I meet these wonderful creatures and thank them for the journey they're about to take us on.'

Lydia climbed unsteadily into the carriage and all but

collapsed onto the seat. It felt so good to sit down she almost groaned in pleasure. Rose took the seat opposite. She was grinning like a schoolgirl.

'It feels like being the Queen, doesn't it?' she giggled.

Lydia laughed. 'Yes, I suppose it does. If the Queen ever fell through a rip in time after being shot at by mad men hunting for a magical book, that is.'

They both laughed then, and the sound of it in her chest felt like a balm. When Dilys climbed into the carriage, she was accompanied by a strong smell of hot apple. Before Lydia could ask the question, Bill appeared at the door. 'You spoil them, Dil,' he said with a slow, exaggerated shake of his head.

'No less than they rightly deserve,' Dilys said, her chin raised and tone playfully reproachful.

Closing the carriage door, he grinned and said, 'Ladies, settle in. Enjoy the ride and we'll be in Cardiff in no time.'

CHAPTER 42

TENBY, SEPTEMBER 1960

*M*aggie closed the paperback with a thwack and slapped it onto the lace-covered table beside her. She looked around her aunt's large, bright guest room and sighed. How anyone could live with so many frills, ornaments and doilies was beyond her.

She got up and pulled back the net curtain to look out onto the sea. It was another warm day, and the beach across the road was filled with holidaymakers making the most of what was left of the summer.

A knock at the door made her jump. They were safe here – there were guards front and back – but she still heaved a sigh of relief when she opened the door and saw Seren instead of the axe-wielding magic hunter of her imagining. The witch was dressed in her usual uniform of black trousers, boots and a thin black sweater. Her hair was pulled back into a tight ponytail, which usually served to emphasise her amazing cheekbones and full lips. Today she was all angles and shadows. Despite her trip to India, she clearly hadn't spent any time in the sun.

Maggie remembered their last conversation. The harsh

words she'd thrown at the witch. She felt her cheeks heat. It wasn't Seren's fault. Her father might blame the Elders, but she didn't. Her fury was reserved solely for the men who hunted for magic they didn't deserve. She should apologise for what she said.

'Can I come in?' Seren asked carefully.

'Oh, of course,' Maggie said, stepping aside.

'How are you holding up?'

Maggie shrugged, glad that Seren was taking the lead but still unsure how she might frame her apology.

'I used to love it here. It was a treat. But now it feels like a —' She faltered. Her aunt had been so kind to them that she couldn't bear to say that it felt like a prison. 'I just miss home. The library. Boudicca …' She trailed off as the emotion caught in her throat. What she missed most was her mother, but she couldn't give voice to that and stay in one piece, so she left it unsaid.

'Well, Boudicca is fine,' Seren said. 'Although clearly missing you both,' she added a heartbeat too late to be truly convincing. 'She's been helping me with my work in the library and has been keeping a close eye on the team working on security. I was worried she wasn't eating, but then I bumped into your neighbour, Mrs Thomas.'

'She looks after Boudicca if we're ever away,' Maggie said, thinking of the small, wren-like woman down the lane.

'Well, she let slip that she's been getting fresh fish from the market for her every day, so I don't think we have anything to worry about,' Seren said, smiling.

Maggie snorted a laugh. Home-cooked fish suppers and witches to hang around with all day – Boudicca was likely living her best life. She missed her though. She'd certainly warmed to Maggie since her mother had disappeared, and being without her now, well, it just didn't feel right.

Maggie sank back into the armchair in the bay window and gestured for Seren to take the other one.

'Do you know any more about what that man was looking for?' Maggie asked.

Seren sighed and shook her head as she lowered herself into the chair. 'The official line is "not yet", but in fairness, Maggie, I doubt we'll find anything now. The energies are strongest in the first twenty-four hours after an incident. We had our people there within the hour, and aside from the cloaking spell Ifan used to get in, there was no trace of anything unusual. I was there myself the next day, and' – she shrugged – 'nothing.'

'Well, we know he was after a book,' Maggie said, aware that she was stating the obvious. 'He was a book dealer, wasn't he?'

Seren nodded. 'That's our assumption, but every book is accounted for, including the new ones.'

'And did they share anything? The books, I mean.'

Seren took a deep breath before she spoke, and Maggie braced herself. 'They're frightened. Some were willing to share, but only to confirm what we already know. They awoke to find Boudicca attacking him. He fled empty-handed.'

Maggie's heart pinched at the thought of her books being afraid. It was all the worse for knowing that they were now without their keeper too. While she wasn't a patch on her mother, she was still their protector. They were her responsibility. She forced herself to get back on track. If they were to figure this out, then she had to know more about Ifan's motives.

'So, you're working on the theory that Boudicca got to him before he could find what he was after?' Maggie asked.

'We have a few theories. The other thought is that whatever he sought wasn't in the library to begin with.'

'And the third possibility?'

Seren shifted in her armchair. It was a tiny movement, especially for a witch who was usually so still, but Maggie straightened her back. If the third possibility made even Seren uncomfortable, then chances were it wasn't good news.

'The other theory is that he wasn't looking for anything at all. Or rather, that wasn't his primary motivation,' the witch said carefully.

Maggie held her breath as she tried to process the thought. Her heart was already pounding, her stomach churning as if they'd put the pieces together before her brain could make sense of things.

'Oh, god, no,' Maggie said, putting her head in her hands as the realisation dawned. 'The other possibility is that he did this just to see if there was a magical library in Pont Nef.'

Seren nodded reluctantly.

The next question seemed to stick on Maggie's tongue. She licked her lips. Cleared her throat. 'And the anomaly?' She couldn't find the breath for more words. She already knew the answer. It rang in her bones, swam through her veins and haunted her dreams. The nightmares in which she was being pursued across a vast, open plain, staggering under the weight of the books in her feeble arms, her legs like lead.

'I'm sorry, Maggie, but the Pont Nefoedd library is now appearing on maps when scried for. Morgan even got a call from the government's magical unit asking about it,' the witch said with a snort of disgust.

'How?' Maggie wanted to scream the word, but it tumbled from her mouth as a breath.

'We don't know for sure. The medallion spell cloaked his presence from the books, but that shouldn't have been enough to destroy the anomaly. As we don't know what caused it in the first place, it's hard to say. There is a theory that the protection was granted through an ancient blood magic spell and that as Ifan was injured and bleeding ...' Seren shrugged. 'As theories go, it's unlikely, but not impossible.'

'So we're sitting ducks,' Maggie said flatly.

'I wouldn't put it like that,' Seren said carefully. She got to her feet in one fluid movement and turned to look out of the window. Maggie waited for her to come to whatever decision she was clearly making about what to say next.

'You're not a child, Maggie, and I'm not going to treat you like one. We're assuming that this revelation – this discovery of a library that the magical community has managed to hide from everyone for so long – well, this will be irresistible to the hunters.'

'And what do we do about that?'

'Some of the Elders want to relocate the library.' Seren held up her hands against Maggie's protest. 'But arguably, with everyone and their dog now able to scry for it, there's nowhere safe. The government unit made their perennial offer to take the books into their' – she mimed air quotes – '"secure facility", but that's never going to happen so long as there are people alive who remember how they betrayed us during the war. If you agree, the library will remain in Pont Nefoedd but with additional, around-the-clock security.'

'So long as *I* agree?' Maggie asked, forcing the words out around the boulder lodged in her throat.

Seren looked confused. 'You're the keeper, Maggie. You have to decide what's best for your library and for you. We've spoken to your dad and he's of the same opinion. This is your decision to make.'

'You mean I'm the keeper until my mother gets home,' Maggie said irritably.

'Of course,' Seren said.

Maggie took a deep breath and ran her tongue over her lips.

'Before you decide, you need to know that this option isn't without considerable risk. Our magic, our boots-on-the-ground security, they can only do so much. We can't guarantee your safety, nor that of your library or family,' Seren said gravely. 'You can walk away from this. There is no stigma in choosing a normal life. And don't think for a second that your mother wouldn't want that for you too.'

Maggie was already shaking her head. There was no choice to make here. Everything had changed since her mother had vanished. She had changed. She barely recognised the version of herself that had been thinking about actually marrying Keith.

'The library stays. I'll not let those bastards get their hands on my books.' Maggie all but growled the last part of the sentence. Anger felt good. So long as she was angry, she wasn't quite so afraid.

Seren studied her for a long moment. 'Very well. We need another day or two to complete the security updates. You need to know that you're going to have permanent house guests. Between the security team and the witches, it's going to feel …' She looked around, searching for the right word. 'Different. You'll also get a security detail for when you need to go anywhere. Think of it like you're a royal, maybe.'

Maggie tried to keep her expression neutral, but inside there was a scream building. How would they even begin to live like this? And how on earth would they hide this from their friends and neighbours? But to Seren she said, 'Fine.'

Seren smiled, but there was sadness in her eyes. 'I'd best get back,' she said, walking to the door. 'I'll be back with a team to take you home on Wednesday.'

'Okay. Give Boudicca a tickle from me,' Maggie said.

'Oh, I nearly forgot,' Seren said, pulling something from

her pocket. 'Boudicca brought me this as I was about to leave. She was very deliberate about it, so I assume it was for you.'

Seren held out a crudely sewn toy mouse. Maggie sucked in a breath. She'd spent hours on that mouse as a little girl. A gift for the cat she'd longed for but who had taken one look at the child she'd been and decided she'd prefer adult company instead. Maggie forced a laugh. 'Tell her thank you from me,' she said. As the door closed behind Seren, Maggie leaned against it and sobbed.

CHAPTER 43

CARDIFF, JULY 1841

*I*t had taken Lydia hours for her body to get used to the rock and sway of the carriage. On the country roads, the journey had been nearly bone-rattling in places, but the closer they drew to the city, the smoother the ride had become.

Lydia ached everywhere. She was bone tired, but sleep evaded her. There had been breaks every few hours, more for the benefit of the horses than the passengers, and Lydia liked Bill all the more for it. He checked their legs, lifted all sixteen feet and spoke softly to each of them every time they stopped. The journey felt impossibly long. How much they took for granted, she thought, in their modern world of cars and trains and buses where forty miles would be an hour's journey, not a day's.

'How long did you live in Cardiff?' Lydia asked Dilys.

'Over twenty years,' Dilys replied, that ghost of a smile on her lips, sadness in her eyes.

'Were you happy there?' Lydia asked, hoping for a lengthy tale that might help pass the time and distract her from her aching bones.

Dilys smiled broadly, taking Lydia by surprise. She looked so much younger when she smiled, and Lydia fancied she could see the young woman she'd once been.

'The first year was the worst of my life. I married a handsome man with an ugly soul, and when he discovered that fortunes were only made through hard work and talent, he took his frustrations out on me. He made such a mess of my face one day that a woman noticed me in the street,' Dilys said, the smile broadening and her eyes softening.

'Dilys, that's terrible,' Lydia said, thoroughly confused by the incongruous reaction. 'I'm so sorry.'

Dilys shook her head. 'Oh, it was. Believe me. But the woman who stopped me in the street became a very dear friend of mine. She was also my introduction to the magical community in Cardiff, so something good came from his wickedness, which is why I can now, finally, smile at the memory.'

'Was he ever punished?' Lydia asked.

Dilys looked out of the window, the sadness back in her eyes. 'After a fashion, yes. My friend taught me how to put a charm around the door to protect myself. It worked too. I'd hear the thunder in his footsteps coming up the stairs, but as soon as he stepped over that threshold, the fury would drain out of him like water down a plughole. I think the magic just diverted his anger, though, because he started to brag about the men he'd beaten in fights at the pub. But one night he picked on the wrong man. There were witnesses. People who saw him start the fight and get the beating of his life for it. He was seen fleeing the pub, but he never came home. They found his body in the River Taff a few days later.'

'I'm sorry, Dilys,' Lydia said.

Dilys nodded in acknowledgement. 'He was a good man once. I mourned that version of him. The version I fell in love with as a girl. What he became, I decided to forget.'

'But you had happier times in Cardiff after that?' Lydia prompted, hoping to get back onto safer ground.

'I did. Close to twenty years of happiness as the companion to the woman who befriended me that day in the street. She was an Elder in the community. I moved back to Hay to care for my parents after she passed away,' Dilys explained, her smiled vanished and her eyes fixed on the scene beyond the window now.

Sensing that the conversation would go no further, Lydia sat back and closed her eyes. She must have nodded off as when she woke, dusk had fallen and they were entering the city. The cooling night air carried on one breath the smell of the sea, and on the next, manure and the acrid bite of burning coal. Lydia pressed a handkerchief to her nose.

Outside, the streets were bathed in the gentle glow of gas lamps and the amber light that spilled from the houses they rolled past. The sound of a fiddle danced into the carriage before its source came into view. A pub, its windows obscured by condensation, its door thronged by a group of soot-streaked men, beers in hand and a cloud of tobacco smoke escaping into the night sky. They were all so thin, she thought, resignation carved as deep as canyons on their faces.

Lydia gasped as a wraith-thin girl with matted brown hair and a baby on her hip approached the men. She couldn't have been more than twelve.

The horses suddenly picked up their pace.

'Do you think the horses know they're nearly home?' Rose asked.

'Without a doubt,' Dilys said. 'A noble, generous animal, destined by nature to be the friend and helper of man, according to Lord Byron. And yet we treat them as we would a table or any other object, ending their gentle lives when they are of no more use to us.'

The air in the carriage seemed to thicken, all traces of the sea air overpowered by the oily smell of burning coal and sewers.

'And God said, "I will send them angels, but give them fur instead of wings so that man may come to know my grace through his own character,"' Dilys said quietly.

Lydia cleared her throat. 'That's beautiful. Is that in the Bible?'

'I have no idea,' Dilys replied, 'but I know it to be true.'

Two short taps on the roof stopped the conversation. The carriage slowed. Peering out of the window, Lydia saw a young boy of about twelve waving excitedly in their direction. Before she could wave back, he disappeared. Next, she heard the rattle of iron on cobblestones.

'How many times, Frank. Lift them as you open them, mun!' If Bill was trying to sound reproachful, he was failing miserably.

After a brief pause, they passed through an archway, the horses' hooves echoing off the stones. One of the horses let out a long snort as the carriage came to a halt. It rocked as Bill jumped down, and Lydia saw the young lad all but throw himself into what she presumed was his father's arms.

'Here we are,' Dilys said brightly.

Bill appeared and opened the carriage door. 'Ladies, welcome to our humble home – and yours, for the duration of your business here.'

Lydia stepped out, grateful for the proffered hand as her aching limbs struggled to remember movement. She stood in a large, enclosed courtyard. A three-storey house stood, windows glowing, to her right. Directly ahead, a long row of stables. Along the far wall was what she assumed must be a barn or storage room, and behind her, the long carriage house. It really was like stepping into a history lesson.

Two other boys, a little older than Frank, appeared from the stables, their faces breaking into smiles as they saw Bill.

'Been a good lad for your ma?' he asked Frank, who had only just let him go.

Frank beamed as he nodded.

'Good lad,' Bill said. He greeted the other two boys warmly, then said, 'Right, you three, see to the horses, please. They've had a long run, so I want them rubbed down, legs and feet checked and double-checked. Put more straw down if you think they need extra.'

A woman of around Dilys's age in a grey dress with a chubby baby on her hip appeared from the door of the house, one hand smoothing down the front of her dress. She smiled politely as she approached, but then the smile turned into an unfiltered grin as Dilys stepped forward.

'You are a sight for sore eyes, Dil chwaer,' she said as they embraced.

'Chwaer?' Rose whispered to Lydia.

'Sister, I think. But don't quote me,' she replied.

'Welcome, ladies. I'm Bill's wife, Margaret, but please call me Peggy.'

'And who's this?' Dilys asked, tickling the baby under the chin. 'New arrival?'

'This is Efa,' Peggy said, bouncing the baby on her hip.

'From the same place as Frank?' Dilys asked.

Peggy shook her head. 'No. Found her on our doorstep, would you believe. Boys had the gates open, cleaning the yard, and ...' She trailed off, still shaking her head. 'Well, she wasn't very well when she arrived, see, Auntie Dil.' She cooed to the baby, her voice full of smiles. 'All skin and bones, she was, with a bad cough too.' Efa broke into a wide, toothless smile as she gazed up at Peggy. 'But we fed her up and cwtched her lots, and now she's all better and ready to go back to her mammy!' Peggy said with a final bounce of the hip, which made the baby giggle.

'She's beautiful,' Lydia said, smiling at the baby. 'Her mother came back for her?'

Peggy shook her head. 'Efa was taken from her against her wishes, but a good friend of ours managed to find her.' Lydia saw sadness flash across Peggy's face, but when she met her eye, she was smiling again. 'So, this time it's going to be a happy ending.'

Bill joined them and leaned over to run a hand over Efa's bonneted head. Then, turning to Lydia, Dilys and Rose, he said, 'And now they are sorted, I can officially welcome you to Chapel and Sons. Make yourself at home, and please, know that you are safe within these walls. We ward them daily.'

Lydia and Rose exchanged a look of surprise. Witches then? Lydia turned to ask Dilys, but she was already walking with the others into the house. As Lydia made to follow, she noticed the sign above the stables. *Chapel and Sons. Embalmers and Funerals since 1790.* She cast another glance at the barn on the far end of the courtyard. *Well*, she thought, *that answers that question.*

The Chapels' house was large but modestly furnished. From the hallway, a door to their left bore a discreet sign with the same gold lettering as the one above the stable. Lydia wondered if that was where the Chapels spoke to the bereaved about the arrangements for their loved ones.

The door to the right was ajar, and as Lydia followed the others down the passage, she caught sight of a simple wooden settle, a table with an oil lamp and a wooden cot next to the remains of a coal fire that was now nothing more than embers.

'I hope you don't mind the kitchen,' Peggy called over her shoulder.

The mere mention of the word made Lydia's stomach rumble loudly, and she cringed at the sound, although nobody else commented. The smell of cooking sailed through the air as they approached.

An hour later, the remains of a hearty vegetable stew mopped up with large chunks of bread, Lydia felt at least partly revived. She had been trying to follow the conversation between Dilys, Bill and Peggy that had started the moment the last spoonful had been consumed, but most of it washed over her tired brain. They hadn't spoken a word yet about where Lydia and Rose had come from, but had Dilys already told them? For now, she decided to just keep up the act until she could ask Dilys in private. Being able to trust these people to provide a safe roof over their head for the night was one thing, but how would they react to the news that two of the women sitting in their kitchen wouldn't be born until well after they'd breathed their last?

Lydia glanced at Efa in her cot by the kitchen hearth and longed to sleep like that. She stifled a yawn and, across the table, saw Rose do the same.

'Well, that will be our first port of call,' Dilys said, answering a question that Lydia had clearly missed.

'Can I show you to your room?' Peggy asked, looking from Lydia to Rose and back again. 'You'll be tired from your trip.'

'That would be lovely, thank you,' Rose said, getting to her feet.

Dilys stayed talking to Bill, but Lydia and Rose followed Peggy, oil lamp in hand, to the second floor, where a row of three doors lined the landing to the right and a single door stood to the left. Their cases were stacked outside the first door.

'I hope you'll be comfy,' Peggy said, opening the door and stepping in to light the oil lamp. The room was furnished much like the one at Dilys's, although it was larger. The glow of the lamp shone onto faded floral wallpaper. An iron-framed bed stood opposite a simple fireplace, above which hung a needlework sampler, although the light was too dim for Lydia to read it. There was a small wardrobe, a washstand with a bowl and jug and a nightstand for the lamp.

'Pot's under the bed, as you'd expect,' Peggy said.

Lydia shuddered at the thought but tried to keep it from her face. She'd added indoor plumbing to her list of things to be eternally grateful for days ago. How Rose had endured it for these long months, she had no idea.

'You take this one, Lydia. I'll just be next door,' Rose said.

After thanking Peggy and saying a weary goodnight to Rose, Lydia retrieved her case from the landing and got ready for bed.

CHAPTER 44

CARDIFF, JULY 1841

*L*ydia knew she was dreaming. She was watching Maggie as a toddler making sandcastles on the beach in Tenby. She turned to peer up at her sister-in-law's pastel-pink townhouse that overlooked the sea. Maggie, all grown up and looking exactly as she remembered her the day she left for Aber, stood in the window, waving to her.

Jolting to wakefulness, the dream collapsed.

'Lydia. Lydia. Are you okay?'

Lydia jumped out of bed and hurried to open the door. Rose stood in the corridor, a frown knitting her forehead and her eyes full of concern.

'I'm fine,' Lydia said, catching her breath. 'I was just dreaming and, well, it felt so real, but …' She trailed off, then stepped aside and motioned for Rose to come in.

'It's a bit of a shock, waking up, isn't it?' Rose said.

Lydia crossed the room and pulled back the curtain that covered the small window. She peered out over the court-yard, which was already a hive of activity. One of the horses was being groomed while it pulled great mouthfuls of hay from nets mounted onto the wall. The carriage they'd travelled in was being polished by two of the other boys. It gleamed in the sunshine, and Lydia wondered how long she'd slept.

'It's a little after ten,' Rose said.

Lydia spun around and saw Rose wince.

'Sorry, I know it's a bit disconcerting, but it's not like I can read your mind or anything,' Rose said sheepishly. 'It's just questions that seem to pop into my head.'

'No apology needed, Rose. I'm only half awake and I just forgot about your new talent, that's all. Shame about the mind-reading though. It would have been handy. Did the spell leave you with anything else? A map to hidden treasure, perhaps?' She'd said it laughing, but Rose looked guarded.

'Well,' she said, wringing her hands, 'there are some other things that I'm noticing, but I'd rather not share them until I've worked out exactly what they are.'

'Oh. Of course,' Lydia said, feeling sightly thrown by the response. She decided to change the subject and asked, 'Is Dilys up yet?'

Rose nodded. 'Oh yes, I heard her get up at dawn. She's in the kitchen with Bill and Peggy.'

'Do they know about us and where we came from?' Lydia said, sinking back onto the bed.

'They do, but Frank doesn't. Dilys said we're not to say anything about the future to anyone, though, just in case it changes things. Even little things, like mentioning phones and so on,' Rose said, lowering her voice.

'Do you know any more about Bill and Peggy?' Lydia asked, feeling like a sneak to be asking such a thing but needing to know.

Rose sat next to her on the bed. 'I think they're Elders. And it sounds like they were all friends when Dilys lived here in Cardiff,' she supplied, chewing her lip. 'I think they must have magic like Dil, but not because they've said anything. I've not seen anything either. It's just a feeling, you know? I can't explain it.'

Lydia didn't know, but she nodded anyway.

'Do they know anything about the hunter Dil saw?' Lydia asked, conscious that her palms were starting to sweat just at the thought.

'I don't think so, but from what they were saying downstairs, it's like the magical community here is always half listening for a knock on the door – or a kick to it in the middle of the night,' Rose said with a shudder.

Lydia sighed. 'Some things didn't change then.'

'Anyway, I came to get you because Dil wants us to go and see a friend of hers. He's got a library, apparently.'

Lydia felt her spirits lift at that. 'Give me five minutes and I'll see you in the kitchen.'

Rose paused at the door, 'Oh, and just to warn you, but Peggy is a bit teary today. Little Efa's mum collected her this morning.'

'Oh, that's lovely news. You don't read stories like that in the history books, do you,' Lydia said, smiling.

Rose grinned in reply before stepping out into the corridor and pulling the door closed behind her.

Lydia dressed as quickly as she could – zips were definitely going on the list of things she missed from her own time. She felt her pulse quickening as she pulled the *Book of Prophecy* from under her pillow and put it in her skirt pocket. A book had got them into this mess, and she'd put money on the fact that it would be a book that would get them out of it too.

CHAPTER 45

CARDIFF, JULY 1841

*H*ad they walked, it would have taken them less than fifteen minutes, but Bill had insisted on taking Dilys, Lydia and Rose in the carriage. Frank had all but begged to come too, but Bill had asked Nate, one of the older boys, to ride with them instead. The lad was tall and broad-chested with watchful eyes, and something about Bill's choice had sent a flash of warning through Lydia's mind. If Bill expected trouble, then she'd happily suffer another journey in a bone-jarring carriage if it meant staying out of sight.

It was market day, and so the going was slowed by other carts and small herds of animals being driven down the road. Lydia shuddered at the sight, trying not to imagine where the poor creatures were being herded to.

The carriage they were travelling in was a much older version than the shiny black one that had brought them here the night before. It smelled of beeswax and old dust. Bill had been apologetic, explaining that the other one was needed elsewhere, but Lydia had barely heard him, her mind focused on what they might find in this library. Maybe this would be her last glimpse of 1841. She tried to commit the scene to memory. Hywel had always loved history, and he would want to know every detail when she got home. Not just how it looked, but the other things. The smells, which at that precise moment were a mix of sewage and baking, and the sounds. She closed her eyes and listened to the vendors in the market calling out their wares, children laughing and, somewhere in the distance, the peal of church bells.

When the horses came to a halt, Lydia opened her eyes and pulled back the curtain. They had stopped in front of a pair of high wooden gates set into a stone wall, above which a thick bank of overgrown shrubs protruded. Only the roof and chimneys of the house were visible. Whoever lived here valued their privacy and security just as much as Bill and Peggy.

Keen to get on with the business of getting home, Lydia made to reach for the door handle, but Dilys put a hand on her arm to stop her. A moment later, Lydia felt the carriage rock as someone, she presumed Nate, jumped from the driver's seat. Then they were pulling forward again, the horses' hooves crunching on gravel. When the carriage came to a halt, Lydia raised her eyebrows in question to Dilys.

Dilys beckoned them to lean in so that their heads were almost touching, then whispered, 'The man we are about to meet is something of a recluse. We can speak freely in front of him. Indeed, we need to tell him everything if we are to have any hope of getting you back to your time.' She mouthed the last word, so it was barely audible, although Lydia doubted Nate had superhuman hearing. 'But remember, no details of the future. I cannot stress that enough,' Dilys said.

Moments later they were standing in the covered porch, the sound of a swinging bell echoing through the house beyond the front door. Lydia heard the approach of slow, unhurried footsteps on tiles. The door moved an inch, squeaking in protest as the swollen wood caught on the frame. The dark green paint was faded and peeling, although the brass knocker shone defiantly against its chalky backdrop. With a final, hefting yank, the door yielded to reveal a tall, skeletally thin woman in an ash-grey dress the same shade as her tightly bound bun. She had a chain around her waist from which hung a set of keys that looked to weigh almost as much as she did. Her dark eyes flashed in obvious surprise, then her lips flattened into a hard line. There was something in the way that the woman glared at Dilys that made Lydia want to step between them.

Dilys, for her part, said nothing. They stood staring at one another for what felt like an age.

The woman in grey cracked first, much to Lydia's satisfaction. 'You'll be wanting to see Mr Montgomery,' she said, holding the door just long enough for the women to step inside before turning to slam it behind them. It bounced against the frame; the glass surrounding it rattled in protest and a small square leaded pane tumbled out and smashed on the tiles. They too were cracked, the pretty mosaic pattern ruined by voids like a prizefighter's smile.

The woman in grey glared at the broken glass as if it had smashed itself to spite her, then closed the protesting door by throwing her shoulder into it. She turned wordlessly and strode towards a wide, curving staircase.

'Mrs Barnes is Montgomery's housekeeper,' Dilys said to Lydia and Rose.

Lydia saw the woman in grey stiffen at the words, her step almost but not quite faltering.

Lydia glanced around as they crossed the large hallway. A length of detached wallpaper bounced idly on the draft from the slammed door. From the stairs, Lydia saw small chunks of plaster lying on the tattered hallway rug. A glance upwards revealed where they had fallen from.

Lydia studied the wallpaper as they climbed. There were patches of fuchsia-pink and peacock-blue flowers clinging to the high corners as if trying to clamber away from their fate. Everywhere else, the paper was so bleached the flowers were just ghosts, all their colour leached away to nothingness, like something left out and long forgotten in the sun.

On reaching the first floor, the housekeeper flung open a door to reveal a large book-lined room. Lydia was almost beginning to feel sorry for the woman, until she glanced up and saw the look of pure, unfiltered hatred on her face.

'Wait in here. Mr Montgomery will be with you presently,' Mrs Barnes said, every word sounding as if it had to be forced between her gritted teeth.

Dilys strode into the room with Lydia and Rose hurrying in her wake. Floor-to-ceiling bookcases covered every wall, the single window and doorway the only interruptions. A large mahogany desk, piled high with papers and books, sat in the middle of the room on a faded, fraying rug. Once the door had closed behind them – it looked as if the housekeeper used the last of her willpower not to slam it – Rose let out a gasp. 'What's her problem?' she mouthed to Dilys.

'She was employed by a very dear friend of mine. There was a falling-out with her employer,' Dilys said evenly.

'And she blames you?' Rose asked, frowning.

Dilys shrugged but didn't elaborate further. Just as Lydia opened her mouth to ask another question, the door inched open to reveal a tall, slight man of about thirty, his hair tied loosely at the nape of his neck.

He had the look of a poet, Lydia thought, from the ruffled cravat at his neck and the faded pink roses embroidered across the collar and lapels of a finely tailored fawn jacket that was frayed around the cuffs. His cheeks were on the hollow side of chiselled, his pale grey eyes fanned with lines and red-rimmed. He was handsome in a way that pinched at Lydia's heart. The quote slipped into her mind unbidden. 'I protest, in the sincerity of love and honest kindness.'

Montgomery stood in the doorway as if frozen, his shy smile fixed in place. Just as Lydia was about to turn to see what he was staring at, a tiny brown hand appeared on his shoulder. She gawked wide-eyed as the hand turned into first one delicate tan-coloured arm, then another. In one swift movement, a tiny marmoset clambered deftly onto his shoulder.

Lydia heard Rose suck in a breath.

'Montgomery,' Dilys said with a bow of her head, then another to the marmoset. 'Ignatius. Thank you both for seeing us. It has been a long time. Indeed, the last time I was in this house, it was to consult Montgomery Senior, and you were playing with a toy horse in front of the hearth.'

Some of the light dimmed in the man's eyes, but his gentle smile remained in place. 'We remember you. My father always spoke very fondly of you and Sophia,' he said, finally crossing the room. His voice was deep, the type that could probably produce a wonderfully rich baritone if he sang, but he sounded slightly hoarse. He cleared his throat.

'My apologies,' he said, gesturing to his throat. 'It's been a while. And please, call me Monty.' He turned to look at Lydia and Rose, and Dilys took her cue.

'Monty, these are my friends. Lydia and Rose.'

Rose looked up at the mention of her name, and Lydia saw Monty's tired eyes widen. Had she not witnessed it, she wouldn't have believed it, but there it was, writ large for all the world to see. She had just seen a grown man fall in love. The sweetness of it made her want to cry. She glanced at Rose, but her eyes were once again on the floor. Her cheeks, though, were already colouring.

'Lydia is—' Dilys began, but Ignatius let out a screech that seemed to wake Monty from whatever trance he had fallen into.

'What?' Monty asked, looking confused.

Ignatius looked pointedly towards the door.

'Oh yes,' Monty said, rolling his eyes.

Without warning, the door closed as if guided by an invisible hand. Lydia, who had seen her fair share of magical feats, felt the hair on the back of her neck bristle. She stared at the door as a haze thickened in front of it.

'We can speak freely now,' Monty said, gesturing for them to sit down. 'Thank you, my friend,' he added with a nod to the marmoset on his shoulder.

Once they were all seated around the desk, Dilys told Monty everything, starting with her visions and ending with their arrival in Cardiff.

'Lydia, perhaps you are best placed to tell Monty about the book,' Dilys said once her story was told.

Lydia reached into the hidden pocket in her skirt and pulled out the little green book. It hummed in her hand, clearly sensing that it was about to become the centre of attention. She placed it gently on the table, but before she could speak, the book had shot across the polished wood to Monty.

'Well, I was going to start by saying that it was quite shy and reluctant to talk, but clearly not,' Lydia said with a nervous laugh.

Ignatius jumped from Monty's shoulder and stroked the cover with his index finger, his head cocked to one side. To Lydia's surprise, the book opened slowly. She held her breath as the pages turned one by one, each one blank. The disappointment settled around her like a damp fog.

'When we were in Aber, the book shared a prophecy,' Lydia said. 'To tell the truth, I remember only the gist of it, not the details. A lot has happened between then and now. Anyway, Dilys and I discussed this at length and decided that it would be best to let the book decide if it wanted to share that prophecy again here,' she said, choosing her words carefully for fear of saying too much.

Monty smiled without looking up from the book. He stroked his long, ink-stained fingers across the blank pages. 'That was wise indeed,' he said absentmindedly. 'To our knowledge, there were only ever three books of prophecy in existence. We remember hearing of the destruction of two. One in 476 AD and the other during the Crusades, 1096 if our memory serves us. And here we have the last of them. I am honoured to meet you, my friend,' Monty said, still addressing the book.

'We need to know how to get Lydia, Rose and the book back to their own time,' Dilys said.

Monty looked up, his eyes flicking to Rose before glancing back to Dilys. Leaning his elbows on the table, he pressed his palms together as if in prayer, then rested his chin on his thumbs, his forefingers tapping his nose.

'There is a lot to consider,' he said at last.

'Shall we leave you to think, Monty?' Dilys suggested.

Monty didn't appear to have heard her, but when Ignatius made a tutting sound, he said, 'Forgive me. Mrs Barnes will have tea waiting for you, if you're able to give me ...' He pulled a pocket watch from his waistcoat and flipped it open. 'Perhaps an hour?' He raised his dark eyebrows in question.

'Of course,' Dilys said, getting to her feet.

As Lydia stood, the *Book of Prophecy* slid back across the table to her. With relief, she slipped it back into her skirt pocket.

Monty was already standing and peering up at one of the high bookcases. Ignatius leapt from his shoulder and scrambled up the edges, which were decorated with exquisitely carved animals.

'Yes, the fourth volume, Ignatius, if you would be so kind,' Monty said, pointing at the top shelf. 'And the Brackerton too. Her early work, if you please.'

The monkey pulled out a book and threw it over his shoulder. The book hung momentarily in mid-air before opening itself and gliding down onto the reading table. Unable to resist, both Lydia and Rose turned to read the cover, but with what Lydia could have sworn was a huff, it slid away from them, coming to rest on the furthest corner of the table. Grumpy books weren't a new phenomenon, then.

A cry from Monty made Lydia turn back just in time to see another book sail into the air. This one was a slave to gravity, and Monty had to dive to catch it.

'Ignatius Walter Archibald Confucius Tellerman,' he sighed. 'What have I said about throwing books! They're not all conscious and able to fly! And even among those that can, many don't like it. They ...'

Lydia and Rose followed Dilys to the door, which opened with a low hiss followed by a whoosh of unnaturally cool air. Mrs Barnes was waiting for them at the foot of the stairs, her expression like granite.

CHAPTER 46

CARDIFF, JULY 1841

The housekeeper didn't so much as blink as the three women descended the stairs. Dilys waited a beat once they were all standing in the hallway, but when the housekeeper said nothing, she turned to Lydia and Rose and said calmly, 'Tea is usually served in the orangery. This way, ladies.'

Mrs Barnes took a step, blocking Dilys's path. The housekeeper sucked in her cheeks, her mouth twisting as if she was trying to eat a particularly bitter lemon. She seemed to come reluctantly to a decision because she curled her lips into a sarcastic smile and said with faux brightness, 'This way, ladies,' drawing out the last word, before turning and striding down a long bright corridor, keys swinging from her belt.

The orangery was a melancholic sight. The ancient fruit trees lining the room stood like sentinels, their gnarled trunks thick and roped with age. Lydia felt a pang of sympathy for the potted trees, their branches sagging under the weight of time, as if mourning their long-lost fruit-bearing days.

Tea had been laid out on a small lace-covered table in the

middle of the room around which three ornately carved chairs were clustered.

As soon as the women stepped into the orangey, the housekeeper stalked out, pulling the double doors behind her. The glass rattled ominously in the old frames but stayed firm.

Lydia let out a breath. Just being around the woman was hard work.

Dilys held up a finger and Lydia caught the ghost of a word on her thin lips, then the pressure in the room changed and the haze she'd noticed in the library surrounded them. She'd seen witches do this before but had no idea Dilys's power extended this far.

'We can talk freely now,' Dilys said, pulling out a chair and lowering herself into it.

'What's the story with the adorable little monkey?' Rose asked.

From the way Rose's cheeks coloured, Lydia could tell it wasn't the question she really wanted to ask. She smiled to herself. So long as young people fell in love at the drop of a hat, there was hope for the world. The thought felt like a comforting hand on her shoulder.

From the way Dilys studied Rose before she replied, Lydia guessed that she wasn't the only one to have noticed the chemistry. Dilys smiled kindly, and then began her story.

'Monty is from a long line of Tellermans. They were a powerful magical family with an unbroken line that they can trace back to ancient Egyptian times. They are quite unique in the magical world. You see, they pass on their memories from one generation to the next.'

'Through stories, you mean?' Rose asked, pouring them all tea.

'Not quite,' Dilys said. 'They inherit the knowledge of every Tellerman who came before them.'

'Wow!' Lydia said, her cup wobbling before it reached her lips. 'That must be an awful lot for a child to deal with.'

'Oh, few have to deal with the knowledge in childhood. There is only ever one custodian, so when one dies, the knowledge awakens in their heir, male or female.'

'What kind of knowledge do they have?' Lydia asked.

'The original Tellermans were scholars in the magical libraries of old, much like your good selves, I imagine. The only thing they don't remember very well is the time before they had this ability. They were forced to flee their homeland in the Middle East sometime in the Middle Ages, but they quickly settled into the magical community here. They were, and still are, trusted advisers to the Elders and scholars in the magical community. I should say that Tellerman wasn't their original name – they adopted that later.'

'Good grief. Why do we need magical libraries when we have them?' Rose said, only half joking.

Lydia frowned. 'And why does Monty need books if he can remember everything?'

'I asked his father the same thing many years ago. He told me it was part habit, part prompt for the memories,' Dilys said. 'They have quite a story, actually, that it is important you know. Back in 1567, Monty's ancestor John found himself working in the court of James VI of Scotland.'

Lydia and Rose both tsked.

'Yes. The very same,' Dilys said. 'Officially, John was an adviser, helping the King and his cronies on something mundane, but as is still the way, the Elders have always had spies in the corridors of power, just in case anyone with an army at their disposal decides to take an interest in our ways.

'Unfortunately for John, around the same time, he also came to the attention of a witch who, to this day, has remained unidentified. She, or he, wanted the Tellermans' knowledge for themselves. We know this only because over a period of weeks, John became the subject of repeated magical attacks. They became so violent, so frenzied, that he confined himself to his home, claiming a bad cold to absent himself from court. His magic was powerful, so there was never any risk of the knowledge being taken, but he sent word to the Elders, asking for their counsel and help in finding whoever was attacking him.'

Dilys took a sip of tea before she continued. 'When the Elders arrived a week later, all seemed to be well. The attacks had stopped, and John had returned to court, summoned by the King to discuss matters in the national interest. By the time the Elders managed to reach him, the damage had been done. He had betrayed us all.'

Lydia gasped, horrified. 'They tortured him?'

'Yes and no,' Dilys replied. 'You see, realising that they were never going to succeed, the witch who coveted the knowledge cursed John and his line. When it struck, every secret John knew came tumbling from his lips. It was a rare misfortune that he was in the company of a king obsessed with witches when it happened.'

Dilys fell silent for a long moment before picking up the story. 'I don't need to school either of you in the horrors that followed. The thousands of innocents who lost their lives. Most possessed no magic at all, but we lost many of our own to the burning times,' she said, her voice fading to a whisper.

'And this John was the cause?' Rose asked, glancing at the door.

'He wasn't to blame,' Dilys said. 'Although they each of them carry the weight of that guilt as if he were. John wasn't tortured by the King, but he tortured himself for the rest of his life.'

'Poor man,' said Rose.

'The Tellermans are gentle people. Imagine how enlight-ened we would be if we had the wisdom of a thousand lifetimes. But once the curse struck them, they couldn't be trusted with the knowledge they carried.'

'Dilys! Why on earth have we told him everything then? What if it gets back to the Reverend Evans and whoever he's told about us?' Lydia asked, her words running into each other as panic bloomed in her chest.

Dilys smiled patiently. 'We are quite safe. The Elders of the time came up with an ingenious way to help the Teller-mans and protect the knowledge.'

'It's the monkey, isn't it?' Rose said, her words barely audible, her eyes unfocused and fixed on the tiles.

'Why, yes!' Dilys said, sounding delighted. 'How on earth did you guess?'

Rose shrugged as she looked up and smiled shyly. 'I don't know. I just sort of feel it.'

Dilys was still beaming as she continued. 'Yes, Ignatius became the living embodiment of the Elders' spell. He has the discernment that the Tellermans lost to the curse. He decides who Monty can trust and who he can't. If Monty encounters someone of dubious character, Ignatius senses it and the Elders' spell overrides the witch's curse, rendering Monty mute. It was a work of magic the world has rarely seen.'

'So he's not a real monkey?' Rose asked, and Lydia couldn't tell if she was incredulous or just disappointed.

'He was a flesh-and-blood marmoset once, but he is likely more spell than monkey by now, having lived such an unnat-urally long life. He would have volunteered for the task in the beginning. It is not our way to compel any living crea-ture,' Dilys said. 'And as you saw, he is also a friend and companion for Monty, as he was to his father before him. Of course, Monty Senior was married and had a child. Though Monty is, I fear, rather a lonely creature.'

'So, Monty was able to speak in front of us because we passed the Ignatius test?' Lydia asked.

Dilys nodded.

'He seems like such a nice man,' Rose said, almost to herself.

'Oh, he is, Rose. His father before him too. They are as kind as they are wise and yet they are haunted by the past.'

A thought struck Lydia. 'I've been a keeper for more than twenty years. Why have I never heard of this story? I did my thesis on the witch hunts. There was absolutely no mention of the Tellermans. I've helped dozens of scholars since then too, but the name, the curse – none of it has come up in our research.'

Dilys's faint smile dropped from her lips. 'Oh dear. I fear that was one of the things we probably shouldn't know.'

Lydia winced. Too late now.

'What does that mean, Dilys?' Rose asked.

Dilys sighed and gave a resigned shrug. 'Monty is the last of his line. He is still young enough to marry, but he is something of a recluse – and, so Bill tells me, a romantic. Only a select few in the community know his story, and nobody wants their daughter to be saddled with a husband that's both cursed and bespelled. It was a different story in his father's day – they still had what was left of the family's fortune – but …' Dilys gestured to the slowly crumbling orangery. 'As you can see, that is rapidly dwindling. From what you say, Lydia, it appears that Monty may well be the last of the line. Maybe their knowledge will end with him. Although please keep that theory to yourself.' Dilys pressed her lips into a thin line, her eyes fixed on the floor as she spoke.

'That's why he's writing,' Lydia said sadly. 'He's trying to share the knowledge because he knows it won't be passed on this time.'

'Poor, sweet man,' Rose said. 'He must be so lonely. I'm glad he has Ignatius. I can't imagine Mrs Barnes is very good company. Actually, how does he speak to her?' Rose asked with a shudder. 'I don't need Ignatius's gift to know she is most certainly not of good character. She must know their story, surely?'

Dilys shook her head. 'The Elders kept the knowledge of the Tellermans' curse a secret. Can you imagine finding out that your wife or daughter was tortured and killed because of one man's indiscretion to a king? They were terrible enough times without people in the community turning against each other too. But that is a moot point as Millicent Barnes isn't one of us. That she found herself in our world was a cruel twist of fate for us all.'

Lydia's eyes flicked to the glass doors as a long shadow loomed. Dilys huffed. 'Speak of the devil,' she muttered, and then released the spell around the room. The housekeeper pulled open the double doors.

'Mr Montgomery is ready for you,' she all but spat, before disappearing the way she had come.

Lydia frowned. The rest of the story would clearly have to wait.

CHAPTER 47

CARDIFF, JULY 1841

When they returned to the library, Monty was standing amongst a sea of books and papers, grinning sheepishly. Rose felt her heart kick up another beat and hoped she wasn't going red in the face. She'd not felt quite right since she'd laid eyes on the mysterious, gorgeous Monty Tellerman.

'Sorry, Rose,' Lydia said, after bumping into her.

Rose startled, realising that yes, she had been standing gawking at Monty and blocking the doorway. She shuffled into the room, her eyes firmly fixed on Ignatius, who was sitting on a tower of books, peeling a grape. How long had he served the knowledge-holders in this line? How many shoulders had he perched on? How many Tellermans had he loved and protected? He glanced up at her, turned to look at Monty and then gave her a wide, toothy grin. Rose felt her cheeks flame.

'I assume, Monty, judging by the satisfied look on your face, that you have already found something of interest to us,' Dilys said, settling herself into a chair.

'I think I have, yes,' he said, grinning.

Ignatius tutted, and Rose stifled a chuckle as a half-eaten grape hit Monty on the chin.

'Sorry, Iggy. I mean, *we* did,' Monty corrected. He mouthed another 'Sorry' to the monkey, who looked suitably mollified. Rose felt her heart squeeze. He was such a sweet man.

'We,' Monty said pointedly with a nod to Ignatius, 'will need to do much more digging, but' – he pointed his finger in the air for emphasis – 'Apollonius of Tyana's lost texts mention spells for creating what he calls tunnels through time. He likened it to physical tunnelling and wanders off into studies of geology more than once, but he was very certain about the possibility. Not, ladies, that I'm doubting your story,' Monty added quickly, holding up his hands.

'And what about getting home to our own time?' Lydia asked.

'On that, we have only a theory, I'm afraid. Our friend Apollonius believed that there are places on the Earth where reality, which he likens to the layers of an onion, are pressed together. Thin places, he calls them. If you find such a place, then with the right spell, you can open a portal, either through time or through reality. If I were a betting man, which I am not,' he added with the merest of glances at Rose, 'I would say that the key to you getting home will be finding one of these thin places.'

Monty looked over at Rose and his smile faltered.

'Can't we just use the one we arrived through?' Lydia asked, already sounding impatient.

Ignatius made a chattering noise from the table before launching himself onto the man's shoulder. 'Good idea, my friend. My grandmother's one, if you please,' Monty said to the marmoset.

Ignatius scaled a bookcase and launched a folded piece of paper at the table. Monty caught it and spread it out.

It was a yellowed map of Wales, hand-drawn and smudged in the corners. Aside from the smudges and the country's outline, the paper was completely blank.

Rose frowned at Monty, who gave her an almost boyish smile in reply.

'Please show me thin places,' he said, touching his hand to the paper.

Rose couldn't contain a squeal of delight as she saw the ink on the map shift. Around a dozen tiny silver circles appeared across the country, place names inked neatly at their sides. Rose read magical texts every day, but there was just something thrilling about seeing a map behave in the same way. Or perhaps, she thought, everything Monty did seemed more thrilling.

'Dilys, can you show me where the ladies arrived?' Monty asked.

Dilys pointed to the spot outside Hay-on-Wye, which was nowhere near any of the circles.

Monty straightened. 'From your story, it sounds as if the book took emergency action in the moment of peril. Probability suggests it unlikely that you were passing a thin place when your attackers struck, and this proves it. In those circumstances, I assume the spell created its own portal, just as one might punch through a plaster wall rather than waste time trying to find a door.'

'It looked ragged,' Rose said, remembering the golden threads dancing in the breeze. 'Like a rip in fabric, all tattered around the edges.'

'Most certainly an emergency measure then,' Monty said. 'Which means it will not be safe to use again. Nature doesn't tolerate disorder for long so will already be working to close the rip. That's why Apollonius likened it to collapsing tunnels. If you used it again, you'd risk getting stuck between times.'

Rose thought her heart might stop altogether when Monty met her eyes and said earnestly, 'I will find you a safer place from which to return to your own time.'

She smiled when she heard his unvoiced question in her mind, feeling like she had just stepped into warm sunshine after an eternity in the cold. Monty's brow registered the slightest frown. He looked to Ignatius, who frowned too. *No,* Rose thought, *you didn't say it out loud, but I heard you anyway.*

'So, Monty,' Dilys said, peering at the map, 'which of these thin places is most suitable?'

Ignatius made a chattering noise.

'Indeed,' Monty said to the marmoset. Turning to Dilys, he replied, 'That, dear lady, will take more time to discern. Plus, we need a spell if you're to use it.'

'Where do we start?' Lydia asked, sounding impatient again.

Monty pressed his palms together, thumbs tucked under his chin, fingers tapping against his nose.

'The spell,' he said at last, drawing out the two words. 'Mother Pennywell is as good a place to start as any.'

Ignatius made a tutting sound. 'Don't be so pessimistic, Iggy,' Monty said. 'There is such a thing as hitting gold on the first strike, you know. We have long precedence for it.'

Ignatius rolled his eyes and started pointedly inspecting his nails.

'Really, Monty? She was an old woman when I left Cardiff. Surely she's no longer this side of the veil,' Dilys said, sounding doubtful.

Monty smiled. 'I think the good lady is immortal. I saw her myself last Easter, and Harold consulted her just last week about this new botanical garden being constructed in London. It's as good a place to start as any,' he concluded, with a glance to Ignatius.

'Then that is where we will begin,' Dilys said, rising to her feet.

Monty shot a glance at Rose, his face suddenly serious.

'I can stay and help with the thin places research,' Rose said, the words out of her mouth before she could stop them. She didn't dare look at Monty.

Dilys's lips twitched but she didn't smile. 'I think that would be a marvellous use of our limited time, Rose. Good thinking. I will ask Bill to collect you on our return.'

Rose nodded and tried to contain her excitement. She risked a glance at Lydia, who looked to be struggling to contain her smirk.

'Monty. Ignatius,' Dilys said with a polite nod. 'We thank you for your time and wisdom. We will be back in a few hours.'

As the door closed behind Lydia and Dilys, Rose turned to Monty. She felt a gentle tap on her arm. Looking down, she saw Ignatius grinning up at her. Beaming, she held out her finger and felt his tiny hand close around it. 'Where shall we begin?' she asked Monty.

CHAPTER 48

ST BRIDES, JULY 1841

*B*ill had been fussing one of the horses when they emerged from Monty's. Nate, he explained, had returned to the Chapels' to oversee a funeral. When Dilys announced the plan to go to St Brides right away, Bill suggested they wait for a day until they could take extra security, but Lydia could tell he already knew it was a lost cause.

They passed the first few minutes of the journey in a companionable silence. Neither of them mentioned the obvious chemistry between Rose and Monty. It was sweet to see, but something about it made Lydia unsettled in a way she couldn't articulate.

'You didn't get a chance to tell me about Mrs Barnes,' Lydia said, keen to think about something else.

Dilys's face hardened.

'It's not much of a story, I'm afraid. She is a convicted criminal and quite frankly lucky that the Tellermans are such generous souls, or she'd have spent the last quarter century in either jail or the workhouse.' Dilys spoke calmly and deliberately, her words clipped.

'Oh my days! What did she do?' Lydia asked.

'She tried to blackmail a dear friend of mine,' Dilys replied, her gaze on the window.

'But why would such an untrustworthy person be working for someone with such a secret?' Lydia asked, not seeing the logic in it.

'She was given a choice. She could have her memories erased and serve her time in jail, or she could work off her sentence in comfort, forever bespelled against sharing anything she sees or hears relating to the magical community,' Dilys said flatly. 'The spell takes the form of a key she can never be parted from.'

Lydia considered it for a moment. 'Sounds like she got off lightly, then.'

Dilys snorted but said nothing more.

Lydia turned her attention to the window. It was a bright summer's day. The air was warm and there was a hint of the sea on the breeze now that they were out of the city.

They travelled the rest of the way in silence, and Lydia settled into the motion of the carriage. She closed her eyes. Away from the city, she could hear the sound of the horses' hooves on the ground, their snorts and occasional whickering. At one point a bumblebee sailed through one window and out of the other, its buzzing a brief but welcome addition to the soundscape. The briny smell of the sea grew stronger the further they travelled, mixed with the scent of freshly cut hay and the occasional hint of flowers. Lydia felt sleep tug at her sleeve. She was warm and safe and being rocked by the carriage.

One of the horses whinnied loudly, clearly distressed. Lydia's eyes flew open. 'I smell burning,' she said, pressing her hand to the sill of the door and peering out. She could see nothing but fields.

The carriage came to an abrupt halt, then rocked as Bill

jumped from the driving seat. Lydia pushed open the door and stepped down.

'The young-un's not keen to go much further,' Bill said over his shoulder as they approached. He was standing at the front, stroking the nose of the pretty bay gelding nearest the carriage. 'He's usually alright with smoke, but there's bad business up ahead,' he said, inclining his head to gesture to the lane behind him. 'It's the bad magic you don't like, boy, isn't it,' he said to the horse as he rubbed the star-shaped blaze beneath his forelock. The horse snorted in reply.

'Stay here with them, Bill,' Dilys said, appearing from the carriage. 'I know my way from here.'

While Bill looked torn between his horses and his friend, he also looked like he knew better than to argue. 'Any point me telling you to be careful, Dil?' he asked.

Dilys raised an eyebrow in reply, then turned and strode down the lane like a woman half her age. Lydia hurried after her. They'd only been walking for a minute or so when the smouldering remains of a cottage came into view. The trees that overhung it were blackened, their canopies transformed to charcoal claws. The roof, which Lydia presumed must have been thatched, was completely gone, and part of the side wall looked to have collapsed into the void it had created. Tendrils of smoke still drifted into the air. The small windows stood like the empty sockets of a skull, the front door, blackened and twisted, hanging on its hinges like a scream.

'Oh no,' Dilys said, breaking into a trot.

Lydia had to run to keep up. She caught up with Dilys in the garden of the ruined cottage.

'Bill was right. There is bad magic here. I can still feel their intent,' Dilys said, curling her lip as if she had just taken a bite of something rotten. She stepped towards one of the large rowan trees that faced the property, which had been spared the flames. She placed her hand on its trunk and closed her eyes.

'Do you think she got out in time?' Lydia asked when Dilys dropped her hand from the tree.

'Mother Pennywell died,' Dilys said. 'They recovered her body from the house just a few hours ago.'

'But how?' Lydia asked, looking from the tree to the cottage and back again before realisation struck. It was sometimes easy to forget that Dilys was a witch. While those she worked with in 1960 kept their magical abilities firmly under their hats, Dilys seemed to keep hers under lock and key in a fortress of her own construction.

'Trees don't need eyes to see with,' Dilys said simply.

A small grey flash of barking fur raced from the bushes and headed directly for Dilys.

'Careful he doesn't bite,' Lydia cried out, but Dilys was already on her knees, her arms open.

'There, there,' Dilys said, scooping up the dog in one fluid movement. 'You have been in the wars too, my friend.'

The rough-coated Jack Russell's fur was charred black across his back, the skin a livid pink, dotted with blisters and red-raw patches that looked to be a mix of fresh and dried blood. His nose and ears were burned too.

'Ci Gwyn, is it,' Dilys said, her voice thick with pity. 'Look at you, bach.'

Lydia saw the dog thump his tail against Dilys's side.

'You know him?' she asked.

'We've not had the pleasure until now, but all of Mother Pennywell's dogs are called after their colour, and I think under all that soot he is probably white,' Dilys said.

Lydia reached out to the dog, who leaned forward and offered up his chin for a tickle.

'Shall we go to the neighbours? Ask what happened?' Lydia suggested.

'No. They will have seen and heard nothing, I'd wager. Will you take Ci Gwyn back to Bill? He won't be safe here and we need to tend to his burns. I doubt there is much point in searching for books in the circumstances, but it would be remiss of us not to try,' Dilys said.

'Agreed,' Lydia said as she took the still-wagging Ci Gwyn from Dilys.

Dilys sighed. 'The garden is extensive, and Mother Pennywell has – had – the field beyond it too. Perhaps there is an outhouse or similar. I'll start there.'

Lydia started to reply, but Dilys was already striding away.

'Come on then, Ci Gwyn, let's get you to Bill,' Lydia said as she turned back to the lane.

CHAPTER 49

ST BRIDES, JULY 1841

*L*ydia left Bill to look after Ci Gwyn and headed back to what was left of the cottage. She crept as close as she dared and craned her neck to peer through the voids that were once windows. She saw nothing but ash and blackness. A lump rose in her throat as she imagined some poor elderly woman perishing here. Hopefully Dilys was wrong about the bad magic. Maybe it had been an accident. A stray spark leading to a gentle drift from sleep into something else. She shuddered and turned away to look at the garden.

Suddenly weary, Lydia sank onto a low stone wall that ringed a magnificent-looking herb garden. Lavender, borage, comfrey, rosemary and dozens more she couldn't identify grew in the neatly tended beds. She brushed her hand over the lavender and inhaled deeply. A memory came of her mother, propped up with cushions in her favourite chair making lavender bags, ready for gifting at Christmas.

Lydia sat still lost in the memory when a shadow crossed her face. She looked up to find the most extraordinary butterfly she had ever seen. With a wingspan almost as big as her hand, it was the colour of a sapphire. Another joined it. It was only slightly smaller than the first, its wings the colour of buttercups, tipped at the edges in a sunset orange. A tiny dark green butterfly danced into the fray, its wings like molten metal. Lydia gasped in delight as she watched them. They were so close she could have reached up and touched them.

'Afternoon, ma'am.'

The voice came from behind her, and Lydia spun around, propelled to her feet by something primal and unconscious. The man was older than her, in his fifties or even sixties, his face weathered and deeply lined. He wore a wide-brimmed hat, which he tipped in greeting.

'My apologies if I startled you,' he said, his voice deep and gravelly, the cadence slow and deliberate.

'No harm done. You're from America,' Lydia said, blurting out the first thing that popped into her mind.

'Guilty as charged,' he replied, holding up his hands in mock surrender. Behind his thick, greying moustache, he might have been smiling, but his eyes, half shadowed by the hat, remained unchanged.

The air felt thick around them, and Lydia prayed that Dilys would come back soon. Something didn't feel right.

'I was watching the butterflies. Did you see them?' she asked the stranger, stalling for time.

'Nope. Can't say that I did, no.'

'Are you staying in the village, Mr ...?'

He watched her for a long moment, his tongue probing the inside of his cheek as if he was considering his answer.

'Thorne,' he said at last. 'And you are Mrs—'

'Her name is none of your concern.' Dilys spat the words like nails from a gun.

Thorne raised his chin and inhaled sharply. He snorted and then spat on the floor.

Lydia backed away until she was beside Dilys.

'You will be held accountable for the evil you committed here,' Dilys growled.

Thorne threw back his head and barked out a laugh.

'Do not speak to me of evil, witch!' he snarled, his dark eyes wild and unblinking. 'You are a plague on mankind and a curse to all God-fearing, right-thinking folk.'

Lydia felt the pressure shift around her. Her ears popped and she looked up just in time to see Thorne, still some six feet away, fling out his arms towards them, his mouth in a wide, yawning curse. Did he mean to push them over? The reality became clear when she felt whatever magic he had sent hurtling towards them rebound off Dilys's protective shield. It knocked him off his feet, and Lydia, her instincts overriding her brain, turned to run while he was down.

'Stay,' Dilys commanded, grabbing her forearm and holding on.

Thorne, hat in his hand, was struggling to his feet, his face twisted in fury. Dilys stepped in front of Lydia, her back ramrod straight, chin lifted, her hands clasped in front of her.

'You would be wise, sir, not to pick a fight you are unable to win,' Dilys said, her tone slow, deliberate and, Lydia thought, surprisingly menacing.

The man probed at the corner of his mouth with his tongue. Lydia could see that it was bleeding. He pressed the back of his hand to the spot, taking his time to inspect the dab of blood. He snorted a laugh.

'And you, woman,' he sneered, eyeing Dilys up and down, 'would be wise to remember your place.'

'You are a disgrace to magic and your line,' Dilys hissed, leaning towards him.

Thorne's eyes flashed with fury, and at his sides, his hands balled into tight fists.

Dilys remained motionless.

'This ain't over, bitch,' he drawled, pointing two fingers at Dilys the way children did when they were pretending to hold a gun. Then he turned and walked into the trees.

Lydia bent forward, bracing her hands on her thighs as she caught her breath.

'Are you alright, Lydia?' Dilys asked, resting a hand on her shoulder.

'Fine,' Lydia managed. 'Was he the one?' She knew the answer, but part of her needed to hear it.

'Yes. He killed Mother Pennywell. The bad magic is clinging all over him like burnt tar.'

'Was he the man from your vision?' Lydia asked.

'Without a doubt,' Dilys replied.

'You were so calm, Dil,' Lydia stammered. 'Thank you,' she added belatedly.

'I must confess to feeling a bit shaky, to tell you the truth, but I will be fine in a moment. It has been a long time,' Dilys said.

'Since you used your magic?' Lydia asked, confused.

'Not quite. It has been a long time since I have come face to face with a Turned. And I have never met one with that much power. We need to alert the Elders at once,' she said, stepping away in the direction of the lane and the carriage beyond.

'Turned?' Lydia asked, not recognising the term.

'Those with magic who turn against the community and use it for the other side,' Dilys said, her pace quickening so that Lydia had to break into a jog.

The sick feeling grew in the pit of Lydia's stomach at the trace of a tremor she heard in her friend's voice.

CHAPTER 50

ST BRIDES, JULY 1841

Thorne kept running until he was sure the witch wasn't coming after him. He had been foolish to speak to the woman in the garden, but if there was a chance that she knew something about the old hag with the dog, then it was worth the risk.

The wind had not been kind to him that morning. The sea was flat as a mill pond and what gusts there were came few and far between, meaning he'd had to get closer than he'd have liked to pick up the woman's scent. There was the faintest hint of magic about her, but ordinaries sometimes picked up traces of power like they would a dusting of pollen as they brushed past a flower.

He made his way through the trees now, snapping off branches as he walked, leaving them hanging limply by woody threads. He should have finished the witch there and then, but he was depleted. The old hag with the dog had put up a remarkable fight, all things considered.

He shook his head in frustration and yanked on a thick, low-hanging branch. When it didn't break, he grabbed at it and heaved until the limb tore free of the trunk with a satis-fying crack.

Breathing hard, he spat on the branch and walked on. The old woman's face from the night before flashed into his mind. She had been terrified at the end – he could see it in her eyes, the last of her powers spent – and yet she'd still refused to tell him. She'd rather die than give up what she knew. *Happy to oblige you, old bitch*, he thought. He sighed and rubbed his forehead. His exertions had come with a cost, albeit a temporary one. He would head back to the city to rest up and recover his strength before continuing his search.

He crossed the road to the field where he'd tethered his rented horse. He'd say that for his client – he wasn't afraid to spend money. The animal had been the finest in the stable.

When he heard the carriage approach, he ducked behind the hedge. He lifted his nose to catch the scent and snarled. The old witch who had just attacked him was heading out of town too. She smelled sickly sweet, like spoiling fruit.

There was another, earthy, peaty smell coming from the same direction, but just as Thorne took another breath, the wind changed, whipping the scent away. No matter. He had what he needed. And the old witch would get what she deserved in due course.

CHAPTER 51

ST BRIDES, JULY 1841

*T*he journey back to Cardiff was tense. Bill had found a blanket for Ci Gwyn, but the little dog had ignored it in favour of Lydia's lap, where he'd promptly fallen asleep, his burnt paws twitching. He would need some serious TLC on those burns, she thought. Did they have vets in 1841? She wasn't sure.

Dilys hadn't said a word since filling Bill in on the attack. While she'd claimed to be feeling fine, exhaustion etched itself into her features. Though Lydia doubted Dilys ever capable of slouching – her back seemed to be held upright by invisible strings – she rested her head against the carriage's sides, her eyes closed. Perhaps it was the dimming light, but she also looked pale.

Lydia was still debating whether or not to risk waking Dilys when the carriage drew up outside Monty's. It rocked as Bill jumped down, and then, moments later, Rose was climbing in to sit next to her. Lydia didn't need to ask if she'd had an enjoyable afternoon as the young woman was positively glowing.

'Did you find anything useful, Rose?' Dilys asked, her eyes still closed but her voice as calm and commanding as ever.

Her question went unanswered as Rose spotted Ci Gwyn. The little dog swiftly abandoned Lydia for her lap. Lydia breathed a sigh of relief. Her hip, bruised from her fall at the cottage, had been crying out for a stretch, but she'd been loath to disturb the wounded pup.

'Rose?' Dilys tried again. 'Did you find anything of use?'

'What? Oh, yes,' Rose replied, tearing her eyes away from the little dog. 'We have a list of potential thin places. But what happened to the poor dog?'

Dilys recounted the story succinctly, and in the telling, Lydia thought, made it sound a lot less terrifying than she remembered.

Rose was quiet for a long moment. 'I don't know what to say. You could have both been killed,' she said eventually, her voice catching.

'Nonsense,' Dilys said firmly. 'But we appreciate your concern.'

'He's the man from your vision, then,' Rose said.

'I think he must be, yes.'

'Do you think he's the man Reverend Evans went running off to tell about us?' Lydia asked.

'Of that, I'm unsure,' Dilys said thoughtfully. 'It makes no difference either way, I suppose. We are still exactly where we were this morning, save for one very important difference.'

'Which is?' Rose prompted as she stroked the small dog's smoky fur, careful to avoid his burns.

'It leaves us still looking for a spell to get you home,' Dilys said flatly. 'But now we are known to the man who is hunting us.'

The three women fell into an uncomfortable silence,

punctuated only by the occasional snore and whine from the dog as he slept. When at last the carriage rolled into the Chapels' yard, Lydia felt weary to her very bones. She stretched her leg tentatively and felt the answering complaint of her hip.

Dilys was already climbing out of the carriage, taking Bill's hand.

'You okay?' Rose asked, patting Lydia's knee. Lydia winced as what felt like a static shock shot through her. Rose didn't seem to notice though.

'Wakey wakey, little one,' Rose cooed to the dog, jiggling her knees to rouse him. Ci Gwyn's eyes opened, and he gave a wide, tongue-curling yawn before stretching his back. He shook himself before jumping to stand on the seat between Lydia and Rose, tail wagging, tongue lolling.

'Oh my god! Rose! Look!' Lydia stuttered, pointing to the patches of snow-white fur covering Ci Gwyn's ears and back. His nose, burned raw and still bleeding when they found him, was a perfect boot-polish black and damp to the touch. He was still grey with soot here and there, but when Lydia parted the new fur, she saw only healthy pink skin.

'Well, I'll be,' Lydia said, laughing.

Rose squealed in delight and opened her arms, just in time to catch the little dog. 'You're all healed!' she giggled as she clambered out of the carriage.

Lydia headed for the carriage door, the smile still on her lips at the miracle they'd just witnessed. Rose was almost running to the house, desperate to share the good news.

The dread fell over Lydia like a dropped weight. She pitched forward, bracing herself against the door-frame as the ghost of gunshots rippled through her mind. She gasped as what felt like every ounce of air bolted from her lungs. She cried out, but there was nobody in the courtyard to hear her.

Tears welled in her eyes as she tasted acid rising in her throat. Just another panic attack, she told herself. *Breathe. Just breathe.*

The dread vanished as quickly as it had arrived, and Lydia forced herself to look on the bright side. Not only were they happening less frequently, but she was also starting to learn how to manage them.

She found Rose, Bill, Peggy and Dilys in the kitchen, surrounding Ci Gwyn, his tail wagging so hard it was a blur.

'Well, look at you!' Bill said, sounding delighted as the little dog jumped up at him.

'Was it you, Dil?' Rose asked, pointing at the dog in bemusement.

'No, dear. I think you did this all by yourself,' Dilys said, the pride lighting up her face like a candle.

When Rose tried and failed to string a sentence together, Peggy steered her towards the nearest chair.

'Can you explain, Dil?' Bill asked.

'I saw it happen as we were talking, Rose, the grace flowing from your hands and into our canine friend. I decided against interrupting as I wasn't sure you were aware you were doing it,' Dilys said.

Rose's mouth was hanging open. 'I'm not a healer though,' she said, but Lydia heard the doubt in her voice.

'I beg to differ, and so does Ci Gwyn!' Dilys said with a rare chuckle.

At the sound of his name, the dog leapt into Rose's lap and licked her chin.

'Eww! Your breath smells,' Rose squealed as she tickled the dog, but she didn't pull away, Lydia noticed.

'Right, I'll go and see where our Frank is. Quicker we find him, the quicker we'll be able to interrogate our witness,' he said, ruffling Ci Gwyn's head as he passed.

When Lydia and Rose exchanged confused glances, Peggy said, 'Didn't Bill say? Our boy Frank can speak to animals.'

Lydia lowered herself into a chair and realised that her hip was no longer sore.

CHAPTER 52

PONT NEFOEDD, DECEMBER 1960

aggie had almost given up hope of ever being able to talk to the book that had cast the time spell. It had taken her weeks to find it the first time, such was its determination to be left alone. She thought she'd played it cool, barely breaking her stride as she went about re-shelving books from her trolley, her heart pumping like a locomotive beneath her ribs. She'd gone back the next day, but the book had found a new place to hide.

The pattern had repeated itself for months. Infuriating though it was, she couldn't force the book to tell her what had happened. And so she did the only thing she could do – she waited.

Maggie flicked on the library lights, not waiting for them to fully blink into life before heading to the kitchenette to drop off the box of teabags and the biscuits that swung in the shopping bag at her side. She wondered idly how many other women her age went to the corner shop with an armed guard walking ten steps behind them.

She scanned the stacks as she went, watchful in a way she'd never thought to be before that man broke in and violated the library. This was meant to be a safe place, but no number of guards or spells could give them back what they'd lost.

The only one who seemed pleased with the new arrangements was Boudicca. Having so many witches around made her almost giddy with delight. At least one of them was happy.

Maggie was filling the jar with fresh teabags when she heard a piercing, strangled yowl. Boudicca! Her heart in her throat, Maggie bolted towards the sound, trying to calculate how long it might take the guards to reach them. The one that had accompanied her to the shop had left her at the front door and had mumbled something, but she wasn't really listening.

The sight that greeted her when she rounded the corner stopped her thoughts dead. There, on the library table, was Boudicca, sitting next to the spell book. Maggie bit her lip. Boudicca, never one to take a risk where the books were concerned, lifted a delicate cream paw and placed it ever so gently on the cover. The book didn't even flinch. Maggie puffed out a long breath. Message received.

Edging forward, she said, 'Thanks for the alert,' as she offered her hand to the cat. Boudicca pressed her head into Maggie's palm, accepting her tickle.

Her eyes on the book, Maggie lowered herself carefully into the chair. She didn't tuck it in as she normally would. If it did go on the attack, every second would count. Boudicca yawned and then flopped theatrically onto her side, the picture of relaxation. For her part, Maggie felt about as relaxed as a bomb-disposal officer. Logic suggested that the book was ready to talk, or else it wouldn't have put itself here, but she'd been brought up to be cautious.

'Hello,' she said, addressing the book. 'It's really nice to

see you. I've been ...' She hesitated, choosing her words carefully. 'Concerned about you.'

The book inched towards her slowly. She let out another
breath and risked a smile.

'Is there something you'd like me to help you with?'
Maggie asked.

The book opened itself so slowly that Maggie had to sit
on her hands to stop herself from helping it. When at last the
cover lay open on the table, exposing the first page, Maggie
waited, heart thumping.

Boudicca stood up and peered at the book too. Nothing
happened. No text appeared. Either it showed you what was
already there or it used the page to tell you something.
Another page turned. It too was blank. As was the next.
Maggie frowned. The pages picked up speed, but all showed
the same thing – nothing.

It was Boudicca who broke the tense silence. She let out a
low, pitiful yowl. It was only then that the penny dropped.
'Oh my days!' Maggie said, the horror of what she was seeing
becoming clear. 'No wonder you were so upset. I am so sorry
for not realising sooner.'

'Realising what?' a voice asked from the doorway. Maggie
jumped, but instantly relaxed when she saw Seren standing
there, her eyes flicking between Maggie and the book open
in front of her.

'Is that who I think it is?' Seren asked, pointing at the
book, her eyes wide.

Maggie nodded. 'Is it okay if I tell Seren?' she asked the
book.

On the blank page, the word 'Yes' appeared in a looping
font.

Maggie cleared her throat of the sadness that had lodged
there like a mournful pebble. She stroked the empty page
with gentle fingers.

'The spell book that opened the portal,' she said, pointing at it. 'Rose didn't just get fragments of the time spell. The book gave her everything it possessed.'

Maggie watched as Seren's usually serene expression morphed into horror. She pressed a hand to her mouth as she rushed to the table. The book turned a few pages as if to underscore what Maggie had just explained.

'No wonder you were so distressed,' Maggie said to the book, stroking its pages.

Seren sank into the nearest chair and bowed her head. They stayed like that for long moments, Maggie contemplating what it would mean for a magical book to give up its secrets and then exist without them. In human terms, it must be akin to losing your reason for living.

When Seren at last looked up, Maggie addressed the book. 'Did you intend for your magic to go to Rose, or perhaps it was an accident?'

The book ruffled its pages, and Maggie knew at once that she'd not phrased her question as carefully as she might have. Ink materialised on the page, sharp, pointed letters that Maggie couldn't read vanishing almost as quickly as they appeared. After a heartbeat, the looping script returned.

There are no accidents in magic.

'Of course,' Maggie said, forcing a nervous laugh. 'I'm sorry.'

The sleeping witch needed the magic for what she will undo.

Seren and Maggie exchanged a puzzled look.

'May I ask a question?' Seren asked the book.

Once the 'yes' had appeared, she said, 'Thank you. Rose is of a magical line?'

Yes. Her father was a Llewellyn, but the girl is unaware.

Seren let out a low groan. 'Well, that explains a lot,' she said with a sigh. 'We wondered why she lasted so long with a powerful time spell in her veins. We put it down to the fact that she was young. Now we know that she held everything our learned friend possessed here – that sort of magic could only have been borne by a witch of powerful magical heritage.'

'But apprentices can't have magic. It's in the rules,' Maggie said, hating how petty she sounded.

'It seems like Rose didn't know herself. Nor did the Elders. Believe me, we vet our apprentices thoroughly. That we didn't find out means that magic didn't want us to know. We would have rejected her had we been aware. As you say, we have that rule so that keepers can remain neutral around the magical texts in their charge.'

Seren addressed the book again. 'You said Rose has to do something. Do you mean in the time she has gone to?'

Yes.

Seren looked to be choosing her words carefully. 'Has she gone forward or back?'

Back.

'Is my mother with her?' Maggie asked, unable to contain herself.

The book seemed to hesitate, but then 'Yes' appeared on the page.

Maggie leaned back into her chair and held her head in her hands as the relief flooded through her. She felt almost giddy with it.

'Are we permitted to know when, or why?' Seren asked.

No.

'Is there anything we can do to help Lydia and Rose return to us?' Seren asked. *Great question*, Maggie thought.

No.

Maggie turned back to the book. 'Thank you for telling us this. What do you want us to do now?'

The page stayed blank for a long time.

Make your peace.
It was then that she heard the gunfire.

CHAPTER 53

*B*ill returned to the kitchen ten minutes later, a shy-looking Frank beside him. Bill's hand was resting gently on the boy's shoulder, although whether to reassure him or to stop him bolting in the other direction, Lydia didn't know. Frank's face was filthy, and she heard Peggy groan.

'What have you been doing, Frank Chapel?' she asked, throwing her hands in the air. 'You look like you've been down a mine!'

There was a playfulness to her tone that turned Frank's wide-eyed, frozen look into a sheepish smile.

'I was playing in the coal house with Tom,' he said, twisting the cap that Bill had tugged from his head and handed to him moments earlier.

Hands on hips, Peggy rolled her eyes. 'How many times?' she said with a shake of her head. She smiled at him, and Lydia wondered at the dynamic here. This orphan boy they'd taken in and who they now loved like their own. 'Well, bath tonight then,' Peggy said with a shrug.

Frank's groan of protest was cut short when Ci Gwyn

shot into the room from the scullery and made straight for him. His whole body seemed to be wagging, and he was whining too.

Frank dropped to his knees and fussed him, then pulled a wooden ball from his pocket and rolled it for the now ecstatic dog. Ci Gwyn shot after it as Frank beamed, delighted.

'Frank, son, this is—' Bill started.

'Ci Gwyn,' Frank said, with a fleeting glance up at his father. 'I know. He told me.'

Peggy's face lit up with pride.

'Good-oh. Well, he saw something that we need to know about, son. Something that might be upsetting for a lad to hear, but ...' Bill paused and threw a questioning look at Peggy, who shrugged resignedly, then nodded. 'We need to know what happened, and this is the important bit, we need to know what Ci Gwyn thinks about *why* it happened. Understand me?'

Frank nodded, his face now serious. He shifted positions, moving from his knees to sit on the floor with his legs crossed. He waited for the dog to retrieve the ball, then patted his knee. He said nothing out loud, but Ci Gwyn, tongue lolling, climbed into his lap and let out a big sigh. Frank sighed too and began stroking the dog's back, his gaze unfocused.

Lydia watched the story play out on Frank's face. First the easy smile slipped from his lips. Fear clouded his young face, eyes wide as saucers, unblinking. He bit his lip and screwed his eyes shut, his head shaking almost imperceptibly. He stopped stroking the dog as his hands balled into fists that he pressed to his eyes. Ci Gwyn whined and stood up, looking into the boy's face, his tail drooping like a limp rag.

Peggy was leaning forward as if at any moment she would rush over and pull the lad away. Lydia knew how she felt. She just hoped that the dog had enough sense to edit his story for a child, although from the look of it, she was doubtful.

'No, go on,' Frank said out loud as he tickled Ci Gwyn under the chin. 'They need to know it all.'

The dog stayed standing but hung his head. Frank resumed his head-to-tail stroking, his own head bowed. Lydia bit her lip – poor lad to have to hear such a story.

'Thank you, my friend. You're safe now,' Frank said at last, sounding so much older than his years.

The dog offered a brief wag of his limp tail. Frank ruffled his head, before getting to his feet.

'Da, can we get him a blanket? He'll be tired after all that talking,' Frank said.

'I'll fetch him one,' Peggy said. 'Come on, Ci Gwyn. Come with me and you can pick your own blanket.'

CHAPTER 54

CARDIFF, JULY 1841

S ilas Thorne shifted in his makeshift seat on the low wall outside the baker's. From here he had a clear view of Chapel and Sons, not that he could see much more than the windowless side of the house that rose above the high wall encircling the property. There was only one visible way in or out. Tall black wooden gates for carriages, a small person-sized door cut into the one on the right. The wall wasn't the only thing protecting them either. He'd walked the perimeter earlier, unable to get too close as every inch was warded – the magic smelled like burning hair and screaming. Or maybe that was just his memory playing havoc with his gift. Either way, it meant he'd need to wait until the old witch came out.

He chewed the inside of his cheek. He should be looking for his target. His client would neither thank him nor, more importantly, pay him for killing some droopy-eyed old crone with ideas above her station, but nobody bested Silas Thorne in a fight and survived to tell the tale. It had never been his way.

Thorne turned his thoughts back to the Chapels' fortress

of a house. Magical folk claimed to like their privacy, but he knew the truth of it. Like every creature bent to the devil's work, they hid themselves away from God-fearing folk – keeping their wickedness secret from the light of the Lord and everything righteous in the world.

Away from the property, the smell of the wards faded, replaced by a more generic stink of magic that rolled off the house like it was horse shit steaming in the sun. He wrinkled his nose as a breeze barely strong enough to move his whiskers delivered another waft of it. He snorted.

He would need to move again soon. The day was drawing to a close and the streets were slowly emptying of the people, carriages and carts that allowed him to blend into the crowd. There was a bar across the street, and while he didn't hold with drinking, it might be his only option until night fell and the darkness conspired to keep him hidden.

The wind picked up, lifting the back of his hat. Thorne wet his finger and held it in the air. He gritted his teeth and cursed the element. With the wind at his back, he would be saved the stench from the house, but it made detecting his new target all but impossible.

He bit back a curse and went into the bar, choosing a seat in the window so that he could continue to watch the Chapels'. Half an hour later, his ale all but gone, he was about to order another when he saw a carriage pull up in front of the gates. He could tell by its motion that someone had just exited on the side nearest the gates. He debated going outside, but the streets were almost empty now, and so the risk of being seen by the visitor was too high.

The carriage moved off to reveal a tall man in fine-cut clothes. His hair was long like a whore's and tied with a ribbon at the nape of his neck. Thorne lifted his nose, more out of habit than expectation, but detected nothing but the stench of old sweat and soured ale.

He continued to watch. Maybe he was a client of these so-called undertakers, but if so, why the hurry? The dead were patient, after all. As he continued to watch, the gate cracked open, and without preamble, the man ran inside. 'Known to them, then,' he said to himself, leaning forward now, his interest piqued.

CHAPTER 55

Frank waited until his mother and Ci Gwyn were out of the room before he began talking. His voice was quiet, and Bill had to ask him to speak up. He started again.

'He lived with a nice woman by the sea. She grew lots of plants and made them into things for people when they weren't well and couldn't afford the doctor. Lots of people went to see her, and Ci Gwyn liked that because most of them made a fuss of him. They used to bring her food too, and he really liked that bit.'

Lydia saw Dilys purse her lips, clearly trying not to ask the boy to speed up. He must have seen it too, because he said, 'Yesterday, they were in the garden after supper, picking herbs that need picking when the moon is out, and a man they didn't know came up to his mam and started asking questions. Ci Gwyn didn't like him. He had magic like his ma, but he didn't smell good. Like meat that makes you sick, he said.

'His ma didn't like him either and told him to go away, but he wouldn't listen. He followed her to the cottage, and she shut the door on him and put the bolt on. But then Ci Gwyn smelled the smell again, and he turned around and the bad meat man, that's what he calls him, was standing right behind them. His mam had a terrible fright, and then ...' Frank swallowed and looked at his father, who put a comforting hand on his shoulder and nodded for him to continue.

'The man was looking for someone. Kept shouting at his mam to tell him where they were. Kept saying things about God being angry and that nature had been ...' The boy scowled, searching for the word. 'Like, insulted or something. He was very angry, and Ci Gwyn went for him, bit the back of his leg, but the bad meat man kicked him and so his ma locked him in the kitchen to keep him safe. He was very upset about that. He said it hurt a lot, being kicked, but his heart hurt more hearing his ma crying.'

Frank stopped and looked at the floor. Bill stepped behind the boy and put both hands on his shoulders. Just the sort of thing Hywel would do, Lydia thought with a pang. Use his presence to reassure. Comfort.

When the boy spoke again, his voice was a whisper. 'Ci Gwyn was biting at the door, trying to get through it, but he could see through the crack. He wouldn't tell me the worst bits, but he said the man kept going on about finding this person. He was hitting his ma and then he used magic, bad magic, and the whole place smelled like rotten eggs and dead things. There was a blue light that hurt his eyes, and then the fire started. His ma had gone quiet before the fire though. He hopes that—' The boy broke off and sniffed loudly.

'Nearly done, son. You're doing well,' Bill said, squeezing the boy's shoulder.

Frank cleared his throat. 'He kept trying to bite the door, but it was burning his nose and the smoke was so thick. Bits of the roof were falling in as well, and one fell on his back and burned him. Then he thought he heard his ma calling him from the coal hole in the kitchen. He nosed the door open and went in to find her, but then he could smell the clean air from the other side, so crawled through it and out into the garden. The house was all on fire, and it was then that he knew he was hurt bad, so he went and hid in the big herb garden at the back. He stayed there until he smelled good magic, he said.'

'Well done, son,' Peggy said from the door. She rushed forward to hug Frank. The boy made a brief show of shrugging her off, before wrapping his arms around her and hugging her back.

'I told Ci Gwyn he could explore upstairs,' she explained when Frank pulled away and cast around, looking for the dog.

'And you're sure he said the man was looking for someone, not something. Not a book, or a spell, or anything like that?' Bill asked.

Frank turned. 'He was sure. The man was looking for a girl, or a lady maybe. He said "her", anyway.'

'Did he say her name?' Lydia asked, her heart thumping. How someone in 1841 could possibly know either her name or Rose's was beyond her, but fear wasn't logical.

Frank shook his head. 'He never said her name, but he did call her a witch,' the boy said with a shrug.

'You did well, son. You can have another half an hour playing,' Bill said.

'Can Ci Gwyn sleep in my room tonight?' Frank asked hopefully.

Peggy sighed. 'You know he can't. I'm sorry, love,' she said sadly. 'But if you have a good wash, get that coal off your face and hands at least, we can leave the bath till tomorrow night if you want.'

Frank beamed at that. 'Thanks, Ma! Can I go now?'

Bill raised his eyebrows at Peggy, but she just shrugged and smiled as she watched the boy race off down the hall.

'His connection depletes him,' Rose said once the front door had banged shut. It was a statement, not a question.

Lydia saw Bill and Dilys exchange a look.

'That's right,' Bill said. 'When we took him in, he was in a terrible state. Couldn't put weight on him no matter how much we fed him. Turns out it was the mouse.' Bill smiled at the three bemused sets of eyes that peered at him. 'On his own, lonely and fending for himself, he befriended a mouse. Lived in his pocket. Talked to each other all day, and half the night, no doubt.'

'It was Mr Monty who figured it out. Once we separated them, Frank got better,' Peggy said, looking wistful.

'But what about his mouse friend?' Rose asked, looking alarmed.

'Oh, don't you worry about him. He lived with us another two years. Died an old boy, cwtched in the bed of hay Frank used to arrange nicely for him every night. Such a sweet, sweet lad,' Peggy said, shaking her head. Lydia didn't know whether she was talking about Frank or the mouse.

'Well, it appears we were off track assuming this man was looking for the same spell we were hoping to find at Mother Pennywell's,' Dilys said, changing the subject. 'Perhaps that is good news of sorts.'

'So he's a hunter of another kind,' Bill snorted.

Lydia opened her mouth to ask a question, but at that exact point the front door flew open and Frank raced down the hall, shouting, 'Mr Monty's here! He's got to speak to you about the anoboly!'

Lydia didn't correct him. She was too busy trying to fight the taste of bile that had flooded her mouth.

CHAPTER 56

CARDIFF, JULY 1841

ose followed the others out of the house and into the courtyard. Nate was securing the bolts on the black wooden gates, and when he stepped aside, there was Monty. She felt her heart jump into her mouth at the sight of him. They had spent just one afternoon together, reading, talking and trying to find the means to send Lydia home, but it might have been a lifetime for how familiar he felt now.

He smiled when he found her amongst the small crowd rushing to welcome him, but she could tell from his expression that there was something very wrong.

How do I break this news to Lydia?

Monty's question sank heavy as a sob in Rose's mind. She tried to hold his gaze as Bill and Peggy fussed around him, steering him towards the parlour.

Rose went to Lydia. She looked grey in the face, as if she already knew what he was about to say. Rose steeled herself. She had to stay calm and strong for her friend. And there was still hope that Monty's news wasn't the worst kind.

Once in the parlour, Bill and Peggy excused themselves,

shepherding Frank out of the room and closing the door firmly.

Lydia stood in front of Monty, flanked by Dilys and Rose.

'Just tell me,' she instructed.

Monty screwed up his eyes for a heartbeat. When he opened them, he sighed. 'Rose and I spent the afternoon researching the thin places using my grandmother's map. After she departed, I decided to cross-reference the thin places with the magical libraries ...' He paused and cleared his throat.

'Please, just tell me,' Lydia repeated, her voice wavering.

'Dilys spoke this morning of the anomaly that keeps your library at Pont Nefoedd hidden from magical means. As predicted, it didn't appear on the map, not even when I asked for libraries of the future.' Monty let out a slow breath, his eyes flicking to Rose and then back to Lydia.

'But then, just twenty or so minutes ago, Iggy saw this.' Monty pulled the folded map from his inside pocket and held it out. There it was, in the top right-hand corner.

Pont Nefoedd Library, May 1859 – December 1960

Lydia buckled like a puppet cut free from its strings. She would have fallen had Monty and Rose not been close enough to catch her. They steered her to a chair, and Dilys took over.

'It's only a faint, give her a few moments,' she said.

Rose tried to swallow down the sob, covering her mouth with her hands, but when Lydia's grief-stricken eyes met her own, she dropped to her knees, wrapped her arms around her friend and gave in to her own tears.

CHAPTER 57

CARDIFF, JULY 1841

Someone was speaking to her, but Lydia couldn't make out what they were saying. She could see them, leaning into her face, their lips moving slowly, deliberately, but it was as if their words were sliding away before they reached her ears.

When the room came back into focus, Lydia became aware of tiny hands stroking her forehead and a hot, wet tongue licking her dangling hand. 'Thank you,' she said to Ci Gwyn, using her now sticky hand to stroke his head, then repeated her thanks to the marmoset, who was standing on her shoulder. In other circumstances she might have felt tickled by the attention, but all she could think of was the thought that she no longer had a family to go home to. A wave of panic crested in her chest. Her breath hitched and she gasped for air.

Dilys, who she now realised was holding her other hand cupped between her own, spoke slowly. 'I am going to give you something to help with the shock. You can refuse, but know that we will have a better chance of putting things right if you are calm and clear-headed.' She waited.

Ignatius stopped his stroking and instead patted Lydia's cheek. She turned her head and looked into Dilys's dark brown eyes.

She nodded her consent. A warm, tingling sensation swept up her arm and through her body, and she was reminded of summer sunshine, the smell of freshly washed cotton sheets and the sound of children laughing. It wasn't as if the news had vanished, more that it had shrunk from the size of a planet to that of a marble. When she looked for the grief that just moments ago had been readying itself to swallow her whole, it wasn't there.

She looked around the room. Monty and Rose were staring at her. Rose's eyes were red and already puffy from crying.

'That will help take the edge off. If you feel it slipping, let me know, and I will top it up,' Dilys said. She turned her attention back to Monty. 'Now. Tell us everything again, in detail. Spare nothing.'

Monty repeated the story, and Lydia found she was able to focus on every word. When he finished, Dilys asked, 'How is the map here in 1841 even capable of knowing what has happened or is about to happen in 1960?'

'And why are the months different?' Rose put in. 'I arrived in 1841 three months before Lydia, but we left 1960 only a day apart. The map is saying something happened to the library in December 1960.'

'In this age we think of time as linear and one way. The very fact that you are both here proves that to be nonsense,' Monty said.

'And the map?' Dilys prompted impatiently.

'Forgive me, yes. From what we know, time is more malleable than our so-called scholars think. It's better to think of it as that onion I talked of earlier today. Layers upon layers of time and reality, where everything is happening all at once. So, you, Lydia, are here in 1841, but another Lydia who is still you is also in 1960, and, heavens, perhaps even 2024. Do you see?'

'We do not know that your library was raided by hunters, only that it ceased to be a library in December 1960.' Monty frowned. 'Or will cease to be a library in 1960.' He shook his head and pressed on. 'For all we know, it might have just been damaged in a flood and closed down.'

Lydia nodded, thinking of the river-fronted property that she'd called home her entire life. They had often talked about moving it one day for its own safety. Perhaps that time had come. Something dark and sinuous uncoiled in her gut, and she swallowed.

'The most important thing to hold on to, dear lady, is that reality is not fixed. Even if the very worst occurred, then that version of reality is not set in stone. There is still hope.'

Lydia tried to smile. Tried to acknowledge his kindness. She wanted to tell him that she understood how difficult it must be for him to have to impart such news. That yes, hope did indeed burn eternal. But her words were gone, consumed by the knowledge that her family were all dead. Her library destroyed. She should have known in the carriage, when she heard not the two shots that had killed Frances ricocheting in her memory but a volley of gunfire that spoke of a massacre.

CHAPTER 58

CARDIFF, JULY 1841

*L*ydia sat silently in the chair, stroking Ci Gwyn. The conversation grew in volume around her. Peggy and Bill had come back into the room at some point, she wasn't sure when. Nor, now she came to think of it, could she remember when the dog had hopped onto her lap. Dilys was still sitting at her side but was now engrossed in conversation.

Every now and then one of them would pause and ask her if she was okay. Did she want some tea? Something stronger, maybe? She smiled weakly and shook her head every time. She remembered the snow globe Hywel had bought for Maggie when she was little. It had a ballerina inside, standing en pointe, her arms and leg forever frozen in an elegant arabesque. Lydia felt as if she too were viewing the world through thick glass and water.

'Is that okay, Lydia? You should get some rest.'

'What?' Lydia asked, startled. Whatever Dilys had just said to her was lost.

Dilys smiled and tried again. 'Monty wants us to visit one of the thin places he identified from the map. It might serve as your portal home, but before we go there, we need the spell to activate it. He and Rose are going to the Elders' head-quarters to check their library, and Peggy and I are going to my friend Sophia's archive. You get some rest, and we will—'

'No!' Lydia's voice was louder than she'd intended, and everyone in the room stopped talking.

'No, thank you,' Lydia said, making an effort to sound calm and collected. 'I don't need to rest, Dilys. I need to do something that will help get me back to my family.' She said the words carefully, as if one slip of her tongue might explode them like bombs.

Dilys patted her hand and nodded, her lips pressed into a resigned smile. 'Very well, we will go to Sophia's together.' Her gaze lingered on Lydia a fraction too long for comfort. *Can she hear the screaming in my head?* Lydia wondered. She lifted Ci Gwyn and set him on the floor before standing up.

'Shall we, then?' she said, offering her hand to Dilys. The older woman nodded graciously but got to her feet without help.

'I expect it will be nice to see your old friend again,' Lydia said, desperate to make conversation and persuade Dilys that she wasn't about to fall apart.

'It would have been the greatest joy of my life,' Dilys said quietly, 'but my Sophia passed many moons ago. Her son, Laurent, lives in the house now, and he will be far from pleased to see me. With any luck,' she added, glancing at the mantel clock, 'he will be at his club, gambling away his mother's money and earning the reputation he so richly deserves.'

Too late, Lydia remembered Dilys telling them about the woman she had been companion to. The woman whose death had predicated Dilys's return to Hay-on-Wye. 'My Sophia,' she had said. Lydia didn't have time to think on it – they had a spell to find.

CHAPTER 59

CARDIFF, JULY 1841

It was another hour before the gates opened again. Thorne left the bar, pushing through the crowd. He emerged on the pavement just as a small, two-horse carriage appeared from the undertaker's yard. He staggered back when the scent hit him. Old roses mixed with a touch of orange blossom. He clenched his fists at his sides as the adrenaline coursed through him, the scent near intoxicating.

He walked casually, careful not to look directly at the carriage. He swept his gaze over it and noticed that it was the same man in the driver's seat. He had a thick, peaty magical smell to him. Thorne snorted and spat on the floor, ridding himself of the offending scent and lifting his head to find the other one, the one that drifted from the inside of the carriage. The one that smelled like more money than he'd know what to do with.

He followed the carriage through the narrow streets. The going was slow to begin with, but it picked up speed as it joined the main road. He thought of the fine horse he'd left stabled in the inn and cursed under his breath. He cast around and quickly spotted a cart pointing in the same direction. Affecting his most genteel manner, he pointed to his knee and asked the owner if he might hop on the back for a few blocks in exchange for a fee. After having to explain that blocks just meant streets, the carter nodded.

Sending up a silent prayer of thanks, Thorne climbed into the flat bed of the cart, leaning side on so that he could watch the carriage ahead. The cloying scent of buttercups caressed his nose, and he turned on instinct, following the smell. The buttery ribbon flowing through the ether led not to a pretty young woman as he'd expected but to an overweight young man with pimples on his face and an unmanly number of ruffles on his shirt. Thorne ground his teeth. If he had the time, he might return for this one just to rid the Lord's green Earth of his kind.

The cart jerked, jolting Thorne from his reverie. He looked up and stifled a roar. The carriage up ahead had vanished. 'Stop!' he bellowed, already preparing to leap down.

As soon as the cart had slowed, he jumped off and began to run, the indignant shouts of the unpaid carter following him.

CHAPTER 60

CARDIFF, JULY 1841

*R*ose could barely believe that she was alone again with Monty – and Ignatius, of course, but the little marmoset looked thrilled too. He sat on the seat between them in the carriage, gazing from one to the other and hopping from foot to foot.

Rose's new sense was going haywire, her mind full of the questions she knew Monty was desperate to ask, tangled around her own. Her mind felt cacophonous, but she couldn't remember feeling happier in her life. She knew it was crazy, but every cell in her body was screaming that she had just met the love of her life. How could that be when said love had been born, she estimated, nearly one hundred and fifty years before she'd entered the world? She had no idea, but life was a strange and mercurial thing.

She looked at Monty, and there it was. The expression that told her she wasn't alone in how she felt. How could two people say so much without uttering a single word? It had been the same this afternoon. They'd spent hours reading and researching the portals that existed in the so-called, 'thin places.' Passing each other books, standing close enough to touch, but neither of them daring to. Rose grinned, her cheeks straining with the breadth of it. Monty smiled back, and his face lost what seemed to be several lifetimes of pain.

Ignatius, clearly frustrated with the lack of verbal communication, pulled Rose's finger. She yielded her hand and allowed it to be steered by the monkey to the place he had been occupying on the carriage seat. He then repeated the action with Monty. Rose giggled. Monty made to speak, but Ignatius tutted at him.

When their fingers remained an inch apart, the monkey shook his head irritably and clicked his tongue rapidly. All subtlety was abandoned when he took to hopping up and down on the back of Monty's hand, screeching. Rose laughed and inched her hand towards Monty's. Their little fingers touched, and she heard him catch his breath. Had he felt it too? The charge that felt like happy lightning?

Rose glanced at his face and saw him staring open-mouthed at their hands. Ignatius leapt away and Rose slid her hand over Monty's before lacing her fingers with his. She had the overwhelming sense that they were blending into each other and that they now shared a hand that was strangely more than the sum of their parts.

When Monty looked at her, there were tears in his grey eyes, but his smile was so pure, so bright, it could have illuminated the entire city. *So, this is magic*, Rose thought.

* * *

THE ELDERS' archive was nothing like Rose had expected. While the house was grand, a three-story townhouse with steep steps leading to a shiny black door, it didn't look anywhere near large enough.

Climbing out of the carriage, she threw a questioning look at Bill. He nodded and pointed at the door.

'That's it alright. I'll be here waiting,' Bill said, already pulling a book from his pocket.

Rose and Monty thanked him, and Rose turned her attention to the horses, giving them each a pat and a word of thanks. She heard Monty call her name and hurried to the steps. When she was only halfway up, the front door flew open and a thin, hooded figure rushed out and barrelled into her. They both wobbled, but Rose's footing was firmer. She grabbed the figure's forearms and felt bones as fine as a bird's beneath the thin coat sleeves.

Rose winced at the touch but held on, despite the cacophony of questions thundering in her head and the feel of a slow-rolling static charge biting at her fingers. And then it was over.

'Begging your pardon, miss,' stammered a young female voice. She sounded terrified.

Rose opened her mouth to ask what was the matter, but the girl was already at the bottom of the steps, her dark coat pulled tightly around her thin frame and the scarf Rose had taken for a hood shrouding her face. Rose stared after her.

'And what have I told you about using the—' The shout from the door was bitten off when its owner, a broad, red-cheeked woman in an apron, saw Rose and Monty on the steps.

Rose scanned the street for the girl, but she was already out of sight. The fear that rolled off her had been palpable – Rose had felt it in her marrow when she grabbed her arms. She sighed. The girl was gone now, and they had work to do.

CHAPTER 61

CARDIFF, JULY 1841

Thorne could smell nothing but the stench of buttercups as he ran. Damn the boy! He sprinted back to a side street they'd just passed. Had the carriage turned while he had been distracted? When he reached the mouth of it, he cursed again. There was no carriage in sight. Retracing his steps back to the main road, he stopped, pulled a rag from his pocket and bent over to blow his nose. When he straightened, sucking in the air as he did so, he smiled as the scent of orange blossoms and summer returned.

By the time he turned into the next street, he was panting with the exertion and excitement that only came with the thrill of the hunt. The scents were so strong now, and their colours ribboned in the air like a map only he could see. He grinned. The carriage stood parked on the opposite side of the street. The tall man who had been hammering on the undertaker's gate was already at the open front door of a smart townhouse, a young woman at his side. The man whistled quietly. *Oh, yes*, he thought. He was about to be a rich man.

Straightening, he continued down the street, scenting the

air and watching as the ribbons of colour dimmed like fading mist in sunlight. When he drew level with the carriage, he bent to tie his bootlace. The carriage driver with the peaty-smelling magic was already reading a book.

Stealing a glance at the house the couple had disappeared into, he caught his breath. His heart thumped in his chest as he doubted the evidence of his eyes. There, fluttering in the air above the front door, were the faint traces of not one colour but dozens. A kaleidoscope of jewelled tones, like streamers in a parade. He lifted his nose to the air and rocked back as the scent of a thousand flowers in full bloom hit him. The Lord was surely smiling on him today. Leading him here with this new discovery only to deliver to him the witch he'd been commissioned to find.

He sent up a prayer of thankfulness, but his lips stilled when he noticed that there was something wrong with the colours. They were fading quickly, as was the way, but the edges of the trail were blunt, as if someone had taken scissors to it halfway up the steps. He gritted his teeth, disappointment quickly morphing into anger. Little bitch had used magic to hide herself. She was taunting him. Laughing at him.

He stood up, needing to move his body before his rage exploded from him. He set off down the road, fists at his side and chest heaving. By the time he reached the end of the street he was calm again. What's more, he had a plan.

CHAPTER 62

CARDIFF, JULY 1841

*A*t the Elder's archive, the housekeeper was full of apologies for her outburst which only redoubled when, finally pausing for breath, Monty was able to take the opportunity to give his name. The poor woman turned an alarming shade of red that bordered on purple, but they were eventually ushered into the library and told to make themselves at home. Somewhat belatedly, Rose thought, the housekeeper told them that the Elder they were here to see was out on business but expected home at any moment.

Rose stood surveying the library.

'Is this it?' she asked Monty, looking around what in other houses in the row might be a formal dining room large enough to seat a dozen people. In place of a table, however, there was a small desk and one row of bookcases against the longest wall.

Granted, the collection at Aber had been the largest in Wales, but what she stared at now could have fit into the office there. Except that the library at Aber was gone. The realisation hit like a blow. Rose closed her eyes and willed away the bubble of grief forming behind her ribs.

'Rose?' Monty's voice was low and soft.

'I'm okay. Just remembering my library,' Rose said, smiling as she realised that the sight of him already made her feel calmer.

'Tell me about it,' he said gently.

Rose hesitated, remembering Dilys's warning, but decided that describing a library wasn't life-altering knowledge. 'It was huge. Probably as big as the whole of the Chapels' house, yard, stables, everything put together. It was in the basement of an old manor house.'

Rose laughed when she saw Monty's eyes light up. She pressed on. 'The office was quite small, though, about a third of the size of this room. When I started my apprenticeship, it was winter, and me and Frances would huddle around the fire in there to do my lessons.' She swallowed as the mention of Frances's name loosed the bubble of grief in her chest.

'Happy memories,' Monty said softly.

'She shouldn't have died like that,' Rose said, her voice wavering.

Monty took half a step towards her, then stopped. Rose heard the question in his head and answered before he could voice it.

'I've no need to forgive you, Monty,' she said, stepping forward and tentatively wrapping her arms around him, careful not to lean on his left side, where Ignatius was hiding in his breast pocket.

Monty loosed a breath, his body relaxing under her touch, and after just a moment's hesitation, he wrapped his arms around her. She drank in the scent of him. Old paper, ink and dust and, inexplicably, sunlight and tea roses. The sensation of their bodies blurring into one swept over her again. It was like finally coming home.

She felt Monty's chest heave and looked up to see his face screwed up in what seemed to be pain.

'What's wrong?' she asked, not daring to break the contact between them.

Monty looked at her, the expression falling from his face like a windblown petal. He shook his head slowly. 'I was just cursing the gods for sending you back under these circumstances. When we have so little time,' he said. Rose saw the sorrow swirl in his storm-grey eyes, and she shook her head.

The sound of muffled voices from the hallway gave them just enough time to spring apart and focus their attention on the books on the table before the door burst open.

She turned and saw an unusually short, rotund man in a berry-coloured waistcoat that was straining at the buttons. He was bald save for a ring of fuzzy grey hair that connected to a fine pair of mutton-chop sideburns.

'Mr Montgomery!' the man exclaimed, and Rose marvelled at how he was able to inject both reverence and surprise into just two words.

'We are honoured by your visit, sir. Honoured. Deeply honoured,' he said.

Rose had been practising her Victorian demeanour since she'd arrived. It had been one of Dilys's first lessons after commenting that young people from 1960 apparently wore every thought on their faces. This, Dilys assured her, would simply not do in 1841. Rose caught herself just in time and stopped her eyebrows heading northwards as the man bowed, actually bowed, to Monty.

Monty smiled awkwardly, glancing at Rose and giving her a roll of the eyes that was definitely more 1960s than 1840s while the man's eyes lingered on the rug they were all standing on.

'Mr Potts,' Monty said, gesturing to Rose, 'I would like you to meet ...' He hesitated, and Rose knew at once that, of course, he didn't know her surname. Interrupting him to supply it wouldn't look good, so she schooled her face into a look of polite neutrality and metaphorically crossed her fingers.

'I can't share her family name for reasons I'm sure you'll understand, but Rose is a visiting scholar. I trust you'll extend to her your full support.'

Nicely played, Rose thought.

It was her turn to be on the receiving end of a bow, granted not quite as low as the one Monty had received, but it was a mark of respect she'd not often seen afforded to women in this age. When Mr Potts lifted his head, she extended her hand. He clasped her gloved fingers briefly and pressed a breath of a kiss to her knuckles before straightening and looking at her properly for the first time.

'Madam, it is an honour to welcome you to our humble library. I am at your service,' Mr Potts said, his voice gruff as an army general's but his tone polite to the point of deference.

Rose heard his questions tumbling around in his mind. *Where are you from? What powers do you have? How have I not heard of you before now? Are you a Tellerman too? What might that mean for the community? A long-lost Tellerman cousin, perhaps? Could it mean that the knowledge will not end with dear Mr Monty?*

Rose smiled as she heard the endearment in the last question. Mr Potts, she decided, was a good egg.

'The pleasure is mine, Mr Potts,' she said, with a nod she'd also been practising with Dilys.

'Please, call me Harold, if you will.'

'Harold then,' Rose said with a nod and a polite smile.

When she caught Monty smiling at her, she knew she'd done okay. Such pride in his eyes. Such—

Harold interrupted the thought by asking, 'Is there anything in the collection of particular interest, Mr Montgomery, sir?'

Monty put his hand on his shoulder. 'Harold, please. How many times? Please call me Monty or else I'll think my father's ghost is at my back.' He smiled kindly at the man.

'Forgive me,' Harold said. 'Old habits and such like. I will try, Mr—' He bit off the word. 'I will try my very best, Monty,' he said with a decisive nod.

'Rose is researching the life and works of Apollonius of Tyana and ...' Monty stopped and shot Rose a sheepish smile. 'Forgive me, dear lady. I should let you speak for yourself.'

'Not at all,' she replied with a measured smile. 'I am happy for you to provide the précis.' The look she exchanged with Monty made her fingers tingle. How could they know each other this well when, until yesterday, they were strangers?

Harold pulled a face that told Rose that his hopes of delivering something of value to his revered Mr Monty had already been dashed.

'On that fellow, sir, we are sorely lacking,' Harold said, striding off to examine a bookcase. 'I do not need to tell you that his works didn't survive. What we do know of the man's work comes courtesy of the Tellerman knowledge, but you will have that already.' Harold's voice dropped to the point that he was all but mumbling to himself as he continued to scan the bookcase.

Rose saw the moment that inspiration struck. Harold, until now adopting the librarian's lilt, his body bowed to the side, head cocked to scan the spines in front of him, jolted back to his full height.

'Oh!' he exclaimed. 'It is a tangential line of inquiry, but I think we do have a grimoire from a witch who wrote a thesis on portals between worlds. Lots of talk about strata and layers in the earth, so a touch too taken with old Apollonius, if you ask me, but I fear it is the closest thing we have. Ah! Here it is!'

'Marvellous!' Monty said, striding over to join Harold,

who held a small leather-bound book, already open. The other man didn't appear to have heard him, lost in his reading. His lips moved as he hovered his finger over the page.

For reasons Rose couldn't articulate, she didn't share Monty's enthusiasm. Was it really going to be this easy? Perhaps it was. She thought of Lydia and felt the emotion catch in her throat at the possibility that her lovely family might not be safe at home, waiting for her, after all.

Monty interrupted her train of thought by holding up the grimoire in front of her. 'Shall we?' he asked, gesturing back to the small reading table they'd passed on the way in.

Rose smiled politely and followed him.

'There are also these,' Harold said a few moments later, placing two more books on the edge of the small table. 'I think the Lovett grimoire is the best of the bunch. I'll leave you to your research, but please, if you need anything at all, please ring.' He pointed to a bell pull near the door.

Monty and Rose thanked him and settled down to read.

CHAPTER 63

CARDIFF, JULY 1841

*A*fter just twenty minutes Rose and Monty had skimmed and rejected the pair of possibles and were ready to read the Lovett grimoire. Although a book about magic, it wasn't a magical text in the sense of being sentient. Part notebook, part journal, the grimoire was a witch's most precious possession, and Rose wondered what had happened to L Lovett. She pushed the thought aside to focus on the task in hand. When craning their necks from opposite sides of the table proved to be too awkward, they moved their chairs side by side to make the reading easier.

While the reading angle was infinitely improved, being in such close proximity to Monty was a huge distraction. Rose could feel the energy pouring from him. His summer scent enveloped her, and she could barely see the page, let alone read it. The inches between them felt like a canyon, and every cell in her body ached to touch him. Beside her, Monty seemed frozen, his eyes on the book but his lips pressed together in a hard line.

'I can't do this,' Rose whispered.

The look of horror on Monty's face felt like a slap. 'No,

no, no,' she said quickly, reaching up to press her hand to his cheek. 'I meant I can't sit here with this gulf between us.' She felt the relief that washed over him as if it were her own.

They both glanced down and then laughed at the matchbox-sized gap between their chairs. Rose moved first, shuffling her chair so that it butted up against Monty's. Then she shifted so that their hips and thighs were touching. Under the table, Monty's foot found hers. She hooked her boot around his ankle, a small patch of her stockinged leg touching his. She then held out her right hand, into which he laced the long fingers of his left hand, and finally, all was right with the world.

He smiled at her. 'You know this would scandalise half of the civilised world, don't you. Two strangers, holding hands. No chaperone in sight.'

'We are anything but strangers,' Rose said, feeling the truth of the words she hadn't planned on uttering.

Monty swallowed hard, but his eyes, serious now, never left hers. He nodded. 'We remember you,' he said quietly, his eyes on hers but somehow unfocused.

He looked like he was about to say more, but Rose shook her head. 'All that matters is now.'

After a brief pause, Monty smiled at her. His nod was reluctant, but she was glad to move on. She couldn't explain what she was feeling either, so, hearing Frances's wisdom echoing in her ears, she decided to focus on the task in hand.

She squeezed Monty's hand, then tore her eyes away from his and began to read.

It took them close to three hours to find the spell. The book was small, the handwriting tightly packed, as if the writer was trying to condense her life's work into the only book she would ever possess. Following the script became easier the more they read, but in places it was still close to impossible to decipher. The spell was buried in a long paragraph describing the witch's attempts to revive a starling. Rose squealed when she found it, remembering too late how such outbursts would be viewed in the Victorian age.

Monty gasped. 'That's it. That's it!' he cried in a stage whisper. 'She used it to send the bird back in time before it hit the barn wall, but the principle is just the same. On that, Apollonius is very clear indeed. Rose, my love, I think we have the means to send you—'

Rose pressed a finger to his lips, cutting off his last word. She shook her head, not able to meet his eye. Standing abruptly, but not letting go of his hand, she said, 'Let's get this to Lydia. She will be beyond thrilled.'

Monty got slowly to his feet. Rose heard the question he was about to ask and tried to talk over it.

'Her family is so lovely, Monty. She has a husband called Hywel, who owns a bakery. He's a sweet man. Big as a bear, but kind, you know. Kind eyes. Gruff voice, probably make a good baritone, and good with their daughter too. She's an apprentice like me, but she's Lydia's apprentice. In their library. I didn't get to see it though, which is a shame as I would have loved to – and did I tell you about the cat? A Siamese called, of all things, Boudicca. It suits her too as she's quite feisty. She didn't like me, which is horrible to think about, but I'm hoping it was the spell fragments and not me. I mean, that's not a good sign, is it, to be disliked by a cat says something of one's character and—'

'You know you can't stay here, Rose, don't you?' Monty said, his voice a whisper.

Rose felt the words like a kick. She would have fallen back on her chair had Monty not pulled her into his arms. They were so close now that Rose swore she could feel his heart beating. While her mind explained the reasoning in a calm, rational voice, her body screamed that she was finally home and exactly where she was meant to be.

She kept her eyes down. Peeking out from Monty's inner lapel pocket, Ignatius stared at her with huge, sad eyes before retreating again. Monty lifted her chin gently, and what she saw in his face broke her heart. There were tears in his eyes, and he looked so pained that she would have given anything to take it away. She'd carry that pain for a lifetime if it would spare him another moment of it.

Defiance surged through her. 'But why? Explain why, Monty. I'm listening.'

'Because, my love, nature has an order, a way of doing things, and you and Lydia, you are breaking her rules.'

'We didn't ask to be here. We didn't ask for any of this, so how can we be acting against nature? If nature and magic are one, then we are exactly where we are meant to be! How can that possibly be unnatural?' Anger was better than pain, and Rose found that once she started, she couldn't stop.

'You are as far away from unnatural as it is possible to be,' Monty said, reaching up to stroke her cheek.

Rose pulled away, unable to bear the tenderness of it. How could a man with the wisdom of ages be so stupid? Or was this just his way of making sure that whatever they had, whatever this was, it stayed temporary? That thought sliced through her as surely as any blade. She clenched her teeth. She would not cry.

'You think I should go back to my own time,' Rose said, only just remembering to lower her voice at the last moment. 'You want me to go back,' she hissed.

'No! Yes! I mean, I think it is the only outcome nature will afford us. The starling in the grimoire. The witch found it dead the next day, which suggests that nature doesn't take well to mere mortals tinkering with her plan.'

Monty stepped towards her, his hands outstretched. 'I would love nothing more than to spend my every waking moment with you, Rose. But if that meant risking your life?' He shook his head miserably. 'I cannot do it.'

'That's a rubbish answer,' Rose snapped. 'I've been here for three months and I've never felt stronger. That starling could have died of anything. Hell, it might not even have been the same bird! If you don't want us to be—' Her voice cracked as the anger gave way to pain again.

Monty pulled her into his arms, cradling her head. She marvelled at how she somehow fit perfectly into the hollow beneath his chin. Like they were made to fit like this. He shushed her, and she was glad not to say the words.

'I would give my last breath to spend even a day with you, Rose. But I will not wager your life on the hope that there is a plan we are not party to,' Monty said, holding her close. 'You are too precious.'

The clock in the hallway chimed, and Rose bit back her reply as she pulled away, ignoring the ache in her chest as her body screamed in complaint at the distance now between them.

'We had better get the grimoire back to the house,' she said flatly.

CHAPTER 64

CARDIFF, JULY 1841

*I*t was dark when they eventually emerged from
the house. It had taken an age to extricate themselves from Harold, who, Rose thought, was clearly lonely.
Thankfully, the old grandfather clock had come to their aid
as they hovered politely near the front door, the nine bongs
giving them the excuse they needed to finally interrupt the
talkative Elder and say their goodbyes.

On the doorstep, the door reluctantly closed at their
backs, Rose scanned the wide street but saw no sign of Bill
and the carriage. An uneasy feeling snaked in her gut, and
she might have reached for Monty's hand for comfort had
she not still been so furious with him.

Beside her, Monty seemed to be uneasy too. Motioning
for Rose to stay where she was, he walked slowly down the
front steps. The street lamps were lit, moths already ringing
the glass around the gentle orange glow of gas light. At the
top of the road, Rose could just see the lamp lighter coaxing
the last of them into flame.

She was still hurt by what Monty had said. She wanted to
stay mad at him, but something wasn't right. She could feel it

in her bones. Bill had been so insistent about waiting for them. She hadn't asked him if he had magic – it wasn't polite – but she wondered now if he was just being protective or whether he was more capable of defending them should the need arise. He would wait, he'd said, no matter how long they were.

Something shifted in the air, and unable to bear it any longer, Rose scuttled down the steps and joined Monty on the pavement, standing as close to him as she could.

'I think we'd better wait inside,' Monty said, placing a hand lightly on the small of her back.

Rose had barely taken a step when she was in the air, hurtling backwards. She slammed into the wrought-iron railings behind her before landing hard, bottom first, on the hard stone steps.

Rose looked up to see Monty sprawled face down on the pavement, his feet scrabbling to find purchase, his hands like claws, his face contorted in rage as some unseen force pinned him to the spot. He roared, the sound of a wounded lion hell bent on tearing out a throat.

A man wearing a wide-brimmed hat sauntered across the road towards them. He was smiling like a child on Christmas morning.

Behind her, Rose heard the front door open. Harold made a noise that was part scream, part gasp at the scene that greeted him. The man in the hat looked up and laughed. He flicked his hand, and Rose saw Harold fly back into the house. There was silence for a beat, followed by the shattering of glass and a shriek of pain.

'No!' Rose screamed as she dragged herself up the wrought-iron railing. The pain in her spine was close to blinding, but she would not let innocent people come to harm as they tried to protect her. Focusing on the pain in her back, she imagined hurling it at the man in the hat as she screamed at him, 'Nooooo!'

Someone cried out, but her vision was already fading. She felt her legs slip on the steps, her arms no longer able to support her weight on the railings. Another lance of white-hot pain shot through her spine and the black spots that had been swimming in her vision merged, pulling her into darkness.

'Rose! Rose!' Monty's voice was tight with panic as he tapped her cheek.

She opened her eyes and the world flooded back to her, Monty's beautiful, angst-ridden face at the centre of it.

'I'm okay. Go check on Harold,' she said, wincing as she tried to find a comfortable position to sit in. There wasn't one. She could already feel the base of her spine swelling against the fabric of her underwear.

'I am unharmed, dear lady.'

Rose turned, gritting her teeth as her spine objected to the movement. She let out a sigh of relief when she saw the Elder walking down the steps, rubbing the back of his head.

There came the sound of thundering hooves on cobblestones, and then Bill was there, throwing himself out of the driver's seat and rushing towards them.

'The blighter's made a run for it,' Harold said. 'Quick thinking on the counter-attack, Mr Monty.'

'Are you hurt?' Bill cut in, looking from Rose to Monty, to Harold and back again.

'Just a bump on the head,' Harold said dismissively. 'Poor Miss Rose is injured though. How on earth did this happen?'

'It's my fault,' Bill growled. He shook his head. 'I fell for the oldest trick in the book. A young lad came rushing up, said there was a horse down in the next street, owner all for calling the slaughter men rather than help it up.' He sighed.

'A lie to lure you away?' Harold asked.

Bill nodded miserably. 'I'm sorry. I should have been here.'

'While we're apologising,' Monty said, addressing Harold, 'I'm sorry, but he grabbed the grimoire before he fled. I am so desperately sorry, sir. It was in my hand as I fell.'

Harold's face hardened into a look of stoic resolve. 'Not your fault, Mr Montgomery. It is, of course, regrettable, but it is a minor volume in the collection and of very little value.'

Rose bit back her response. If only Harold knew that they had in fact found the very thing they'd been looking for – a portal spell to send Lydia home.

'Was it the same man who attacked Dil and Lydia at St Brides?' Bill asked.

'He matched the description, so I assume he must be,' Rose said.

'Come on, Harold,' Bill said. 'I'll see you back safe inside before I get these two home.'

It was Rose's turn to inspect Monty for any damage. He had a nasty-looking scrape across his chin from where he'd landed on the pavement, and when he lifted his hand to brush her hair from her face, she saw a second graze across his palm.

Rose leaned into Monty's chest and closed her eyes. Ci Gwyn had been so sure that the man who killed Mother Pennywell had been looking for a person. The man who had just attacked them certainly fitted the description, but why had he stolen a book?

Monty's words slammed back into her memory like a wrecking ball. *'It was in my hand when I fell.'*

'Ignatius!' she shrieked. He had been in Monty's pocket! It all happened so quickly there would have been no time for the tiny marmoset to have escaped, and while Monty wasn't a big man, his weight would have surely crushed—

'Rose!' Monty said, holding open his jacket. Tucked in the

inside pocket, Ignatius, though from his expression clearly unhappy, was alive and well and definitely not squished. He held out his hand, and when Rose reached towards him, planted a kiss on her fingertip.

'Oh, thank God!' Rose exclaimed, sniffing.

'You can't crush a spell,' Monty whispered as he closed his jacket.

Rose swallowed a sob and made a garbled hiccupping sound. Monty smiled at her and handed her a handkerchief.

Bill returned and crouched down beside them. 'I take it you found something, then?'

'We did,' Monty said, sounding close to incredulous. 'If I was a betting man, I would have put the odds at a million to one, but ...' His eyes drifted to Rose. 'We had a stroke of remarkable luck.'

'There was a spell in the book to open a portal,' Rose whispered, allowing herself a smile. Lydia was going to be thrilled.

Bill sighed and shook his head. 'I'm not sure what's worse. Not finding it or finding it and losing it,' he said ruefully.

'But we read the spell,' Rose said, failing to see the problem. 'And Monty retains anything he reads, so he can just write the spell down when we get back.'

Bill and Monty exchanged a look, and, with a sinking heart, Rose realised that there was something she was missing.

'The book was imbued, Rose,' Monty said with a sigh. 'It means that a tiny part of the spell was woven into its pages. The spell in my memory is useless without it. I'm sorry. This is all my fault. I should have taken more precautions.'

'The only person to blame is that hateful man who attacked us,' Rose said, feeling the fury build in her chest again.

'Come on, let's get home before anything else happens,' Bill said, looking up and down the street.

Rose could feel her back continue to swell, the nerve endings screaming even while she sat. Setting her jaw against the pain, she allowed Monty and Bill to help her to her feet and down the last few steps to the pavement. Sweat trickled down her neck and back.

The carriage steps might have been mountains for all her faith in her ability to climb them. She swallowed, trying to think. Monty touched her shoulder and raised an eyebrow. He was getting good at asking questions without speaking.

'Yes, please,' she said.

He lifted her gently, one arm wrapped around her back, the other scooping up her legs behind the knees. The nerves in her back screamed. Bill helped them into the carriage, a steadying hand at Monty's back as he negotiated the steps he couldn't see beneath the folds of Rose's skirts.

Monty made to lay Rose on the seat, but she whispered in his ear, 'No. I want to sit like this. With you, please.'

She looked at him. His face was in shadow, but she felt his smile like a warm glow that spread through her own body. He lowered them both gently, holding her to his chest. Rose sighed.

'Do you feel it too?' she asked. 'It's like we're two snowmen, melting together in the sunshine to make one big puddle of water.'

She felt Monty's breath catch. 'I would have preferred a more cheerful simile,' he said, his breath a warm caress in her hair. She could tell that he was trying to lighten the mood, but she was done with pretending. There was so little time. Anything could have happened to him just now.

'But yes, Rose. I feel that too. I felt it the moment you walked into my library. You felt like the memory I've been searching for my entire life.'

As the carriage pulled off, Rose winced, the movement jarring her back and sending what felt like bolts of furious lightning up her spine.

'Are you—' Monty began, looking down at her face in the darkness.

Rose cut him off, first finding his neck with her hand and then pulling his face towards her so that she could kiss him. He only hesitated for a heartbeat, propriety lost to desire and the magic of knowing that no power on the Earth was ever going to separate them now.

CHAPTER 65

CARDIFF, JULY 1841

*T*horne didn't stop running until he was back on the main street. Exertion was usually a good way of dealing with his rage when there wasn't an unnatural to vent his fury on, but it wasn't helping today. He ducked into an alley, bending double in the darkness to catch his breath.

'Bitch!' he roared, taking aim at a stack of wooden crates, his kick sending them skittering across the cobbled floor into the filth he could smell in the darkest corners.

Eve's sin was in them all, like rot in an apple, ruining the world for good, God-fearing men like him.

It was only then that he remembered the book in his hand. He'd had to duck to avoid the spell and had only just shielded himself in time. The book had been at his feet, and he'd grabbed it instinctively.

He sniffed the cover, and the sickly-sweet scent of lavender and honey caught in his throat. He recoiled. He should burn it. Wipe it from the earth like the stain it was. He gritted his teeth and exhaled slowly through his nose. The Lord was testing him right enough, but he was also a god of love. Of compassion. Thorne straightened up and wiped his nose with his sleeve. He would follow the Lord's example and extend some of his compassion to himself. With thoughts of a hot meal and maybe the company of a whore in need of some Christian education, he tossed the book into the alley.

CHAPTER 66

CARDIFF, JULY 1841

'It makes no sense, though,' Peggy said, throwing her hands in the air as she paced around the parlour, her tone one of utter exasperation.

Lydia tried to stifle a yawn but failed. They had been sitting here for hours now, ever since Bill had stormed through the front door, Monty in his wake carrying an injured Rose in his arms like the hero in some romance novel.

With Rose lying propped up on the chaise longue and Dilys in the only armchair in the room, everyone else was sitting on dining chairs. Monty had positioned his as close to Rose as possible and could barely tear his eyes away from her. Ignatius had abandoned him for Rose and lounged on her shoulder, absently twisting loose strands of her hair as he followed the conversation, wide-eyed as only a marmoset could be.

Rose's newfound healing ability worked more slowly on herself than others, but she was looking more herself. The colour was returning to her face, and Lydia fancied that she didn't wince as much when she shifted position.

While the initial panic over Rose's injury had subsided, they were still at sixes and sevens over the motive behind this most recent attack.

'Nobody's suggesting it makes any sense, Peg,' Bill said wearily, 'but we can only go on the evidence we have. Ci Gwyn said this Thorne character was looking for a person.'

Lydia glanced down at the dog lying asleep on Dilys's lap and smiled as his lip twitched as he dreamed.

Bill pressed on. 'Who's to say that this man even has a single motive? It wouldn't be the first time we've encountered someone willing to trade in people rather than things.'

Monty blanched at that and reached for Rose's hand.

'I think he was looking for me,' Rose said quietly, as some of her newly returned colour drained from her cheeks.

When nobody answered, Dilys tutted. 'We have been so consumed by the events of the last few days that we have forgotten where we started from.'

When again nobody spoke, Dilys huffed. 'Rose arrived in Hay-on-Wye just over three months ago. Then, less than a week ago, Lydia arrives. We make plans to travel here but have to bring them forward because—'

'Of me,' Lydia said. 'He's looking for us both,' she added, her eyes on Rose. 'That's why Thorne attacked me in St Brides, and now Rose. Ci Gwyn said Thorne was going on about something unnatural. Someone that had upset the balance of nature. Well, two women out of their own timeline should do that, surely.'

'Poppycock!' Dilys said with a snort. 'You are both here,' she added, looking pointedly at Rose, 'because magic decided you needed to be here. In this time. In this place. Magic does not make mistakes.'

Lydia couldn't miss the glance that Rose aimed at Monty. It looked as if Dilys had just handed her the card to win the hand. Monty's face softened and a tiny smile tugged at his lips. Was Lydia imagining it, or was that the faintest of nods? Whatever was passing between the couple, because that was as clear as the nose on your face too, would have to wait.

Peggy groaned. 'So why steal a book then, Dil?'

'I don't know, Peg. Perhaps he thought it would help in some way,' Dilys suggested.

Peggy blanched and went to the window. 'You think he's watching us?' she said as she fussed with the curtains, making sure there were no gaps.

Bill let out an exasperated breath. 'Well, that stands to reason, love, doesn't it? Either he followed us from St Brides or he knows the location of every magical house in Cardiff and just happened to run into Rose and Monty tonight.'

'There's no call for sarcasm, William,' Peggy snapped.

'Maybe he's an opportunist and just took the book once he knew he couldn't fight Monty,' Rose said, smiling up at the man in question.

Monty smiled back, but then frowned. 'Don't you mean Bill?'

Rose shook her head. 'No, Bill didn't arrive until a few moments later. It was you who warded him off with a spell, wasn't it?'

'Not me, my love,' Monty said. 'His magic had me pinned to the floor until he came under fire and fled. Only then was I released.'

Bill was shaking his head. 'Rose is right, I didn't get there in time. It must have been Harold.'

Rose frowned, but Dilys was on her feet, a sleepy-looking Ci Gwyn already curled up on the seat she had just lowered him onto.

'There is no more we can do tonight,' she announced.

'There will be a council meeting in the morning. We will know more then,' Bill said. 'But for now, can I suggest that we all get some rest.'

Lydia got gratefully to her feet. She was bone-weary and felt sick to her core. She hoped whatever Dilys had given her earlier for her panic wouldn't wear off in the night. She was certain that functioning at any level would be almost impossible without magical help. All she had to do was stay calm until she could figure out how to get back to the 1960 where her family might still be alive and well.

'If it's all the same to you, Monty,' Peggy said, 'I think it safer if you stop with us tonight.'

Monty looked about to protest, but Peggy jumped in and added, 'Besides, I don't like the thought of my Bill taking the horses out again this late, so it would be a kindness to us if you'd stop, please.'

Lydia mumbled her goodnights and headed for the door. She had the vague sense that she was missing something, but she was too exhausted to think about it.

CHAPTER 67

CARDIFF, JULY 1841

It took Rose a few moments to orient herself. There was buttery sunlight spilling in around the curtains and a warm breeze that brought with it the smell of the sea, but curiously, not the stench of the city. But it was the scent of tea roses and long summer days that made a grab for her heart. She gasped, the memory of the previous night's events flooding back to her.

Lying beside her, his sleeping face the picture of contentment, was Monty. She bit her lip to stop herself from reaching over to kiss him. Who knew when he had last found the peace of sleep – she wouldn't deny him that, no matter the heat that was steadily building in her core.

The memories of the previous night washed over her. Dilys, closing the parlour door. Bill and Peggy smiling wistfully at them. While, admittedly, Rose and Monty had done nothing to hide their feelings for one another, they'd not intended to broadcast them either.

Dilys had pulled up a chair and sat in front of them. 'I met the love of my life thirty years ago. We faced many challenges, just as you do now. We made mistakes. We rowed.

Sometimes furiously. But there is one thing that we got right. We didn't waste a second of the time we had together. Not a moment of it. Only death parted us, and in the years since, my greatest comfort has been the knowledge that we didn't wait. We didn't let propriety or custom or anyone else's rules get in the way of our love. And if you will forgive the bluntness that my age affords, nor should you.'

Monty had reached for Rose's hand, and she'd heard his question. It rang in her mind now like a joyful bell, mixed up with the new memories they had made together until dawn had broken and they'd fallen into an exhausted sleep.

'As an Elder,' Bill said, 'I can of course hand-fast you, if that's what you want, but to be clear, it matters not a jot to us. There is no judgement in this house, only joy in the face of love.'

Rose had only dimly registered the lack of pain in her spine as she'd jumped to her feet, pulling Monty to standing. As Dilys and Bill stepped away, Monty had rested his forehead against hers and held her face gently in his long fingers. Rose placed her hands over his.

'You really mean to stay, don't you,' he said, his eyes searching hers.

Rose hadn't answered out loud. She didn't need to. She knew he knew, so just raised her eyebrows at him.

'You must understand, Rose, I am almost penniless. I am twice cursed, three times if you count my terrible housekeeper, and in most normal ways, I will make the worst possible match for you.' He swallowed hard before continuing. 'We are already bound to each other by a force that, I confess, I am at a loss to name. But if this is what you want, I will marry you joyfully and with my heart bursting with love.' Monty's eyes were shining in the little cave they'd made of gentle hands and falling hair.

Minutes later, they stood in the garden, in the moonlight,

with Dilys, Peggy, Ci Gwyn and Ignatius as witnesses as Bill blessed their union and then, with a hastily found scarf, tied their hands together. A robin sang from the apple tree high above and Rose blew him a kiss for the pre-dawn serenade. Then she turned and kissed her husband.

'I think I might have been drunk last night,' Monty said beside her, his eyes still closed. 'I dreamed I married an unbearably bossy time traveller who—'

Rose leapt on him, giggling, then silenced him with a long kiss.

'Good morning, wife,' he said, the playfulness replaced with a look of such love that Rose felt her stomach flip over.

'Good morning, husband,' she said. The word felt so strange in her mouth, and she guffawed.

'Oh! Like that, is it?' Monty teased, flipping her over and showering her face and neck with kisses.

They froze when someone knocked softly on the door. 'Rose. Are you awake?'

'Lydia,' Rose mouthed to Monty. How was she going to explain this? She hadn't meant to exclude her last night, but it had all happened so fast, and Lydia had already gone to bed. It had seemed rude to drag her from it again. Besides, Rose was certain that she wouldn't approve of her decision to stay here. Far from it, in fact.

Rose sighed and edged from the bed, but then Peggy was outside too. Rose stilled, holding her breath until, blessedly, both Lydia and Peggy retreated down the corridor.

Rose let out a breath. Monty chuckled and resumed his work, covering her neck in kisses. 'Now, where were we?' he asked.

* * *

WHEN ROSE and Monty appeared in the kitchen some hours later, they found Lydia sitting alone with a book. Rose squeezed Monty's hand, uncertain of the reception they'd receive.

'I hear congratulations are in order,' Lydia said, getting to her feet and walking towards them, her hands outstretched. Rose loosed a breath in relief.

'I'm sorry, we should have woken you. It just all happened so quickly, and I didn't want to be rude, or insensitive,' Rose said over Lydia's shoulder as she hugged her.

'Oh, don't be so silly. I'd have been there like a shot, but I am grateful too that you let me sleep,' she said.

Rose thought she detected a note of disappointment in her friend's tone, but she was clearly doing what she could to take the sting out.

Stepping back, Lydia smiled at Rose. 'If it's any consolation, I think I knew from the off that you wouldn't be coming home with me. Don't ask me why. You just always looked so right here.'

Rose smiled but wasn't sure what to say. Monty rescued her from the moment.

'Where are the others?' he asked.

'Ah. Council of Elders. Dilys has gone as a witness to tell them what happened at St Brides. I said I'd stay behind to update you two and make you both breakfast.' Lydia glanced at the mantel clock, which declared it to be one fifteen, and added, 'But we can call it lunch.'

'What happened at Sophia's archive?' Rose asked as Lydia busied herself frying eggs.

'Oh yes, we didn't get to that last night, did we. Well, we got lucky in one way. The son was out, as Dilys suspected he might be. He likes to frequent the gentlemen's clubs in the city, apparently. I'll leave that to your imagination.'

Monty tsked beside her and Rose leaned over to plant a kiss on his stubbly cheek.

'The butler was sweet though. He remembered Dil looking after him when he was a tot. He let us in, and we spent hours in the basement going through boxes, but we found nothing. Anyway, the son came home earlier than planned, and Walt – that's the butler – had to smuggle us out the back door. So Sophia's archive was a bit of a washout.'

'Who's Sophia?' Frank asked, trotting into the kitchen. 'Can I have an apple, please?'

'A dear friend of Dil's,' Lydia said, before disappearing into the scullery, Frank at her heel.

Monty stroked his thumb over the back of Rose's hand. When she looked up into his face, he raised his eyebrow and gave an almost imperceptible nod.

'Oh!' Rose mouthed, the penny finally dropping. She sent up a silent prayer of thanks to wherever Sophia was taking her eternal rest. Waste not a minute, Dilys had said. She didn't intend to.

CHAPTER 68

CARDIFF, JULY 1841

*L*ydia was in the cool of the stable, learning how to groom a horse, when Dilys and the Chapels returned. The day had felt almost impossible to fill. The house was already spotless, the garden bereft of a single weed, and so when Frank had offered to teach her, she'd jumped at the chance.

After thanking the boy and Modron, the infinitely patient horse, for the lesson, she jogged over to meet them. Ten minutes later, they were all in the small garden of the Chapels' home.

The old apple tree provided welcome shade from the late-afternoon sun and there was a cooling breeze rolling in off the sea. Dilys and Peggy shared the only bench. Rose and Monty sat together on a checked rug, Ci Gwyn between them enjoying belly rubs. Lydia sat on an upturned apple crate. Only Bill was on the grass, basking in the sunshine.

Bill, Peggy and Dilys had appeared exhausted when they arrived, and now, sitting in the garden, it looked as though the sunshine and mint tea had done little to revive them. The news they'd brought from the Council of Elders had depressed them all.

'I can't believe I'm about to say this,' Rose said, shaking her head, 'but this Thorne chap is, for want of a better description, a witch finder.'

'You understand us perfectly,' Peggy said. 'Our people found his name on the port records this morning. He's been here a week. He didn't even bother to use a false name.'

'Have the Tellermans knowledge of a Silas Thorne, Monty?' Bill asked.

Monty cocked his head to the side and frowned, almost as if he were listening to someone. 'We know of a line of _Haw_thornes. They were renowned for their ability to sense magic through smell. They disappeared for a few generations, and the next memory we have of them is a Matthias Hawthorne. Alas, he came to our attention not as a friend of the community but as a witness for the prosecution during the Manningtree witch trials. He was declared a Turned by the Elders, a warrant issued, but he disappeared. Some said to the New World, which' – he spread his hands – 'would fit. I suppose they might have shortened the name to Thorne at some point,' he said thoughtfully.

'Do you know what turned them?' Peggy asked.

Monty shrugged. 'Money. Greed. Fear. Who knows. We have no knowledge of it, save for the trial.'

'I just don't understand why someone with magic would go hunting down his own kind,' Peggy said.

Bill shrugged. 'Well, we can't blame the New World for it. They had turned before they fled, but I'm sure the religious fervour of the puritans didn't help much.'

'He sounded quite religious,' Lydia said ruefully.

'Many of the Turned act under the mistaken belief that they are doing God's work by ridding the world of witches,' Dilys said, her voice as smooth and calm as ever.

'He'd have a job!' Peggy said. 'Does he mean to kill us all? Or just the vulnerable ones like Mother Pennywell who can't fight back?'

'I think you'll find, love, that he does God's work best when there's a bounty on the witch he's looking for.' Bill's tone was dripping with sarcasm.

'So much for greed being a sin, then,' Rose quipped. 'I wonder who was paying him to look for us, though?'

Lydia shifted her weight on the apple crate. She had wondered the same since last night's revelation. She had tried to puzzle it out, had even tried to ask the *Book of Prophecy* about it, but it remained stubbornly blank. She supposed she should be angry at the book. If it had known about the raid on her library in 1960 and had escaped to 1841 to survive, she wished it had just gone with Rose. If Monty was wrong and there was nothing she could do to change the future, then she would have preferred to have been with her family when it happened. At least they'd have been together.

She stroked the book through the pocket of her skirt, smiled when it hummed softly in reply. She couldn't find any anger towards it. Even now, it still felt like the only thing connecting her to her home.

'When did you say he arrived?' Monty asked, pushing himself up to sitting.

'Saturday the third of July. He docked at Bristol and came straight to Cardiff,' Bill said.

'And Lydia, you arrived when?' Monty asked, turning to look at her.

'Friday the fifteenth,' Lydia replied.

'You mentioned earlier that the Elders had mapped his movements,' Monty said. 'Retrospectively, I mean.'

'Right enough. Eleri has the sight, so once we had his name and his signature on the port documents, she could tell us where he went,' Bill said, pushing himself up to sitting.

'We know he went to St Brides to commit murder two nights ago, but where else did he go?' Monty asked.

'Nowhere, except there and the city,' Bill replied.

'What about Hay-on-Wye?' Monty asked, glancing at Rose and then Lydia.

'No,' Peggy said. 'He only went as far as St Brides.'

'I might be barking up the wrong tree here,' Monty said, 'but even if Rose and Lydia are his targets now, I don't think they're the people he originally came here to find. Remember, the crossing from America would have taken him at least three weeks. If Rose alone had been his target, then why didn't he track her to Hay?'

Lydia bit her lip. The effects of Dilys's calming spell had been slowly ebbing away all day. She could ask for another, but she needed to think, and the magic, while calming, dulled her senses and her mind. If she had any chance of getting home, of saving her family, she needed her wits, no matter the price to be paid.

'Do they know where he is now?' Rose asked.

'Newport,' Bill said. 'We think he's heading towards Bristol. Maybe he plans to board a ship. We've got people following him, so there's a chance he'll pay for what he did to Mother Pennywell, God rest her.'

Everyone seemed to talk at once, and the noise level in the small garden felt close to unbearable. Lydia had had enough. She stood up.

'Monty,' she said, loud enough to stop the conversations dead. 'If the worst has happened to my family, is it possible to go back to a point in time before all this?' She stayed on her feet, determined to have her answer.

He considered the question for a moment before replying, 'Most certainly, yes. In fact, what we know about the theory of time travel tells us you need an anchor memory to return to.'

'So, I can't go back to a future I can't remember,' Lydia clarified.

'That is the theory, yes,' Monty said.

'Monty, dear, what do you know about—' Dilys began, but Lydia cut her off.

'I want to go now,' she said. 'You said there was a thin place nearby, and I want to see it. Now.' Her voice was calm, authoritative and, to her own ears, far stronger than she felt. The calming spell was fading quickly now, like a bubble shrinking inwards towards her centre, leaving the frayed edges of her nerves exposed to the salty air. Grief nibbled at her fingers, making her hands tremble. She didn't want to think about how she'd feel when that magical point of light blinked out entirely.

Nobody moved. Nobody spoke. Lydia set her jaw, determined not to back down. It had to be now. She had no idea where this certainty had come from, but she knew it to be true. She'd go on her own if needed.

Rose jumped to her feet. 'Then let's go,' she said, coming to stand beside Lydia.

CHAPTER 69

CARDIFF, JULY 1841

*L*ydia focused on standing up straight when Monty got to his feet and Bill and Peggy started making plans. Every muscle in her body wanted to collapse with the relief, but she had to stay strong. Only Dilys didn't move immediately. She gave Lydia a rare smile and a nod of what Lydia decided was approval before rising to her feet.

'How far is it?' Lydia asked, realising that the only thing she remembered was someone saying there was a portal nearby.

'It's in St John's Baptist Church in town,' Bill supplied. 'Look, love, you do know, don't you, that without the spell to open it, the portal will be useless?' he added, his tone gentle, brow knitted in concern.

'I know that, Bill. I just need to see it, that's all,' Lydia replied.

'Hopefully, they'll be able to recover the book when they catch this Thorne bloke. They don't know about you two, and the time thing, by the way. As far as the other Elders are concerned, Rose needs the book for her research, so they're also searching for any similar spells that might help,' he said with a smile Lydia knew he meant to be reassuring.

'If we hurry, we can make it before Evensong, and we can have a quiet word with Reverend Price about staying behind afterwards,' Peggy cut in.

Lydia bristled at the mention of another clergyman. Would he sell them out to the highest bidder too – or worse?

'Don't worry, he's practically one of us,' Peggy said, smiling. 'No magic, but the kindest heart. He's the one who brought us Frank, not to mention all the others we've fostered. He found little Efa's mother too, and helped her get a position where she can keep her baby. He'll help us, no questions asked.'

As Peggy bustled off, Monty stepped into her place. 'I do not want to add any negativity, dear lady, but the map only showed us the location as being somewhere within the church. It might be in the crypt, or in the middle of a pillar, even, and so there is no guarantee that we will even be able to see it, let alone access it when we find the spell. People had a habit of building churches on energy centres, but often lacked the knowledge of how to properly align things,' he finished with a roll of his eyes and a shake of his head.

'I know, Monty. My expectations are low to non-existent, but I will feel better just for trying,' Lydia said, reaching out to squeeze his arm. Rose had picked a good man.

* * *

The early evening seemed reluctant to let go of the day's heat, and Lydia's feet felt hot and sticky in her boots. A rivulet of sweat meandered down her back as she walked beside Dilys, the pair sandwiched between Bill and Peggy in front, Monty and Rose behind.

It was the first time Lydia had walked outside. There had

been some debate about whether they should take a carriage, but as they were trying not to draw attention to themselves, they decided against it. The Chapels' black funeral carriage was too well known.

The thought of Thorne escaping justice by simply sailing back to America made Lydia's blood boil. She tried to hold on to the anger, picturing his sneering face mocking them. She thought of the poor old woman he'd murdered. Was she his first? She doubted it. She tried to stoke the anger, because every time her fury cooled, the void opened and threatened to swallow her whole – transporting her to a reality where she would never again see her precious family.

The *Book of Prophecy* hummed in the pocket of her dress. It seemed adept at reading her moods. She brushed her hand against it through the fabric. *If only your friend had let me stay with them*, she thought, and the anger slipped from her grip.

'It looks so different, doesn't it?' Rose said, appearing beside her. She leaned in to whisper to Lydia. 'I came to Cardiff Castle on a school trip, and they talked about the history, but never in my wildest dreams did I think ...' She let the sentence hang in the air.

Lydia looked up to see the castle across the road. It looked the same as the one she remembered. She wondered what people might think if she told them about the Cardiff of her time, with its cars, buses and mopeds.

'Rose, my love,' Monty called.

'Back in a minute. My husband calls,' Rose said with a giggle.

Lydia walked on alone, her eyes on the castle. At the gate, a small group of people lingered. Their clothes hung around skeletal frames, but it was their body language that broke Lydia's heart. They looked so defeated. As if life had dealt them one last rotten hand by keeping them this side of the veil. She remembered the grandeur behind those walls from her own school trip. The exquisite decorations, the frescoed ceilings, the gilding. And yet, outside the castle, the men and women who toiled on the Marquess of Bute's land lived in squalor. She choked down a sob and reached into her pocket for the book.

Ahead, Bill and Peggy turned into the aptly named Church Street. Dilys lingered on the corner and motioned for Lydia to go on. St John the Baptist Church loomed in the distance. A tall narrow Gothic tower with battlements gave it a fortified appearance. Lydia wondered why she'd never noticed them in her time. Above the arched doorway in the centre of the tower, a leaded window mimicked the door's shape but soared three times its height. Perched above the window, a clock kept a steady vigil, marking the passage of time for the faithful and the wayward alike.

Time. Lydia swallowed, her mouth suddenly dry as crypt bones. Her nerves felt frayed and exposed at the edges. She pressed her hands together to stop them shaking. Her family would not die for another one hundred and nineteen years and five months, but with a certainty that Lydia couldn't explain, she knew she was rapidly running out of time.

CHAPTER 70

CARDIFF, JULY 1841

*R*ose could barely feel the cobbles under her feet. With her arm tucked into Monty's, she might have been walking on air. She'd never expected to find someone to love. Hoped for it, yes – who didn't – but expected? No. It had always felt beyond the likes of her.

Yet here she was. Happier than she'd ever hoped to be. If that meant giving up some comforts from the twentieth century, she'd gladly do it. They were married! The thought made her giggle, and Monty turned as she tried to swallow the sound before it left her lips.

'We're married!' she whispered to him, barely able to maintain her composure.

'We are!' he said, beaming at her. 'We need to get you a ring,' he added, frowning down at her gloved hand. 'Would you think it bad luck to have my late mother's?' He barrelled on before she could answer. 'Or I could get you a new one. Yes, that would be better, perhaps. A fresh—'

Rose stopped walking and pressed a finger to his lips. 'I would be honoured to wear your mother's ring. We are our own fresh start, my love. I don't need a new ring for that.'

Monty looked like he wanted to cover her in kisses right there in the street but held himself back. Instead, he said, 'I love you, Rose Tellerman,' his eyes like hot smoke behind his long lashes.

Rose heaved in a deep breath and tried to remind herself that they were in public. 'I love you too,' she whispered.

'Rose! Monty!' Dilys's voice was sharp.

Rose looked up to see that the others had already turned into a side street. She waved apologetically to Dilys. They really had fallen behind.

'Oh dear,' Monty said. 'We're in the bad books. Come on. The quicker we find this you-know-what, the quicker we can get home.' The corner of his mouth hitched by a fraction, but Rose felt her blood heat in response.

They hurried along Church Street, walking as swiftly as the cobbles and propriety allowed. Rose felt the skin on her neck and back prickle, and she halted. She spun around, conscious of her heart pounding in her chest.

'What?' Monty said, his eyes wide.

Rose scanned the faces of the passers-by. Nothing.

'Rose?' Monty said, her name a question.

She sighed, feeling silly. 'It's nothing,' she replied. 'I thought I heard a question. Or felt something.'

'What was the question?' Monty asked, his expression serious.

'It sounded like ...' Rose scrunched up her face, trying to remember, but everything felt foggy. Up ahead, she saw the others were making their way back to them.

'Ignore me. I'm sorry,' she said hastily, not wanting to make a fuss. Thorne was miles away. The Elders had galvanised the community to find him and the spell. All they needed to do now was find the nearest portal for when the time came.

Rose could tell there was something wrong the moment

they stepped into the church. Peggy and Bill were standing at the back, their heads bowed together in conversation with Dilys.

'Jack's not here today,' Bill explained. 'The vicar, I mean. Or Reverend Price, to give him his full title. His wife, Lilly, delivered their fourth child this morning, apparently,' he added, scowling.

'Bill,' Peggy scolded. 'These things can't be helped. We should celebrate a new life, especially one born into such a beautiful family as theirs.'

Bill looked suitably admonished. 'Aye, right enough. But we've no chance of staying behind with him in Jack's place,' he said, eyeing the man in black marching up to the pulpit.

Before anyone could respond, the service began. Rose found the sermons close to insufferable, the focus entirely on man's wickedness and the punishment that awaited sinners who didn't repent. From the body language and mutterings of the congregation, she suspected this wasn't what they were used to. It was a relief to lose herself in singing during the hymns, her cheeks glowing with pride and joy as Monty whispered in her ear, 'You have the voice of an angel, my darling wife.'

When the service ended, they filed into the aisle with the rest of the congregation, but then stepped away from the main door to wait. Rose glanced up. Above the main doorway was a wide landing. Its far end was dominated by the grand window they'd seen on their approach, and directly above their heads, a thin rail was all that separated the space from the main body of the church. Taking a step back, her heel knocked against the first step of the open staircase that led up to it.

'I think we might have to come back when Jack's here,' Bill said. 'We need the place to ourselves to search properly.'

'No. It has to be now,' Lydia said, her jaw set.

Rose glanced behind them and saw the reverend was just a few rows away. In his black-and-white vestments, he reminded her of a young Border collie herding sheep. The fact that he was swinging his arms, palms up, added to the general impression that he was ushering his flock out of the door as swiftly as possible. They were out of time.

The reverend gave them a hard stare as he drew parallel, and Bill sprang into action.

'Reverend,' he said with a bob of his head. 'We've not had the pleasure, but we're friends of—'

Before Bill could finish, Rose saw the reverend blink hard. So hard, in fact, that he screwed up his face for long seconds. Beside her, Bill let out a controlled sigh and turned to stare pointedly at Dilys.

'Of course! I was left a note telling me all about your visit. Please, take your time. I am almost late for supper, so I will leave you in the capable hands of the Almighty,' the reverend said. His voice had the same nasal tone they had been subjected to during the service, but his diction was stilted, almost mechanical.

'Dilys Lloyd,' Bill said under his breath as they watched the reverend walk slowly away, mount the steps and disappear, pulling the heavy wooden door closed behind him. 'Was that absolutely necessary?'

Rose squeezed Monty's hand to keep from laughing at the serene expression on Dilys's face.

'Yes,' she replied simply. 'I don't hold with lying, William. You know that, and if I am not mistaken, you were about to concoct some story about why we needed to be here.'

Bill opened his mouth to protest, but Dilys continued. 'So, in place of a lie, I merely gifted him a memory. Our business here will be completed by the time it dissolves,' she said, smiling innocently.

'Shall we get on with it, then,' Peggy said pointedly. 'Some of us would like to get home for supper too.'

'Why don't we split up then,' Bill said. 'There are four aisles and four of us with magic. Monty, you take the middle. I'll take the far left, and Peg, you and Dil take one of these each.' He pointed to the aisles to the right. 'We'll meet down the front when we're finished and then start on the vestry and any other rooms.'

'I want a look up here,' Lydia said, already halfway up the stone steps that led to the wide landing of the tower. Rose watched her for a moment until Monty tugged at her hand. She moved, allowing herself to be guided while she watched Lydia ascend. It was a silly thing, she knew, but she suddenly, desperately wanted Lydia to wave at her from the railing.

Monty cleared his throat and she turned, feeling foolish.

'Are you ready, Mrs Tellerman?' he said playfully as he turned towards the central aisle and looped his arm through hers.

It took Rose a moment to catch on. 'Oh!' she mouthed.

'We'll need to do it legally at some point, if you can stomach the hypocrisy of all this,' Monty said, waving his hand around the church.

'For you, I can do anything,' Rose whispered.

Awe, love, and intense heat filled Monty's eyes, prompting her to grab his hand and, laughing, all but tow him down the aisle. They needed to find this portal quickly.

CHAPTER 71

CARDIFF, JULY 1841

*L*ydia was shaking by the time she reached the wide landing of the tower. She could feel the last remnants of the calming spell still clinging to her – or was it her clinging on to it? She could no longer tell. All she knew was that it was now a tiny speck of light in the ocean of blackness that swirled around her. She needed to be on her own for a moment. Needed to think clearly away from the concerned glances and meaningful looks the others exchanged when they thought she wasn't looking. She had never felt quite so useless in her life. Without the magic to sense it, she couldn't even help look for the portal that might one day soon send her home. She was a librarian without a library, and as such – pointless. *The Book of Prophecy* pulsed against her skin from inside her skirt pocket. *Okay*, she thought. *Not entirely pointless.*

She studied the landing. It was around twenty feet square and dominated by the vast arched window they'd seen from the street. The sun was setting, and a sliver of shadow near what she presumed was the door up to the rest of the tower seemed to grow before her eyes.

It was markedly warmer here than it had been in the main body of the church. Lydia tugged at her high collar as the heat and fatigue conspired to drain the last of her energy. Spying a chair in the corner, she walked wearily over to it and sat down. Leaning her head back, she gazed at the panelled ceiling. She counted the petals on the blue-and-gold decorative flower at its centre. Eleven. She squinted, trying to make out the shape of the flower's centre. She was pretty sure it was a rose, but her eyelids were so heavy. Her head rolled, and she jolted back to waking. Now was not the time to give in to the fatigue. She'd have time to sleep when they got back to the Chapels'.

Lydia stopped mid-stretch as her eyes snagged on a pinprick of light hanging in the air just beyond the landing's wrought-iron railing. The whole church was bathed in the golden rays from the setting sun, but this was different.

Getting up, she walked to the centre of the landing, her eyes fixed on the spot. From here, it looked like a puddle of molten silver. Could it be the—The book vibrated in her pocket, more urgently than before, breaking her train of thought.

Lydia pulled it out, her eyes still on the light. What had been the size of a penny was now the diameter of a teacup, and it was growing. Her heart kicked up, adrenaline pulsing through her body as she smiled. It had to be the portal!

She could hear the others chatting from the church below her. What were the odds that she'd spot it before four witches. She sent up a silent thank you to Lady Luck then opened her mouth, ready to call out and claim her victory, but changed her mind. They'd all risked their lives to help her get home. She'd give them a few minutes – someone was bound to spot it any moment now.

The book vibrated again in her hand. She headed back to the chair and sat down. All they needed now was for the

Elders to recover the spell book Thorne had stolen and she could be on her way home.

If she could make it back to a time before the raid on Aber, then there was a chance that she could protect the anomaly that kept her own library hidden and her family safe. She could be going home as early as tomorrow. She wondered how long it might take the Elders, or whoever they'd sent after Thorne, to travel from Bristol, but the book vibrated again.

Lydia ignored it, her thoughts on which memory, and therefore, which point in time she'd return to. She smiled. *Yes*, she thought. *That day had been perfect.* The book flipped open on her lap, its covers slapping her thighs. As she glanced down, the smile fell from her lips. She sucked in a breath and only just managed to stifle a scream.

CHAPTER 72

CARDIFF, JULY 1841

*R*ose trailed behind Monty, feeling like a spare part. The others were nearly at the pulpit. Thanks to her distracting him, Monty, Ignatius now visible on his shoulder, had been lagging in his own search and was now clearly trying to catch up. She sincerely hoped that the portal wasn't in the crypt. Much as she had loved the library in Aber, she'd had enough of being underground.

Rose sat on a pew and gazed up at the arched red ceiling. How on earth did people build such things? she pondered, marvelling at mankind's skill and ingenuity. She was lost in her thoughts when the skin on her neck prickled as it had in the street.

Getting swiftly to her feet, she hurried after Monty, suddenly feeling as if the distance between them was an uncrossable chasm. He smiled at her as she slipped her hand into his, and her heartbeat slowed to a normal rhythm.

'You checked in there?' Monty asked when he joined the others at the front of the church, pointing to the choristers' pews.

Rose didn't know who replied. She could hear the others

talking, but their words seemed to flow around her, slipping away before she could grasp their meaning. She stepped away and leaned against a pew just as a flash of heat surged through her. The air felt thin, her breath hard to catch. She felt something skitter across her arm. *No.* Fear caught in her throat, all but closing it. She knew this sensation. When she felt something hot and oily slither across her cheek, she cried out and spun around, looking desperately for Monty.

It was then that she saw Thorne leaning against the font at the back of the church. Rose felt the darkness descend just as it had in Pont Nefoedd. Her last thought was that Thorne was grinning.

CHAPTER 73

CARDIFF, JULY 1841

*L*ydia was on her feet, heading for the stairs, when Ignatius shrieked, stopping her in her tracks. Had he seen the portal? Her gut offered up an answer as what felt like a cold lead weight landed in the pit of her stomach. That had been an alarm call.

She took half a step forward, her legs reluctant to move. She clutched the book to her chest and wondered if it could hear her heart hammering. She flattened herself against the wall and inched towards the inset door to the tower.

'Oh, dear god! Rose!' Monty's voice was a strangled scream.

Lydia's heart leapt into her throat. Whatever was happening, she had to help, but instinct pinned her to the wall. She fixed her eyes on the portal, as big as a dinner plate, hanging just six feet from the edge of the landing.

'Bill! Bill! Grab her legs, I can't hold her!' Monty panted, sounding frantic.

'Peg! Dil! See if there's something to tie her down with,' Bill yelled.

'Noooooo!' Monty's guttural scream tore through the church.

Using every drop of courage she could muster, Lydia pushed herself off the wall only to be thrust back against it by a flash of near-blinding white light that sent a shockwave through the church. The windows rattled as dust and small fragments of stone and plaster fell to the ground around her.

Lydia clamped her hand over her mouth to stop herself from screaming when she saw her. Rose, haloed in ethereal silver-blue light, was floating high above the pews, her head tipped back, her body naked and limp as a rag doll. Her expression was one of serenity itself, but Lydia recoiled at the sight of the words and symbols that snaked across her flesh. The black ink coiled around her limbs and torso, sliding over every inch of her, a living, writhing thing that seemed possessed of a will entirely separate from her friend.

Lydia tasted acid in the back of her throat. Looking up, she saw the portal widen as Rose drifted towards it. Of course. It was so obvious now that she was looking at it. Lydia kicked herself for not realising sooner. Rose had told them about the words under her skin and how Seren had called them spell fragments. Pieces of magical shrapnel that had embedded themselves in Rose when the spell went off. But they were nothing of the sort.

Lydia shook her head at the wonder of it. Rose was the portal spell. Given her other newfound gifts, hell, she might even be the whole damn spell book.

Tears welled in Lydia's eyes. Everything was going to be okay. She was going home. Today. All Lydia had left to do was hand the *Book of Prophecy* over to the Elders here in 1841, and the world would be spared from the horror of the wars and suffering of a century. While what was happening to Rose was certainly something of a spectacle, she knew her friend was in no danger. It all made sense now. The rightness of Rose here in 1841, her new-found abilities to hear unspoken questions, the healing power and who knew what else. She stared in awe at her friend as she drifted ever closer to the portal – Rose had claimed her magic at last, and she was utterly magnificent. Lydia bit her lip, feeling giddy at the joy of it all. This was why they were here. They were going to put right the wrongs of the last century.

'Star-crossed lovers. A tale as old as time.'

Lydia's blood ran cold as Thorne's voice reverberated around the church.

CHAPTER 74

CARDIFF, JULY 1841

*T*his couldn't be happening! Lydia's mind refused to accept the evidence of her ears. Thorne was on his way to Bristol. The Elders were on his trail and had told Dilys and the Chapels as much, only hours ago.

'Don't get me wrong,' Thorne drawled, his voice menacingly casual, 'I'm enjoying the show and all, especially now that the witch has revealed herself for the devil's whore she is, but I'm also on a tight schedule.'

Even from where she was hiding, Lydia felt the air pressure change. She risked a breath, relieved that her friends had at least shielded themselves.

'Enough games!' Thorne spat the words, and Lydia's ears popped as the pressure dropped. What had happened? Had he just knocked out their shields? Lydia was desperate to know, desperate to help, but what could she do against such magic?

Thorne was speaking again. 'If I had the time, I would make you all pay right here and now. Just being here is a desecration of His house, but your reckoning will need to wait.'

Lydia risked a glance at Rose floating serenely in the air just below the portal. The words and symbols of the spell still snaked around her, but the pace had slowed. *It's waiting*, she thought.

'You leave her alone,' Monty snarled from below, his voice so full of fury, Lydia almost didn't recognise it.

Thorne barked out a laugh. 'For the wisest man on God's green Earth, you sure are stupid,' he said with a chuckle. 'I have no interest in the witch. Who you whore yourself with is none of my concern, unless she's diseased, and then we have an issue.'

A roar reverberated around the church. Lydia inched forward and peered down to see Monty wild-eyed and frozen inches from Thorne, his hands outstretched as if lunging for the man's throat. To Lydia's horror, Bill, Peggy and Dilys looked to be held in place too. This couldn't be happening!

'My client is a collector of exquisite magical antiquities, and while you're not top of their wish list – that little lady still evades me – the lost Tellerman heir is second,' Thorne crowed.

Lydia felt her breath hitch in her chest.

'Did you assume that nobody would gossip? Or find a way of breaking the punishment spells meted out by your so-called Council of Elders?'

Lydia saw the realisation flash across Monty's face. Thorne had to be talking about his awful housekeeper, Mrs Barnes. Dilys had been right then.

'Enough of this,' Thorne said, waving his hand dismissively. 'It's time to go.' He grabbed a still immobilised Monty by the collar.

Lydia shoved the little book back into her skirt pocket as she scanned the landing, looking for something to throw at

Thorne. If she could at least slow him down, then maybe one of the others might have a chance.

She had just lifted a plaque from the wall, staggering under its unexpected weight, when all hell broke loose.

CHAPTER 75

CARDIFF, JULY 1841

*R*ose was only dimly aware of the scene playing out beneath her dangling feet. She could feel the spells surge through her veins, and she wondered idly if magic would replace her blood entirely now that she was— She paused. What was she, exactly? She was no longer what she had been before; she knew that. Maybe no longer entirely human. Was she a witch, then? A small, forgotten part of her purred from the pit of her soul, like a long-abandoned stray cat who had finally found a warm hearth and a kind lap to call their own. She smiled.

Below her, someone screamed. She tried to tune it out, not wanting anything to interrupt her euphoria. She wasn't just magic. She was love itself.

'I love you, Mrs Tellerman.' The memory of Monty's words punched through her thoughts, and she gasped back to consciousness.

On the ground below her, Thorne had an immobilised Monty by the collar, already dragging him towards the door as Dilys, Peggy and Bill hammered their fists against the containment spell that held them.

Rose harnessed her fury, gritted her teeth and summoned a disarming spell. It shot from her fingers in a torrent of words and symbols, bursting Thorne's magic like a sharpened pin to the skin of a balloon.

Monty reacted first, pushing Thorne to the floor with a furious roar. Thorne fired off a spell as he fell, but Monty ducked into the row of pews to avoid it.

Dilys was first to shoot back, her spell an arc of pale blue light that cracked the air as it shot towards Thorne. It missed him by inches. When he retaliated, it was clear that, unlike Dilys, his intention wasn't to disarm and contain. The pew behind which Dilys had taken shelter exploded into dust.

Peggy and Bill were crouched either side of the front pews, emerging only long enough to hurl spells as if they were cannon balls. A movement caught Rose's eye. Monty was crawling along a row of pews, clearly intending to take Thorne by surprise.

Rose needed to end this before anyone got seriously hurt. She reached for a disarming spell, but the portal spell, still coiling around her arms, reared up and snagged it at the last minute. Words and symbols collided, launching bits of magic into the air, like sparks from a struck flint. Cursing under her breath, she tried again, but it was no use.

Stifling a snarl of frustration, she cast around, looking for Lydia. The only way to be free of the spell was for Lydia to use the portal. The spell responded to her thought by squeezing ever tighter.

'Rose!' Lydia's voice was hoarse and barely audible over the air-splitting hiss and crack of magic from the church below them.

Straining against the spell, which felt intent on keeping her as close to the portal as possible, Rose glided towards the open landing of the tower.

'Lydia, you need to jump through the portal. Until you do,

I can't use my magic to save them,' Rose said, her voice tight and her breaths increasingly hard won as the spell, desperate for release, coiled up around her throat.

Lydia's eyes were wild and terrified. She held up the little book, shaking her head furiously. 'I have to give the book to the Elders first. The prophecy! It's back! In the book! It just showed me, just like it did in Aber! This must be the reason I'm here, Rose. To stop the wars and end the suffering that's to come!'

Rose gasped, and the spell tightened around her, claiming the space that had once been the air in her lungs. Black dots swam in her vision. On the ground, she heard someone curse loudly. There was no time.

'No time, Lydia! Go!' Rose spluttered.

'But you don't understand, Rose. My father and brother died in the war! Think of the millions who perished. We can stop it from ever happening!' Lydia pleaded.

'Save your family, Lydia. Go! Now!' Rose choked out the words, lacking the breath to explain any more. There wasn't time.

Rose saw her friend's eyes fill with tears. She was already shaking her head. 'You can't ask me to choose!' she wailed.

A noise made them both turn to see Thorne heading for the steps to the landing.

'Do you want him in 1960? Go!' Rose bellowed as she shoved Lydia hard in the back with what felt like the last of her strength. Lydia stumbled, then pressed the book into Rose's hand, her eyes a plea.

'Go!' Rose wailed.

For a terrible moment, Rose didn't think Lydia would do it. The portal hung six feet in front of the landing, making it at least thirty feet from the pews and the hard, cold stone of the church floor. Unless the others had slowed him, Thorne would be here in seconds.

The portal spell tightened around Rose's throat, quivering in anticipation. She held her breath as she watched Lydia clamber up onto the wrought-iron rail, and then, with a look of something close to blind terror on her face, she flung herself towards the swirling disc of silver light.

The spell sprang from Rose's body, and she gasped as the last tendrils released her and the full power of her magic surged through her veins. The spell enveloped Lydia in a cloud of words, and then, with a flash of blinding light, Lydia and the portal were gone. Rose flexed her fingers and glanced down at her hands. As she'd suspected, so too was the *Book of Prophecy*.

CHAPTER 76

CARDIFF, JULY 1841

*R*ose lifted into the air just in time to see Thorne appear at the top of the steps. She shot a bolt of energy towards his chest, and he tumbled backwards. She had no desire to kill, but if he broke a bone in the fall, she'd not lose any sleep. She'd heal him before handing him over to the Elders for trial.

Suddenly aware of her nakedness, she sheathed herself in a simple white dress as she drifted to the edge of the landing, expecting to see him lying prone on the tiles below. Thorne was nowhere in sight.

She recoiled as a spell exploded off a shield she hadn't consciously conjured around herself. The feeling was familiar though, instinctive. She smiled as she recalled the confusion over who had shielded Monty from Thorne's first attack at the Elder's residence. Mystery solved.

Monty and the others were crouched behind the pillars on the far left of the church by the side doors. Rose gained height, soaring into the middle of the church for a better view. Thorne had vanished. Somewhere in the distance, a door banged, the unmistakeable sound of wood flung against stone. Let him run. She'd find him.

Bill and Peggy heard it too. Bill sprinted to the front door while Peggy burst out of the side. Thorne was about to be the most hunted witch hunter in the magical community.

Rose floated down, running to Monty almost before her bare feet touched the ground. He swept her into his arms and held her. She drank in the sunshine and ink smell of him.

'You did it, my love,' Monty said, cupping her face in his hands. 'And became your true, magnificent self in the process! My darling Rose has finally bloomed.'

Rose giggled and wrinkled her nose. She felt fabulous. Her husband was safe. Lydia was back in 1960 with her family, and Rose was exactly where – and when – she was meant to be. If Dilys was right, and magic really didn't make mistakes, it certainly had a convoluted way of moving souls around the celestial board. Working out why this had all happened this way would be tomorrow's challenge, though. Right now, she needed to help Bill and Peggy track down a killer.

'Magnificent indeed,' Dilys said as she walked stiffly over to the couple.

'Dil, are you hurt?' Rose asked, scanning her friend from head to toe and back again.

'Just a bruised hip,' she said with a smile. 'I know you are itching to give chase, but hadn't we better get Monty back to the Chapels', Rose?'

Rose felt Monty still beside her. His indignant question landed in her mind, and she winced. Dil was right though. While Thorne was still at large, Monty was at risk. As much as she wanted Thorne behind bars, or whatever the magical equivalent was, her priorities were clear.

'Monty, my love—'

Rose didn't finish the sentence. A spell containing more

fury that she'd thought possible slammed into her back. She felt her shield reassert itself, but not before her forehead cracked against the nearest stone pillar.

Spinning around, she saw Thorne on the pulpit. Monty saw him too, and they attacked at the same time, the wooden structure exploding before their eyes, but Thorne was already on his feet and running for the side door.

'Dilys!' Monty cried out.

Rose glanced down and gasped at the sight of her friend lying awkwardly between the pews.

'I'll see to her. Go!' Monty instructed.

Rose took to the air, soaring high into the church, scanning for Thorne. She cursed under her breath. Was the man a chameleon? A movement in the choristers' stalls caught her eye, and she was moving, drawing on as much magic as she could muster.

Her head swam with the effort of it, although she doubted the bang to the head was helping matters. She landed and raced towards the ornamental wooden screen that sectioned off the stalls, her eyes fixed on Thorne's hat, the only bit of him that remained visible. Her head was still swimming, and when she called for the attack spell, it came more slowly to her hands than it had before. She had to end this – and quickly.

What happened next was the stuff of nightmares. Rose saw Thorne step out from behind the screen. He raised his hands, and the spell, so filled with fury that the air caught light around it, lanced towards her. She had already fired back, abandoning the intent to just contain at the last moment and adding enough power to injure Thorne in the hope that it might slow him down.

But then she was falling sideways into the pews, an agonised scream echoing in her ears. Her brain put it all together just before she hit the ground – Monty had pushed her out of the path of Thorne's spell and taken the full force of his malign fury.

She scrambled around on her knees, her hands slipping on the tiles. Monty lay, unmoving, just a few feet away. This wasn't happening. It couldn't be happening.

Someone else was firing at Thorne. Thorne screamed and cursed, but Rose barely heard it. Panic clawed at her throat as she realised that her hands and dress were covered in blood. Her husband's blood.

Ignatius crept from Monty's inside pocket and let out a piercing wail.

'Monty! Monty!' Rose whispered his name as she turned his head to face her. His skin was deathly pale save for the scorch marks that fanned up his left cheek and eye.

Ignatius threw his arms around Monty's neck and squeezed his huge brown eyes closed as if trying to block out his friend's ruined face.

Rose pressed her fingers to Monty's neck and heaved a sigh of relief as she felt a fluttering pulse. 'He's alive,' she announced.

Dilys, panting with exertion, crouched down to join her. 'Oh, thank God,' she said. 'Thorne went out the side door. I saw him leave this time,' she added as she gingerly lifted Monty's jacket to peer at his chest.

Rose felt her throat constrict as she saw the blood blooming across Monty's white shirt. She steeled herself, before easing it up to inspect the gaping wound below. She gagged at the sight. Thorne would have done less damage had he been wielding a scythe.

Dilys got to her feet and hurried away, returning moments later with an altar cloth. She pressed it to the wound, and Monty winced.

Ignatius trilled just before she heard Monty speak.

'Rose.'

'I'm here. I'm here,' she said, stroking his face.

'Monty!' Bill's shout from the doorway was accompanied by the sound of two sets of running feet.

Rose turned her attention back to her husband.

'Oh, Monty,' she whispered as she kissed his forehead. She wanted to take him to task for his heroics – there had been no need for him to try and protect her like that – but that would need to wait.

'I'm sorry, my love,' Monty said, his voice cracking. 'It was just instinct. I couldn't shield in time. I took a direct hit,' he said, his face contorted in pain.

Bill and Peggy knelt at Rose's side.

'We leave you for five minutes and look at you,' Bill said to Monty. It was typical of him to try and use humour to defuse a situation, but the catch in his voice sent a shard of ice through Rose's heart.

'Rose, my love,' Monty said, reaching up to cup her cheek in his palm. 'You need to prepare yourself, my sweet. I'm so sorry.' Rose felt the world tilt on its axis as her husband's smoke-grey eyes filled with tears. How could she find the love of her life and lose him less than twenty-four hours after taking their vows?

Her own eyes filled with hot tears, and she was dimly aware of Dilys struggling to her feet.

'You'll sort out the necessary papers for Rose?' Monty asked Bill. He groaned. Swallowed hard. 'For the house and what's left.'

'No!' Rose ground out the word through gritted teeth as she leaned into Monty's face. Clinging to his neck, Ignatius turned his head away. Monty stroked the marmoset with what looked to be a great effort.

'Enough, Monty. You are not going to die. Do you hear me. I have not come all this way to find you, fall in love with you and marry you only to lose you now. It's a big no. No!'

Monty tried to laugh, but it turned to a grimace, his face twisting in pain. Rose glanced at the altar cloth beneath Dilys's hand. It was already soaked through. Peggy saw it too and hurried off, running back moments later carrying an armful of cloths and vestments.

Rose stroked Monty's face as she focused all her attention on her healing magic. It was still so new she had no idea how it worked. Intent – and love – would have to be enough.

Monty cried out, and she leaned closer. He was struggling for breath. Rose tried harder, willing the healing to hurry up and fix him.

'It has been the honour of my life to meet you, Rose Tellerman, let alone have the privilege of calling you my wife,' Monty said. Every word seemed to be an effort now.

Rose made to still him – he needed to conserve his energy for healing – but Monty took her hand in his. His skin was cool to the touch, and she could feel the strength ebb from his grip.

Monty smiled up at her as fresh tears rolled from the corners of his eyes and tracked into his hair.

'Will you please transcribe the last of the Tellerman memories from my notes? Ignatius will help you, won't you, Iggy,' Monty said, his voice fading.

'You can transcribe them yourself,' Rose said shakily. Monty was growing paler before her eyes.

Panicked, Rose cast around. 'You tell him!' she said to Bill. 'Please! Tell him he can do it himself when he's healed! Tell him, Bill. Please.'

Beside her, Peggy choked back a sob. Turning back to Monty, Rose saw Ignatius standing on his back legs, his belly pressed to Monty's ruined cheek as he patted his temple, then, with tiny, trembling fingers, he lifted Monty's eyelid to reveal a fixed, unmoving eye.

The howl that left Rose's lips sounded like nothing a human could make.

CHAPTER 77

PONT NEFOEDD, JUNE 1960

'*Mam!*' The voice was close, loud, and sounded more than a little exasperated.

Lydia turned to see Maggie at the end of the stack, hands on her hips, head cocked and eyebrows raised. Lydia blinked. She was in her library, in row four. She knew that much, at least. She also knew that her daughter was rolling her eyes at her. Nothing new there. But what had she just been doing? Her heart was hammering like she'd run a marathon and her stomach felt like she'd just stepped off a rollercoaster at the fair.

Maggie's tone changed. 'Mam, are you alright?' she asked, rushing over and putting a hand on her back. 'You're as white as a sheet and you're shaking. Let's get you sat down for a minute,' she added, guiding Lydia out of the stacks.

Lydia's legs felt like jelly, and she was glad of Maggie's arm. As she sank into the hard-backed chair, she had a flash of an old-fashioned kitchen. A Jack Russell hopping onto her lap. She put her elbows on the reading table and noticed that she was holding a small teal-green book.

The memories came in a torrent. Dilys with an armful of

flowers. The cave. A tall, handsome young man with a tired face and kind eyes and a marmoset perched on his shoulder. The neat little room in the Chapels' home. Thorne.

'Rose!' Lydia said, trying to stand up. She wobbled as her legs refused to comply with the sudden command, and Maggie leapt up to steady her.

'Mam! It's alright,' Maggie said, guiding her back to sitting. 'Take a minute.'

Lydia waited for the room to stop spinning around her. She remembered it all now. The raid on the Aber library. Frances's murder. The car chase. The spell. Chief among the memories was the marrow-deep grief that had rippled through more than a century to find her when her family had—A sob caught in her chest, and she flung her arms around her daughter, drinking in the smell of her freshly washed hair and borrowed perfume.

She was home. Lydia pulled back and inspected her daughter. She'd bought that dress for her twenty-first birthday party.

'What's the date?' Lydia asked.

Maggie rolled her eyes and laughed, assuming it was a joke. 'Hmm, let me think,' she said, rubbing her chin and trying not to smile. 'Oh yes, it's the twenty-second of June 1960, which happens to be my twenty-first birthday!' she said playfully. 'See, Mam, if you'd only planned it better, I could have been twenty-one on the twenty-first,' she added, laughing.

Lydia made a noise that wasn't a laugh or a sob but something in between. She'd done it. She'd come home to a point in time before the Aber raid and before whatever had destroyed the anomaly that kept them safe here. She had changed the future. Or one version of it at least.

There was a soft thud on the table, but before Lydia could turn, she was all but wearing a cat. Boudicca yowled and purred, clinging to Lydia's chest while madly butting her head into her chin.

'Good grief, Boudicca, it's like you've not seen her in a week!' Maggie quipped, a taint of longing in her tone.

The cat was purring and kneading her paws into Lydia's shoulder. When Lydia wrapped her arms around her, Boudicca made to bite the end of the book in her hands. The *Book of Prophecy*!

No! She'd handed it to Rose before she jumped. Told her to get it to the Elders at once. The prophecy had been there, which meant that they had had a chance back in 1841!

Tears welled in Lydia's eyes as she remembered the first time she'd given the book to Rose only to have it materialise in her lap minutes later.

She clamped her hand over her mouth as the thought struck her, heavy as a kick to her gut. *If I'd stayed and taken the book to them myself, I could have changed the world.* Tens of millions of lives lost just to the wars. So much suffering. A sob ripped through her, and she felt the world slide into darkness.

'Lydia. Lydia!' The voice was sharp. Clipped. Familiar.

Someone was tapping her cheek. Lydia opened her eyes to see Frances peering at her through her bubblegum-pink spectacles.

'You're alive.' Lydia's voice was an incredulous whisper. Was she dreaming? Sleep seemed to be pulling at her edges, coaxing her back into oblivion.

'Of course I'm alive, dear girl,' Frances replied, patting her on the shoulder. 'Alive and well and here to enjoy Maggie's party, which we'll get to once you stop having a funny turn. Can someone get her a glass of water, please? Quick as you like,' she instructed. 'Did she fall, Maggie?'

Maggie said something Lydia didn't catch.

'Where's Rose?' Lydia asked. Her words felt slurred and syrupy on her lips.

'Who's Rose?' Frances asked, confused.

'Your apprentice,' Lydia sighed. Talking was such an effort.

'You mean Cheryl, Lydia. Are you sure you didn't fall and bang your head?' Frances asked, her long fingers already probing Lydia's skull for bumps.

Frances went on, not waiting for a reply. 'Cheryl is still checking in books at the new facility. I'll be having a word with Morgan when he arrives. I know security is everything, but moving the Aber library without notice is unprecedented. As for rousing me from my bed at three a.m., well, that was just bad manners.'

Lydia sighed but said nothing. The words were just too hard to form. She closed her eyes and surrendered to the darkness. *Just for a moment,* she told herself.

When she opened her eyes, Seren was leaning against the reading table in front of her, the *Book of Prophecy* clasped between her palms. Boudicca sat at her side, her feet buttoned into a neat square. From the stillness in the room, Lydia knew they were alone. Her face crumpled as a sob caught in her chest.

'I should have stayed and seen to it myself,' Lydia cried, covering her face with her hands. 'I could have stopped it! All of it!'

'No, Lydia,' Seren said quietly. 'Our friend here,' she said, holding up the book, 'has told me a little of what I need to know, and that was never for you to do. You are a keeper of magical texts, and you kept your charge safe from harm.'

'But it showed me the prophecy!' Lydia forced out the words between sobs. 'Twice!'

'Because it needed you to know what was at stake. And so that you could have hope for what is to come.' Seren was kneeling now, her voice soft and earnest as she rubbed gentle circles on Lydia's back.

Lydia opened her mouth to reply, but she had no words. Nothing Seren could say could convince her she had done the right thing.

'Lydia, listen to me. The prophecy is useless if the Ethereal isn't incarnated here on Earth. So, even if you had taken the book to the Elders, it might not have made a shred of difference. Some things are just too monumental to change.'

'But my father! My brother! And all those millions of people! What my Hywel had to endure,' Lydia sobbed into her palms as Boudicca paced, rubbing her head across Lydia's hands.

Seren rose gracefully to standing, her hand still on Lydia's back. She sighed heavily.

Lydia felt the pressure change around her, but before she could speak, the spell wrapped itself around her, soft and warm as a lover's embrace. She felt something loosen in her chest and sucked in a breath. As she released it, she had the strangest sensation that something else was leaving along with it. She sighed. Whatever it was, it could wait.

'Lydia?'

Lydia opened her eyes to see Seren studying her face. She leaned back in her chair and Boudicca hopped onto her lap, purring.

'Did I nod off?' Lydia asked with an embarrassed chuckle.

'Just zoned out for a second,' Seren said lightly. 'I was talking magical theory, though, when we're meant to be partying, so the fault is mine. Are you feeling okay?'

Lydia frowned. 'I'm feeling great. Shall we go up?' she said, scooping Boudicca into her arms and getting to her feet.

Seren smiled and made to follow, but Lydia stopped in her tracks when she spotted a small teal-green book on the reading table.

'Oh, is that a new one?' she said, nodding towards it.

'Er, no. Maggie checked it in, I think,' Seren said.

'Ah, okay. Just leave it on the table and I'll shelve it tomorrow,' Lydia said, already halfway to the door.

Seren smiled. 'Don't worry. I'll do it. You've got a party to enjoy.'

EPILOGUE

CARDIFF, OCTOBER 1841

*R*ose got to her feet and stretched her aching back, spreading her arms wide. Glancing down at the desk in front of her, she smiled as she watched the ink dry on the page. Her handwriting was getting better, and she could now write for hours before the cramp set in.

She inspected her hands, ink-stained to such a degree that no amount of scrubbing ever removed every trace. There was little to love about Victorian clothing conventions for women, but she was glad of the gloves. She waggled her fingers and then, yawning, interlaced them before pushing her arms up into another delicious stretch.

How many years would she need to wait until the type-writer was invented, she wondered, for what felt like the millionth time. She loosed a long sigh as she sat back down and leaned forward to rest her elbows on the desk. A brush of soft fur tickled her arm.

'Oh, there you are,' she said to the marmoset.

Ignatius made a low churring noise by way of reply, his eyes already turned to inspect the page.

'We can add another seventeen pages to the list,' Rose

said, wholly failing to keep the pride out of her voice. It had been a productive day. 'I reckon by tomorrow evening we'll be able to send this one for binding. What do you think?'

'I think, my love, you are, as ever, wildly optimistic. It will be Thursday at the earliest,' Monty said from the other side of the desk, the side of his mouth twitching as he tried and failed to look serious.

Rose felt the familiar tug in her chest as she looked at him. How could he possibly be hers, and yet, here he was. And here she was. They had both defied the odds stacked against them.

She thought back to that moment in the church. The looks that Dilys, Peggy and Bill had exchanged that for a heartbeat knocked the breath from her lungs and her hope along with it. But she would not lose him, and her newly awakened magic agreed, bursting from her like an exploding bomb of love and longing and propelled by a will so strong it sometimes terrified her.

It had still taken Monty weeks to recover, confined to bed and barely conscious. Rose had spent long, agonising nights too afraid to close her eyes in case somehow the magic healing him needed her conscious intent.

Nothing lasts forever, not even the worst of times, and soon those endless, sleepless days and nights were behind them. Twelve weeks on, and Monty looked not just recovered but reborn. His face had lost its hollowed look, and his eyes were no longer shadowed and bloodshot. He had colour in his cheeks and even his hair shone. Rose pushed back her chair, not taking her eyes from his.

They had just stepped into each other's arms when Dilys pushed open the library door and strode into the room. She rolled her eyes, but Rose caught a ghost of a smile tugging at her lips.

'There's no time for all that,' Dilys said, trying to sound

reproachful. 'Thorne has been spotted,' she added, with the practised air of one used to choosing her words and her timing carefully.

'Where?' Monty gasped.

'Liverpool,' Dilys said. 'He is in a boarding house and looks to be in no immediate hurry to move on. Our people are watching him, naturally.'

Rose felt her pulse quicken. She licked her lips. 'Dil …' She drew out the name slowly but left the rest of the sentence unfinished.

Dilys raised her eyebrows. 'Will I finish writing up the last of the volume and get it to the binders?'

'Would that be a terrible imposition?' Monty asked, slipping his hand into Rose's and squeezing.

'While overseeing the repairs to the house, training the new housekeeper and making sure Ci Gwyn is properly pampered?' Dilys asked, already turning.

Rose held her breath.

Dilys paused at the door and smiled at them. 'It would be my absolute pleasure,' she said with a nod.

After a beat, she added, 'Come on now. You had better start packing. You have a witch hunter to apprehend.'

* * *

THE END

THE FIRST ETHEREAL

The *Book of Prophecy* has been waiting patiently.

But now the time has come.

A witch who's lost her powers, a super empath living her last life and a secret library where the books whisper of a magical being that could just save them all...

Read on for your free sample of, The First Ethereal.

THE FIRST ETHEREAL

CHAPTER 1

*L*illy woke with a start, her heart hammering. As if stumbling out of thick fog, it took her mind a few seconds to realise that she was at home in her bed. She reached out her hand and found the wall against which her single bed was pressed in the tiny bedsit flat. Had someone called her name?

'Lil,' whispered a familiar voice from the darkness, his voice hoarse.

Lilly's heart slowed. She pushed herself up and groped for the bedside light, the chill air giving her instant goosebumps.

She squinted, her eyes struggling to adjust to the brightness and then her mind to comprehend what she was seeing. After a moment she said, 'Jack. What the hell? Who are you meant to be this time?'

He was dressed as a 1970s rock star, complete with skinny black jeans, cowboy boots and a tight shirt. His usually short-cropped fair hair had been replaced with a thick mop of unruly dark waves that stretched past his shoulders. To complete the look, he was holding a microphone stand and posing as if the photographer from NME was standing behind her. She laughed in spite of herself.

'Steven Tyler?' she asked while trying and failing to suppress a yawn.

Jack rolled his eyes. 'Not even close. Ian Gillan. Smoke on the Water. Get it?'

It took her a minute to make the connection. 'Oh no, really? Again?'

'Afraid so,' he said with a grimace and then instantly transformed back to his usual uniform of white T-shirt and jeans before slumping down into the flat's single armchair. 'I was just trying to cheer you up in advance.'

She smiled at him, grateful for the gesture but already bone weary at the thought of another night on a camp bed in the community centre. 'How long do you think?'

'About fifteen minutes before the sirens go off, give or take. I gatecrashed the emergency services meeting and they're mobilising the pumps and boats again. If you ask me, this one will be worse than the last few – the river looks like it's bloody possessed.'

Lilly sighed and scanned the tiny basement flat, which was one square room with a chunk taken out of the far corner to squeeze in a bathroom. It had been her haven once. Even at sixteen and desperate to find anywhere to live that wasn't her parents' farm, she'd been impressed by the crisp whitewashed exterior of the old Georgian house, the window boxes stuffed full of cheerful pink geraniums and the modern Scandi interior that convinced her to trade square footage for style. Three years had passed without incident, but in the last twelve months she'd been evacuated seven times as the river surged to levels no one had thought possible. So far, her flat had only been flooded once, but something told her that it was only a matter of time before the damage would necessitate more than a few weeks of drying time and a new carpet.

Reluctantly, Lilly flung off the thick duvet and padded over to the suitcase that served as her wardrobe. 'Did you let them see you?' she asked Jack as he filled the kettle and spooned coffee into her travel mug.

'Nah,' Jack said. 'Everyone was so stressed out I thought it best to keep a low profile. I will though when we go to the community centre, unless of course you want to get a reputation for talking to yourself,' he added with a smile.

Lilly had been able to see Jack for as long as she could remember. They grew up together, although he always looked to be a few years older than her. When Lilly had a scooter, Jack had a bike. When she had a bike with stabilisers, Jack had one he could do wheelies on. The older she got, the older Jack appeared. The perpetual big brother.

Her parents had tolerated what they dismissed as her 'imaginary friend' when she was very small, but their patience had quickly run out as it did with most things. There was no place for magic or mystery at the farm, even for a child. Arguing the point proved futile, so she had just stopped talking about him to avoid the consequences, but he remained as real and as corporeal to her as any living person. She knew that if he allowed it, other people could see him too – they just couldn't remember him for longer than a few seconds.

Lilly was well aware that Jack wasn't human in the sense that other people were. When she was little, she once asked him if he was a ghost. He'd just laughed and said he was her friend. She only ever broached the subject once after that and he said there were rules about how much he was allowed to tell her. Having always hated arguments, she decided it was as good an explanation as any. He was her only friend, after all, so she wasn't going to push her luck.

Lilly reluctantly pulled off the T-shirt she was wearing once she'd found a long-sleeved top, sweater and jeans to put on, then pulled her long auburn hair into a bun.

'You've lost more weight, Lil,' Jack said flatly. Lilly could almost feel his eyes on her bare back, inspecting her. She shrugged and ignored the comment. She wasn't in the mood for that particular debate tonight. Thankfully, he let it drop.

By the time the flood siren sounded twenty minutes later, Lilly had everything she considered essential stuffed into her backpack. Jack had spent the time putting anything that they couldn't take with them hopefully out of reach of any flood-water. Lilly's drawing board he'd balanced on top of the shower unit. Her printer, lamps and kettle had been given refuge on top of the kitchen cabinets.

Picking up her art portfolio and her rucksack she scanned the room. The routine was horribly familiar now.

'Ready?' Jack asked, relieving her of the rucksack and then handing her the travel mug of coffee.

Lilly nodded sadly.

'You've shielded yourself? There's going to be some seri-ously high-octane emotions out there tonight,' he said, putting his hand on her shoulder and studying her face.

It had been Jack who had taught her how to control her 'gift'. As gifts went, she thought it was probably about the worst sort you could get. A kind of super-empathy that meant she felt the emotions of any living soul within about a ten-mile radius. Worse, she seemed to be tuned to the lower vibrations of pain and misery because she could never recall feeling anyone's joy or elation. It wasn't just an awful gift – it was a defective one to boot.

Had it not been for Jack teaching her how to protect herself and switch off all but the emotions that were hers, she guessed she'd be living in a cave, half mad – or worse.

'Yep,' she said, 'hatches all well and truly battened down.'

He looked worried so she tried to smile reassuringly, but the truth was that she felt sick to her stomach at the thought of having to spend a night crammed into a hall with half of the town. Shielding herself was one thing, but short of making herself invisible like Jack, she still had to cope with being in a crowd of people for hours on end. Sucking in a deep breath, she grabbed her coat and keys and they headed out of the door.

THE FIRST ETHEREAL

CHAPTER 2

*T*he wail of the siren sounded indecently loud in the darkness as they stepped out of the house. Street lights had been routinely turned off after midnight since the power shortages had begun and while they were usually turned back on during emergencies, whoever had responsibility for flicking the switch had clearly not yet received the memo.

Lilly handed Jack her travel cup so that she could find the torch she kept in her coat pocket. As she did, a strong gust of wind caught the side of her portfolio case and almost dragged her off her feet. Instinctively, Jack threw his free arm around her.

'Thanks,' she said, feeling suddenly close to tears.

'Always said a strong gust of wind could have you over,' Jack said, only half joking. 'Come on, you'll feel better once we're back in the warm. If we hurry, we might get a spot at the back again.'

Perched on the Welsh-English border, Pont Nefoedd was a hilltop market town built high above the banks of the river

Wye. Three steep hills connected the Old Road at the base of the town, where Lilly lived, to the New Road at the top which was bounded by the start of the forested mountains. The town, which could trace its history back to Roman times, had never flooded before. It was a fact the news-readers liked to trot out when reporting on the unprece-dented nature of the country-wide flooding. The implication was that if even Pont Nefoedd could flood, then nowhere was really safe.

Lilly and Jack were halfway up the hill, the wind and rain blessedly at their backs and the glow of the community centre just a few hundred yards ahead of them, when Lilly felt her vision blur. 'No,' she muttered, but it was too late. As her heart slammed into high gear, she felt her breath hitch high in her chest as her back slicked with sweat and her legs turned to jelly.

When she opened her eyes, she was leaning against a wall. Jack was holding her arms and staring at her in the glow from the now working street lights, his brow knitted together. At least she was still on her feet, she thought.

'Did you have another one?' he asked, scanning her face, although for what, Lilly wasn't sure.

The question confused her for a second until, like frag-ments of a torn photograph, the pieces of her memory rearranged themselves. Her stomach reacted first, lurching as if she was about to vomit. Swallowing hard, she took a deep breath as the picture in her mind settled into coherence.

Realising she'd not answered his question she said, 'I saw someone,' then faltered as her eyes swam with tears. 'I saw someone I loved very much being,' the last word was a choked whisper, 'beheaded.'

Jack pulled her into a tight hug and planted a kiss on top of her head. She held on tightly, anchoring herself as if without him she really would blow away on the next gust of wind. She breathed in the scent of him, wild honeysuckle and summer meadows, and tried to forget the smell of blood and sawdust that had so recently overwhelmed her.

'It was so real, Jack,' she said quietly. 'I felt the rough wood under my hand as I climbed the steps up to the execution platform, the weakness in my knees, the nausea. I could even smell the sawdust, the sweat of the guard behind me and the blood. There was so much blood.' When she lifted her eyes to meet his she saw that he was on the verge of tears too.

'Drink this,' Jack said, pressing her travel mug into her hand.

After fumbling with the lid, she took a swig of her coffee. It was still close to scalding and she winced, but the pain helped to ground her. She hadn't wanted to kick off another argument, especially now she was facing who knew how long in the evacuation centre again, but neither could she go on like this. The nightmares were bad enough, but now it no longer seemed to matter whether she was asleep or awake for these horrors to attack her. Only the day before she'd had to abandon her shopping basket in the market after a particularly brutal episode had sparked a full panic attack that her bent double and gasping for breath.

'I need to know, Jack,' she said, holding his gaze. 'Please, I can't go on being hijacked like this. I feel like I'm losing my mind.'

Jack looked away quickly, but Lilly reached up with her free hand and gently turned his face to look at her. 'Please.'

She held his gaze and after a moment he nodded slowly. 'But you have to be sure,' he said.

'I am sure,' Lilly replied, hoping that he could read the absolute conviction in her eyes, but not her fear.

'Okay, but not here eh? Let's get in the warm first and then I'll tell you,' he said. 'I promise.'

'Okay,' Lilly said and pushed herself away from the wall. Her legs felt weak, but there was no way she'd admit as much to Jack. After months of nagging and pleading he was actually going to tell her what was happening to her and she wanted nothing to get in the way.

THE FIRST ETHEREAL

CHAPTER 3

*B*y the time they reached the community centre there were already a dozen families settling themselves onto the camp beds that would be their temporary home for the night, but possibly longer. Lilly remembered the first time they'd been evacuated. The children had been wide-eyed with the adventure of it all, racing around excitedly despite the best efforts of their anxious-looking parents to contain them. There was no such excitement in the air tonight, just the howls of over-tired toddlers and the loud sobs of one little boy who had forgotten his favourite teddy in the rush. Even the pets seemed fed up with the repeat performance. A Siamese cat yowled loudly from its carrier, while an old chocolate Labrador turned in circles trying to get comfortable on a makeshift bed of thin blankets and what looked to be its owner's padded coat.

'Lilly isn't it?' asked a stocky man wearing a bright orange tabard with 'volunteer' stamped back and front. 'You'll have to remind me of your last name,' he said, smiling, although Lilly could see the tiredness on his face.

'Jones,' Lilly said quietly, 'And this is my friend Jack Smith.'

He gave Jack a nod of acknowledgement and Lilly watched as he added her name to the list on his clipboard. He frowned, his pen hovering over the paper as if he had lost his train of thought, then said quickly, 'Great. Well Lilly, you know the routine by now unfortunately. Grab yourself a spot. There's tea and coffee in the kitchen next door so just help yourself.'

As the volunteer strode away, Lilly turned to Jack. 'That never gets old, you know.'

'What, people forgetting me the instant they've met me?' Jack said.

'Yep. You're like a wizard,' she said, yawning. 'I wish I could do it.'

After finding two beds together in the corner, they dumped Lilly's things and went into the kitchen. Lilly longed to sleep. What she had come to think of as her waking night-mares always left her feeling physically and emotionally drained, but now that Jack had at last promised to explain things to her, she had to stay awake.

After helping themselves to coffee they were drawn to the small crowd of people standing around the large wall-mounted TV watching the news. The banner at the bottom of the screen read, 'live from Venice'. The reporter, a polished thirty-something in a suspiciously new-looking rain jacket, was standing in a boat next to an elderly man wrapped in a foil blanket. As the camera pulled back, the old man heaved back a sob before being comforted by a younger woman, herself in tears.

'So, there you have it,' said the reporter, his voice wobbling slightly. Making a visible effort to contain himself he said, 'The Adriatic has finally claimed this unique, magnif-icent city. A UNESCO World Heritage Site, beloved by honeymooners and tourists the world over, but now lost to us all under the waves. Feeling that loss, of course, most acutely, are the people who called this beautiful city their home. Here on this boat and the handful of others in this final flotilla of evacuees are the last of the Venetians.'

The last sentence comes out in a hurry as if he too is holding back a tide that might any second overtake him. The camera panned to take in a half-dozen small boats before the shot switched to images of the inundated and now forcibly abandoned city.

'Not just us being washed out of our homes then,' said an elderly man standing next to them. 'Poor buggers,' he added, shaking his head before, with shoulders drooped, he left the room.

Lilly lingered, hoping that the next item might be news of the UK-wide flooding, but instead it was a report on the nationwide state of emergency in Australia prompted by record-breaking bush fires. Images of charred koalas, sheep and kangaroos filled the screen before being replaced by aerial shots of log-jammed highways and still smouldering towns that look like something out of Mad Max.

The newsreader said, 'As the scale of this latest disaster escalates, the focus is now on evacuation. Both New Zealand and Indonesia have said that they will review the Australian government's request for emergency refugee status for its citizens over the coming months, but that no change in their initial decisions to refuse the application would be forth-coming in the short term. Humanitarian aid in the form of medical supplies, food and water would, though, continue.'

Lilly became aware of Jack's hand on her arm, then realised that her breathing was coming in short hiccupping gulps. As the newsreader began reading out the daily death toll from the sepsis crisis, Jack gently steered her out of the kitchen. 'How's that shielding holding up?' he asked quietly.

Lilly forced herself to take a deep breath, centring herself and checking that everything she was currently feeling belonged to her and nobody else. 'All mine,' she said breathily, 'the misery, despair and anger is one hundred percent coming from me,' looking up at Jack and seeing what she considered to be similar emotions mirrored in his own face.

'How one species can quite so spectacularly screw up an entire planet in so short a space of time is kind of beyond me,' he said, almost spitting out the words.

Lilly didn't have the words to reply. They had talked about this so many times but always seemed to circle back to the same point of hopelessness. Lilly felt hot tears fill her eyes and a split second later, Jack pulled her into a hug.

'At least the troubles haven't spread here yet,' Jack said, referring to the frequent riots that had been blighting most of the big towns and cities for months. If he'd intended to point out a bright side, Lilly thought, he'd majorly missed the mark.

'Come on, why don't you get an hour's sleep at least,' Jack said, tucking an escaped strand of her hair back behind Lilly's ear. 'And no, I'm not trying to get out of telling you about the dream stuff – I promise. But you look done in.'

Lilly nodded her agreement and led the way back into the main hall. Although her back still ached at the memory of the last night she'd had to spend on the emergency camp beds, she decided that she was probably tired enough to sleep on the floor if she had to. She sat on the bed, pulled off her boots and laid down. The last thing she saw before sleep overwhelmed her was Jack pulling a blanket over her shoulders.

When she woke a few hours later, the first feeble rays of watery winter sun were filtering in through the gaps in the mismatched curtains. Her eyes felt puffy and with a sinking heart she recalled snatches of the latest dream.

'Hello, sleepyhead,' Jack said quietly from where he sat on the bed next to hers, 'that was another rough one. The nuns, right?'

Levering herself up, she nodded, caught off balance for a second that Jack knew exactly what she'd just been dreaming about. This time she had been sitting in the street, fat cold cobblestones beneath her and crippled with pain all over her body. She had been freezing and soaked to the skin. Two figures had hurried towards her, lanterns swinging in the darkness. They had started to lift her with strong but gentle hands, their kind words as comforting as their touch, but when her hood slipped back and they had seen her disfigured face caught in the swinging lamplight, they called her a whore and let her fall back onto the cobblestones. The physical pain was blinding but had been eclipsed by her sense of heart shattering despair.

Before she could ask him, he said, 'I don't see all of the dreams, just the ones where I was ...' he hesitated slightly then added, 'close by.'

Swinging her thin legs off the bed so that she could sit facing him, Lilly held her head in her hands and rubbed at her temples, trying to kick her brain into gear and process what Jack had just said to her while still struggling to banish the image of the pinched, pious-faced nuns from her mind.

Failing, she said, 'I don't understand. How did you know?'

Jack hesitated for a beat but then said, 'What you're going through, it's called the Remembering.' He paused as if waiting for some kind of recognition. She racked her brain, but she'd never even heard the term before. Pressing on, he said, 'So you see, Lil, they're not just nightmares or panic attacks ...' He paused again and Lilly felt a mixture of irritation and apprehension rising in her chest. If he's hoping to avoid having to spell it out, she thought, then he's bang out of luck.

'What do you mean?' she asked, lifting her head so that she could look at him. She probably knew Jack's face better than her own. She studied it, trying to figure out the expression in his gold-flecked green eyes.

'What I mean is that what you're seeing, feeling, they're ...' He hesitated and Lilly cursed herself for not being sharp enough to fill in the blanks for him. 'They're memories,' he said at last; the last two words were almost a whisper directed at the floor. She let the silence stretch, unsure about what to say. He raised his head, lifting his eyes hesitantly to meet hers.

The realisation dawned slowly. 'Memories?' she asked. Her mind wrestling with the idea of what he might be trying to tell her. Jack nodded slowly and Lilly took a few deep, deliberate breaths, conscious that her heartbeat had broken into a trot and may at any point bolt into an all-out gallop. Willing her voice to stay level, she added, 'As in past lives?'

'Yes, Lil, you're remembering your past lives,' he said, sounding relieved to finally say the words aloud.

Lilly exhaled as if she'd been winded. She scanned the hall, feeling suddenly trapped by the thirty or so people dotted around the cavernous space. Some were still sleeping, others were huddled over their phones and talking quietly in small groups at the front of the hall. Quelling the compulsion to bolt from the room, after a few fumbled starts she said in a whisper, 'So, just to be clear, you're telling me that all these horrific, terrible, murderous dreams that make the worst horror films feel like a trip to Disneyland are real?' She shivered, but when Jack reached out to take her hands she snatched them away. He had known this. For the past nine months, he'd known this, but he hadn't told her.

'Well, yes and no. Yes, they happened, but no, they're not

real. They can't hurt you – they belong to a life that's long past,' Jack said in an urgent whisper. Taking her face tentatively in his hands he said, 'Please don't be mad at me, Lil. I couldn't tell you until you were ready. There are rules, you know that.'

Lilly felt her eyes brim with tears and she pulled away, turning her head away from him and wiping her face on her sleeve. Then, all at once, as if she was watching a hundred horror films on fast forward, a barrage of terrible scenes flashed before her eyes at lightning speed. The sensation made her giddy and she held her head in her hands to steady it.

Jack sat down next to her and put his arm around her shoulders. 'That's just the data coming in – it's nothing to worry about. It's normal,' he said. He was doing his best to sound calm, but she could hear the tension in his voice, feel it in his fingers as he gently rubbed her back with hands that were trembling.

Lilly had no idea why she was so upset. It wasn't like she didn't already believe in past lives. When your best friend is invisible to everyone but you, reincarnation is not much of a stretch. As she considered it, she supposed that it was knowing that her current life wasn't an anomaly. Just another miserable existence in a long and seemingly endless line. Granted, it was a million times better than it was growing up on the farm – that was hell on Earth – but she was far from happy. She couldn't even claim to be content. Apart from Jack, she had no one. The world was dying around them and she sometimes felt like she was the only one who felt it – this impending, unquestionable sense of everything ending. They had already lost most of world's wildlife; entire ecosystems were collapsing almost overnight, yet everyone else just seemed to want to carry on as normal, like toddlers *la-la-la*-ing with their fingers in their ears.

There were so many days when she didn't even leave the flat. Daren't turn on the radio or TV. Instead, she would sit and draw new worlds for herself on paper, so she supposed she was no better than the rest of them. Weren't they all pretending the truth wasn't real?

'So, these flashbacks, will they stop now that I know?' she asked, pulling herself back to the present.

Jack made a face halfway between a grimace and a wince but shook his head. 'Sorry, Lil, no. If anything, you may have more than you've been getting.'

Lilly's stomach lurched in complaint. The hope that this milestone would bring some relief withered as quickly as it came to bud.

'But why now?' she asked. He stopped rubbing her back and she heard him catch his breath and hold it for a long moment.

'Now that's the question I was hoping you wouldn't ask me. Not yet anyway,' he said quietly. She didn't need to be an empath to spot sadness in his voice. Preoccupied with a thread on the knee of his jeans, without looking at her he said, 'But now that you've asked, I have to tell you. The thing is, Lil, I'm pretty sure you're going to like this answer even less than you liked the last one.'

CONTINUE THE STORY NOW

WWW.ELWILLIAMSAUTHOR.COM

PRAISE FOR THE FIRST ETHEREAL

"I can't recommend this book more highly. I absolutely loved it. An intelligent, generous and ambitious novel.'

— Z. ARDEN

'Eerily predictive…thought provoking and magical at the same time.'

— S. ANGEL

'Beautifully told, The First Ethereal will stay with you for a long time. '

— WOSSY

'An amazing story filled with love! I could not put it down! I fell in love with the story, and oh my, the plot twist!'

— K. ARBUCKLE

PRAISE FOR THE FIRST ETHEREAL

'Beautifully written story with engaging and relatable characters that'll keep you turning the pages till the very end. Timeless in its message but particularly relevant to society today, but also fun and easy to read.'

— DAVID

'Wow...what an imagination....I just loved this book. It keeps you guessing right up to the end.'

— J.KINNAIRD

'A beautifully told modern fairy story.'

— LYNNE H

'I'm struggling to put into words how much I loved this book and why. It's so relevant and rooted in reality while still being full of real magic, with a sprinkle of hocus-pocus for good measure!'

— MRS. T

'The First Ethereal' offers a narrative unlike anything I've seen before. Highly recommend this gem for a magical and charming reading experience.'

— EMMA S

'Read it all in one sitting. Couldn't stop reading it! Very different story line but very good. If this is your genre, you won't be disappointed!'

— MARILYN S

PRAISE FOR THE BLESSING OF CROWS

'I loved this sequel to The First Ethereal. A breathless race to save a peaceful world from the evil trying to consume it, full of twists and turns. Beautifully written and impossible to put down.'

— J. OAK

'Another uplifting, gripping and beautifully written novel and I've loved catching up again with Lily and her friends as they fight to continue living in a world of peace and love. I highly recommend you read the first book in the series to meet the characters and read about their fight to achieve the Ethereal world.'

— BRACKNELL LIBRARY SERVICE

'This was the novel I needed to escape the turbulent times we are experiencing and I enjoyed every minute of this fast moving, immersive story.'

— D. PENKITTY

'Magical and captivating...It ended up being my binge-read book. Exciting plot, fast-moving as always and had me hooked until the very end.'

— PEPPIE

'Ever since I read the first book, The First Ethereal, I've been desperate for a sequel! Being able to dive into the new age of Ethereal, the challenges it faces and more surprising twists and turns, was an absolute treat. And the underlying message of the negative impact humanity is having on earth isn't lost either.'

— M. WARD

'I could hardly put this book down and sped through it. I loved the first book and was excited to see what happened next. The premise of trying to preserve vibrations and energy is so very simple on one level and yet allows for complexities enough to make a twisty-turny plot.'

— E. BURKE

'A sequel that doesn't disappoint! Another page turner which brings back old friends & continues the themes of The First Ethereal with some surprising twists & turns along the way. Great read again!'

— B. EVANS

ACKNOWLEDGMENTS

Writing an acknowledgment for my third book feels like a dream. Had someone predicted this five years ago, I'd have laughed, but life clearly had other plans.

I am eternally grateful to my darling husband, Stuart, for his unwavering encouragement and support, for always being my first reader, my sounding board, and my all-round cheerleader. He also makes sure I survive on more than coffee and toast! My love and thanks too to my bestie, Katie Brunskill, for always being there.

I hadn't thought about writing about the librarians aka the keepers of the magical libraries until Nicola Sparkes wrote to me just after I published The First Ethereal suggesting it. Thanks for the prompt, Nicola, I hope you like the result!

As I mentioned in the author's note, The Magic Keepers had its own schedule and refused to be rushed, despite my inherent impatience. That it morphed from a short story to a full-blown novel is thanks to the feedback from my first beta readers: Judith Oak, Barbara Evans, Jo Shock, Niki Toogood, Nicola Sparkes, Alice Heath, Theresa McAdden, and Rachel Sheldon.

Thanks to Rebecca Fearnley for the alpha read and to Toby Selwyn for the meticulous editing and for being such a joy to work with. That the story comes wrapped in such a gorgeous cover is thanks to Nell Wood, and a big thank you to Layane Moura for the map in the special edition. I can now tick, 'book with a map in it' off my author goals list!

Writing a time travel story was never on my project list. I was terrible at history in school and while I'm fascinated now, I'm still rubbish at remembering dates. My heartfelt thanks therefore to Dai Hill at the Museum of Cardiff who helped to bring life in 1840s Cardiff alive for me with such enthusiasm.

Last, but by no means least, a massive thank you to everyone who's read the first two books, rated, reviewed, passed them on to friends, borrowed them from the library, chatted with me on social media, or had a natter at an event. Your feedback and encouragement mean the world to me. Words are magic, and yours are the spells that keep me writing.

ABOUT THE AUTHOR

E L Williams is the author of the urban fantasy duology "The First Ethereal" and "The Blessing of Crows", as well as the standalone novel "The Magic Keepers". After years of advising on sustainability (and secretly wishing she could save the world with a well-muttered spell), Emma now weaves tales where nature and enchantment collide.

When not crafting magical worlds, she's either nose-deep in a book, spying on the local wildlife, or employing stealth tactics to smuggle 'just one more' houseplant past her ever-vigilant (but surprisingly tolerant) husband. Her ultimate goal? To own more books than the local library, rescue ALL the animals, and turn her home into an indoor jungle – though not necessarily in that order.

Thank you for reading The Magic Keepers. If you enjoyed it, please help other readers find it by leaving a review.

KEEP IN TOUCH

To be the first to hear news of the next book, please head over to the website (www.elwilliamsauthor.com) and join the Readers' Club. You'll receive a short monthly update, plus occasional giveaways, free short stories, and interviews with inspiring people.

You can also find me social media, usually blathering about books, dogs, plants, and the joys of writing fiction in stolen moments. I love a natter, so do come and say hello. You'll find me @elwilliamsauthor on Instagram, TikTok and Facebook